# Caught Up

*Also by Liz Tomforde*

Mile High
The Right Move

# LIZ TOMFORDE

# Caught Up

HODDER

First published in Great Britain in 2023 by Hodder & Stoughton
An Hachette UK company

16

Copyright © Liz Tomforde 2023

A CIP catalogue record for this title is available from the British Library

Paperback ISBN 978 1 399 72859 1
ebook ISBN 978 1 399 72858 4

Typeset in Plantin Light by Hewer Text UK Ltd, Edinburgh
Printed and bound in Great Britain by Clays Ltd, Elcograf S.p.A.

Hodder & Stoughton policy is to use papers that are natural, renewable
and recyclable products and made from wood grown in sustainable
forests. The logging and manufacturing processes are expected to
conform to the environmental regulations of the country of origin.

Hodder & Stoughton Ltd
Carmelite House
50 Victoria Embankment
London EC4Y 0DZ

www.hodder.co.uk

October 10th (*Caught Up*'s release date) would have been my dad's birthday. Kai and Monty are for him because he was the blueprint for writing my two favorite fictional dads.

And to Allyson—Miller is for you.

# Playlist

Caught Up – USHER 3:44
Wild – Carter Faith 3:36
Juice – iyla 3:27
Save Me The Trouble – Dan + Shay 3:20
3:15 (Breathe) – Russ 3:03
Wild as Her – Corey Kent 3:18
Lil Boo Thang – Paul Russell 1:53
Lovely – Arin Ray 2:57
Best Shot (Acoustic) – Jimmie Allen 3:12
Miss Shiney – Kaiit 3:11
Stay Down – Brent Faiyaz 3:26
Come Over (Cover) – JVCK JAMES 2:21
Grateful – Mahalia 3:05
I Just Want You – JAEL feat. Alex Isley 4:00
Snooze – SZA 3:21
If You Let Me – Sinéad Harnett feat. GRADES 3:51
Until The End Of Time – JVCK JAMES /
 Justin Timberlake 5:22
BRB – Mahalia feat. Pink Sweat$ 3:37
My Boy (My Girl Version) – Elvie Shane 3:25
So Gone – Vedo 3:01

# I

# Kai

"You've got to be kidding me, Ace." Monty drops the scouting report onto his desk in the hotel room. "You fired him on a game day? What the hell are you planning to do with Max tonight? It's your night on the mound."

I made sure to bring my son in for this meeting partly because I didn't have anyone else to watch him and partly because I knew Monty was going to be pissed I fired another nanny, but would be less furious with Max's chubby-cheeked smile staring back at him.

"I don't know. I'll figure it out."

"We *had* it figured out. There was nothing wrong with Troy."

Like hell there was nothing wrong with Troy. After my early morning workout with the team doctor and training staff, loosening up my shoulder for tonight's start, I came back to my room to find my son with a diaper that was hours past due for a change. Add that to the weeks he spent fanboying over my teammates instead of focusing on his job, and I was done.

"Not the right fit," is all I say in response.

He exhales a long, defeated breath and Max giggles at my field manager's frustration.

Monty eyes him from across the desk, leaning in. "You think this is funny, kid? Your dad is making me go gray."

"I think that's all you, old man."

My fifteen-month-old son smiles back at my coach while sitting in my lap, all gums and baby teeth. Monty drops the tough guy act as I knew he would because Max is a soft spot for him. Hell, he's a soft spot for the entire team, but especially for the man sitting across the desk in this hotel room.

Emmett Montgomery, or Monty as we call him, is not only the field manager of the Windy City Warriors, Chicago's MLB team, but he's also a single dad. He's never told me the details of how his family came to be, but I would be shocked if his situation were anywhere as absurd as mine. That is, unless he also had a past fling fly across the country almost a year since he last saw her, only to drop the bomb that he's a dad and she wants no involvement before leaving him as a single parent to a six-month-old baby boy.

I try not to take advantage of Monty, knowing he and the entire organization have bent over backwards to make my new family situation work, but when it comes to my kid, I refuse to compromise on who takes care of him while I'm working.

"I'll talk to Sanderson," I offer, referring to one of the trainers on staff. "He'll be in the training room all night. I can get Max situated there. As long as no one gets hurt, the room will be quiet. He can sleep."

Monty rubs his thumb and forefinger over his brows. "Kai, I'm trying here. I'm doing everything I can for you, but this isn't going to work unless you have childcare we can all rely on."

Monty only uses my first name when he's wanting me to take his words to heart. Otherwise, he and the whole team call me by my nickname—Ace.

But I *have* taken his words to heart. They're the same ones he's been preaching to me for the past three months, ever since the season started. I've already rotated through five nannies. And the reason for that is because, well . . . I'm not sure I *want* to make it work.

I'm not sure I want to play baseball anymore.

The only thing I'm positive of is that I want to be the best possible dad for Max. At this point in my life, at thirty-two and after ten years in the majors, nothing else matters to me.

A game that I once loved, that I thought of as my entire existence, I now view as time away from my family.

"I know, Monty. I'll figure it out when we get back to Chicago. I promise."

He exhales another defeated sigh. "If your brother weren't also on my roster, you'd be the biggest pain in my ass, Ace."

I roll my lips in, trying not to smile. "I'm aware."

"And I'd trade you if you weren't so damn talented."

I can't help but laugh at that one because he's full of shit. I'm one of the best pitchers in the league, yeah, but regardless of my talent, Monty loves me.

"And if you didn't like me so much," I add for him.

"Get out of here and go talk to Sanderson about watching Max tonight." I stand from my seat, situating my son over my hip before turning to leave his hotel room. "And Max," Monty calls out to my kid, who can't respond to him. "Stop being so dang cute all the time so I can yell at your dad every once in a while."

I roll my eyes, leaning in close to speak to my son. "Wave goodbye to Monty and tell him he's getting grumpy and kind of ugly in his old age."

"I'm forty-five, you dick, and you can only hope to look this good in thirteen years."

Max giggles and waves at my coach, having no idea what we're talking about, but he loves Monty as much as Monty loves him.

"Hi!" Max hollers from across the room.

Close enough.

"Hi, buddy." Monty laughs. "I'll see you later, okay?"

I didn't think I'd ever be as close to a coach as I am to Monty. Before last season, I was playing for the Seattle Saints, the team I was drafted to and spent the first eight years of my career with. I respected the staff there, and I liked the field manager enough, but our relationship was all business.

Then, last season, my free agency brought me to Chicago, solely because my younger brother is on the roster—starting shortstop for the Warriors, and I missed playing ball with the little shit. When I met Monty, I instantly liked him, but our working relationship became more like family when Max came into my life last fall. I can't thank him enough for what he's done for me. It's because of him, understanding the kinds of sacrifice it takes to be a single parent, that made this situation work.

He told the team executives that my son would be traveling with me this season, and he wouldn't be taking no for an answer. Knowing if he was denied, I'd be going into early retirement. I refuse to be without my kid for half the year when his own mother abandoned him at six months old. He needs someone constant and stable in his life, and I won't let something as trivial as a game be the reason my son doesn't have that.

I should probably stop firing everyone we hire so I can make Monty's life a little easier, but that's a different conversation.

My brother, Isaiah, jogs down the hall and hops into the elevator right after us. His disheveled, light brown mop of hair is still formed into whatever shape the bed he slept in gave it. I've been up for hours, between waking with Max and getting my morning workout in, but I'd bet good money he just left his bed.

And I'd bet my life there's still a naked woman in it.

"Hey, man," he says. "Hi, Maxie," he adds, blowing a raspberry on my son's cheek. "Where are you guys going?"

"Gotta go beg Sanderson to watch him tonight during the game."

Isaiah doesn't say anything, simply waits for me to elaborate. "I fired Troy."

He laughs. "Jesus, Malakai. Make it a little more apparent you don't want to make this arrangement work."

"Troy sucked and you know it."

Isaiah shrugs. "I mean, I prefer your nannies to have tits and a strong desire to sleep with me, but besides that, he wasn't terrible."

"You're an idiot."

"Max . . ." Isaiah turns to my son. "Don't you want an auntie? Tell your daddy that your next nanny needs to be a woman, single, twenties or thirties. Bonus points if she looks banging in my jersey."

Max smiles.

"Wouldn't mind being a mother to a thirty-year-old man," I add. "Is okay with a disgusting apartment. Knows how to cook and clean since you're a literal man-child and refuse to do so."

"Mmm, yeah, she sounds perfect. Keep your eyes out for someone just like"—the elevator doors open—"that."

My brother's attention is glued straight ahead when we arrive on the lobby level.

"Shit, I missed Sanderson's floor. *Shoot*," I correct. "Don't say *shit*, Max."

My kid is too distracted to listen to me curse as he chews on his fingers and watches his uncle. Said uncle stays standing in the middle of the elevator, dumbstruck.

"Isaiah, are you getting off or not?"

A woman walks onto the elevator, standing between him and me, which makes his sudden state of shock a bit more obvious. Pretty girls tend to make him stupid.

And this one is real pretty.

Dark chocolate hair falls over tanned skin that's covered in intricate black ink. And there's a whole lot of skin. She's got a little tank or bra thing under a pair of cutoff overalls, thick thighs spilling out past the frayed hem. Those thighs don't have the same artwork that covers her arm and shoulder though.

"Hi," Isaiah finally spits out, all dazed and distracted.

Reaching behind her, I lightly smack him on the back of the head, because the last thing he needs is another woman in another city to keep him occupied. I've lived the life he's currently indulging in and now I have a fifteen-month-old on my hip to show for it. I need the added responsibility of my younger brother following in my footsteps like I need a root canal for fun.

"Get off the elevator, Isaiah."

He nods, waving and walking backwards into the lobby. "Bye," he says with hearts in his eyes and not to me or my son.

The woman in the elevator simply lifts one of her two Coronas in a farewell.

"Floor?" she asks, all raspy and deep before lubricating her throat with a swig of beer. She reaches past me, pressing the floor I just came from before looking back over her shoulder for my answer.

Eyes are jade green and thoroughly confused, a tiny gold septum ring shines just under the bridge of her nose, and now I get why my brother turned into a dumbstruck teenage boy because suddenly I am too.

"Should I just guess? I can press them all if you'd like and we could take a nice long elevator ride together."

Max reaches for her, finally snapping me back into reality as if I've never seen a good-looking woman before.

I twist my hip to keep him from getting his little fingers tangled in her hair in a way that sounds awfully fun right about now, but this woman is not only drinking one beer at 9 a.m. on a Thursday, she's drinking *two*.

I clear my throat and press Sanderson's floor myself.

Miss Double Fisting on a Weekday flips her hair over her shoulder as she retakes her spot in the elevator next to me. Regardless of her morning beverages of choice, she doesn't smell like booze. She smells like a cake and suddenly, I have a sweet tooth.

Out of my periphery, I catch her looking at Max with a little smile.

"You've got a cute kid."

*You've got a cute everything,* is what I want to say in response.

But I don't because, as of last fall, that's no longer me. I no longer have the luxury of flirting with every pretty woman I pass on the street. I don't have the chance to throw back a beer at 9 a.m. I can't take a random woman back to my hotel room without exchanging names, intending to never see them again because said hotel rooms are cluttered with cribs, highchairs, and toys.

I especially don't need to be throwing out flirty statements to *this* kind of woman. It doesn't take a mind reader to know she's a wild one.

"Does he speak?" she asks.

"Him?"

She laughs to herself. "I was referring to you. So, you just make it a habit of ignoring people who talk to you?"

"Uh, no." Max goes to grab her again and I turn further away to keep him from grabbing a stranger. "Sorry. Thanks."

My kid catapults his body across my waist, continuing to reach his chubby fingers towards her, going for either her or one of her beers, I'm not quite sure.

The woman chuckles to herself again. "Maybe he knows you need one of these."

She offers me her second Corona.

"It's 9 a.m."

"And?"

"And it's a Thursday."

"We're judgy too, I see."

"Responsible," I correct.

"Jesus," she laughs. "You need something stronger than a Corona."

What I need is for this elevator to move a little quicker, but she might be onto something. I do need a beer. Or ten. Or a few hours rolling around with a naked woman. I can't remember the last time I did that. It sure as hell hasn't happened since Max came into my life, and that was nine months ago.

"Dadda." Max squishes my cheeks together before pointing towards the woman again.

"I know, buddy."

I don't know shit.

All I know is my kid won't stop trying to throw his body off mine to get to her. Which is weird, because in general, Max isn't big into strangers and even more so, he isn't all that comfortable with women.

I blame it on the fact the one who gave birth to him left him to be raised by a single dad, a reckless uncle, and a team of rowdy baseball players. The only presence of a woman that's stuck is my buddy's fiancée, but even then, it took him a minute to warm to her.

But for some reason, he's into this one.

"Come on, Max," I exhale, readjusting him. "You've gotta stop squirming."

"I know it's weird to offer, but I can hold him if you wa—"

"No," I snap.

"Geez."

"I mean, no, thank you. He doesn't do well with women."

"Wonder where he got that from."

I shoot her a pointed glance, but she just pops her shoulders and takes another swig.

Max laughs again. At literally nothing. This kid is just oddly into her, and this elevator ride is taking too fucking long.

"Did you get your smile from your mama?" she asks him, tilting her head and admiring him. "Because I don't think your dad knows how to."

"Funny."

"I'll pretend that wasn't sarcastic and you actually have a sense of humor."

"He doesn't have a mom."

The space goes eerily silent the way it typically does when I say those five words. Most people are concerned they crossed a line because his mom passed away tragically, not because she didn't tell me she was pregnant then showed up six months post-partum to flip my world upside down before leaving.

Her teasing tone immediately shifts. "Oh God, I'm so sorry. I didn't mean—"

"She's alive. She just isn't around."

I can physically see the relief wash over her. "Oh, well that's good. I mean, that's not *good*. Or maybe it is good? Who am I to say? Goddamn, this elevator is taking forever." She slaps a palm over her mouth, her eyes darting to Max. "I mean, gosh dang it."

That finally makes me chuckle, a small grin sliding across my lips.

She softens a bit. "He *does* smile."

"He smiles a whole lot more when he's not being berated by a stranger in an elevator while she's double fisting beers first thing after she wakes up."

"Maybe she never went to sleep." Another casual pop of her shoulders.

*Dear God.*

"Maybe they should stop talking about themselves in the third person like a couple of pretentious a-holes."

9

The elevator finally opens on the floor she needs.

"Maybe he should loosen up every once in a while. He's got a cute-ass kid and an even cuter smile when he shows it." She lifts her Corona to me before chugging the rest and exiting the elevator. "Thanks for the ride, Baby Daddy. It was . . . interesting."

That it was.

# 2

# Miller

I love butter. Imagine being the person who created God's greatest gift to mankind. I could kiss them for their discovery. With bread? Perfection. Melted onto a baked potato? Heaven sent. Or my personal favorite, baked into my famous chocolate chip cookies.

Now, you might be thinking it's a chocolate chip cookie, they're all the same. Wrong. Dead wrong. I might be known throughout the country for my ability to fix a Michelin star-seeking restaurant's underperforming dessert program, but I wish one of these fancy restaurants would say "fuck it" and let me bake them a goddamn chocolate chip cookie for their menu.

They'd sell out. Every night.

But even if they'd let me fancy up a classic like that, that recipe is mine. I'll lend out my creativity and my tips and techniques. Hell, I'll even create an entire fresh and inspiring dessert menu for a restaurant that has a yearlong waitlist for a table. But the classic recipes, the ones I've honed for the last fifteen years, the ones that make your body melt into a sigh as soon as the sugar touches your tongue, reminding you of home, those are mine.

No one is asking for those recipes anyway. They aren't what I'm known for.

But I'm fairly certain that the only thing I'm going to be known for is the mental breakdown I'm about to have in the middle of this Miami kitchen, simply because for the past three weeks, I haven't been able to create a single new dessert.

"Montgomery," one of the line cooks calls out. He, for some reason, doesn't feel the need to call me by my title, so I haven't concerned myself with learning his name. "Are you coming out with us after our shift tonight?"

I don't honor him with eye contact as I clean up my work-station and pray that the soufflé in the oven makes it through without sinking. "I'm going to assume you forgot my title is Chef," I say over my shoulder.

"Sweetie. You just bake cakes. I'm not calling you Chef."

As if a record scratched, the entire kitchen goes silent, every prep cook freezing with their tools in hand.

It's been a while since I've been disrespected in my profession. I'm young, and at twenty-five, it's not easy to stand in a kitchen of adults, typically men, and tell them what they're doing wrong. But over the last couple of years, I've earned a reputation, one that demands respect.

Three weeks ago, I won the James Beard Award, the highest honor in my industry, and since being named Outstanding Pastry Chef of the Year, my consultation services have been booked solid. I'm now sitting at a three-year-long list of kitchens I'll be spending a season at, including this Miami stint, fixing their dessert programs and giving them a shot at earning themselves a Michelin star.

So yes, I've earned the title of Chef.

"You coming, Montgomery?" he starts again. "I'll buy you a beer or something with an umbrella you'll probably like. Something sweet and pink."

How this guy isn't picking up on the fact his co-workers are silently begging him to shut up is beyond me.

"I know something else sweet and pink that I wouldn't mind a taste of."

He's only trying to get a rise out of me, to get the one

woman working in the kitchen to snap, but he's not worth my time. And luckily for him, my timer beeps, pulling my attention back to my work.

Opening the oven door, I'm greeted by blazing heat and yet another sunken soufflé.

The James Beard Award is only a piece of paper, but somehow, the weight of it has crushed me. I should be grateful and humbled that I won an award most chefs strive for their entire lives, but the only thing I've felt since winning is a crippling pressure that's caused my mind to go blank, rendering me unable to create anything new.

I haven't told anyone I'm struggling. I'm too embarrassed to admit it. All eyes are on me more than ever before and I'm flailing. But there will be no hiding in two months' time when I'm featured on the cover of *Food & Wine* magazine's fall edition, and I'm sure the only thing the article will have to say is how sad the critics are to see yet another new talent unable to live up to their potential.

I can't do this anymore. As embarrassing as it is to admit, I can't handle the pressure right now. It's just a bit of burnout, a creative rut. Like writer's block for a pastry chef. It'll pass, but it sure as hell isn't going to pass while I'm working in someone else's kitchen with the expectation to teach others my craft.

With my back to the staff so they can't see my newest fuck-up, I plop the soufflé ramekin on the counter, and as soon as I do, a hand lands on my waist, every hair on my neck standing up in alarm.

"You've got two more months here, Montgomery, and I know a good way to pass the time. A way to get the staff here to like you." The line cook's hot breath brushes the back of my neck.

"Get your hand off me," I say coolly.

His fingertips dig into my waist, and they feel like my breaking point. I need to get away from this man and this kitchen. I need to get away from *every* kitchen.

"You've got to be lonely, traveling around the country the way you do. I bet you find a friend to keep you warm in that little van of yours in every city you visit."

His palm slides down my lower back, heading towards my ass. I snatch his wrist, turning my body and kneeing him in the balls, hard and without a second of hesitation.

Instantly, he keels over in pain, a pathetic whimper escaping him.

"I told you to get your fucking hand off me."

The staff is silent, letting their co-worker's cries echo off the stainless-steel appliances as he remains folded in half. Part of me wants to make some comment regarding how little his dick felt against my knee, but his actions made it obvious that he's overcompensating already.

"Oh, come on," I say, unbuttoning my chef's coat. "Get off the ground. You look pathetic."

"Curtis." Jared, the head chef, turns the corner in shock, staring down at his line cook. "You're fired. Get the fuck up and get out of my kitchen."

Curtis, as I've come to learn his name, keeps holding his balls and rolling around on the ground.

"Chef Montgomery." Chef Jared turns to me. "I am so sorry for his behavior. That is completely unacceptable. I promise you, that's not the kind of culture I'm cultivating here."

"I think I'm done here."

For a multitude of reasons, I'm done. The line cook who will never be hired in a high-end restaurant again was simply the straw that broke the camel's back, but I know in my bones I won't be any help to Chef Jared's menu this summer.

And I sure as shit don't need others to learn that I'm struggling. This industry is cut-throat, and the moment critics learn a high-end chef, let alone a James Beard recipient, is drowning, they'll start to circle like vultures, blasting my name in every one of their food blogs, and I don't need that attention right now.

Chef Jared cowers slightly, which is strange. The man is revered in the food world and is twice my age. "I completely understand. I'll make sure you're paid out for the entire contract, including the next two months."

"No. No need to do that." I shake his hand. "I'm just going to go."

Curtis is still on the floor, so I offer him a simple middle finger as I make my exit because yes, I'm an awarded pastry chef who sometimes still acts like a child.

As if my inability to do my job wasn't suffocating enough, the moment I'm outside, the late June humidity chokes me. I don't know what I was thinking when I agreed to spend my summer working in a South Florida kitchen.

Quickly hopping into my van parked in the employee lot, I crank the AC to full blast. I love this van. It's completely renovated inside and out with a fresh coat of deep green paint on the exterior and my own little kitchen on the inside.

I live in it while I travel the country for work, hair down and without a care in the world. Then when I get to my destinations, I turn on work-mode and spend the following months with my tattoos covered, being referred to as "Chef" for ten hours of my day.

It's the weird juxtaposition that I call my life.

And if we're being honest, it's not exactly what I saw myself doing. I had once dreamt of running my own bakery, making all my famous cookies, bars, and cakes that I had baked for my dad while growing up. But I was lucky enough to be plucked fresh out of school to train under one of the best pastry chefs in Paris, followed by another internship in New York City.

My career took off from there.

Now, it's bite-sized tarts, mousses most people can't pronounce, and sorbets that we all like to pretend are more fulfilling than ice cream. And though there are parts of the high-end world that feel pretentious and ridiculous, I'm grateful this is where life has taken me.

My career is impressive. I know this. I've worked endless hours to be impressive, to reach these borderline unattainable goals. But now that I've achieved most of them, I'm floating without direction, looking for the next checkmark to chase.

And that's exactly what my chaotic mind has reminded me over the past three weeks. I either maintain success or quickly take my spin through the ever-revolving door that names the newest and hottest chef in the industry.

With my mind reeling, I merge onto the highway headed towards my dad's hotel just as my agent calls.

I answer on the Bluetooth. "Hi, Violet."

"What the hell did that little prick do that made you, of all people, quit a job early? Chef Jared called me to apologize and tried to forward three months' pay for you."

"Don't accept that check," I tell her. "Yes, his employee is a raging douche, but the truth is, I wouldn't have been any help to him this summer anyway."

She pauses on the line. "Miller, what's going on?"

Violet has been my agent for the past three years, and though I don't have many friends due to my hectic lifestyle, I'd consider her one of them. She manages my schedule and lines up my interviews. Anyone who wants to write about me in their food blog or have me consult on their menu must go through her first.

And though there are very few people I can be honest with about what I'm dealing with, she's one of them.

"Vi, you might kill me, but I think I'm going to take the rest of the summer off."

If the Miami highway wasn't so fucking loud, you'd be able to hear a pin drop.

"Why?" Her tone is frantic. "You have the biggest job of your career in the fall. You have the cover booked for *Food & Wine* magazine. Please don't tell me you're backing out of that."

"No. God no. I'm still doing it and I'll be in Los Angeles by the time my next job starts, I just . . ." Shit, how do I tell her that her highest-paid client is losing it? "Violet, I haven't been able to create a new dessert in three weeks."

"You mean you haven't had the time?" she assumes. "Because if you're needing more time to perfect the recipes for the article, I could understand that."

"No. I mean I haven't made something that didn't fall apart in the process or burn to shit in the oven. It'd be comical how bad I am at my job if I weren't on the brink of a mental breakdown because of it."

She laughs. "You're fucking with me, right?"

"Violet, a five-year-old with an Easy Bake Oven could make a better dessert than me right now."

The line goes silent once again.

"Violet, you still there?"

"I'm processing."

Taking the exit for my dad's hotel, I wait for her to speak.

"Okay," she says, calming herself. "Okay, this is fine. Everything's fine. You're going to take the next two months to breathe, gather yourself, and get out to Luna's by September first."

Luna's is Chef Maven's restaurant that I'll be consulting at in the fall. Maven did a seminar while I was in culinary school, and I've been dying for my chance to work with her, but she left the industry shortly after we met. She became a mother, then came back into the food world by opening a restaurant named after her daughter and asked me to come help with her dessert menu. The interview for *Food & Wine* magazine will be taking place in her kitchen in Los Angeles, and I couldn't be more excited for the opportunity.

At least, I *was* excited until everything turned to shit.

"You'll be at Luna's by September first, right, Miller?" Violet asks when I don't respond.

"I'll be there."

"Okay," she exhales. "I can sell this. You're celebrating your new award by spending the summer with family and you're looking forward to being back in the kitchen in September. God, the blogs and critics are going to be up my ass about this, wondering where the hell you are. Are you sure your dad isn't sick? I could spin that."

"Jesus, Violet," I laugh in disbelief. "He's perfectly fine, thank God."

"Good. That man is too beautiful to be dying so young." Finally Violet laughs through the receiver.

"Gross. I gotta go."

"Tell Daddy Montgomery I said hello."

"Yeah, I won't be doing that. Bye, Vi."

The Windy City Warriors, Chicago's professional baseball team, have been in town for a couple of days. My dad has been the field manager, which is essentially the head coach, for the past five years. Before that, he worked with their minor league team after being snatched up from our local college back in Colorado.

Emmett Montgomery rose through the baseball ranks quickly. As he deserved to. He was already on the fast track to making a name for himself in the sport when everything changed for us. He gave up everything to become my dad, including his thriving career, refusing to leave his local coaching job until I graduated from high school and was off doing my own thing.

He's one of the good ones. In fact, I'd argue he's the very best.

It's been just the two of us most of my life and, though you'd think I left home at eighteen to spread my wings, I really did it so he could. I knew then, just as I know now, that the moment I stop moving, he'll tie himself to whatever city I settle in to be close to me. So, for his sake, I haven't stopped running since I left home at eighteen, and I have no plans to. He's given up everything for me. The least I can do is make sure he doesn't give up any more.

I stop at a convenience store, grabbing a couple of Coronas, one for me and one for him, before trading my kitchen pants and non-slip shoes for a pair of cutoff overalls and flip-flops. I peel off my long-sleeved shirt, replace my septum ring to its rightful home, and take the furthest parking spot from the entrance to the stunning hotel my dad is staying at.

Even after watching him coach in the majors for the past five years, I still can't get over seeing him like this. We never had fancy or expensive things growing up. He didn't make a lot of money being a college coach, and he was only twenty-five when he became my dad. In a lot of ways, we grew up together.

He fed me mac and cheese from the box more nights than not because he wasn't the most proficient in the kitchen. Which is why, when I was old enough to, I took over in that department, learning to cook and finding my love for baking. I lit up whenever I impressed him with a new recipe, which, let's be honest, was every single time. He's easily my biggest fan.

But seeing him here, thriving, doing what he loves most and being so good at it that he's already got a World Series ring, makes me infinitely proud of how well he's done without me around.

I want to make him equally as proud, especially after everything he sacrificed for me, and I have the opportunity to. After being one of the youngest recipients of the James

Beard Award, I've been booked for an eight-page spread in *Food & Wine* magazine, including the cover and three brand-new featured recipes that I can't find the inspiration to create. All happening in two short months when I get to LA for my next project.

No pressure, whatsoever.

I twist the cap off one of the beers to swallow down the sky-high expectations I put on myself as the elevator opens on the lobby floor. The two men inside don't get off, so I slide in between them.

The one to my left has a head of light brown hair and what seems like the inability to keep his jaw from hanging open.

"Hi," he says, and I don't know what it is about him, but I can almost guarantee this guy plays for my dad. He's somewhat tall, athletic build, and looks freshly fucked.

My dad's roster tends to be equally as invested in the women they take home from the field as they are in the game itself.

"Get off the elevator, Isaiah," the man to my right says, and while yes, they're both objectively good-looking, this one is offensively attractive.

He's got a backwards hat on, dark-rimmed glasses, and a toddler in his arms with a matching cap for goodness' sake. I try my hardest not to look too closely, but I can see the dark hair spilling out around the edges, ice-blue eyes framed by those glasses. Scruff slopes over his jawline, screaming "older man," and that alone is my kryptonite.

Then you add the cute-ass kid he's got slung on his hip and he's almost begging to be drooled over.

"Bye," the man to my left says as he gets off the elevator, leaving me to ride with the two cute boys to my right.

"Floor," I ask, taking a swig of my beer as I press the number for my dad's room.

There's not a chance in hell he didn't hear me, but still, Baby Daddy doesn't respond.

"Should I just guess?" I ask. "I can press them all if you'd like and we could take a nice long elevator ride together?"

He doesn't laugh or even crack a smile which is a red flag if you ask me.

His little boy reaches for me, and I've never been one to fawn over kids, but this one is especially cute. He's happy, and after the morning I've had, a toddler smiling at me like I'm the greatest thing to ever exist is surprisingly what I need.

His cheeks are so chubby that his eyes almost disappear from his beaming grin as his dad continues to ignore me, pressing his floor number himself.

*Well, okay then.* This should be fun.

The longest elevator ride of my life has me concluding that the gorgeous man I rode with has a giant stick up his ass. And when I make it to my dad's room and knock, I couldn't be more thankful that our brief encounter is over.

"What are you doing here?" my dad asks, his face lighting up. "I thought I wasn't going to get to see you again this trip?"

I hold up both beer bottles in faux excitement, one empty, one still full. "I quit my job!"

He eyes me with concern, widening the opening into his room. "Why don't you come in and tell me why you're drinking at 9 a.m."

"*We're* drinking," I correct.

He chuckles. "You seem like you might need that second one more than me, Millie."

Crossing the room, I take a seat on the couch.

"What's going on?" he asks.

"I suck at my job. I don't even enjoy baking right now because I'm so bad at it. When have you ever heard me say I don't enjoy baking?"

He holds his hands up. "You don't have to justify it to me. I want you to be happy and if that job wasn't making you happy, then I'm glad you quit."

I knew he'd say that. And I know when I tell him that my new summer plans consist of driving around the country and living out of my van to get some fresh air and a fresh perspective, he'll say he's happy for me even though there will be concern laced in his tone. But I'm not fazed by his concern. What I'm worried about seeing is disappointment.

In the twenty years he's been my dad, he's never once shown it so I'm not sure why I constantly look for it. But I'd work my ass off and stay in every miserable kitchen for the rest of my life if it meant I could avoid disappointing him.

I'm self-aware enough to know that I have an innate need to be the best at whatever checkmark or goal I'm chasing. Right now, I'm not the best and I don't want to give anyone the opportunity to watch me fail. Especially him. He's why I strive for perfection in my career, which is a stark contrast to the wild, unattached, and go-with-the-flow attitude I have towards my personal life.

"Are you done for good?" he asks.

"Oh, God no. I'm taking the summer to get my groove back. I'll be back and better than before. I just need space without prying eyes to get it together, and to give myself a little break."

His eyes lighten with excitement. "So, where are you spending this summer break?"

"I'm not sure. I've got two months and my next job is in LA. Maybe I'll take my time driving to the West Coast and see some sights along the way. Practice in my kitchen on wheels."

"Live out of your van."

"Yes, Dad," I chuckle. "Live out of my van and try to figure out why every dessert I attempt to create since I won that fucking award has been a complete and utter disaster."

"Every dessert is not a disaster. Everything you've made me is phenomenal. You're being too hard on yourself."

"Basic cookies and cakes are different. It's the creative stuff that's giving me a hard time."

"Well, maybe it's the creative stuff that's the problem. Maybe you need to go back to the basics."

He's not in the food world the way I am so he doesn't understand that a chocolate chip cookie isn't going to cut it.

"You know," he starts. "You could come spend the summer in Chicago with me."

"Why? You'll be on the road half of the time for work, and when you're home, you'll be at the field."

"Come on the road with me. We haven't been in the same place for more than a few days since you were eighteen and I miss my girl."

I haven't had a holiday, weekend, or more than a single evening free in seven years. I've been endlessly working, killing myself in the kitchen, and even tonight, my dad's team has a game in town. It never dawned on me to take the night off to go watch.

"Dad—"

"I'm not above begging, Miller. Your old man needs some quality time."

"I just spent three weeks in a kitchen full of dudes, one of whom was practically begging me to file a sexual harassment complaint with HR. The last thing I want is to spend my summer around another team full of men."

He leans forward, tatted arms propped on his knees, eyes wide. "Excuse me?"

"I handled it."

"Handled it how, exactly?"

"With a swift knee to the balls." I take a casual sip of my beer. "Just how you taught me."

He shakes his head with a small laugh. "I never taught you that, you little psycho, but I wish I had. And now I'm even

23

more adamant about you coming on the road with me. You know my guys aren't like that."

"Dad, I was planning . . ." My words die on my tongue when I look up at him across the couch. Sad and pleading eyes, tired even. "Are you lonely in Chicago?"

"I'm not going to answer that. Of course, I miss you, but I want you to come hang out with me for a couple of months because you miss me too. Not because you feel obligated to."

I don't feel obligated. Not in that regard, at least. But everything I do, in some way, is an attempt to erase the guilt I have towards our situation. To repay a debt he paid by giving up his entire life for me when he was only twenty-five years old.

But I'd be lying if I said I didn't miss him too. It's why I ensure all my jobs overlap with his travel. I pick kitchens in big cities with MLB teams that my dad will be coming through for work. So of course, I miss him.

A summer with my old man does sound nice, and if having me nearby for a bit will make him happy, it's the least I could do after everything he's done for me.

Except there's one problem.

"There's no way upper management would allow that," I remind him. "No one on the team or staff is allowed to have family members with them while they travel."

"There is one family member who's allowed to travel with the team this season." A sly smile slides across his lips. "I have an idea."

# 3

# Kai

**Monty:** *Leave Max with Isaiah and come back to my room. We've gotta chat.*
**Me:** *Am I leaving Max so you can yell at me?*
**Monty:** *Yes.*
**Me:** *Cool, cool. I'll be sure to rush right over for that.*

"I found Max a new nanny," is the first thing he says before I've even closed the door behind me.

*Huh?* I take a seat across the desk in Monty's hotel room, eyeing him with confusion. "How? I fired Troy an hour ago."

"I'm just that good, and you're going to hire her because you clearly have shit taste in nannies since you won't stop firing them all, so I'm taking over."

"Her?"

"My daughter."

My eyes shoot to the framed photo sitting next to him. It's the same picture he has back in his office in Chicago. The same photo he props on his desk in every city we visit.

I knew the girl in the picture was his daughter, that much was clear, but even though he and I are close, he's never told me much about her. I always assumed it was because he felt guilty leaving her and traveling for work as much as we do. That, or he knows talking about his kid who he misses will only reaffirm what I already believe—that it's nearly impossible to do this job as a single parent.

The girl in the photo can't be more than thirteen or fourteen years old. She's in that awkward phase we all had in our early teens, donning both braces and acne. Dark hair is slicked back in a tight ponytail, visor shading her face and a bright yellow T-shirt with number fourteen centered on the front. Softball player, with her too-big sleeves cinched together with some sort of band on each shoulder. A pitchers' glove rests on a single knee as she poses for her season photo.

Monty *would* have a softball-playing daughter.

"She's free for the summer and I want her to travel with us," he continues.

Makes sense, she's out of school for the summer.

"Yeah, but Monty, this is my kid we're talking about."

"And mine." His brows raise, daring me to say something against this plan. "It's not a question, Ace. I'm telling you this is happening. I'm tired of you finding something wrong with every single person we hire. We're doing background checks every few weeks for someone new, and changing names on the hotel rooms and plane manifests is becoming a pain in the ass for the travel coordinators. She's Max's new nanny, and the best part about it is she's my kid and you can't fire her."

*Shit.*

"She's only free until September so we'll have to find someone else to finish the last bit of the season, but we'll cross that bridge when we get there."

It's clear there's no getting out of this. I owe him for everything he's done for Max and me, and he fucking knows it.

If I have to leave my son with someone who isn't me, I guess this isn't the worst possible solution. This is a nanny that's probably too young to give a shit about a bunch of pro baseball players, and her dad will most likely be watching her like a hawk anytime she's not taking care of Max, which takes that responsibility off my shoulders.

What's two months? *Just double the time I've gone without firing someone.*

"Can she drive?" I ask.

His brows furrow in confusion. "What?"

"Like if something happens to Max while I'm not around, can she get him to the hospital?"

"Yeah . . ."

Okay, that's good. She's at least sixteen. That photo is probably a couple of years old at this point.

"Is she responsible?"

"She's . . ." he hesitates. "She's responsible at work."

Weird answer.

The door to his hotel makes that noise when the electric lock is being undone by a keycard. Over my shoulder, dark hair enters first as a woman walks in backwards, using her ass to open the door.

Chocolate hair. Frayed hem to her shorts. Thick thighs.

She turns around and Miss Double Fisting from the elevator is standing in my coach's hotel room. And she's double fisting again, only this time it's with a couple of coffee cups.

I adjust my glasses on my face to make sure I'm seeing this correctly. Green eyes connect with mine.

"You." The word comes out part seething, part shock.

She sighs, her shoulders dropping. "I had a feeling it was going to be you."

*Huh?*

"Ace, meet my daughter, Miller Montgomery. Max's new nanny."

My head whips back in his direction. "You're kidding me."

"Miller, Kai Rhodes. You'll be taking care of his son this summer."

"Absolutely not," I quickly interject.

Miller rolls her eyes, handing her dad one of the two coffees.

How is this possible? She sure as hell isn't thirteen or fourteen. She's a full-grown woman who drinks beer and apparently doesn't sleep. The acne is long cleared up, leaving tanned, flawless skin, and her braces have created perfectly straight teeth in a mouth that says whatever the hell it wants.

She looks like a Miller, though. That wild tomboy thing she's got going for her with her cutoff overalls and tattoos.

"She's not watching my kid."

Miller takes the seat next to mine and points at me with her thumb, giving her dad a look that says, *this fucking guy*.

Monty laughs—traitor.

"You two have met already, I see."

"Yeah, she was double fisting beers in the elevator at 9 a.m."

"*Dear God*." She throws her head back, and that raspy voice mixed with the sexual way my brain took that phrase has my cock betraying me. "They were Coronas. Do you know the alcohol content in those? That's some people's form of hydration."

"I don't care." I face her dad. "I won't leave someone like that in charge of Max."

"Lighten up, Baby Daddy." She takes a casual sip of her coffee—or rather her chai tea latte per the tag on her paper cup.

"Don't call me that."

"I had a beer to celebrate me quitting my job this morning. You're acting like I was doing lines of coke off the handrails in the elevator, which yeah, now that I'm saying that out loud, I realize sounds oddly specific, but I promise I've never done that."

I turn back to Monty. "This your kid?"

"The one and only," he says with pride.

"How old are you?"

"Twenty-five."

28

I didn't realize Monty became a dad at such a young age. That'd put him at . . . twenty years old when she was born? Damn. I thought this was hard at thirty-two.

"How old are *you*?" she asks.

"I'm asking the questions here. I'm trying to figure out if it's worth risking my kid's safety just to hire you and get your dad off my back."

"And I'm trying to figure out if it's worth ruining my summer by spending the next two months working for a guy with a giant stick up his ass."

"I'm being responsible. I don't have a stick up my ass."

"Probably been lodged so far up there and for so damn long that you forgot it was even inside of you."

"Miller," Monty interjects. "You're not helping."

"Do you have any childcare experience?"

"Adult children, yes."

I shoot a pointed glance towards Monty. "We don't know if Max will even like her. You know how he is with women."

"He was practically throwing himself at me in the elevator. I think we're fine in that department."

"I'm pretty sure he was going for your bottles. They look a lot like his."

"You're not going to get over the beers, are you?"

"No."

"Okay." Monty claps his hands together. "This is going to be interesting."

"Do you smoke?" That voice of hers suggests she might.

"No, but it seems you might drive me to if this is how the rest of the summer is going to go."

"Miller," Monty interrupts like a stern dad breaking up a fight between his kids. "Thanks for the coffee. Can you give me a minute with Kai?"

Miller sighs, quickly tying her long brown hair up in a knot on top of her head, giving me a better view of the artwork on her arms and shoulders. It's mostly intricate line-work making up a sleeve of florals. Almost like the outlines of a coloring page.

Max will like those.

"Fine." She stands from her seat, taking her chai with her, that sweet scent of dessert wafting from her again before she turns to me. "But so you know, I'm doing this as a favor. So, try to be less of a dick about it, yeah? See you later, Baby Daddy." She stops at the door, her hand on the knob as she cocks her head in contemplation. "Or should I say, *Baseball* Daddy? Oh yeah. Much better. Baseball Daddy, it is!"

She leaves us alone with that.

I shake my head in disbelief. "Your daughter is unhinged."

"She's the best, right?" Monty's chest rumbles at my annoyance.

"You can't be serious about this. There's no way she's the right person to take care of Max."

He leans back in his chair, tattooed hands crossed over his stomach. "I'm not just saying this because I'm biased, but you'd be lucky to have her. She might be my wild child and not know what the hell a filter is, but when it comes to work, she's the most driven person I know. She will do everything for your boy."

I toss my head back. "Come on, man. Let's be serious about this."

"I am being serious. Trust me on this, Kai. I know my daughter. If for some reason, she ever gives you a *valid* reason to fire her, I'll even offer to be the one to do it. That's how much faith I have in this situation."

Staying silent, I eye him, searching for any sign of bullshit.

I might not know Miller, might not trust her, but I do trust Monty with both my life and my kid's. And I know he'd never put Max at risk, even if this situation benefits him.

I can't believe I'm even considering letting him talk me into this, but I owe him. "She gets one strike," I say, holding a single finger to reiterate.

"Baseball puns, Ace? You're better than that."

"Shut up."

He puts his hand out to shake mine. "One strike, and she's outta here!"

"Okay, way too far."

I put my palm in his, but before I can pull away, he tightens his grip, willing my eye contact.

"I'm gonna give you a word of advice, son. Knowing her, she'll make sure you have the time of your life this summer, both you and Max, but don't even think about getting attached to her."

My brows cinch in confusion. "Did you not see that interaction?" I free my hand, gesturing towards the door Miller left through.

"I did, and I'm telling you this, not as her dad but as your friend. She will leave when the summer is over. I love my daughter to death, but she's a runner and the last thing she wants is to get caught."

Monty should know me well enough by now that the last thing *I* want is for her to stay. In fact, if it weren't for Max growing up far too quickly, I'd be wishing the summer away already.

"Trust me, Monty. You have nothing to worry about."

He hums, unconvinced.

Standing, I tuck my chair into the opposite side of his desk. "See you at the field."

I'm almost out the door when he stops me.

"And Ace," he calls out. "Keep your dick in your pants. We all know how fucking fertile you are, and I'm too young and too goddamn attractive for someone to be calling me Grandpa."

"Jesus Christ," I huff, leaving his room.

# 4

## Kai

Max makes a jumbled sound that I've come to know as meaning "snack" as he points towards the kitchen in my hotel room.

I adjust him on my hip. "You want a pouch?"

He points to the kitchen again.

"Can you say *pouch*?" I prompt, but he just keeps pointing in that direction.

I grab his favorite flavor of pureed fruit, undoing the top and letting him feed himself as I carry him around my room, tidying up before Miller comes over to watch him for the first time.

"Is that good, Bug?"

He smacks his tiny lips together.

He still only has a handful of words in his vocabulary, but it's wild when I get to hear them. It's even wild to watch him feed himself though he's been doing it for months. It might sound pathetic, but the small changes I see in him as he learns and grows are the most exciting moments of my everyday life.

And right on cue, I have to push away the lingering disappointment and questions, wondering what moments I missed for those first six months of his life when I didn't even know he existed.

I should probably put him down. Let him chill in his highchair or something but I'm always a needy little fucker on game days. I hate knowing I'm leaving him behind for the rest of the day. I miss dinner with him, and bedtime. So yeah, I'm a bit helicopter-y on afternoons I have to go to the field.

A knock sounds at the door and I find myself checking out my room, making sure it looks okay before answering it for my coach's daughter. Except when I open the door, it's not Miller waiting for me on the other side. It's my brother.

"What are you doing here?" I ask as he barrels inside.

"Heard the new nanny is hot." He looks around my hotel room, for her I guess. "And a woman, thank fuck."

"Don't curse in front of my kid."

Who am I kidding? Max is being raised by a baseball team. He's heard worse already.

"Sorry, Maxie," Isaiah says. "Thank frick. Better, Dad?"

I roll my eyes.

"So where is she?"

"How do you even know about her or that she's hot?"

"So, she *is* hot? I didn't actually know that. I was *manifesting*."

Isaiah takes a seat at the small kitchen nook, his feet up on the stool next to the one he's sitting on. I tend to get the biggest rooms on the road because I have another person living with me, and all of Max's stuff eats at any available space I have. Additionally, there's always an adjoining room connected to mine for Max's nanny to stay. Now that Troy's gone, it's empty, but Miller will stay in there while I'm at the game tonight.

"She's not *not* hot."

"Oh my God," my brother says, accusatorially. "You're gonna bang the new nanny, aren't you? So cliché, my guy."

"No, I'm not. And neither are you because not only is she Max's new nanny, but she's also Monty's daughter."

Every muscle in Isaiah's body freezes. "You're kidding me. Monty has a hot daughter? How old is she?"

"Twenty-five."

"And she's good with kids?"

"Doubtful. She's like a goddamn hurricane, but Monty's adamant about me hiring her, so I don't really have a choice." Isaiah nods in understanding. "How the hell do you know about her? I've only just met her."

"The team's group chat is going off." He holds up his phone and I adjust my glasses to look at it. "You should take it off mute every once in a while."

**Travis:** *Heard Max's new nanny is a woman. Fucking finally, Ace.*

**Cody:** *Troy was cute, but his replacement is cuter. I think I saw her in the hallway earlier. I wouldn't mind her being my nanny. Feed me. Tuck me into bed. Take my temperature too.*

**Isaiah:** *She's not a nurse, you idiot.*

**Cody:** *I call dibs on her being my seatmate on the plane.*

**Travis:** *What the hell? That's my seat.*

**Cody:** *Wait until you see her. You'll understand.*

**Isaiah:** *You can have the plane seat. I call dibs on everything else.*

An odd sense of annoyance rattles through me because this is Monty's kid and Max's new caretaker. She's not here for them. They're acting like a pack of starved dogs going after a single bone when, in reality, they have a buffet in every city we visit.

I would know. I used to have a buffet too.

"Okay." I usher him off the stool. "You need to leave before she gets here."

"No way. At least one of the Rhodeses needs to make a good impression and you're too stressed and grumpy lately to do it."

"If there's one Rhodes I can count on making a good impression, it sure as hell isn't going to be you. Max will do it." My brows cinch. "And I'm not grumpy, you dick."

I'm just *tired*. Tired of doing it all alone. Tired of feeling like I'm not doing enough.

"Really?" Isaiah asks with a huff of a laugh. "Because you used to be the happiest dude I knew, but I couldn't tell you the last time I saw you genuinely having fun. Back in the day, you were a bigger flirt than me, with shockingly more game. When's the last time you let that side come out?"

"There are ways to have fun other than screwing around in every city."

Like watching the same YouTube video of farm animals singing and dancing on repeat. Or playing peekaboo behind a napkin for an hour straight in an attempt to get Max to stop crying while he's teething. My new definitions of fun.

"Yeah, but that way is the *most* fun." A smirk quirks on his lips.

In my twenties I was a massive flirt, and I did my fair share of fucking around, but responsibilities crept into my life again, shifting my priorities. The flirty side pops out occasionally, when I'm out at work events alone, but then the reminder of who's waiting for me at home brings me back to reality and I squash my former self.

But I'm not getting into that conversation with my little brother right now because as much as I love him, he'll never understand. Our teen years were terrible, but he has no idea just how hard they were because I sheltered him from it all. It's what I do. I take care of my responsibilities.

"Are you feeling okay?" I ask.

"Huh?"

"You look sick. Maybe you should call out tonight. Stay home. Watch my son."

He rolls his eyes. "Says the guy who plays once every five days."

"Exactly. And look how much I get paid for it. I'm *essential.*"

Isaiah barks a laugh. "I'm the shortstop. I play every single game. There are four more starting pitchers waiting for their night."

"Which is why I should retire early. The Warriors will be fine without me."

His brown eyes narrow. "You're just running in circles hoping one of your points sticks, huh?"

"Worth a shot."

"If Monty's daughter is anything like him, she'll be great with Max. What are you so worried about?"

A knock at the door sounds, cutting off that conversation. "You'll see."

Isaiah turns back to me with a mischievous smile. "Who is it?" he calls out in a sing-song voice.

*Shut the fuck up*, I mouth.

"Don't curse in front of my nephew."

"Your favorite person in Miami," Miller deadpans from the hallway.

"Sexy voice," Isaiah whispers, and I find myself annoyed that he noticed.

He opens the door, casually leaning on the frame and blocking my view of the girl in the hall, but I watch as his spine stiffens before his head whips around to me, slack jaw and wide brown eyes.

I know that guy better than he knows himself, so it's not hard to understand that he's silently asking why I didn't tell him that Miller is the girl he fell in love with from the elevator this morning.

"Isaiah, Miller. Miller, Isaiah. My brother."

"Buy one, get one. Fun," I hear her say, but I still can't see her because my brother is frozen in the entryway.

"I'm the uncle," he finally blurts out.

She laughs, a deep throaty sound that goes straight to my dick. "I put that together from the whole brother thing."

"Isaiah, move."

"Yeah. Welcome. Come on in." He ushers her inside as if

36

it were his room to welcome her into. "Can I get you anything? Water? A snack? My number?"

She completely ignores him.

As soon as he's out of the way, she comes into view, still wearing those cutoff overalls and I'm not quite sure what's so fascinating to me about her thighs, but they're thick and muscular, the kind you get from years of playing softball.

And I can't stop imagining how blissfully constricting they'd feel around my waist. Or even better—my face.

But then I remember this is Monty's kid I'm thinking about, and I have to close my eyes to keep myself from looking at her.

"You good, Baseball Daddy?"

Isaiah cackles.

My eyes shoot open to find her looking at me like there's something very, very wrong with me and clearly there is if I'm looking at *this* woman like *that*.

She's borderline certifiable.

"Yeah." I clear my throat. "This is Max." I nod my head towards him, shifting my hip so he can see her better.

"Hi, Max," Miller says, her eyes softening.

That wild-girl edge I saw this morning is calmer now, maybe for Max's sake or maybe for mine, I'm not sure, but a small amount of my hesitation about this situation eases away.

Max blushes, burying his head into the crook of my neck, knocking off his little ball cap in the process. He's being shy, vastly different from his desperation to get to Miller this morning, but he's not afraid of her the way he is with most strangers. I think he's simply aware of her attention, and even though he's acting like he doesn't, he likes it.

But there's a part of me that's loving that my son wants me regardless of the pretty girl calling out his name.

"He's being shy."

"That's okay, Max. I tend to have that effect on boys."

My eyes dart to Isaiah. Case in point—my brother, who is frozen like a statue in the kitchen, silent but mesmerized.

"Should we show Miller all your stuff?" I ask my son.

Max reaches up to use his hat to cover his pink cheeks, but it's on the floor so his giddy smile is pretty obvious behind his arm.

"Come on, Bug." I take his empty pouch, setting it on the kitchen counter before placing him on his feet.

"Bug?"

"It's his nickname. The first time I ever saw him, he was wearing a onesie that was covered in a pastel bug print. So, Bug kind of stuck."

With Max's hands in the air, I hold on to each of them with my own, letting him use me to balance himself as he takes slow, wonky steps into the kitchen.

"He's not walking on his own yet?"

My head snaps up to Miller, looking for a judgmental glare to accompany her statement, but there isn't one. In fact, nothing in her tone was judgmental either.

It's a me thing, thinking others are judging my parenting skills or my son's progression. He's fifteen months old. Maybe he should be walking. Maybe he should have more words in his vocabulary. I don't fucking know. To be honest, I don't *want* to know because I'm doing my best. Am I failing as a parent? Possibly. But he's healthy and I'm trying.

"Not yet. It'll happen any day now, though." I shift my attention back to Max as he continues to take shaky steps into the kitchen, not letting her see the concern on my face that I'm screwing up this whole "dad" thing.

"That's kind of nice. I'm glad I don't have to worry about him running away on me," she chuckles.

Looking up at her, I catch her watching my son with a soft smile. She's not judging us.

She's not judging me.

"He's a hell of a crawler though." Letting go of his hands, Max immediately folds onto the ground before he takes off crawling. "He'll be on his hands and knees most of the time."

"As all men should be."

Isaiah makes his presence known with a childish squeak of a laugh. "I like her," he says.

"Well at least one of the Rhodes boys does."

"Two," I interject.

A flash of confusion and maybe a bit of hope washes over her face.

"Max."

She barks a laugh, and that fucking sound is so frustratingly sexy to me that I have to clear my throat and turn away from her.

"Emergency numbers," I say, pointing to the list attached to the fridge. "Mine. The team's travel coordinator. Hotel front desk. The local hospital—"

"You added 9-1-1."

"They're emergency numbers."

"I think I've got that one down already."

I continue down the list. "Your dad."

"Got that one too."

Isaiah barrels his body between us, pen outstretched. "Mine," he says as he sprawls his number on the very bottom, ten times the size of the rest. "Text me anytime. Call me. Emergency, non-emergency." He blocks me by turning his back to me, arm leaning on the fridge to create a barrier she can't see behind. "I'm Max's favorite and I have a feeling I'll be yours too."

Miller chuckles. "Thirsty."

Well, that's new. I'm used to women falling for my brother's charmingly easy playboy thing.

Isaiah doesn't move, keeping his body between ours. "I like to call myself eager."

"Parched. Dehydrated," she continues.

"Desperate," I add for her.

"Hey." Isaiah holds up a single finger. "If I wasn't getting any, I'd let you call me desperate, but I'm doing just fine in that department, so I would say I'm *enthusiastically available*."

"Sounds like you keep yourself plenty busy then. No need to try for your coach's daughter, right? Don't think he'd like that all too much." Miller tilts her head.

Isaiah stiffens, his voice dipping to a whisper. "Please don't tell your dad."

"Then please don't make it awkward for me while I'm watching your nephew."

Okay, maybe there are three Rhodeses that like her.

"You heard the woman." I usher him to the door. "Stop harassing her and leave so Max can get to know her."

"But I wanna get to know her!" he says as I push him out of the room.

I shut the door behind him, turning back to the kitchen. "Sorry about him."

"Was I too direct?"

"Nah. A little rejection is good for his overgrown ego, but by turning him down you probably made him fall in love with you. So, good luck with that."

"Great," she deadpans before finding Max sitting at her feet, staring up at her.

She gets down on her haunches, making herself as eye level as she can. "Hi, Bug."

Max smiles and I lean against the wall, watching them.

"What do you say? Wanna hang out with me while your dad is working? We can watch his game and make fun of how tight his pants are."

"You'll be watching?"

"The game? Or your ass?"

"Both."

Miller's greens dart to me over her shoulder.

*Shit.* The old me popped out without thought, two seconds after she gave my brother a warning for hitting on her.

A smirk lifts on her lips, but she doesn't fully answer my question. "Yeah, I'll be watching."

"Shit. *Shoot*," I correct myself. "You probably have tickets. You should go to the game. Hang out with your dad afterward. I'll get Sanderson from the staff to watch him."

"It's fine." She waves me off, clearly not picking up on the fact I'd rather have Sanderson watch him tonight. I trust him enough and, that way, Max will be at the field where I am. "It seems I'll be around all summer now. Plenty of baseball to watch."

*Yeah, we'll see about that.*

Part of me wants to set her up for failure, give her dad a reason to fire her, but her failing only hurts Max in the long run.

Right on cue, as that disapproving thought passes through my mind, Max reaches his hands up for Miller to hold him. She takes him with ease, and he buries himself into her shoulder, something he never does with strangers, least of all a random woman.

My son looks over to me, a little grin on his lips as if he were silently telling me that, despite my best efforts, she's staying.

Taking my hat off, I give myself a moment between pitches, running my thumb over the small photo of Max I keep tucked into the inner band.

Travis calls for change-up, but I shake him off. I was lucky enough that this guy skimmed my last change-up. I'm not risking it again.

Two outs and the third is coming two pitches from now. Bottom of the seventh inning and we're up 3-1 on Miami. That run pissed me off. I lost focus and pitched right into the batter's pocket, where Miami's second baseman sent it flying into the bleachers past right field.

Thankfully, no other runners were on the bases, but that's the last time I think about Miller fucking Montgomery while I'm on the mound.

It's her first night with Max, and I'd assume from the glimpse I got of her this morning, it'll also be her last. There's no way she won't fuck this up.

Travis, my catcher, changes his call, giving me what I want—a four-seam fastball. I need this inning over. No unnecessary runners on the bases, no extra time spent running through pitch sequences. Just up and down. Three at-bats. Three outs.

Giving him a nod, I straighten my body and align my fingers over the laces of the ball in my glove. Deep breath and I go through my mechanics, sending a fastball high and outside. Just high and outside enough that the batter swings and misses, earning me my second strike.

He's pissed at himself, and I love that. I can see the frustration even from the mound. And when Travis gives me my next pitch, I know he's going to be real pissed when I get my final strike on a slider.

It's similar to my curveball, but my slider is deadly. This is only the second season that Travis has been my catcher, but he knows this is how I like to end an inning. It's effective, and right now I need efficiency so I can get back to the dugout and check on my son.

Like clockwork, the batter swings as the ball takes a downward curve, cutting inside.

Three strikes. Three outs. Inning over.

Travis meets me halfway between home plate and the

pitchers' mound, connecting his catcher's glove to my own. "Damn, Ace. You're going to bruise my palm with that speed. How's the arm?"

I round my shoulders. "Still feels good."

I would add that I've got at least another inning in me, but I wouldn't dare speak that out loud. Superstitions and all that.

"That's what I like to hear."

"Let's go, big bro!" Isaiah jogs in from his position between second and third base, smacking my ass with his glove. "What's gotten into you tonight?"

I steadily jog to the dugout with them. "Just ready for this game to be over. Would like for it to happen as quickly as possible."

"Fucking hell," he laughs. "Is this because of the hot nanny?"

"What the hell did you say, Rhodes?" Monty yells out as we pass him, taking the stairs into the dugout where I'm met with ass slaps, shoulder claps, and endless praise for tonight's pitching.

"Nothing. I don't think I said anything." He looks around. "Nope, didn't hear anything either."

"Good. I like you a whole lot better when you don't speak." He palms the back of my head. "Nice pitching, Ace."

Nodding, I find the first staff member who isn't busy.

"Sanderson," I call out to one of our trainers as I take a seat on the back of the bench, high enough to give me a view of the field. "You got your phone on you?"

His eyes bounce to mine nervously, probably because he knows better than to speak to a pitcher between innings. In fact, I typically don't talk at all, and my teammates know not to break my focus once I take a seat on the bench, but tonight is the exception.

Seven innings down which makes this the seventh text I've sent to Miller. Only I can't be the one to do it because there are too many cameras focused on me in the dugout.

"Send a text for me," I call out before rattling off Miller's number I memorized this afternoon.

"What should I say?"

"Checking in. Ask her how Max is and remind her she can bring him here if she's having trouble with him. You can take him off her hands, right?"

"Ace!" Monty calls out. "Stop texting my daughter and focus on the goddamn game."

"Hey, you're the one who not only raised an absolute wild card, but also hired her to watch my son. This is your fault."

A crack of a smile peeks through his lips.

Sanderson clears his throat. "She texted back." He reads from his phone with absolutely no inflection in his voice. "She says, 'Tell Kai if he doesn't leave me alone, I'm going to feed his kid all the sugar I can find in this hotel, sit him in front of a screen so he can get brainwashed by whatever the hell a Cocomelon is, then leave his grouchy ass to deal with Max all night.'"

"Not funny." I go to grab his phone.

"Ace," Monty says under his palm so outsiders can't read his lips. "Cameras."

Exhaling a resigned sigh, I say, "Text her back and tell her she's fired."

Monty chuckles under his breath.

Sanderson holds up his phone for me to read as texts continue to roll in.

**Miller:** *I got fired in the third and sixth innings too! This must be a new record.*

**Miller:** *Tell him his change-up should get him fired. That was ugly.*

**Miller:** *Oh, and tell him his baseball pants aren't doing anything for his ass.*

**Miller:** *Actually, don't lie. His change-up though, that's not a lie. It really was ugly.*

"Jesus," I huff out, shaking my head. "Just ask her if my kid is alive."

Sanderson's phone dings. "Alive."

A small weight lifts from my chest. Seven innings down, two to go.

"I can't wait to meet her," I hear Travis chime in from down the bench, talking to my teammates.

"About time Max got a hot nanny," my brother says.

"About time *we* got a hot nanny. We deserve this," Cody, our first baseman adds. "This is far more exciting for the boys than it is for Maxie."

Monty turns around to rip my teammates a new one, but I beat him to it.

"Watch it," I say from my isolated seat. Standing, my jacket falls from my shoulder as I project my voice loud enough to be heard from the other end of the dugout. "I'm going to say this only once, so listen up. No one better try anything with her. I don't give a shit if you think she's God's gift to this team, she's not here for any of you. So let this be the one and only warning that if you mess with her in any way that makes her feel uncomfortable or unwelcome, you will be answering to me. You think Monty is scary when it comes to his kid?" I chuckle condescendingly. "You don't even want to know what I'll be like if you fuck with mine, and messing with Miller, or anyone who is watching my son, is the same thing as messing with Max, so don't fucking try it."

Sinking back onto the top of the bench, I re-cover my shoulder with my jacket to keep it warm.

The dugout is eerily quiet, probably because my teammates are shocked to hear me speak. Baseball's unspoken rules and superstitions are no joke—you don't mess with them, but making sure Max is okay is more important than any superstition.

"Yeah!" my brother calls out, breaking the awkward silence. "Only Ace is allowed to make her feel unwelcome, isn't that right, Coach?"

"Isaiah, stop being such a kiss ass and get on-deck. You're batting next."

"Yes, sir!"

He swaps his hat for his batting helmet, scurrying out of the dugout to the on-deck circle, while I sit and wait for this goddamn game to be over.

# 5

## Miller

"Max, there's your dad." I point to the television screen across the room.

He squeals and claps, his eyes wide with excitement.

"Is your dad the best baseball player ever?"

His icy blues grow and glint, so I'll take that as Max's version of a yes.

"I wonder who's gonna break the news to Babe Ruth and Willie Mays?"

He giggles, though I know he doesn't have any idea what I'm asking.

Over the past few hours with him, I've learned that I'm the funniest person to ever exist and if he keeps laughing at everything I have to say, I'm going to need an ego check by the time the summer is over.

When my dad proposed the idea of me nannying for his pitcher's son, I was hesitant. I've never really spent time with a kid before, and sure, there are some major fears of not being good at this role, but what's different about this job compared to all the others is that, no matter if I'm the best or not, I'm directly helping my dad. Other goals I strive for are to impress him, reassure him I'm doing something with my life after he gave up his. But this, this is me having the opportunity to make his life easier.

Max continues to look at his dad on the TV as he stands in some kind of contraption that keeps him upright and level with the counter so he can hang out with me as I get his dinner together. He reaches for his sippy cup of water, chugging it back while I cut up a bit of avocado and brown some toast, putting it on his food mat so he can eat and make as big of a mess as he'd like.

I'm not sure if I suddenly gained a knack for working with kids or if Max is the easiest fifteen-month-old to exist, but he's really boosting my confidence here. In his own way, he responds to my questions, as long as the answer is yes or no. He eats the food I put in front of him and was fully entertained by the castle of wooden blocks I made earlier.

As if I wasn't already convinced that Kai was the problem and not the nannies themselves, spending my afternoon with Max is proving my point. They've got an entire MLB organization catering to their new family, but I'm starting to feel like maybe Kai isn't all that eager to make this situation work.

My attention is pulled back to the television. Top of the eighth and the Warriors already have two outs. Number twenty-one is on the mound, looking stunning in that royal blue uniform. Scruff slopes over his sharp jaw, perfectly proportioned lips, full brows. He must be wearing contacts at the moment, but his usual glasses really add to that "uptight but fuckable" vibe he emanates. Clark Kent look-alikes do it for me apparently.

Kai shakes off a call and then another before accepting the third option his catcher gives him.

I roll my eyes. I'm glad to know I'm not the only one Kai likes to disagree with.

Winding up, that tall and lean body stretches out, releasing a curveball that's speed is surprisingly fast for the type of pitch, but it moves so much over the plate that there's no denying it's a curveball. And it's a nasty one too.

Third strike. Third out.

"Max, why didn't you tell me your dad was so good?"

He smacks his lips around the bit of avocado before smiling at me, all green baby teeth.

"Dadda." Once again, he points his avocado-covered finger at the screen as a camera zooms in on Kai jogging off the field.

The guy is annoyingly easy on the eyes. His cap is pulled low over his brow, but the blue of his hat makes his piercing eyes shine even from here.

"Kai Rhodes is having a heck of a season," one of the announcers says in the background. "He looks better at thirty-two than he did at twenty-two."

I'm assuming they're talking about his talent, but there's no denying that Kai Rhodes looks damn good at thirty-two.

Another voice cuts in. "I'd say those fans in Chicago are feeling awfully lucky right about now. He signed with the Warriors last season to play with his brother one final time before moving into retirement in the next handful of years, but with how he's playing lately, retirement is the last thing anyone is thinking about. And I'd assume it's not even on Kai's radar."

The little boy next to me with dark brown hair and wistful blue eyes looks at the screen in awe as his dad slips into the dugout. Not only does Kai look like a superhero, I think he might actually be one to his son.

You can see it in the way Max looks at his dad. In the way Kai looks at him. I'd bet good money Kai thinks about retirement every single day.

"Max," I say, pulling his attention back to me and the food on his mat. "I made you something."

I'm versed enough to know that crust is a hard no for most kids, so while cutting it off, I made it a little more exciting by turning his square of white bread into a piece of doggy-shaped toast.

Look at me using my kitchen skills on day one of this gig. Who the hell needs cookie cutters?

"Woof! Woof!" Max barks, pointing at the bread.

"Do you like doggies?"

He slaps at the toast in excitement before tearing off a leg and popping the bread in his mouth.

Glad to know I'm still in debt from pastry school when I could get this kind of reaction by cutting some store-bought bread into the shape of a Labrador.

I lean my elbows onto the counter to get on his level. "Max, what do you think is wrong with me?"

Damn. Loaded question for a fifteen-month-old. I guess I really am losing it.

He doesn't answer, continuing to chew away at the bread and avocado. Little does he know there are people in certain parts of the world willing to pay twenty-five dollars or more for some avocado toast and he's over here mashing it into his mat long before it ever makes it to his mouth.

I rephrase my question. "Do you think I'm going to get my life together by the end of summer?"

He looks at me with shiny eyes.

"Do you think I'll stop sucking in the kitchen?"

He giggles.

My eyes narrow. "Do you think I'm going to figure out these recipes?"

He smacks his lips as he chews before giving me his biggest smile.

"Wow." I straighten. "Hanging out with you is going to be excellent for my self-confidence. Did you know that?"

He squeals and I chuckle, brushing his hair away from his eyes. "All right, little man. I'll be sure to keep phrasing my questions so I like your answers."

My phone dings on the counter. The eighth time in eight innings.

**Unknown:** *This is Sanderson ... again. Ace wants to know how Max is doing.*

I can't help but roll my eyes at the unknown number accompanying the exact question I received during all seven of the previous innings. Kai is ridiculous, pulling these poor employees into his overprotective insanity.

**Me:** *Good. He's sleeping really well after the whiskey I slipped into his bottle.*

**Unknown:** *Oh okay. Well, um ... Ace wants me to tell you that you're fired.*

**Me:** *Weird. I was fired three times already tonight, yet I'm still at the hotel with his son.*

**Unknown:** *I'm sure he'll reach out again in the ninth.*

**Me:** *I'm sure he will.*

When I agreed to this gig, I wasn't fully convinced I was ready to spend my summer taking care of anyone other than myself, but I said yes because my dad is almost impossible to say no to. Whatever convincing I needed was solidified by Max and how easy he is to be with, but his dad's overly concerned parenting style is causing me to question my decision.

My attention falls back to the little boy who is an absolute mess covered in avocado.

"Max, is your dad the most overbearing parent of all time?"

He squeals and from now on, I'm taking that as a definitive *yes.*

"That's what I thought."

# 6

## Kai

Still in most of my uniform, I jog down the hall to my hotel room. As quietly as possible, I enter the darkened space, Max's noise machine covering up whatever sounds I do make as I hurry to his crib.

He's okay. In fact, I'd say he's better than okay, sleeping soundly in a cozy pair of pajamas with his favorite lovey in his fist that I didn't even tell Miller about.

I don't know why I didn't tell her about the tiny fox-shaped comfort he's obsessed with. Max doesn't sleep without the thing, but even though I'm glad he's getting some rest, I can't lie and say I'm completely stoked that she seemingly did fine without my guidance.

Following the light filtering through the crack under the adjoining door, I tap my knuckles against the barrier between Miller's room and mine.

"Come in," she says just loud enough for me to hear.

Opening the door, I find her sitting on the mattress, legs crossed, attention on the TV. Max's baby monitor sits on the nightstand where she can check on him while she watches the Food Network without any sound.

"Does this make sense to you if you can't hear it?" I gesture towards the TV, but Miller doesn't look in my direction, keeping her eyes on the screen.

"It makes way more sense with the sound off. I only wanted to see how they made their frittata. I don't need the backstory about how their great grandmother had a chicken farm, so it inspired them to create this dish for their children on the first day of school, ya know?"

"I have no idea what you're talking about."

Mesmerized by the woman on the television, she barely glances my way to wave me off before doing a double take, her eyes falling right back to my body.

"Are you still in your uniform?"

"Had to rush over here and make sure my kid was still breathing."

"You texted all night. Lighten up a little, Baseball Daddy." She refocuses on the screen, but then her brows furrow and her attention finds mine again. "You know, this uptight control freak thing is making it really hard to imagine myself watching Max all summer long."

I cross my arms over my chest. "Is that supposed to deter me?"

Her eyes narrow. "For someone who says they like my dad so much, you're hell-bent on making his job hard, huh? You act like this towards any person who comes within a ten-foot radius of your son, they quit, or you fire them, only for him to bend over backwards to do it all over again for you."

*Well . . . shit. That's annoyingly perceptive.*

And because I hate that she's calling me out on day one, I deflect. "If he's so important to *you*, where have you been? I've been playing for him for a year and a half and assumed you were a kid, not a full-grown woman, because you've never come around before."

"I'm not around *because* he's important to me."

I nod my head as if I understand. "That makes no fucking sense."

"Emmett Montgomery would give up his apartment, his dreams, and his career if it meant he could live near me. Work keeps me busy, keeps me from staying in one place for long, so we see each other on the road a few times a year. This is the first time in my adult life I have some free time and he wants me around. I owe him, so could you stop making it so difficult to pay him back?"

"What do you mean you owe him?"

She waves me off. "Maybe one morning we could get drunk together and I'll explain it to you then." Miller grabs her phone from the nightstand, holding it out for me to see. "Look at this video of Max. Look how happy he is."

On the small phone screen, a video plays of my giddy son sitting on the couch, pointing up to the television screen where he can see me pitching. He's never been to one of my games and, for all I know, this might be the first time he's ever seen me play. The constant repeat of "Dadda" makes my chest physically ache as he watches me do something I've loved my entire life, but all that changes at the end of the video when I watch him cuddle up to his new nanny.

I can feel my face fall in conjunction with my stomach. He's never been so comfortable with someone else so quickly, never had a woman in his life that he wanted to cuddle up to.

It scares the shit out of me.

Because as much as Miller has freaked me out today, what scares me more than anything is how Max will react in two months when she's gone, if this is how much he likes her on day one.

She continues to scroll through picture after picture of him, Max smiling as widely as his little mouth allows, and when she's done with her slideshow, without a word, I head back to my room.

"That's it?" she asks.

I linger back into her space. "What else do you want me to say?"

"I don't know. How about 'Thank you, Miller. I'm not surprised my son loves you already because you're the easiest person to get along with' or maybe you could try to get to know me. Anything really."

"I don't want to get to know you."

*What's the point when she's leaving soon?*

Her head jerks back from my words. "Did the fucked-up social skills come with fatherhood, or were you born this way?"

I don't say anything, continuing to lean my shoulder on the door leading from her room to mine.

"You do realize you're the issue here, right? Your son is easy."

Again, I don't respond.

She doesn't have to tell me that. I'm self-aware enough to know I'm the problem. I know I'm overly protective. I know Max is easy, but he's also my only family outside of my brother, and I'm his. He's all I've got.

Miller exhales a tired sigh, and it sounds awfully like she's tired of me. "You're just not going to respond? Cool. Do you need anything else?" She gestures towards my body. "Do you have any post-game therapy you need to do before I call it a night?"

"No, I'm done."

The lie slips easily off my tongue. My body is going to pay for pitching into the eighth inning without taking care of my shoulder, elbow, or wrist tonight. I should be going for a midnight swim or spending the next hour in the training room, letting them run me through stretches and mobility work. Instead, I got on the first bus to leave the arena without even giving the equipment guys my uniform.

Miller laughs and it's without humor. "God, you finally say something and it's bullshit."

I should've known better than to lie to her about my post-game routine. She was raised by a baseball coach.

She stands from the bed, handing off the baby monitor as a physical sign that she's done for the night. "I had fully planned on playing Mary fucking Poppins this summer, but there's no way I can deal with you for two months." She casually grabs her things from around the room. "I thought I could do this. Max is great, but you—" She shakes her head. "You are not."

What is she doing? And where does she think she's going? My entire game, I expected her to fuck up so I could fire her, but now she's leaving on her own accord.

And all I can think about is that little boy in the next room who is sound asleep after happily spending his day with this girl who's going to leave because of me.

I step in front of her, between her and the door. "Where are you going?"

"As far away from you as I can get. This whole overbearing single dad thing was kind of hot at first, but now"—she motions up and down my body—"this is exhausting."

She steps to the side, reaching for the door to the hallway, but I move with her, blocking the exit.

"Please move."

"Where are you going?" I ask again. "It's late."

She throws her head back for a moment to compose herself. "I have a house rental I need to pack up so I can drive to Chicago tomorrow."

"Oh." Well, that's a good sign. She's heading back to my city. "So, I'll see you on Sunday then? At my house."

She chuckles and it's laced with so much frustration. "First, you don't want me to watch your son. Now, you do. Make up your mind, Rhodes. Which is it?"

Great fucking question. Does she think I have a goddamn clue what I'm doing? I want Max to be safe. *I* want to be the one to keep him safe, but I can't be with him 24/7. I want him to be happy, but I also don't want him to get his heart broken when this woman leaves in two months.

I lift my hat off my head, running a frustrated palm over my scalp before flipping it, brim to the back. "I don't know, Miller."

"Oh my God." She throws her hands up. "I'm so done with you. Move."

She bolts to the other side of me to get to the door. Without thinking and without words I reach out to stop her, but she moves one way and I move the other far too quickly so that both my hands land on her tits instead of my intended destination—the safety of her upper arms.

We freeze by the door, my hands cupping her.

Miller's greens bounce down to my hands then back to me. She pauses for a beat, not saying anything until finally she clears her throat. "You gonna keep them there all night, or . . ."

"Shit." I jerk my hands away, letting them settle at my sides, forming them into fists to resist accidentally touching her again because holy fuck, she felt good to touch.

My skin is buzzing; my nerves are on fire. I almost forgot what a woman's body felt like, how delicious the weight felt in my palm. My fingers are tingling to remember again.

God. How fucking pathetic am I that an accidental tit grab is the most action I've seen in well over nine months?

"You need to touch them again?" Miller asks and it's when my attention snaps to her that I realize my eyes have been trailing all over her body, thinking, fantasizing. "If touching my boobs makes you chill the fuck out, please, be my guest."

"Sorry . . . I . . . It was an accident."

"You're acting like you've never touched a set of tits before. You have a kid. I do hope there was some boob grabbing on the night you made the little guy."

"I'm sure there was, it's just . . . Sorry."

Miller softens, no longer trying to escape, but now I feel like a creepy old man standing in front of her door, refusing to let her leave after manhandling her without permission.

I move to the side, giving her a path to go, and wordlessly, she does.

"Will I see you in Chicago?" I desperately ask before she's fully out the door.

Miller pauses for a moment before turning back. "Kai," she exhales, her voice all gentle and I can tell from the tone alone that I won't like the answer I'm about to get. "I've got a lot going on this summer, things I'm far too stressed about. I can't handle your stress on top of my own. I thought I could do this for my dad, I wanted to do it for him, but I don't think it's going to work out." She offers me a placating smile. "You've got an awesome kid. For both of your sakes, I hope you can learn to loosen the reins."

*Fuck.*

There are so many questions I want to ask. What is she stressed about? What can I do to change her mind?

Then there's the other part of that equation—Monty.

God, my brother was right. I am a grumpy dick because who else would ruin this for Monty of all people? He's been so good to me and my family and all he wanted was to spend the summer with his daughter.

And my son. *Fuck.* My son liked her.

How many nights have I stayed awake, worrying about what being raised by an all-male baseball team is going to do to him? He genuinely liked a woman for the first time in his short life, felt comfortable with her, and my own bullshit scared her away.

I watch Miller leave down the hall, watch her get into the elevator, and I'm stuck wondering about how only hours ago I was wishing her away and now that she's gone, I find myself desperate for her to stay.

# 7

## Miller

"Dad, you don't need to make up the couch. I'm sleeping in my van tonight."

Bending to reach my toes, I stretch out my back, needing some relief after my twenty-hour road trip. The last thing I want to do after sitting for so long is to sleep on a couch. The mattress in my van is far more comfortable.

"You can take my bed," he insists.

"I'm not sleeping in your bed."

"And you're not sleeping in your van in downtown Chicago."

I exhale a resigned sigh. "Can we figure it out later?"

"Fine. How was your drive?"

"Good. Easy."

"And how long are you staying in town?"

I knew that was coming, but anything I have to say, he won't want to hear. I only decided to drive up to Chicago from Miami to placate him, but my original plans of slowly making my way out to the West Coast are back on. He's going to be spending most days at the field or in other cities for games, so what's the point in sitting around Chicago if I'm not traveling with him to help with Max?

He rounds the kitchen in his apartment, pulling out a few ingredients even though he knows two minutes into him cooking, I'll be the one taking over. Emmett Montgomery is great at a lot of things. Cooking is not one of them.

"Want to talk about what happened the other night?" he asks.

"Nope."

"Okay. Let's talk about it anyway."

"Kai's too much," I quickly blurt. "That guy has no chill whatsoever."

My dad's back vibrates in a chuckle as he stands over the stove, cracking eggs into a pan.

Without hesitation, I follow.

"You should stick to coaching," I tell him, fishing out a few eggshells before they cook into the whites.

"You should be grateful I'm terrible in the kitchen. It's the reason you're doing something so amazing with your life. The cover of *Food & Wine* magazine, Millie? Incredible."

His voice drips with pride as it always does, but I'm trying not to think too much about the article or the award I just won. I need to get back into the kitchen and practice without anyone breathing down my neck.

It's probably for the best that Kai is too difficult to help. I have other things I need to focus on.

I grab the spatula from him, officially taking over. "Can we talk about something other than baking?"

"Sure. Let's talk about Kai."

"Smooth."

"What happened the other night?"

I shoot him a pointed glance. "I just want to let you know that you have terrible taste in people because your favorite player is the worst. He told me he didn't want to get to know me after I spent the entire day taking care of his son."

Then proceeded to call my phone countless times, but I haven't listened to the voicemails. I assume they were forced by my dad, and I don't need to hear his coerced apologies.

Grabbing some fruit from the fridge, I cut it up, keeping an eye on our eggs while throwing a couple slices of bread into the toaster, diving right back into taking care of him the way I did growing up.

"He's a little protective," my dad admits.

"Understatement of the year."

"And he's used to doing everything on his own. He practically raised his brother and he's only two years older than Isaiah."

*Wait. What?*

My attention darts to him, but I quickly avert it. He loves Kai and for my own pettiness, I don't want to learn why.

"He's got a lot of pressure on him, Miller. He's Max's only parent and he's maybe the best pitcher I've ever seen, let alone coached. The MLB life is almost impossible to live when you're a single dad."

Without knowing, those words fall onto my chest, sitting heavy. I've carried them around for years, all too aware of what he gave up for me.

My dad was also in the majors before I came along, but unlike Kai, the second he became a single parent, he left the league. He settled in a small town in Colorado. Coached at a shitty college with an almost non-existent budget. Stayed when the bigger offers started rolling in. Raised me on my own. Was home every night. Made it to every school function, every one of my softball games.

All the while he was talented enough to make millions of dollars playing a game he loves. But instead, he gave it up because of me.

"He needs your help, Miller. He doesn't know how to ask for it and I'm not sure if he knows how to accept it, but if there's anyone who could bulldoze their way in, it's you."

I burst a laugh. "I'm not sure that's the compliment you're intending, Dad."

"I don't want him calling it and retiring early."

The hits keep coming. He doesn't want Kai to give up his life for Max the way he had to give up his life for me.

Clearing my throat, I plate our breakfasts and meet him at the table. "Where's Max's mom?"

"No idea. Last fall, right before playoffs, she showed up out of nowhere, left Max at Kai's place, and a couple of days later she skipped town. Didn't want any part of her kid."

"*Shit*," I exhale.

"He tried to retire the next day," my dad continues. "Came to my office, told me what happened, and asked what kinds of fines he was looking at for breaking his contract early. We were about to go into the playoffs, and he was ready to walk just like that." He snaps his fingers. "No hesitation in taking on this whole new responsibility."

That makes me dislike him a little bit less. And it makes his overprotective, overly annoying parenting style make a whole lot more sense. Max didn't have anyone and suddenly, Kai stepped up, ready to be his everything.

It reminds me of the man sitting across the table from me.

"I can't spend my summer with someone like that, Dad. He's unbearably uptight. The guy has no idea how to chill the fuck out."

"He's a good man, Miller. Good heart, takes care of his family. He just needs a reminder that he has to take care of himself sometimes too. And if there's anyone who knows how to let loose and have a good time, it's you. Maybe that'll rub off on him."

"You want me to rub up on him?"

"*Off*, Miller. I said 'off.'"

I pop my shoulder. "I like my version better."

"Millie," he begins, setting his fork down. "Please, for me, give him another chance. Kai needs your help. He might not say it, might not fully realize it yet, but you'll be good for him. Both of them."

*Fuck my life.* This man, who has given up so much for me, knows I can't say no to him.

"You want me to force myself into their lives when he told me he didn't want to know anything about me?"

"Yes."

I huff a laugh. "I'll think about it."

A moment of silence passes between us, unspoken words lingering in the air before my dad finally breaks the silence and speaks them out loud.

"If you decide to stay, have fun. Make him have fun, take care of his boy, but don't forget that you're leaving at the end of the summer, okay? Kai is grounded and attached, and he has a good reason to be. But you, my girl, are the most no-strings person I know."

"You're just full of compliments today, aren't you," I joke, but he's right. I always leave, knowing I won't have to deal with the sting of homesickness when I go. At least for anyone but him.

"In a way, Kai is lucky," he continues. "That he doesn't miss Max's mom, and that Max won't remember her when he's older. But the stakes are a lot higher when kids are involved. Take care of them, but don't give them someone to miss."

He's asking a lot of a girl who, up until ten minutes ago, was contemplating leaving town at her earliest convenience.

"Dad, that was a very long, drawn-out way for you to tell me not to have sex with your pitcher."

"Well, my way sounded a whole lot more poetic than that, but yeah, don't have sex with my pitcher."

# 8

# Kai

"Max!" Indy exclaims as soon as she opens the door to her new house.

"Kai too," I remind her with a laugh.

"Yeah, yeah." She holds her hands out for my son. "You too."

Max reaches for her, so I hand him off before she covers him in cheek kisses, and I follow the sweet sound of my son's laughter into the house.

"Hey, man," Ryan says when we find him in the kitchen. "Thanks for coming early."

I put my hand in his, the other going around him in a hug. "Thanks for hosting early."

"Well, you're the only one in season right now. Figured we should cater to your schedule."

Ryan Shay is the captain of the Devils, Chicago's NBA team. We share the same agent, and he was the first athlete I met in my new city when I moved here eighteen months ago. Until this spring, when he and I both bought houses outside the city limits, we had also shared the same downtown apartment building.

We've been friendly since we met, but it wasn't until Indy, his new fiancée, came into his life that we became *good* friends. He was admittedly closed off, not willing to let anyone too close before her. I'm not sure if he even had a real friend other than his twin sister, but since he and Indy have been together, he's constantly having people over to their new home.

And every Sunday evening, the two of them host family dinners with guests including his twin sister, Stevie, and her fiancé, Zanders, starting defenseman for Chicago's NHL team. Zanders' blue line mate, Rio, is a constant here, as are my son and I. The other guys sometimes bring a few of their teammates too and Isaiah tags along if he doesn't have any other plans lined up.

Unlike my brother, I look forward to Sunday dinners all week because more than anyone else in Chicago, I feel like these people get me.

Zanders and Stevie are expecting, and Ryan and Indy are trying for their first. They're always excited for Max to be at the house and I don't feel like I'm bringing the party down because I have my fifteen-month-old with me the way I feel around my teammates sometimes.

"Hi, Maxie," Ryan says as Indy rounds the kitchen island for her fiancé to say hello to my son as well.

They've been trying to conceive for a few months now with no luck, so I'm happy to give them all the time with Max they want. They regularly ask to babysit, and Indy is the only woman Max feels comfortable being left with.

Well, she *was* the only woman. Before Miller.

"Who do you guys play tonight?" Ryan turns back to the stovetop.

"Cincinnati."

"No Isaiah?" Indy asks, bouncing Max around the kitchen.

"I'm fairly certain he's still in whoever's bed he landed in last night. Sunday mornings are typically a no go for him."

And family breakfast is typically a no go for the Shays unless I have a Sunday night game. They've got some weird thing about breakfast that they like to keep it to themselves, but they made an exception today.

"Is your uncle a little playboy?" Indy asks my son, which gets him giggling. "Yes, he is. He's a playboy, huh?"

65

"You talking about me, Ind?" I hear as the front door closes.

"No, Zee, not everything is about you."

"Good luck convincing him of that," Stevie says, hand on her belly.

"Hello, my beautiful, radiant best friend." Indy hugs her future sister-in-law, all while holding my son on her hip.

"If by radiant you mean hungry and cranky all the time, yes, I'm *so* radiant."

"The most radiant," Zanders says with a kiss to the top of her curls.

After hellos are said, the girls take my son into the back-yard to play in the fresh air while I hang back with Ryan and Zanders in the kitchen.

"How's Max doing?" Ryan asks, pouring the three of us mugs of coffee.

"Good. He's good. He's been a champ this season with the travel and living in a hotel room part-time. He's easy. I'm lucky."

I drink down half my mug and hand it back to Ryan for a refill.

His brow arches, filling it up again. "We all love Max, but this is probably the only time you're able to bitch about being a single parent. So, let's hear it. Other than you clearly being exhausted."

He hands my coffee back over.

"Please don't ask me to complain to you of all people, when you and Indy are trying so hard to become parents."

"Kai, we all have our shit. Just because we're dealing with our own stuff, doesn't mean I can't hear about yours. Besides, we're having fun trying."

Hesitating, I eye them both. It seems weird to complain about the person you love more than you knew your heart was capable of loving. Max is the best thing to ever happen to me, but being a single parent is still the hardest job I've ever had.

"He pissed on me the other day," I admit. "I'm talking all over me. Dripping down my shirt while I was trying to change him. I'm pretty sure it hit the ceiling, sprayed the walls."

"Jesus." Zanders' eyes go wide.

"Just you wait, Zee. You might want to rethink your wish for a boy."

"You *should* rethink wishing for a boy," Ryan cuts in. "No way in hell do we need another one of you running around."

"Love you too, brother," Zanders adds with a smile and a middle finger.

"At least he's cute," Ryan says, looking out the window as my son plays with his fiancée and sister. "Kind of makes up for the pissing in the air thing."

"He's cute as hell, but the kid's got the worst taste in entertainment. His latest obsession is this show about a fruit salad dance party. Like a bunch of fruit and veggies have eyes and mouths but they don't talk, they just dance to rave music. I swear to God whoever created that was dropping acid at the time. Whenever it's on TV I feel like I'm in a fever dream."

Zanders' face scrunches in horror.

"I tried to turn it off and he screamed his head off until it was back on. The radishes were twerking."

"How does a radish twerk?" Zanders asks, his mug to his lips.

"I don't know, man. I don't fucking know." I shake my head. "And last week I had to track how many times he took a shit. I literally had to write it down. The first thing on my mind every morning was this kid's shit because he hadn't taken one in a couple of days."

A small smile spreads on Ryan's lips but he tries to cover it with his coffee mug; all the while Zanders stares at me like I told him someone kicked his dog.

"And the sleep schedule. Those naps are the most sacred times of the day. If one of my teammates tries to mess with his sleep schedule, I'll lose it on them. I'm talking 'use their balls as a speedbag' kind of lose it on them. He's miserable if he's not sleeping properly, and those are the only moments of the day where I have my own time without feeling guilty."

"You feel guilty?" Zanders asks.

"All the time." I exhale a long breath. "All the fucking time. If I'm not with him, I feel guilty for being gone, but if I'm with him all day without a moment to myself, I feel guilty for wanting a bit of my own time. And the anxiety. I'm so afraid something is going to happen to him when I'm not there, or something will happen to me, and he'll be left without anyone."

Zanders takes my mug from me and adds a healthy pour of Baileys into my coffee.

"What are you doing? I have a game tonight."

"You're in the bullpen tonight, and you need that," he says, adding a splash into his mug and his future brother-in-law's.

Ryan nudges my shoulder. "You know Indy and I—we're always here to help you. Whenever you need a break. We've got you."

"I shouldn't want a break, though. I had a break for the first six months of his life."

"Jesus, Kai," Ryan exhales. "You can't be punishing yourself for that. You had no idea he even existed. You have no balance in your life. 'Dad' is just one of your titles."

"And the other is 'Starting Pitcher'. My time is split between baseball and him, and when I'm focused on one instead of the other, I'm constantly feeling guilty that the other doesn't have my full attention."

*Shit.* Talk about word vomit. I try not to complain because I don't have much to complain about. Max is the greatest part of my life, but I won't lie and say I'm not tired. I'm tired of worrying all the time, tired of wondering if I'm messing everything up.

"You know," Ryan begins with a small laugh. "For a split second, when I first introduced you to Indy, I was so concerned she was going to like you. You used to be a lot like her. A walking ray of fucking sunshine. Little did I know, six months later you'd be as grumpy as I used to be."

"I'm not grumpy," I state in a tone that sounds real fucking grumpy. "I'm exhausted. I became a single dad at the beginning of the off-season last year. I had it handled when baseball wasn't an issue, but now . . . If I could just retire early—"

"No."

"Shut your mouth," Zanders adds.

"You're not retiring early," Ryan continues. "For being your age, you're surprisingly at the top of your game. You're not calling it quits. You just need to figure out how to ask for help and learn to accept it. How's it going with Troy?"

I avert my eyes from his. "I fired him."

Pausing for only a moment, he bursts out a laugh. "Of course you fucking did." Opening the kitchen window that faces the backyard, he calls out, "Blue! Kai fired the nanny!"

I hear her footsteps racing inside the house. "Was it before or after Wednesday?"

"Thursday, I think. Why?"

"Goddammit!"

Ryan cackles. "Thank you for that."

"What am I missing here?"

"Indy and I bet on when you were gonna fire him. Had a feeling it was gonna be this week. She bet on the first half of the week, I bet on the second."

"You're making bets on Max's childcare now? Love that for me."

Stevie follows Indy inside, holding Max's hands above his head to help him walk. "What does the winner get?"

"Blue owes me a blow job." Ryan smiles into his coffee once again.

"Gross." Stevie grimaces.

Indy tosses her hair over her shoulder. "Joke's on you. Little do you know, I like giving you blow jobs."

"Yeah, little do I know. There's no way I would know that, huh?"

Ryan rounds the kitchen island to pick up Max, he and Indy doting on him. Zanders joins Stevie in setting the table, with him not so sneakily copping a feel every so often.

As much as I feel connected to these guys, us all being professional athletes settled down, they both have partners they can lean on. Someone else to help lessen the burden. They'll luckily never understand what it means to go through the hard stuff alone. But maybe worse than that is going through the good stuff and not having someone to celebrate those moments with. No one else heard Max's first word. No one else saw the first time he crawled.

And in this moment, watching the four of them, I couldn't feel more single.

That is, until the other very single guy of the group comes bursting through the door.

"I'm here!" Rio DeLuca, Zanders' teammate, busts through the house with his boombox on full blast, making his grand entrance. "What did I miss?"

"Kai fired another nanny," Ryan explains before throwing my kid in the air, catching him mid-laugh.

"Yeah, well, about time. It's been what, two weeks since he got hired?"

"Four."

"Record for ya, Kai?"

Is it? Wow, I'm not sure.

"I already hired someone else. She watched Max in Miami."

Conveniently, I leave out that she's now gone as well, but my tendency to hastily fire any and everyone is quickly becoming everyone's favorite joke.

"She?" Stevie asks.

"She."

Rio turns down his boombox. "Who is *she*? And is *she* single?"

Is she? I have no idea if Miller is single. I learned she doesn't live anywhere in particular so I can't imagine how she'd make a relationship work, but maybe her partner is a nomad like her.

"I'm not sure, actually."

"Let's say, hypothetically, she's very single. Very *available*," Rio continues. "Would she be into me?"

"No."

"Geez, Kai. Answer a little quicker next time."

"I mean, I don't know. She's my coach's daughter so I think it's best if no one in my life"—I motion around the room—"tries to find out."

"Coach's daughter, Kai?" Indy wears a knowing grin. "Interesting. I do love that plot line."

"Nothing about this is interesting, you hopeless romantic."

"Hopeful," she corrects, pointing towards Ryan. "The new term is '*hopeful* romantic'."

"Yeah, well, whatever kind of scenario you're creating in your head right now about me and the new nanny, let me squash it for you. Monty hired her without me knowing and I couldn't exactly say no."

"Bullshit," Ryan barks out. "You've never let something like pleasing your coach be the reason you compromise when it comes to Max. You like her."

"No, I don't. I kind of can't stand her, but it doesn't matter either way because she's already gone."

The entire house is wordless once again.

"What the hell is wrong with you?" Ryan asks, breaking the silence. "You have a game tonight. What are you going to do with Max?"

I raise a suggestive brow at him and his fiancée.

"Oh, no. Don't look at us like that." Indy waves her hands at me. "We love Max, but we're not enabling you. What was wrong with this one? Did you not like the way she breathed? Was she too nice? Did you not agree with her favorite color?"

"Max liked her too much already."

She's also way too fucking tempting to be glued to my side all summer, but I leave that part out.

Indy blinks at me blankly. "You're ridiculous. You need to call her and get her back here."

I already did. Right after she left. I didn't get a chance to explain that she's done *too* good of a job with my son, but even if she gave me the opportunity, how pathetic would it be for me to admit that my attitude towards her is due to Max growing so comfortable with her that it made me nervous. In the one day Miller was with him, he was the most content he'd been with any nanny before, and I fucked it up all because I'm afraid. Afraid of her being around, but even more afraid of her leaving.

"I tried," I admit. "About fifteen times, but she's ignoring me."

"Oh, you're *so* gonna sleep with her." Zanders laughs. "Hate sex or make-up sex. One of the two."

"No, I'm not."

"No, he's not," Rio adds. "Because if Kai meets someone, I'm going to be the only single one left, and I refuse to be the old, sad, single one. Well, besides Isaiah, but he doesn't count. He likes being single."

"Rio," Indy coos. "You're still a baby, but when you get old, you could come live with us, and we'll take care of you. Ryan will cook us breakfast and you could be our platonic third wheel."

"I'm not cooking him breakfast," Ryan cuts in.

"And I'm not anyone's third wheel. And don't even tease me about living with Ryan Shay, Ind. That will very quickly turn into a two-wheel situation, and you won't be one of them."

Ryan huffs a laugh under his breath.

"All right, let's eat. I gotta get home. I'm hoping Monty can convince Miller to give me another chance before my game tonight."

"Her name is Miller?" Stevie asks, taking a seat at the table, stretching out her legs and rubbing her stomach. "She sounds cute."

She is cute. In the same way a tornado is cute. Or a pack of starved lions. Super cute.

"Oh my God," Rio chastises my silence. "He didn't even try to deny it! I *am* going to be the only single one left. I'm going to have to move into my best friend's house and grow old with Ryan freaking Shay."

Zanders makes a plate for Stevie as we all take our seats. "You don't sound all that upset by that."

Rio pops his shoulders. "Never said I was."

Everyone gathers around the table, and I pull out the high-chair I store for Max here before taking my seat as well. My friends take their turns feeding my son or entertaining him. His blue eyes are bright as he laughs and smiles at the group of professional athletes making silly faces at him.

And though, yes, sometimes I feel single as hell around these people, I couldn't be more grateful for them pulling me into their fold and giving me a place in Chicago that feels like home.

73

# 9

## Kai

Five minutes to three o'clock, a forest green Mercedes Sprinter comes rolling up my driveway. Besides the fact I already know who this is because security at the front gate had to call me and clear her, this van screams Miller.

As does the way she's blaring music from the speakers and driving a little too fast for my liking. A fucking travel van. I bet the nomad herself lives in it too.

I was surprised when I got the call that she was here, but I'm thankful she came back.

Miller parks, hops out of the driver side, and rounds the front.

"What the hell is that?" I ask, arms crossed, leaning against a pillar on my front porch.

"This old girl?" She proudly pats the hood. "My van."

"You have a van."

"Yep. Live in it sometimes too."

"Of course you do."

She mirrors my posture, leaning on her car with crossed arms, a peek of a smile tugging on her lips. I'm sure she loves the satisfaction of knowing she can get under my skin with something as simple as not having a permanent residence, but I truly have no clue as to how someone could live so unattached.

Miller's tanned and tatted arm glistens under the early July sun, the glint of light reflecting off her septum ring. Max's new nanny has yet to figure out the concept of a real shirt because, once again, she's only wearing some kind of strapless piece of fabric as a bra, almost like a bathing suit. It's flimsy and barely there, but the rust orange color looks nice underneath the denim one-piece.

"Overalls again, huh?"

She's got a different pair on, and this time they're baggy and full-length, covering her thighs I tend to daydream about.

"They're easy."

"You know who else wears onesies?" I gesture to the baby monitor in my hand where a sleeping Max can be seen.

She huffs a laugh. "Shut up."

"Seriously though, those seem like the biggest pain in the ass to take off."

"So, you're thinking about taking them off of me?"

"No—"

"At least get me inside first, Baseball Daddy. We're in public."

I can't help the small smile tilting on my lips as I lean my shoulder on the pillar, thankful she's up for bantering with me after what went down the other night.

Miller takes the steps leading up to my porch, bypassing me for the front door, but I gently grab her wrist to stop her, pulling her back until her chest bumps into mine.

My voice is low and sincere. "I'm sorry. About the other night."

Her gaze dips to my lips for a split second, but I catch the movement. I especially catch how she licks her own lips after looking at mine. "And?"

"And thank you for coming back. I appreciate what you're doing for us. For me."

"And?"

"And . . . you're good with Max."

"And?"

*What the hell?* "And . . . I don't know what else you want me to say, but I am sorry for how overprotective I've been with him. It's just that he's all I've got."

Miller's set shoulders drop. "Remember that time you grabbed my tits?"

"Okay." Reaching around her, I grip the doorknob to usher her inside. "Great talk, Miller."

She puts her hand on mine, stopping me, her tone growing serious. "That was your one fuck-up, Rhodes. Treat me like my presence is a burden to your summer again, and I'll walk out this door and never come back."

A small smile tilts on my lips. "Yes, ma'am."

"Don't smile. You're too old to be smiling. You're sure to get wrinkles just from doing it once."

Shaking my head, that grin grows as I open the door of my house for her.

She enters first and, from behind, I watch as she takes in the first glimpse of my home. I bought this place a few months ago, so there are still some boxes tucked in various corners, but overall, we're moved in. The house is a nice size. Perfect for Max and me. I'm not sure if Chicago is our long-term spot, but I like the idea of picking a place and setting roots. Especially now that I have a son. Once he's old enough to start school, I don't plan on moving him.

God, that thought is depressing. He's only fifteen months old and I already feel like I'm missing out on too much time. What am I going to do when he's too old to be traveling with the team? When he's in school? Leave him in Chicago while I travel for work and hire someone else to raise him?

I want to be involved. I want to be a good dad. I want him to be surrounded with unconditional love from his family. The last thing I want is for him to feel the weight of too many responsibilities at too young of an age the way I did.

I want his life to be easy. At least, in a reasonable way. I want him to learn how to work hard, to earn things in his life. But the big stuff, like finding a way to get to school when you live across town, figuring out where your next meal will come from, or forging your dad's signature on paperwork because you don't want anyone to know you and your little brother live alone. Yeah, my kid will never know what that's like.

Rounding Miller's body, I face her in the foyer. "Max's room is down that hall. I'll let you explore on your own once he's awake from his nap, but the main part of the house is this way." Hands in my pockets, I nod towards the opposite side of the house. "Come."

"*God*," she moans, head falling back. "I can't wait to hear you say that in the bedroom."

*Jesus.*

I wouldn't know where to start figuring out how this woman's mind works, how she makes these connections. She loves to throw me off balance, to get a rise out of me. But this is my house. I'm in charge here, and I'm tired of this twenty-five-year-old woman making me feel like a teenage boy with no retort for the pretty girl who spits out the most asinine statements.

Instead of backing up or shaking my head at her as I typically do, I take a step into her, invading her space before leaning down to keep my voice low but clear. "If you're as terrible of a listener in the bedroom as you are in real life, Miller, I can promise you this, you wouldn't be allowed to come."

Those pretty lips part, jade eyes wide.

"Two can play this game, Montgomery. Now, let's go." I nod towards the other side of the house once again.

Her lips press together, holding back a grin. "You keep talking like that, Kai, and I'll be ditching the 'baseball' part and just be calling you 'daddy'."

A laugh bursts out of me, a smile mirroring the one on Miller's mouth.

Her eyes track my face as she stands only inches from me. It feels only slightly sexual, but more so satisfied. Like she's proud of herself for getting me to laugh.

"Thanks for helping me out with him today," I add, needing to voice a bit of my appreciation for her coming back before she can leave the two inches that separate us.

She nods, following behind as I lead her through the other side of the house. Max's bedroom is in the furthest corner, done purposefully in hopes that he'd be able to sleep through whatever noise is happening in the main part.

"My room is down that hall, as is a guest room. Living room. Dining room," I continue, rattling off the open spaces as we pass them. Turning the corner, we leave the main family room. "Here's the kitchen, and if you come this way, you'll find—"

I stop in my tracks, no longer hearing Miller's sandaled feet slap against the hardwood. Her back is to me, eyes on the kitchen.

"This is your kitchen?" she asks.

"Yeah."

"Kai, it's stunning."

Is it? I guess it is, with its butcher block countertops and brand-new appliances. There's plenty of storage, white cabinetry, and black finishes. But I've never thought much of it because I, for one, never use it.

"It's what the contractor had picked out, but it works."

"It works?" she asks with a breathy laugh. "This is my dream kitchen. Is that a convection oven?"

"I have no idea."

She leaves her spot, opting to explore, her hands roaming over the electric buttons. "It is."

Miller continues to open cabinets and drawers because of course she does. The woman wouldn't know what a boundary was if she tripped and fell right over one.

She comes up empty in almost every drawer before continuing to the fridge. It's embarrassingly bare, but I just got back from a road trip so I'll chalk up my lack of groceries to travel and ignore that I've been too exhausted to set up a grocery delivery or even go to the store myself.

"Kai Rhodes," Miller gasps. "Is that beer in your fridge?"

"Will it still be there by the time I get home, or should I plan on you emptying me out?"

Miller glances at the stove to check the time. "It'll probably be there. It's after three. Too late in the day for my drinking habits." She closes the fridge, leaning on the counter next to it. "Would you mind if I borrowed your kitchen tonight?"

I shrug. "Go for it. Just try not to burn my house down. And I uh . . . clearly don't have much to cook with."

"I won't be cooking, but I'll get some groceries delivered. I'll get you stocked up too."

After how I treated her the other night, I figured I'd have to be on my hands and knees to get her to watch my son again, but she's being surprisingly . . . *pleasant*. What the hell did Monty say to her?

"I mean, you'll be paying for it obviously," she continues.

"Obviously," I chuckle. "I'd appreciate that. I haven't had the time. There's an emergency card you can use in that drawer." I point to the small drawer by her hip. "As well as all the phone numbers you need. Max's pediatrician, local hospital, my buddy Ryan's number is there if you need any help. He lives ten minutes down the road. I also laid out Max's nighttime routine. He's eating regular foods now as you know from the last time you watched him, but if he gives you any trouble while you're putting him down, you can give him a bottle. I already prepped it for you. Just add water."

"So organized, Baseball Daddy. I bet you're one of those people who knows where their birth certificate is, aren't you?"

"You don't? Miller, that's something you should definitely know the location of."

This woman, who is about to be responsible for my child for the next two months, can't even locate one extremely important piece of paper.

*Max likes her. She's Monty's daughter.*

"I'm going to need you to say something reassuring right now because I'm about to leave a human in your hands and I'm not having much faith."

"I'm fun."

I can feel one side of my mouth tugging upward. "Is that supposed to be reassuring?"

"I'm also very good at poker."

"Well, thankfully my fifteen-month-old doesn't have much money to his name."

She slides her palms against the counter. "And I look good in your kitchen."

I attempt to hold back, but fuck it, I like sparring with this woman. "That you do."

There's no question there. Miller looks damn good in my kitchen when I allow myself to look.

"Does your boyfriend know what a flirt you are?"

"Oh, come on, Kai. You're better than that. Be direct. Ask me if I'm single." There's a sly smile on her lips, a smile that screams she likes flirting with me as much as I do her.

There's something about Miller, something so fierce about her personality, that my gut knows loyalty is deeply ingrained in her. So, no, she wouldn't be flirting with me if she had a boyfriend.

"No need to ask. I've already got my answer."

"Oh yeah? And what's that?"

I miss letting loose and flirting with a beautiful woman, remembering how easy life used to be, and Miller makes it pretty easy to get caught up in pretending I still have the freedom to be that man.

But I fucking don't. There's a kid in the next room reminding me of that.

I clear my throat, not answering her question. "Call security at the front gate when the groceries get here. They'll come and drop them off."

She looks around the room. "It's fancy out here, Baseball Daddy."

"It's safe."

"Glad to know I don't have to worry about anything dangerous getting in."

She might not have to worry, but I do. Because with Miller Montgomery, my coach's daughter, standing in my kitchen looking like *that*, I'm afraid something very dangerous has already gotten in.

These seats are the fucking worst.

Before I signed my contract last year, I should've amended that the bullpen needed more comfortable chairs. Eight and a half innings and my ass is numb as I wait and watch for my team to pull out the W at home.

Isaiah is playing his ass off. His defense is tight and locked in. He hit a two-run homer in the fourth and another double in the seventh, bringing in a run and giving the Warriors a comfortable lead. I was going to invite him over after the game to have one of those beers that may or may not still be in my fridge, but with how well he's doing, Mr. Popular is about to get a whole lot of attention he's not going to want to pass up.

It's not that I'm not a team player, but I hate bullpen days. Besides my forty pitches thrown to get my arm loose and active between my starts this week, I don't do anything here other than watch.

We sit somewhere off the foul line for the entirety of the game when I could be sitting at home, spending time with my son. This is where it gets hard for me. On my starting nights, I can justify the time away, but nights like these, I wish Max were here too.

With my hat in my hands, I absentmindedly run my thumb over Max's picture. It's a habit, but also a good reminder when work becomes too much, none of it really matters. He does.

I love the game, I really do, but I love my son a whole lot more and I don't know how to find that balance.

Maybe if his mom hadn't left him the way she did I'd be handling all of this a whole lot better. I'd be more hands-off perhaps. But most of the time I feel like I need to overcompensate, to be both parents and just hope that Max doesn't notice the gaps.

"Ace." One of our relief pitchers pats me on the back. "I like this no-work thing. You think you can go another eight innings on your next start?"

Chuckling, I lean back in my chair, crossing my arms. "I'll try my best."

Taking a seat next to me, he offers me a bit of his chew, but I decline, holding up my seeds instead.

"Your brother is going to be insufferable after tonight."

"God," I exhale. "Tell me about it."

And right on cue, post-game in the training room with the music blaring, my little brother waltzes in like the arrogant fucker that he is.

Isaiah slowly unbuttons his uniform to the song, the jersey with his number nineteen falling to his still cleated feet. "I'm here, baby!"

Lying back on a training table as I get my shoulder rubbed out, I watch, trying my best not to laugh. But it's pretty difficult not to when he's got the whole room on his side, cheering him on as he strips down to the music, high from our win and his personal game.

"Rhodes, you're on my table tonight," Kennedy, one of the trainers, says. "I'm rubbing you down."

Isaiah stops mid-dance, his eyes going wide with excitement because well, he's in love with Kennedy.

"Kenny . . . are you serious?" He follows her to her table like a love sick puppy dog.

"Yep. Strip down and hop up."

My brother's attention darts to me, his mouth hanging open but smiling at the same time. Kennedy rarely volunteers to work on Isaiah because the kid can be a colossal pain in the ass.

Looking at me, he points to her then to himself as if she has no idea how obsessed he is with her.

I can't help but laugh at him from across the room, but then my doctor's thumb digs into my rotator cuff and wipes my smile right off my face.

"Is this part of my reward for having a good game?" Isaiah asks Kennedy as he strips down to nothing, his cup clattering to the floor. "Just how much are we talking here with this rub down?"

"Jesus, Rhodes." Kennedy turns away from him as quickly as possible, covering her eyes. "Leave your goddamn compression shorts on. This isn't that kind of massage." She peeks over to me. "Ace, what the hell is wrong with your brother?"

"I wish I knew, Ken."

Isaiah uses both hands to quickly cover his dick while standing bare-ass naked next to Kennedy's training table. "Well, you said to strip down and I got excited."

I motion to what he's covering. "Clearly."

The entire room falls into a fit of laughter. Isaiah pulls his shorts back on and hops onto the table with his stomach down and his calves exposed.

"I just thought," he continues. "Finally, my Kenny is going to realize I'm the guy for her. After all these years and all this tension, it only took a two-run homer for her to open her eyes."

Kennedy's voice has no inflection. "There's no tension."

Isaiah smirks, looking over his shoulder at her. "Baby, there's tension. You could cut it with a knife. You'll see one day, Kenny. You're gonna want a real man, and *I'm* a real man."

Kennedy's elbow digs into Isaiah's right calf.

"Oh, holy fuck!" he screams, biting into the padded table to muffle the sound. He lets out a strangled whimper, his voice cracking. "Kenny! Kenny!"

"That's it, baby. Let it out like a real man."

The entire room is in hysterics as my egotistical brother melts into the table, squirming to get away from her. "You like hurting me?" he asks, sitting up and getting out of her reach. "Little do you know I like pain. Some might even call me a masochist in the bedroom."

Kennedy is trying her hardest to hold back her smile. They've worked together for three years and my brother has tried his best to get her in his bed. It hasn't worked. Though, the girl used to have a diamond on her left ring finger, and this season she doesn't, so who knows, maybe that's reignited his determination.

"If you like pain so much, get back on this table." She pats the cushion.

"Kenny, you've had a long day. I'm good. I don't want you working too hard."

She laughs, shaking her head and walking away. "Wimp."

My doctor continues to stretch out my throwing arm as I speak to my brother. "You're going to drive her to quit one day."

"Nah," Isaiah says, his voice growing louder as he walks to my table, looking down at me. "She's in love with me. She has absolutely no idea, but she is. And clearly, I'm in love with her."

"Clearly. Since you flaunt a new girl in your bed every night while staying in the same hotels as her."

Isaiah pops his shoulders. "We have an understanding."

I chuckle.

"I'm surprised you stayed for PT. I figured you'd be rushing home to get Max away from the hot nanny."

"Yeah, well, I'm trying to work on *loosening the reins* per Miller's request."

"We're taking requests from Miller now? Interesting."

"She's not so bad, I guess."

Isaiah's brows shoot up, a mischievous smirk on his lips. "She's not so bad, huh? Who are you and where's my overbearing big brother?"

I use my free hand to flip him my middle finger.

"You know, I was thinking, maybe I should come over tonight. Make sure Miller is okay. If she doesn't like your house, she can stay at mine."

Kennedy walks by, shaking her head.

"As a friend," Isaiah quickly adds for her to hear. "As a friend, Kenny!"

"You're an idiot and she's not staying at my house."

"But Max's nannies have always lived in your house."

"And Max's other nannies didn't have a dad they could crash with who lives thirty minutes away."

They also didn't look like Miller, talk like Miller, or have me wanting to flirt back with them every time they open their damn mouth. Additionally, they didn't have my throwing hand putting in extra work while in the shower because flashes of her thick thighs and green eyes won't leave my fucking daydreams.

# 10

# Miller

My body jumps as the front door unlocks, the whisk in my hand clattering around the metal bowl when I drop it.

I lost track of time. Apparently, I've been in the kitchen for hours, ever since I put Max to bed, but the time flew as I got lost somewhere between the butter, sugar, and flour. Kai's kitchen is a disaster. I fully intended to clean up by the time he got home, but that sure as shit won't be happening now. I watch on the monitor as he checks on his sleeping son before leaving the bedroom, headed straight for me.

I wonder how pissed he's going to be. I bet he'll get all red in the face, furrowed brows with wide icy eyes. Flustered Kai is my favorite, and I seem to do a wonderful job of pulling that side out of him.

But I'd enjoy this moment a whole lot more if I wasn't so flustered myself.

Nothing is working. I've attempted four new recipes tonight and they've all been hopeless disasters. The groceries I had delivered? They're gone, besides the ones I purchased to stock Kai's lacking pantry and fridge. Not even a stunning, state-of-the-art kitchen can bring out my creativity. My last hope is the crème fraiche cheesecake I've been working on, but even that is feeling bleak.

"What the hell happened?" Kai's voice drips with panic.

Turning, I attempt to wipe off some of the flour from my apron but it's no use. I'm covered. "How'd your game go?"

"It was fine." Kai doesn't make eye contact with me; instead, his attention continues to wander over his disaster of a kitchen.

The long exhale that leaves me blows a strand of hair from in front of my eyes, but it falls right back onto my face. "I suck at my job."

He pauses his confused perusal, his face softening. "Well, my son is alive and you haven't burnt the house down . . . yet. I'd say you're doing okay."

"That might be the nicest thing you've ever said to me, but no. Not this job. Not watching Max, but my real job. I suck at it."

Just then, the oven's timer beeps. Using the dish towel thrown over my shoulder, I pull out the cookie sheet to find my garnish burnt to a crisp.

"Fuck my life. This is supposed to be a black sesame crumb."

"Looks like you nailed it. It's definitely black."

My eyes narrow at the giant baseball player who looks far too good leaning a shoulder on the fridge and watching me.

"It's not even the main dessert. It's just a garnish. I can't even get the garnish right. What is wrong with me?" I toss the cookie sheet onto the counter.

I'm not a crier. I don't get attached enough to cry, but I had an attachment forming to what I thought was going to be the recipe to pull me out of my rut. Head falling back, I close my eyes, attempting to swallow down my disappointment.

That is, until I feel two long arms, corded with muscles, swallow me whole in a hug. My eyes pop open to find a gray T-shirt pulled taut over a chest that my face is buried in.

"You're okay," he says, soothingly. It's spoken in a way he might say those words to his son if he fell and bumped his head. It's gentle and steady, and works far too well on my chaotic brain.

I melt into him, my arms sliding around his lean waist. "You smell good."

His chest rumbles against my cheek. "I showered after the game this time."

"Does that mean you trust me with your son?"

"Don't ask me that, Montgomery. You're in a fragile state, and I'd have to lie to you so I don't feel bad."

"Kai?"

"Hmm?"

"Why are you hugging me?"

He exhales, my body moving against his with the movement. "I don't know. You seemed like you needed one. I've been told I'm a fixer so I guess it was instinct."

He might be onto something because I have a feeling if there were something that could fix me, it'd be the deep timbre of his voice accompanied by his stable hold.

"What's going on?" he gently asks, rubbing a hand over my bare back.

"I'm a joke. No one is going to hire me again. They're going to pull me from the cover, all because I can't make a goddamn garnish for a goat milk fromage blanc which is basically just a garnish in and of itself. I can't even make a garnish for the garnish! I hadn't even gotten to the cheesecake yet."

He pauses, clearly lost for words. When he finally finds them, he hits me with, "Well, if we're being candid here, who the hell wants goat cheese as a dessert anyway?"

I chuckle into his chest. "It's so hot that you somewhat understood that."

"Want to explain to me why the tattooed nanny without a filter is speaking like she owns a Michelin star restaurant?"

Pulling away from his hold, I instantly miss the reassurance. With just that simple hug, I understand a bit of what it is about Kai that my dad likes so much. He's solid. He's stable.

"Sorry." I gesture to his shirt that's now as covered in flour as I am. "I don't own a Michelin star restaurant, but I do help kitchens earn them."

Behind his glasses, I can see the confusion.

"I'm hired out as a contract employee. Chefs hire me for three months at a time to come into their kitchens and fix their dessert programs, typically in hopes of earning a star. Some chefs are excellent at both their dinner and dessert menus, and some just don't have the knack for the sweets. That's where I come in."

"So, Miami . . ."

"I was working in a kitchen there, but I kept fucking everything up. I decided to take the summer off to get ready for my next project. It's my biggest one yet."

"And what is this cover you're so worried about?"

"The cover of *Food & Wine* magazine. And I'm assuming the headline will read something to the effect of"—I gesture in front of me, as if I were spelling it out—"Miller Montgomery. Can't bake for shit."

He nods in understanding. "It's catchy. I think it'll sell well."

A bit of my internal frustration leaves me with the laugh that bubbles from my lips. Like a shot to the chest, the realization hits me that I could potentially like Kai. Especially if he keeps acting all charming and supportive instead of being overbearing about his kid.

"Well, if it counts for anything, I'm thoroughly impressed."

"Oh good." I drop my shoulders. "I'll expect an excerpt from you in my interview. 'Baseball pitcher from Chicago wonders who the hell would want goat cheese as a dessert, but is impressed nonetheless.'"

"Texas, actually."

"Hmm?"

"I'm from Texas. Austin, to be specific."

It's something so small. Such a minuscule fact in the grand scheme of it all, but hearing Kai willingly share information beyond his son's favorite snack or sleep routine holds a weight I didn't expect.

"Country boy, huh?"

The mental picture of him in Wranglers, much in the way he wears his baseball pants, is doing all sorts of things to my imagination.

"Miller."

"Hmm?"

"You're sexualizing me in your mind right now, aren't you?"

"Absolutely."

The corner of his lips tick.

"Your parents, are they still in Texas?"

He begins to gather the dishes I made a mess of, completely ignoring my question. "Why don't you head out. I'll clean this up. I don't want Monty to chew my ass out tomorrow at practice because you woke him when you got home too late. Thanks for your help tonight. I hope Max was okay for you."

"He was an angel. I truly have no idea where he inherited that from."

Kai's back vibrates, but he doesn't give me the satisfaction of hearing his laugh.

"And so you know, I'm not staying at my dad's."

Standing by the sink, Kai's eyes dart to mine over his shoulder.

"I'm staying in my van in his parking garage."

"Downtown?"

"Yeah."

"No."

A disbelieving laugh escapes me. "Excuse me?"

"You're not staying in a garage in downtown Chicago, Miller. You can stay in my guest room."

"No thanks."

"Miller." His tone bites. "Do not fight me on this."

I roll my eyes. "You might be a dad, but you're not mine."

"Do you need me to call yours so he can tell you how out of your goddamn mind you are?"

"Really, Kai? You're going to call my dad and tell on me? I'm a little too old for that, don't you think?"

"If that's what it takes to keep you safe, then yes. You're being ridiculous. Stay in my guest room or sleep on his couch. Why would you live in your fucking car?"

Because it keeps me detached. It's my own space, one with wheels that can take me far away from anything or anyone. My career isn't conducive to relationships. I love my dad, but I refuse to get attached to having him so close. He needs me to stay away so he can live the life he was always meant to live before I came along.

Kai pulls his hands out from the sink, drying them on a towel. "You going to tell me what this is all about?"

"No."

"Cool." He nods his head. "Good talk."

The tension from our argument begins to dissipate when a smile creeps across my lips.

"Don't make me laugh right now. I'm annoyed with you." He points an accusatory finger at me. "I have plenty of space in my side yard. If you're so hell-bent on living out of your car, will you park there at least? I have water and electrical hookups, and then I'd know—"

"Okay."

His brows shoot up, surprised I'd give in so fast, I guess. "Yeah?"

"Yeah."

"Good." He exhales a long breath, turning back to the sink. "And just so you know, the only reason I care about this is because it'd be really hard to get a new nanny this late in the season. It has absolutely nothing to do with you as a person. I just want to make that clear."

That smile I was trying to hide is fully exposed now. "Charming."

"Now help me clean up from the tornado that came through my kitchen while you tell me more about this job you suck at so badly."

Using the nearest dish towel, I wind it back, whipping it against his ass.

"Nice try, Miller. But it's all muscle. I didn't feel a thing."

Taking the space next to him, I dry as he washes, and I don't point out that he has a perfectly good dishwasher two feet away because I like having an excuse to stay. He listens intently as I ramble about my job, asking detailed follow-up questions, and it's then I realize he's doing exactly what I asked him to do.

He's getting to know me.

I already accepted that I was staying for the summer, but as we stand in his kitchen, cleaning together, it feels like the moment that Kai has accepted I'm staying too.

My dad's smile beams under his baseball hat as he drives us to the airport. It's the happiest I've seen him in a while, reaffirming I made the right decision to spend my summer near him.

I've been parked outside of Kai's place for a week now, but I head to my dad's each morning so we can share breakfast together. It's enough of a compromise for him since I'm not staying at his apartment.

"This is nice," he says. "It feels like the old days when you were a little girl and you'd come to practice with me and hang out in the dugout."

"Because you bribed me with ice cream."

"It was worth the investment." He peeks over at me, his brown eyes wistful as if he were reliving my entire childhood. "Missed you, Millie."

I squeeze his shoulder. "Missed you too, Dad."

My phone dings in my lap with another unsaved number. To be candid, most numbers in my phone are unsaved and unknown. What's the point? I don't stay in one place long enough to save them.

**Unknown:** *Are you and Monty on the way?*

**Me:** *Who is this?*

**Unknown:** *Really, Miller? You've been watching my son for a week and you haven't saved my number in your phone yet?*

**Me:** *Gonna need you to narrow it down a bit more. Could be anyone, really.*

**Unknown:** *I'm the guy who looks devastating in his baseball pants. Your words, texted to me last night. Scroll up in your messages.*

**Me:** ...

**Unknown:** *I'm the guy you're mooching water and electricity from.*

**Me:** *Baseball Daddy?*

**Unknown:** *You on your way?*

**Me:** *Yes, pulling into the lot now.*

**Unknown:** *Good. And Miller?*

**Me:** *Yeah?*

**Unknown:** *Save my number in your phone. You're stuck with me for a bit.*

"What are you so smiley about?" My dad laughs.

I quickly flip my phone over to hide the screen in my lap. "What?"

His brown eyes glint, a knowing smile trying to erupt on his lips, but I ignore him, hopping out of the car outside the private airport terminal at O'Hare International airport.

The plane is surrounded by line-crew putting away baggage, team travel coordinators checking off the manifest, and photographers taking pictures for the team's social media.

And right there at the base of the aircraft stairs are Kai and Max.

Kai is rocking the backwards hat today, painfully handsome in a tee and shorts that cut above his knees. It's the first time I've seen his legs and I'm not sure what I was expecting, or if I was expecting anything really, but they're thick, cut, and corded.

Didn't know a man's calves could be hot, but here we are.

And he's got . . . Is that a thigh tattoo peeking out past the hem of his shorts? Who would've thought stick-up-his-ass Kai had some ink?

My dad stays back to talk to one of the pilots. A line-guy takes my luggage for me, and Max essentially hurls himself at me as soon as I'm close enough.

"There's my guy," I laugh. "Missed you, Bug."

He giggles, his chubby hands roaming over my face, gently touching my septum ring. I pretend to bite his finger and his laugh explodes, falling into my shoulder before he begins to trace the ink there. I've quickly learned it's his favorite thing to do while I'm holding him.

I find Kai leaning against the stairwell, hands in his pockets and watching us. "Hi."

His blue eyes are soft. "Hi."

My dad steps up, joining us. "Hey, Ace."

Kai clears his throat, standing straight. "Monty," he says, with a hand in his and his arm thrown over his back.

Icy eyes dart to me from behind his glasses while he hugs my dad.

"You waited for me to board, honey?" My dad pats his cheeks with a palm. "So sweet of you."

"You wish, old man. I was waiting for your daughter so my teammates don't eat her alive when she gets to the back of the plane."

My dad turns to me. "You don't want to sit up front with the coaching staff?"

"So I can watch you go over game film all flight? No. I'm good."

"Fine." Throwing an arm over my shoulders, he kisses the top of my head. "Have fun, Millie. See you in Houston."

"You're not going to warn her about the boys?" Kai asks as my dad starts up the stairs. "Tell her to stay away from them?"

I roll my eyes at the pitcher.

"Have you met my kid? I should've warned the boys about *her*. She can take care of herself."

With that, my dad takes the stairs and boards the plane.

"You hear that?" I ask. "I can take care of myself."

Kai takes my tote bag, which is full of my favorite cookbooks, sliding it down my arm and carrying it for me as I carry his son. "I just don't want any of them to mess with you, *Millie*."

I hold a single finger up. "You're not allowed to use that name."

Over the past week, I've gotten him to crack a few smiles, but he doesn't showcase one right now. He simply nods towards the aircraft stairs with a bit of concern etched on his features.

I have no idea why he's being so weird. Kai should know by now that I have no problem looking out for myself. It's just a few baseball boys. What's the big deal?

"Hot Nanny alert!" one of them calls as soon as I step on board.

From the back half of the plane, where the players sit, twenty-five pairs of eyes peek out into the aisle or over the seat in front of them, wide and excited smiles.

Oh.

Still holding Max, I pause right there in the aisle for everyone to see me. "This is what you're worried about?" I ask Kai over my shoulder.

"Literal children."

I hold my hand up in a small wave to the back of the plane. "Miller," I say, introducing myself. "Hot Nanny works too."

"No, it doesn't," Kai says, loud enough for the entire team to hear him.

We make our way down the airplane aisle, passing my dad, who is simply shaking his head at me, but he's got a smile plastered on his mouth.

The seats up front are taken by every man that works for the team, until . . . Is that a woman?

She looks tiny in this airplane seat, decked out in black leggings, running shoes, and a team issued quarter-zip. Her hair is the prettiest shade of auburn, falling around her elbows, but I can't see what her face looks like because it's buried in her phone at the moment.

She's staring at a photo of a hand? A ring? I'm not sure.

"Hi," I say, stopping at her seat, and pulling her attention to me. "I'm Miller."

Holding out my hand that isn't holding Max, she cautiously shakes it, looking around in confusion.

"I'm glad I'm not the only woman here," I continue as Kai waits patiently behind me. "What's your name?"

She's skeptical, her freckled cheeks tinted rose. "Kennedy. I'm one of the athletic trainers."

"Kennedy," I repeat. "I'm looking forward to painting each other's toes, syncing cycles. You know, all the stuff we girls like to do."

"Jesus," Kai exhales behind me.

Kennedy finally cracks a smile that's accompanied by a small laugh. "Yeah," she says. "Looking forward to it."

I nod towards her phone. "Pretty ring."

Her smile falls. "It is."

And with that, Kai ushers me to the back of the plane.

Past the exit row, heads follow me as I pass each of them, attention bouncing from me to Max to their teammate.

"Was that you I heard, Isaiah?" Kai asks from behind me when we reach his brother's seat.

Isaiah wears a naughty smile. "I don't know what you're talking about."

"Her name is Miller," he scolds. "Start using it."

"Miller," Isaiah says, dragging out my name and patting the seat next to him. "Saved you a seat."

"So did I!" The man across the aisle from him jumps in, eagerly sitting up. "I'm Cody. First baseman." He holds his hand out and I shake it.

"Sorry, Miller," another guy says, sliding into the seat next to Cody. "This spot is taken. I'm Travis, by the way. Catcher."

"Trav!" Cody pushes him. "Get out of here."

"Looks like you're sitting with me." Isaiah pats the empty seat next to him again for me to sit.

Wordlessly, Kai slides a large hand around my waist, pulling me into a row behind them all. "You're with me, Montgomery."

I like the way that sounds far too much. Almost as much as I'm enjoying the way his arm feels heavy and possessive around my waist.

"Fine. Then I get Max." Isaiah holds his hands out for his nephew, who essentially catapults his body to get to him. "Am I your favorite person ever?"

Max giggles, showcasing his baby teeth.

Cody slips into the aisle. "Maxie! I thought I was your favorite."

"Bug!" another player calls out. "I missed you!"

The team surrounds Isaiah's seat, entirely entranced by Kai's son, and I couldn't be happier to see how much these guys love him.

It's an odd situation, having a baby travel with a team of professional athletes. The hours are tough, the road can be an escape for some guys, and I know the organization has changed a lot of the travel schedule to cater to the Rhodeses. In a short time, I feel oddly protective of that little guy, and seeing this team fawn over him instantly does something to my chest.

The back of the airplane is clearly for Max. A crib is anchored into the floor with black-out curtains pushed against the fuselage, ready to pull around him while he sleeps. And he even has his own play area on the opposite side of the aisle.

The Warriors really did go all out to make this work.

"This is our spot." Kai gestures to the row behind his brother, one side empty, the other with a carrier strapped into the aisle seat. "Max is pretty good about sleeping on the flights. If it's a day flight, this is his play area." Kai motions to the empty spot across from the crib. "Don't feel like you need to hang out with him on the plane. I'll be with him and if I need to go over film with the coaches or something like that, Isaiah can watch him."

"But I like watching him."

Kai's attention darts to me. "Okay. I just don't want to burn you out on him."

"I don't feel that way at all. I like spending time with him."

Kai doesn't say anything, simply looks at me with a softness I've only seen him wear around his son. "Okay."

"Please take your seats. The boarding door is closing." The flight attendant's voice booms over the PA system.

Isaiah goes to hand his nephew over, but Kai motions to the carpeted aisle floor.

"Put him on his feet. Let's see if he wants to get some steps in." Kai gets down on his haunches and holds out his hands, hoping Max will take his first steps in order to reach him.

Instead, Max grips the armrest as if his life depended on it before falling back. It's clearly his naptime, because Max isn't much of a crier, but as soon as he hits the ground, he begins to wail.

"All right, Bug," Kai says, picking him up to soothe him. "We'll get it next time."

He bounces him, rubbing his back until Max sucks in enough air to calm himself down. It only takes a few minutes, and once the crying stops, Kai gets him strapped in his carrier for takeoff before sliding into the empty seat beside it. I take the free row opposite them with a perfect view to watch the baseball player smile down at his kid, Max looking equally in love, staring up at his dad with tired and teary eyes.

Kai brings his son's hand to his lips, peppering kisses on his palm, finally pulling a sweet giggle from the typically happy boy.

I've never thought about having kids before, but I'd be shocked to find a woman whose ovaries *aren't* doing all sorts of cartwheels watching Kai Rhodes know exactly what to do to make his son feel better.

# 11

# Kai

As soon as my brother is settled in my room, I softly close the hotel door behind me, hoping not to wake Max. I almost knocked on the door between my room and Miller's to ask her to watch him for one more hour before calling it a night, but when I had gotten back from my game, she was nose deep in her cookbooks and laptop, searching for inspiration, I'm sure.

Last week, after she told me about her job, I googled her name. Surprisingly, I hadn't done that before. I suppose because she's Monty's daughter and I already knew she was more than I could handle, I didn't think there was much more for me to find.

I was wrong.

The Internet was littered with her name. *Impressive* isn't a strong enough word to describe Miller Montgomery's career. Her accomplishments are unheard of for someone her age. She's been featured in articles, won prestigious awards, worked under some of the biggest names in her industry before becoming one herself. But it was the pictures that shocked me more than anything. Her in a crisp white chef's coat, hair in a slicked back bun. No nose ring, tattoos covered. She was hardly recognizable from the girl I met in the elevator just weeks ago.

She shows up every day in a different pair of overalls, typically with her feet bare, but after seeing her professional side online, there's a part of me that feels privileged that Max and

I get the lesser-known side of Miller, no matter how wild it may be.

She likes my son. My son likes her, and that makes *me* like her just a bit more.

After my last start on the road, I lied about not needing to cool down from the game. This time, I can't. I pitched into the seventh inning tonight and my shoulder is screaming. I doubt I'll be able to pick up Max with my throwing arm tomorrow.

Heading to the top floor of our hotel in Houston, I grab a couple of towels and make my way outside to the rooftop pool, needing to get a few laps in to cool down my muscles. It's late, after midnight, and the pool is closed to the public, but it's never stopped me before. I live for the peace of a solo swim after a game.

Only tonight, I'm not alone.

Steam from the neighboring hot tub rises behind her, but she sits with her feet dangling in the pool. It's a warm July night, and the summer moon provides just enough light to outline her. Miller in a two-piece suit. A strapless forest green piece of fabric covers her chest, and her bottoms are pulled up so high over her hips, every inch of her thighs that I like so much are exposed.

She's fucking stunning, all earth tones and tattooed skin glistening under the moonlight.

Opening the gate, I make plenty of noise so she knows she's no longer alone.

"Breaking and entering, Rhodes? Not very responsible of you."

"Maybe I've got a wild streak you don't know about."

She chuckles a hearty laugh. "Yeah. Okay."

Little does she know, pre-dad Kai was as wild as her.

"I figured you'd be in your room looking for inspiration in one of those cookbooks you're traveling with."

She nods towards the summer moon sitting just above the city line in the distance. "This feels pretty inspirational."

She's not wrong. It's stunning out here.

Both the view and the girl I shouldn't be looking at.

I drop my towels onto a nearby lounge chair and in my periphery, I watch Miller as she begins to stand, pulling her legs out of the water, my eyes wandering every inch of that wet skin.

"Where are you going?"

She gestures to the hotel. "Giving you the pool. I figured you'd want it to yourself."

"You should stay."

Okay . . . I have no idea why I suggested that.

She hesitates, but doesn't answer me. Simply retakes her seat, her red-painted toes dipping back into the water.

Pulling my shirt over my head, I toss it on the chair before adjusting the waistband on my trunks. I catch Miller's greens taking their time tracking every ridge of my stomach and chest from across the pool, only the glow of the lights under the water allowing me to see it happen.

It's been so long. So fucking long since I've noticed a woman's attention on me. So long since I've been looked at in a way that makes me feel like a man and not just someone's dad. I preen under her gaze, my chest expanding from the attention.

"You have tattoos." It's a statement, but her voice holds a bit of surprise in the tone.

Looking down at my ribs and thigh, I note the ink she's studying.

"I always thought you were judging me for mine."

*Fuck.* Was I? Maybe I did, but it wasn't that she had tattoos or a septum ring or anything about the way she looked. I assumed if a woman were to ever watch my son, she'd be a sweet old lady with a knack for crafts and gardening. I didn't expect a foul-mouthed firecracker who's also a badass in the kitchen.

"Nah. I like yours. They suit you."

Miller's lips tick.

"Drinking at 9 a.m., though? I was judging you for that."

She chuckles and her raspy laugh is the last thing I hear before I dive headfirst into the deep end of the pool. I swim across the length to the shallow end where she sits before popping out of the water to find myself a foot or so in front of her, raking a hand through my hair to move it from my face.

"Dear God, Kai. No wonder you have a kid. Just looking at you like this would get any woman pregnant."

I huff a laugh. "Let's not joke about anyone getting pregnant again, please. I'm doing a terrible job raising one. I couldn't handle another."

She sits up straighter. "What are you talking about?"

It's too late to get into that conversation. I'm too tired. Too sore. My mind is too exhausted to think of anything other than loosening my shoulder and falling into bed. I'll have to be up with Max in a handful of hours, but Miller's dark green bathing suit, wet and suctioned to every crevice of her body, has me eager to pull an all-nighter just to stare at her.

*Monty's daughter. Monty's stunning-as-fuck daughter.*

With that, I duck under the water and swim the length of the pool again, stretching out my shoulder and hoping the distance between us will help me forget how beautiful that woman is.

But with my eyes closed, she's all I can see, and when I come back up for air on the shallow side and find her sitting there, leaning back on her palms, I know the image won't be leaving my mind for far too long.

"You should know by now that ignoring me isn't going to make me forget, Kai." Her tone is even, confident. "You're a fantastic dad. And if someone needs to tell you, I'll be the one to do it."

I don't believe her, but there's no point in arguing. "Thank you."

"Who's watching him right now?"

"Isaiah."

"Where's his mom?"

A startled laugh escapes me and I slip under the water for a moment to gain my bearings. "It's a little late for that talk, don't you think?" is what I say when I come back up.

"Nope. I think it's the perfect time."

I turn away from her, pacing and pushing my way through the water. The view is stunning from up here, the entirety of the city below us. The night is warm, the water is calming, and this almost naked woman has my lips feeling real loose.

"Seattle, I'd imagine. But I'm not sure."

Before I know it, I hear a small splash as Miller enters the water behind me. She swims to where I stand before she pulls herself out and takes a seat on the ledge, forcing me to look at her.

*Forced.* I laugh to myself. Sort of feels like a privilege to watch Miller Montgomery dripping wet in a bathing suit.

Her voice is softer than it typically is. "What happened?"

Water drips down her body, some of it falling between her tits and my attention is glued. She knows it too and like some kind of sex hypnotist, she scoots slightly closer and asks again, "What happened with Max's mom?"

"Are you using your body to distract me?"

"Is it working?"

I scrub a palm over my face because, yes, it's working. A little too fucking well. "She was um . . . someone I was casually seeing when I played in Seattle. I met her at a local restaurant the team frequented. Ashley was our server. It was never anything serious, and it was over as soon as I signed with

Chicago. Just a fling, or so I thought. I moved to the Midwest in the fall, and just about a year later, she showed up at my apartment with my six-month-old son in her arms."

"She never told you she was pregnant?" Miller's brows are pinched, anger evident.

"She didn't know until after I had already left. But, no, I don't think she had planned to ever tell me."

"I hate her."

I chuckle. "I don't."

"How could you not?"

"Because she genuinely believed she was doing the right thing, however misguided it was. She didn't want me to think she was trying to trap me or take my money, so she had planned to do it on her own, but six months in, she realized she didn't want to be a mother. That's when she showed up."

Miller scoffs. "I'll hold a grudge for you then since you're being sane and reasonable. That's fucked, Kai. You missed out on six whole months."

"I know I did, and I think about those six months every day of my life. What I missed, what Max learned without me around. I don't hate her, but I am angry with her for not telling me about him sooner. When she showed up in Chicago, there was no question in my mind that I would be the one to raise him."

"And you were sure he was yours? Just like that?"

Lifting my brows, I wait for her to connect the dots. Max has my steel-blue eyes, my dark hair. There's no mistaking that he's mine.

"Okay," she laughs, holding up her hands. "Stupid question."

"I've already missed so much, I'm afraid to miss any more."

The space goes eerily quiet, the silence screaming.

"Sorry," I apologize. "It's too late to be getting deep on you."

"It's never too late to go deep in me, Baseball Daddy."

A startled laugh bursts from my lips, breaking the tension. "You're ridiculous."

She smiles and I like it far too much. I want to stare at her, tell her too many things when she's looking at me like that. So instead, I dip under the water and swim away until I feel her on my heels, taking my same path in the pool.

Popping out in the deep end, I tread until she breaks the surface as well. "What the hell are you doing?"

"Following you around this goddamn pool until you tell me the rest."

"The rest of what?"

"The rest of the story. Why you don't trust anyone with your son. Why you don't trust me." She uses her arms and legs far more than she needs to, just to stay upright in the water. "Also, I'm not a great swimmer, so if I drown, that's on your conscience for life."

"I do trust you."

She stills, those green eyes going wide before she slowly starts to sink.

"All right, Michael Phelps." Reaching out, I wrap an arm around her waist and pull her into my body. "No need to sacrifice your life here. I'll talk."

Our legs tangle under the water, our skin sliding against one another. The water is plenty warm, but I feel the line of goose-bumps scatter up Miller's spine underneath my palm. Hand snaking around her hip, her legs hook around my waist, eyes slowly dipping to my lips because they're far too close to hers.

I clear my throat, swimming us back to the shallow end.

When I reach the height she can stand, I still don't let go. When she tries to remove her legs from my hips, I tighten my grip. She feels good. Too good. I truly have no idea how long it's been since I've had a woman's body on mine, but I don't want it to end just yet.

"You trust me?" she whispers.

"I think so."

"Why?"

"God, I have no idea. You're like a bull in a china shop so maybe I'm just clear out of my mind."

Slowly, I walk her back to the ledge, depositing her to sit, but I don't leave. I stay standing between her open legs, my palms flat on the concrete bracketing them.

"Ask your questions."

"Why have you fired every one of his nannies?" She doesn't hesitate, but I do.

My head drops, Miller's thighs right there in front of me, and I have to fist my hands to keep from touching them.

"Can I tell you why?" she quietly asks. "I think you want to stop playing baseball. I think you're so worried you're going to miss out on the big moments, that Max's caretaker is going to be the first one to experience them. I think you're so hung up on what you did miss that you're desperate not to miss any more."

Inhaling through my nose, I back away in the water because we're far too close and she's seeing far too much.

"I know what it's like to notice your parents' absence," I tell her. "The day I was drafted, Isaiah was the only one in the crowd for me, and it was the same thing when it was his turn. I was also the only one there for him when he got his driver's license or when he had his heart broken for the first time. The last thing I'll ever be is an absentee dad. I won't miss the important stuff, and even more, I don't want to miss the everyday, insignificant moments. I want them all."

Silence falls over us as Miller kicks in the water, her foot brushing my leg.

Her typically confident demeanor turns soft. "Where were your parents?"

"My mom died."

"So did mine."

My eyes jerk to hers as she sits on the ledge.

"Cancer," she says.

"Car accident."

"And your dad?"

All right, that's too much for tonight. "Long story."

She seems to understand my need to change the subject. "You need to have a little fun in your life."

A smile ticks up at the memories. "Trust me, my twenties were plenty fun. Once Isaiah was settled in the league, I lived it up. I was stupid and reckless, and I don't need to go back to that now that I have a son to raise."

"You don't need to go back, but you could find a balance between then and now. Now, you're all grumpy"—she lowers her voice, mimicking me—"'I equally hate playing baseball and people who watch my kid.'"

"I don't hate baseball. I love it, actually. I just hate that it takes me away from Max."

"And the people who watch your kid?"

My mouth twitches. "To be determined."

She laughs, smacking me in the chest with the back of her hand, but I catch it before she can pull away. "How old were you when your mom died?"

The tone in the air shifts again.

"Five."

"Geez," I exhale. "I didn't realize Monty was so young when he lost his wife."

"Oh, they were never married. Actually, they had only been seeing each other for about a year when my mom died." Miller slips off the ledge, into the water between my body and the side of the pool. "He's not my biological dad."

*What?*

She swims away from me, but like she said, she's not a great swimmer, so she doesn't get far. She's been chasing me in the pool all night, but for once, I'm the one determined to catch her.

"Keep talking," I urge as she crests the water.

"He adopted me." She wipes the water droplets from her face. "The day before she died, my mom asked him to adopt me. It was a ridiculous thing to ask of him. He was twenty-five years old, playing professional baseball. I was simply his girlfriend's kid, but he did it anyway. My mom was a single mom, raised me on her own up until then. My biological father was a one-night thing. Monty adopted me, we changed my last name to his because she wanted us to. He left the league and took a college coaching job to take care of me because I didn't have anyone else. It's the most self-less thing anyone has ever done for me, and I feel terrible about it."

I'm frozen in place, standing in the shallow end of the pool, stunned by the vulnerability Miller has never worn around me. She uses humor to dissipate tense situations, but she's not right now because Monty deserves a moment of recognition. She wants me to understand how good he is. How important he is to her.

I fucking love that guy.

"He's worried you'll retire the same way he did," she continues.

It's something I think about daily. It would take away a lot of the stress I carry. Sure, I'd be giving up a career I love, but it'd be to do a job I love even more.

"Don't," she whispers. "Take it from the child of someone who gave up exactly what you're thinking of giving up. Max will live with that guilt for the rest of his life."

This is why she came back last week. This must be what Monty told her to give me another chance.

"Miller, I'm exhausted. All the fucking time."

"Let me help you. Let me help you find the balance."

She's serious about this, about the guilt she carries. But why? I know Monty. I know the kind of man he is. He'd give up everything for his kid, the same way I would. How does she not get that? There's a different kind of love that comes into your life when you have a child. Monty didn't sacrifice his career, he simply changed directions because of how much he loved that little girl. So much so that he carries her softball photo to every away game so he can place it on his desk to see her.

Her eyes bounce between mine, pleading, but before I can answer, the blinding light from a flashlight roams over her face.

"Hey!" a security guard yells. "The pool is closed!"

Turning, I use my body to cover Miller's, my back to her, partly to get the light off her face, but mostly because I feel real possessive seeing her in this little green bathing suit and I have no plans to share the view.

She falls into a fit of laughter behind me.

"Sorry about that!" I hold my hands up, out of the water. "We'll go."

Miller continues to giggle.

"I'm holding you responsible for this one, Montgomery. Here I am, spending *one* night with you and already getting in trouble."

"Trust me," she chuckles. "I have plans to get you in a whole lot more trouble than that."

That's exactly what I'm worried about.

# 12

# Kai

We've been on the road, making our rounds to play the Texas teams. We haven't had a day off since we left Chicago, and I haven't had a chance to speak to Monty alone. The boys are rowdy as they make their way down the tunnel, headed to the field, but as the team gets ready for warmups, I sneakily slip into the visiting coach's office.

"Hey, Ace," Monty says, barely looking up at me as he stands over his desk, rifling through scouting reports. "What can I help you with?"

Quietly closing the door behind me, I round his desk, and without saying a word, I pull him into a hug.

He stills for a moment with his hands full of papers, but I don't let go. Eventually, he drops them on his desk and returns the embrace. "You okay?"

Yes. No. How do I tell him how impressed yet annoyed I am at the same time? How do I voice how grateful I am for what he did for Miller without sounding attached as fuck to his daughter?

Pulling away, I push him in the chest. "Fuck you."

Monty laughs, holding his hands up in surrender. "I'm getting some real mixed signals here, man."

"You talked me out of retiring when you did the exact same thing for the same fucking reason."

Monty's brown eyes soften, his chest moving in an exhale. "She told you."

"Yes, she told me, and you should've too."

"Take a seat."

Annoyed, I do as he says, sliding into the chair on the other side of the desk.

Monty settles back in his seat, steepling his fingers under his chin. "I didn't tell you because you and I are not the same."

"We are exactly the same in that regard, Monty. You retired to take care of your kid. Why can't I?"

"Because I wasn't you, Ace. I didn't have your level of talent. I wasn't your age. I didn't have the kind of help you have. Why do you think I've been so adamant about the organization making this work for you? I know how hard it is. Fuck, Kai, I know what you're going through, but you're not alone in this. *I* was."

*Shit.*

"I didn't tell you because you're looking for a reason to retire," he continues. "I wasn't going to give you one. If you didn't love playing anymore, I'd help you pack your bags right now, but I see it. The look you have on the nights you're pitching. How much you love being with Isaiah again. You still love the game."

"You do too. Clearly. Otherwise, you wouldn't have coached for the past twenty years. So why did *you* leave if you loved it so much?"

"Because Miller was five years old, and she had just lost her mom."

My eyes dart to the framed picture on his desk. A pre-teen Miller in her yellow softball shirt with a giant number four-teen on her uniform. Knowing what I know of the woman now, my chest aches at what she went through at such a young age.

Taking off my hat, my thumb dusts the photo of Max I keep tucked in there.

Monty sighs with resignation. "She was in kindergarten

and had lost the only parent she had ever known. She needed me."

"Do you regret quitting? Is that why you don't want me to do the same?"

"Not for a second. I needed her as much as she needed me, but it was different for Miller and me than it is for you and Max. I was looking for direction at that point in my life, and I'm a much better coach than I ever was a player."

My eyes stay glued to her photo.

"You have the help I never had. You and Max have so many people behind you. Your brother, me, this entire team."

*Miller*, I silently add.

I can see it from the weeks she's been here how protective she is of Max, how much she cares for him already, but I won't say that out loud for her father to hear.

"What is quitting going to do? Keep you home to make sure Max is happy? You know what makes a kid happy? Watching their parent fulfill their dreams. Baseball is still your dream, I know it is. Stop viewing it as the enemy and let yourself enjoy it. All of it—the team, the travel, the fans. Once it's gone, it's gone."

Keeping my eyes on Miller's photo, her words ring through my mind. How she doesn't want Max to feel the guilt she does, how she wants to help me find a balance between the two loves in my life.

"Kai, look at me."

I do so, finding Monty across the desk.

"I love both you and your son. You know that. You're the best pitcher I've ever had on my roster, but I wouldn't ask you to stay if I didn't think it was the right thing for you both. I want you to have the opportunity I never had. You've got a hell of a lot of people in your corner."

For someone who has always felt alone in my responsibilities, never having anyone else to rely on, it's not easy for me to see the help around me. But it's there. There's not a single soul on this team or staff who wouldn't go out of their way for me or my son. I tend to wallow in self-pity, telling myself I'm alone in this, but I'm not.

I nod. "Sometimes I forget to look."

"Well, you spent a lot of years looking and coming up empty, so I don't blame you, but that's not the case anymore."

Silence lingers between us.

"You good?" he asks.

"Yeah."

He gestures towards the field. "Good. Go get your ass in the bullpen."

Chuckling, I stand as he does the same. When he takes my hand to shake, he tugs on it, pulling me across the desk to throw his arms around me in a hug, but as I leave, he stops me.

"Ace, what was that hug for when you first came in?"

I hold his eye contact, making sure he hears my words. "For taking care of Miller when she needed it. You're a good man, Monty."

"Ah fuck," he breathes out, chuckling under his breath. "You're getting soft on me."

"I can't help it. Something weird happens to your emotions when you have a kid."

"Tell me about it." Monty shakes his head, rubbing his eyes with his thumb and forefinger, trying to be discreet about it. "Get out of here. I need to get my shit together so I can go out there and pretend I'm a lot tougher than I actually am."

"It's hotter than Satan's asshole," my brother complains as he warms up his arm next to me, throwing down the foul line to Cody.

# Caught Up

I do the same, stretching out my shoulder and throwing at twenty-five percent speed to one of the other starting pitchers who will be hanging out with me in the bullpen tonight.

"I don't miss Texas for a lot of reasons," I say. "But these bullshit temperatures are pretty high up there if not the number-one reason."

Isaiah catches the ball, holding on to it as he turns to me. "Do you ever feel weird coming back here?"

I couldn't care less about being back in my home state. Both Seattle and Chicago feel more like home than this place does. I spent my teen years grinding while I was here, trying to get my brother into college on a scholarship, figuring out a way for us to get to practice and school all while hoping to make him feel the love and support our dad couldn't provide.

I keep my ball in my glove, facing him. "Nah. Do you?"

"Not weird, but I kind of miss it. I have some good memories growing up and playing ball here."

I swear it's that dad thing I was talking about, getting me all emotional, but there's a flood of relief that flows through me knowing my little brother can look back at that time in our lives with nostalgia. I thought it would fuck him up. I thought me *raising* him would fuck him up, but he seems to be doing all right.

Leaving my spot, I throw an arm over his shoulder and palm the back of his head. "Yeah, man. We did have some good times here, huh?"

"Hey, Rhodes!" someone yells from the quickly-filling stands. "Your ass looks good in those baseball pants!"

Isaiah's smile grows as he investigates the crowd behind me. Following his line of sight, I find the owner of that raspy voice wearing those cut-off overalls, sunglasses, and holding my son.

God, she looks good. In a sea of royal blue and red, she's all denim and earth tones.

But what is she doing here? The game is about to start and she's got Max situated in her overalls like some kind of kangaroo. When I look a bit closer I can see him wearing the mini version of my jersey the team bought for him with his arms and legs slathered in sunscreen.

My brother turns around to show off his butt, looking back at it. "This old thing?"

"Not you," she shouts back, nodding in my direction. "I'm talking about the hot single dad over there! Number twenty-one."

"Him?" Isaiah asks, throwing a thumb towards me. "He's old as hell."

"I'm two years older than you, you dick."

"What can I say?" Miller yells to the field. "I've got a thing for older guys!" She punctuates that with an admiring whistle of her lips.

My smile is painfully big as it covers my face, partly because Miller calling me hot in front of my brother does something stupid to my ego, but mostly because Max is here and he's never been to one of my games.

I jog over to them as they stand in the first row behind the barrier between the field and the fans.

"What are you guys doing here?" Max turns to look down as he sits in Miller's overalls, his cute, chubby-cheeked smile finding me. "Hi, Bug!"

"I thought you might want to have Max nearby seeing as you're in the bullpen today."

My eyes dart to hers. "Where are you sitting?"

She points to a seat off the foul line, the first one on the side of the bullpen. A spot where I'd be able to see them both all game.

"How the hell did you score that seat?"

"I know somebody who works for the team."

My head jerks to the field where Monty stands in front of

the dugout, but he stares straight ahead, wearing his sunglasses and chewing his gum as if he wasn't just looking over here.

Max reaches back for me. "Dadda!"

"Hi, little man! I missed you this morning."

Miller unhooks one of her overall straps and pulls him out.

"You look like a kangaroo wearing him like that."

"But like a hot kangaroo, yeah?"

She passes Max to me over the barrier as I stay silent, not answering her question that'll get me in trouble. Because yes, her carrying my son around, even if she's doing it in a weird Miller way, is one of the hottest things I've ever seen.

"There's my guy." I pop a couple kisses on his cheek. "Are you my little kangaroo?"

He giggles.

"Look at you in your jersey," I say, running a soothing hand over his back where our last name is. "You're ready for the game, huh?"

Max falls onto my shoulder, burying his head in the crook of my neck and knocking his tiny baseball hat off his head. I catch Miller watching him—*us*—with a soft smile.

"Max-a-million!" Isaiah exclaims. "Are you here to watch your uncle absolutely dominate on the field?"

My brother takes my son from me, running him to the infield and showing him off to the rest of the boys. Max smiles while my entire team dotes on him, as if we don't have a professional game we need to focus on in less than an hour.

With my hands up on the barrier between the field and the stands, I watch as Isaiah holds his nephew on his hip, running him around the bases, only to be greeted by the rest of the team at home plate.

My heart physically aches, but it's not from the time away or the missed moments with my son. It's because for the first time since Max came into my life, I feel like I could have it all.

A small hand lands on mine as it sits on the padded barrier, and I look up to find Miller watching me.

"He's never been to one of my games before," I tell her, my voice a bit hoarse. "Thank you for bringing him, Mills."

A single brow lifts. "*Mills*, huh?"

"Don't try to ruin the moment with humor, Montgomery. I'll call you whatever the hell I feel like."

"Yes, Daddy."

The woman next to her coughs into her fist, reminding us that she's there.

"*Baseball* Daddy, I mean."

I simply shake my head at her.

I've quickly learned that Miller isn't great with sentimental moments, so instead of saying anything in that regard, she simply squeezes my hand. I squeeze back, the two of us having a silent conversation in the crowded stadium. Her telling me she's backing up her promise to help me find balance in my life and me finally accepting some help.

"I'm going to go show him around the dugout." I lean down, picking up Max's hat, but as I walk backward, I keep my attention on her. "I don't see you wearing number twenty-one. Where's your jersey?"

"I'm more of a fourteen gal myself."

Her softball number.

I keep my mouth shut to not let out that I've looked at that photo of her on her dad's desk too many times and know the reference well.

"If you're going to start coming to my games, I better see Rhodes on your back and I'm not talking about my brother."

"Is this some athlete kink you got? Need to see a girl in your jersey?"

The old flirty side of me that I've kept hidden and locked down for the most part since Max came into my life is itching to break free.

I pop my shoulders. "I like to see pretty girls in my jersey. Like to take it off them too."

Miller's lips part, a shocked and satisfied grin lifting on the corners. "Well, with that kind of promise, I'll be sure to wear it next time."

My chest heaves in a laugh she can't hear because I'm too far away now, and though Miller's blatant comments are meant to rile me up and they hold no guarantees behind the words, I can't deny that they make me feel like my old self, the one who was happy and light without the weight of more responsibilities than one person could handle alone.

Only, the best part of it all is that my son is here, and I still feel that way.

The training room is packed post-game because besides the flight home, we finally have the day off tomorrow. Most of the guys are getting their treatment done tonight so they don't have to meet with a trainer or team doctor in the morning before the flight. I'm one of those guys, looking forward to sleeping in as much as my son will allow, so with an exercise band tied around a pole, I pull it away, giving my rotator cuff some light work.

Typically, I'd be rushing out of here, especially after a loss, hoping to get back to the hotel in time to put Max down for the night, but for the first time all season, I don't feel the need to make up for those missing moments.

Because I got to see him all game.

Sitting on Miller's lap, he'd wave at me in the bullpen every few minutes until he passed out in the third inning, sleeping against her chest. I'm fairly certain my kid was drooling all over her, but she didn't seem fazed. She simply rubbed his back as he napped, reapplying sunscreen on his little body when the time came, and kept a mini fan on him for all nine innings.

I got to be there when he woke up, reacclimating to his surroundings, and when he looked up at the girl who had him in his arms, that sleepy smile bloomed.

He loves her. It's obvious in the way he looks at her, in the way he reaches for her when she's near. She brings him a comfort he was missing, and she equally brings me the same, knowing how well they get along.

"Kenny, please," my brother begs, following his favorite trainer around, slipping between tables to stay on her heels.

"I'm not working on you."

"It's your literal job to work on me."

Kennedy ignores him, wrapping ice around Cody's knee.

"Kenny," he whines like the child he tends to be.

"Sanderson is free. Hey, Sanderson!" she calls out. "Rhodes needs some work."

"No—"

"What's hurting?" he asks, stepping up.

My brother's eyes widen. "Nothing."

Kennedy falls into laughter behind him. "C'mon, Isaiah. Tell him what you wanted me to rub out."

Sanderson holds his hands up. "I swear to God if you say your dick, I'm quitting on the spot."

"Jesus Christ," I huff, shaking my head because well, I'm fairly certain that's exactly what my brother was about to say.

"No. God no. It's my ass."

"Your *glutes*," Kennedy corrects.

"My *glutes*."

"Hop up." Sanderson pats his table. "Let's take a look."

Isaiah shoots Kennedy a death glare and holds her attention while he gets on Sanderson's table, ass up.

She wears a satisfied smile when Sanderson starts working an elbow on my brother's glutes, but when Isaiah starts giving the trainer genuine direction and making sounds of discomfort, Kennedy's face falls.

"Isaiah, are you actually hurting?" I ask.

"Yeah. What did you think, I was asking Kenny to work on me just so she'd touch my butt?"

"Yes," most of the room says in unison.

"You all suck, but no, I just think she's good at her job."

"Hey," Sanderson scolds.

"You too, man."

My brother stiffens on the table in pain, his entire body going rigid as Sanderson works an elbow into his glute muscle.

Kennedy watches from above him for a moment before putting a hand on the back of Isaiah's shoulder, her teasing tone gone. "I got you next time, Rhodes."

"Thank God because next time what I need rubbed out is my di—"

"You always make me regret it."

He peeks his head out from the table, shooting her a cheeky smile.

A knock sounds on the training room door before Miller enters, eyes closed. "Everyone decent?" she asks before peeking one lid open to see the entire team somewhat dressed. "Dang it."

She holds both of Max's hands above his head, letting him use her for balance as he practices his wobbly steps into the giant open room.

"Look at those big steps!" Isaiah says, sitting up on the edge of the table.

"Nice work, Maxie!" Travis, my catcher, chimes in.

Hurrying to the door, I get on my haunches only a few feet away from him, holding out my hands. "Come on, Max. Let's see it."

I wait, hoping this is the time he finally gains the confidence to take his first steps.

When Miller releases him he pauses, wobbly as fuck, and when he tries to take that first solo step, he simply falls back on his butt, his diaper taking the brunt of the impact before he gets to his hands and knees, crawling to me equally as happy for himself as if he were to walk.

I chuckle, picking him up. "Good try, Bug. We're getting there."

Miller stands by the door, all warm and glistening from the sun she got, and suddenly an overwhelming urge to kiss her rolls over me. She's so pretty and so ridiculous sometimes but seeing her with Max today, and knowing she brought him so I could have the two things I love in one place, has me feeling far too attached to the girl that only a couple of weeks ago I wanted gone.

"Meet in the lobby at eight," Cody announces. "Monty, close your ears," he adds, directing his words to my coach who just walked in. "We're getting drunk tonight, boys. Maybe a few of you might even get lucky. We're going dancing and we're not going back to the hotel until the sun comes up."

"I know nothing," Monty says, plugging his ears before tossing a quick kiss on his daughter's head and ducking into the adjoining office.

"Kenny, you coming?" Isaiah's voice holds so much hope.

"No."

"Cool. Cool." He looks up to Miller. "Hot Nan—"

His eyes meet mine, and I don't even have to say anything for him to know that if he finishes that sentence, I'll kick his ass.

"*Miller*," he corrects. "You in?"

Miller's attention darts to me. "Are you going?"

I nod towards my son, letting that speak for me.

She turns back to my brother. "I think I'm going to stay back."

I like the idea of that far too much, that she wants to stay in because we are. But she's twenty-five years old and I'm sure this summer away from work is nothing like she had envisioned. The last thing I want is for her to resent us.

"You should go. All you've done this summer is chase around my fifteen-month-old." I nod towards my brother. "This wouldn't be much different."

"Fuck you very much." He adds two middle fingers for dramatic effect.

Max laughs at his uncle.

"Great," I deadpan. "Can't wait for him to add *fuck* to his limited vocabulary."

"That's okay. I'll help you get Max down for the night," Miller says.

"I got him. You should go."

"Listen to Ace," Travis pipes up. "You should come out with us, Miller."

My head jerks in his direction, not liking the way he said her name, all soft and wistful like that. Travis is a good guy, a good teammate, but I don't need him talking to Max's nanny that way. I don't need him looking at her like that either, as if she might be the prettiest girl he's ever seen.

She is, but he shouldn't be noticing.

My attention then finds my brother, wearing the most devilish smile on his face.

What the hell is that look for?

Miller turns back to me. "You sure you don't mind?"

*Fuck.*

I swallow down the regret. "Yeah."

"Kennedy," she says. "Are you sure you don't want to go?"

Kennedy hesitates, which is surprising. She's never once gone out with the team, not wanting to blur the lines between work and fun. Something not a single one of the men on staff has ever had to worry about.

"I'm going to pass," she eventually decides. "Thanks for the invite though."

Isaiah scoffs. "I always invite you and you never thank me for the offer."

Kennedy completely ignores him.

"You're going too, Ace," Monty says, strolling out of his office. "I've been wanting to hang out with this little guy and tonight seems like the perfect opportunity."

"Nah, it's cool. I'm going to head back with him."

Monty lifts his brows as if he were silently reminding me of the conversation we had earlier today.

*Find the balance. Enjoy it while you still have it.*

I look from him to his daughter.

There's a naughty tilt to her lips. "You should come."

I choke on my own saliva because Miller is fucking Miller and said that with so much innuendo, it'd be impossible not to pick up on the alternate meaning.

"Fucking gross," Monty mutters.

"Let's stop cussing in front of my kid."

"Yeah, stop fucking cussing, Monty," Isaiah calls out.

Monty shoots him a dangerous look.

"I mean . . . you should say whatever you'd like, sir."

My coach takes my son from me. "I'm hanging out with Max tonight whether or not you go out and have some fun."

Watching my kid fully content with the man who has adored him since he came into my life, I look back to Miller. Her green eyes are lifted and expectant, waiting for my answer.

For once, I don't feel like I'm missing out on anything because I got to have him nearby all day. I don't feel guilty for wanting to go have fun with my teammates. The only guilt I have is due to my coach's daughter occupying a bit too much of my brain space lately.

"Okay," I say, looking right at her. "I'll come."

That sly smile lifts.

"Let's go!" Cody pipes in. "Daddy is coming out! Fucking finally!"

There's a shit ton of noise and cheers, being far too hyped for a team that just lost the final game of a road series, but I haven't been out with the boys since last summer.

The energy in the training room is wild as the guys get their things together, wanting to get back to the hotel as soon as possible, but I keep my eyes on Miller, who stands there, infinitely proud of herself for getting me out for the night.

# 13

# Kai

My hand itched to knock on the door between my room and Miller's, wanting to walk down to the lobby with her, wanting to show up in front of my teammates together in hopes they'd understand she's off-limits for tonight.

She's off-limits always.

For them and for me.

Instead, as soon as Monty was settled in my room to watch Max, I headed down to the lobby alone, forcing myself to wait for her there while pretending to be entirely unaffected by the prospect of having a night away from the house or hotel with the girl I, annoyingly, can't stop thinking about.

The entire team seems to be down here already, drinking pregame beers and all too excited to have a night off without needing to be at the field tomorrow. I find Isaiah on a couch and as soon as my ass hits the cushion next to him, he's holding out a fresh beer, top popped already.

"Never thought this would happen again," Isaiah says, clinking his bottle to mine. "You coming out with us."

"It's a one-time thing."

He doesn't say anything, simply brings his beer to his lips, but I can feel the unspoken words he's dying to say swirling around us.

"What?"

"I just find it interesting that the night you decide to join us is the same night Miller is."

"There's nothing interesting about that."

"Really? Because I thought it was especially interesting how suddenly, after Travis invited her, you were in too."

I find our catcher hanging out with Cody and a few other of our teammates. I like Trav a lot, he's a good guy and a good baseball player. He's also twenty-six years old, a lot closer to Miller's age than me, and doesn't have someone else that he revolves every minute of his day around.

I'm not surprised that he might be interested in her. Hell, I think anyone would be interested if they knew her, but I hate that if Travis's interest was reciprocated, it'd make a whole lot of sense.

"He into her?" I ask as casually as possible, taking a pull from the bottle.

"Would it bother you if he were?"

I shoot my brother a side glance. "Answer the question."

"You answer mine."

Rolling my eyes, I stare straight ahead once again. "It would only bother me because she's here for Max. I don't want it to get in the way of her taking care of my son."

My brother barks out a laugh. "Oh my fucking God. You're so full of shit." He scrubs a hand over his face to hide his disbelieving grin. "Don't put this on Maxie. I saw the way you were looking at her in the stands today."

"I wasn't looking at her. I was looking at my kid."

"You can lie to anyone else, including yourself, but don't try to bullshit me. I've known you since the day our wonderful mother blessed the world with me, and I haven't seen you watch a woman the way you watch Miller in far too long. Hell, maybe ever."

*Fuck my life.* I thought my lingering glances were sly, but I can't lie and say I haven't found myself looking at her anytime she's in the same room as me. The way she is with Max, the odd juxtaposition of her as a person—polished and put together in the kitchen then reckless and wild outside of it—makes me want to learn everything there is to know about her. It doesn't hurt that she's fucking stunning and her blatant statements about the way I look make me feel equally as desired.

I try to save the lie anyway. "She's good with my son. So, yeah, of course I like watching them together, but it's only because Max is happy."

"I make Max happy. Monty makes Max happy, but I don't see you looking at us like you want to fuck us against the wall."

"Fucking gross, Isaiah."

"I'm just saying, it's okay to admit that you might be interested in more than Miller's babysitting skills."

I shake my head. "It doesn't matter. She's leaving."

Out of my periphery, Isaiah's cheeky smile lifts. "Fucking knew it." His voice isn't low at all. "Fucking *knew* it. Glad to know the Rhodes' family jewels are still functioning because I was getting worried there for a minute."

"Can you please shut up?" I look around to make sure no one else heard him. "I haven't slept with her, Jesus."

"Well, get on it. You said it yourself, she's leaving."

I take another swig of my beer. "We're done talking about this."

"I think she's into you too."

That gains my attention. "You think so?"

He gestures to me. "This insecure dad thing doesn't suit you."

"I'm not being insecure."

*I'm completely insecure.*

"I'm being realistic. Miller is young and successful. She doesn't stay put for long. I'm inching towards retirement and have a kid who will always be my priority. Women like that don't go for guys like me."

Isaiah's eyes are wide and unblinking. "You whiny little bitch. You need to get laid and find some of that swag that left when Max showed up at your door. I never thought I'd see the day where I'd have to be Malakai Rhodes' personal hype man but here we go." He sits up straighter. "First of all, having Max is a bonus, not a deterrent—"

"I never said he's a deterrent."

My brother holds his hand up to stop me. "I know you didn't, but you're thinking other women might view him that way. We don't give a fuck about those women. There are people out there, let's take the hot nanny who is living in your side yard for example, who will look at you being a father as a major check in the pro column. And the retirement thing— you're a professional athlete. Of course, you're close to retirement. We all are. You're making it seem like you're in your seventies and about to sign up for an AARP card. You used to have girls falling at your feet. Remember who the fuck you are. You're Kai Rhodes, starting pitcher and sexy as hell."

I raise my brow at him.

"And I'm only saying that because minus the eye color and glasses, you look a lot like me. Come on, man. Remember my prom date who only said yes to me because she wanted to ride in the same limo as you?"

"Krista?"

"Kaitlin." He sighs, eyes looking up towards the ceiling. "Who I thought was the love of my life until I realized she was in love with my big brother, as was every other girl I wanted in high school."

"You find a new love of your life every other week."

He waves me off. "All I'm saying is, there would be a horde of women who would happily get you out of your self-inflicted dry spell."

"Don't need a horde of women."

"Of course, you don't. Because you're only interested in one."

I shake him off, my voice low. "She's Monty's kid."

Just then, the elevator doors open on the lobby level, and like the magnet she's become, my attention finds her as soon as she's in the room. That dark hair is curled, falling over the tattoos I've begun to memorize, and instead of Miller's typical overalls, dark denim jeans act as a second skin, so tight I can see every striation in her thighs. A cream-colored tank dips between her breasts, her typically bare lips are painted in red, and her eyes are set on me.

"Does she look like a kid to you?" Isaiah asks, trying to gain my attention, but it does nothing to take my eyes off her. "I didn't think so. She looks like a grown-ass woman who knows exactly what she wants." He pats my leg as he stands from the couch. "And that, my brother, would be you."

Miller keeps her jade green gaze attached to mine from across the room and it does all sorts of things to my head and my dick. If I could pull my eyes off her, I imagine I'd find a few of my teammates checking her out as well. Not that I could blame them, she's fucking stunning and that red around her lips has me daydreaming of seeing it smeared around my cock.

But then Travis steps up to offer her a beer, pulling her attention away from mine, and earning one of her smiles.

"And yes," Isaiah says, walking backward to join the rest of the boys. "To answer your question. Trav is interested."

*Fucking hell.*

"Let's go!" Cody yells into the lobby. "Cars are here."

Miller says something to my catcher, which causes Travis to join the rest of the team filing outside, but she stays put, lingering behind. I stand and do the same, waiting for the lobby to empty.

Miller's eyes take their time trailing up my body until finally, they connect with mine. "Hi," she says, her red painted lips lifting.

"Hi there."

"You look hot."

I didn't think too much of my jeans and button-down while I was getting ready, but now I'm categorizing this as an outfit I need to repeat at my earliest convenience.

"You don't look half bad yourself, Montgomery."

Understatement of the fucking year. She always looks good. In the overalls, the chef's coat, or this sinfully tight pair of jeans. I've just spent our time together trying not to notice.

A twinkle glitters in those green eyes, a slight color creeping on her cheeks. She pulls her bottom lip between her teeth, and fuck if I don't want to pluck it out of there and bite it myself. It makes no sense. She's wild, far too carefree for my liking. Not to mention, she's Monty's daughter. I can't stand half the things that come out of that mouth, but for some reason, I can't stop imagining what it might taste like.

"I'm now taking *not half bad* as your highest compliment yet." Her head tilts. "How was Max at bedtime?"

The sudden shift in conversation causes me to pause. I'm not sure why, but I didn't expect her to ask about my son, especially when she's got the night off to go out and party with the team.

"He was out like a light. I think the field wore him out in the best way possible."

Her lips curve in a smile. "We had fun at your game."

"Hey!" Isaiah calls from outside. "Kai, we're leaving! Hot Nanny, let's go!"

I shoot him a disapproving glare from across the lobby. "I swear I'm going to kill him if he keeps calling you that."

Miller pops her shoulders. "At least someone is willing to call me that."

She turns on her heel, headed straight for the exit.

Isaiah's reminders ring in my mind, Miller's blatant words too. I've always brushed off her forward flirting, chalking it up to her love of getting under my skin. But I don't want to brush it off anymore. For one night, I want to pretend I can be the guy who can get a woman like her, the guy that doesn't have a hundred responsibilities at home weighing him down.

For one night, I don't want to think about whose daughter she is, and I sure as hell don't want to think about her leaving in less than two months.

My steps swallow hers, chasing after her. Reaching around Miller for the handle of the door, I pull in, holding it closed with my chest to her back and my arms caging her in on either side.

I lower my lips to her ear. "Is that what you need to hear, Miller? That I think you're hot? Do you really need to hear me say I can't keep my fucking eyes off you when you're in the room, or have you finally picked up on that?"

Her body stiffens and from behind, I watch her throat move in a long swallow. "No. I like watching you beat yourself up over wanting to look at me. It's much more satisfying to know I piss you off than it would be to know I turn you on."

A small laugh rumbles in my chest. "Well, much to my frustration you, Miller, are excellent at both."

# 14

## Miller

**Violet:** *How's the break? Are you making progress in the kitchen? How are the recipes coming?*

   **Me:** *The break has been great.*

   **Violet:** *And the answers to my other questions?*

"A line-dancing bar?" Isaiah complains as soon as we walk through the door. "Cody, what the hell, man?"

Cody's smile is beaming like a kid on Christmas, taking in the giant open room. The dance floor is fittingly Texas-sized with a live band on the stage in front of it. Everywhere I look I'm bombarded by denim, flannel, and cowboy boots, including the brand-new pair donned on Cody's feet.

"It's not a line-dancing bar. It's just a good ole' country bar." He takes a deep breath through his nose, a ridiculously excited smile on his lips as he heads straight for the bar. "Let's go, boys."

They follow suit.

Before I can leave the entryway, an oversized hand lands on my hip, fingertips gripping into the denim. Instinctively, I know it's Kai, mostly due to the possessive grip matching the vibe he's been putting out since we left the lobby of the hotel.

"Does everyone just do what he says?" I ask as the team swarms the closest bar top.

"He's the planner. Always has a plan for our time off. He rented a boat when we were in Tampa. Broadway show in

133

New York City. A trip to Niagara Falls when we were in Toronto. And a country bar in Dallas, apparently."

Turning, I face him. "And where were you for all those outings?"

"At the hotel with Max."

"But not tonight."

Behind his glasses, Kai's steel-blue eyes wander my face before dipping to my lips. "No. Not tonight."

"Ace!" one of the boys calls out, holding up a shot glass filled to the brim with amber liquid.

"Fuck," Kai mutters, looking over my shoulder at the bar. "I can't be doing shots."

"No. I'm sure at thirty-two there's no way your geriatric liver could handle it."

"Are you calling me old, or are you trying to goad me?"

"Both." I begin walking backward to the bar. "The other night you told me you had a wild streak. I want to see it. C'mon, Baseball Daddy, it's time to find the other half of that balance I promised you—the fun."

He leisurely wanders my way, but his long legs move much quicker than mine. With a single finger hooked into the waistband of my jeans, he not only stops me from getting farther away from him, but he pulls me back until my chest slams into his.

Oh, there's no doubt in my mind, tonight is going to be fun.

He wets his bottom lip with a slick slide of his tongue. "What kind of fun are we talking about here?"

*Jesus.* I'm trying to hold it together, I really am, but all I can think about is climbing his giant body like a tree.

He chuckles at my frozen state, unhooking his finger to turn my hips back to the bar. "Come on, Mills. Show me how the youngins shoot the shots."

"God, you're a thirty-two-year-old Boomer, aren't you?"

"Proudly."

When we reach the bar and join his teammates, Travis takes the spot next to me, and I can feel the annoyance radiating off Kai's body as he stands behind me.

Little does he know, Travis already told me back in the hotel lobby that the boys were all planning to rile up Kai tonight by conveniently never allowing him a moment alone with me, and who am I to interrupt team bonding, no matter how weirdly it's done.

"Kai," Isaiah calls out, holding up two shots.

He sighs, but he leaves to join his brother.

"Cinnamon whiskey." Travis slides me one of the glasses.

A shiver rolls through me at the thought. It's one of those "will not touch" liquors after puking my brains out from it on my twenty-first birthday. But there's a smile on Kai's lips, a lightness about him as he laughs with his brother, so fuck it, for tonight, cinnamon whiskey will be my liquor of choice.

It burns going down, and it takes everything in me to keep from gagging, but then I catch Kai staring straight at me as he throws back his own, and I refuse to let him know I'm suffering.

There's only one instance in which I can see myself gagging in Kai Rhodes' presence, and it sure as hell isn't from liquor.

He steps forward, wiping his thumb across the corner of my lips to catch a rogue droplet of liquor. "You okay? You were so confident only a minute ago. You're not going to gag, are you?"

I pop my shoulders. "Hopefully later."

He shakes his head—his typical move when I've said something that's caught him off guard. "You flirting with me, Montgomery?"

"Have been since we met. You gonna start flirting back?"

"Miller," Isaiah interrupts before I can get Kai's answer. "Can I have this dance please?"

When I agreed to this, I didn't realize *I'd* be as annoyed with the lack of solo time. But Kai should know, it doesn't matter which of his teammates it is, I have no interest in anyone else here. There's been a single dad on my mind far too much for me to have the brain space for anyone else.

Isaiah's smile is expectant, so I agree, putting my hand in his to allow him to lead me to the dance floor with a few of his other teammates.

"I have no idea how to dance to country music," I shout over the live band.

"Me neither. I think we're all going to look like idiots, but why not, right?"

Smiling, I look up at him only to make the mistake of directing my attention back to the bar.

Kai looks lethal, already with a beer in his hand, and the smile I was wearing falls when I catch his stare. He tracks me, his eyes dropping to where my hand is in his brother's, before he pulls his beer to his lips.

We join the crowd for the next song.

"Here's the thing." Isaiah swings an arm over my shoulder and pulls me close, speaking into my ear. "I'm not into you."

I bark out a laugh.

"I mean, don't get me wrong, that'd be different if I thought I had a shot in hell, but as it stands, I like my balls right where they are, and Monty scares me enough as it is. My big brother, however . . ."

Both our attention finds him at the bar, jaw ticking.

"Kai is probably the only guy on the team who could spend time with you without Monty losing his shit. And I think he likes you. We all think that, but he doesn't do a very good job at going after what he wants anymore. He tends to sit back and take care of everyone else, so . . . I just thought . . ."

"You'd force his hand?"

He shrugs. "Us men are simple creatures. Jealousy does wonders. I figured I'd take you for a twirl, let a few of the guys have a song or two and maybe we'd get the less attractive Rhodes brother to be selfish for a moment and stand up for what he wants. And I'm only roping you into this because, and correct me if I'm wrong, but you want him too."

I don't correct him. "Travis already told me what you guys had planned."

"So, are you in?"

As the music begins, I cast one more look in Kai's direction. I wasn't lying earlier when I told him he looked hot, and the jealous thing he's rocking right now only adds to it. Sure, my dad warned me not to give him someone to miss, but Kai knows I'm leaving in less than two months and still, he's looking at me like *that*. Maybe what he wants is a little unattached fun with the nanny for the rest of the summer.

"First of all, your brother is hotter than you."

Isaiah chuckles.

"But, yeah, I'm in."

With a sneaky smile on his lips, Isaiah spins me out before pulling me back in as the music takes over the crowd on the dance floor.

Six songs later and I've concluded that my dad's players are all surprisingly good on their feet. I've had a turn with six of them, Cody being the most fluid, as if the pair of brand-new cowboy boots on his feet suddenly gave him the ability to dance to fast-paced country music.

Every player has made their way out here, either to dance with me or someone else, and then there's Kai, still at the bar with the perfect sightline to me and his teammates.

"Goddamn," Travis says next to me, hands on his hips to catch his breath. "I thought he'd be out here by now. I'm a catcher; my knees are shit. I can't be dancing with you all night."

"I think maybe you guys read him wrong. He doesn't seem to give a shit, which defeats the purpose of this prank."

"Nah." Travis shoots a glance back to the bar. "He changed when Max came. Now he likes to play the role of a martyr. He'd never let any of us get away with a single dance with you if this were last season."

The music switches to something slow as couples begin to pair off once again.

"Ah fuck." Travis slides a hand on my lower back to pull me into him. "I swear to God if Ace hates me after this, I'm punching Isaiah straight in the face for coming up with this idea."

Over his shoulder, I find Isaiah at a table, wide and excited eyes bouncing from us to the bar. I refuse to look over there. This was fun at first but now it's sort of awkward to try to goad a guy into making a move when he clearly doesn't plan to.

As Trav turns us, I immediately catch Kai shift from the bar, standing before heading straight for the dance floor.

With every step he takes, his eyes are locked on mine from across the room, but when he reaches the dance floor, he doesn't come to interrupt. Instead he heads for his brother, who is sitting at a table on the outskirts, leaning down to speak into his ear.

Isaiah's eyes widen as he looks at the front door.

"What's going on?" I ask Travis, nodding behind him to the Rhodes brothers.

He follows my line of sight, then tracks Isaiah's.

"Oh, shit," he breathes, ushering me to the table Isaiah has occupied all night. "What are they doing here?"

Kai's eyes bore into Travis's hand on the small of my back while he takes a sip of his beer, elbows casually perched on the high-top table in front of him.

I want to smack him. I also really want to kiss his stupid handsome face, but he's going to have to be the one to do something about it. I've spent the past two weeks telling him how attracted I am to him.

"They start their series against Texas tomorrow." Isaiah turns back to the dance floor. "Cody!"

The first baseman is mid-dance with a cute guy wearing a black cowboy hat, and he shoots daggers towards Isaiah for the interruption.

But then Isaiah motions towards the door again and instantly Cody is at the table with his teammates. "Dean Cartwright is here? They couldn't have picked a different bar?"

"What's going on?" I look around all four of them for an answer.

"Daddy over here beat the shit out of that one"—Isaiah points to a group of men with eerily similar builds to the ones I'm with—"last year when we played Atlanta."

"I didn't beat the shit out of him." Kai takes another pull from his bottle, eyes locked on the inches that separate me from his catcher.

"You cleared the benches after delivering a right hook to Dean's jaw that knocked him on his ass."

"It was your throwing arm, Ace. Do you know how much money that's worth?"

Kai pops his shoulders. "He deserved it."

"What did he do?" Kai's eyes finally flicker up to meet mine at my question.

He doesn't answer right away, so Travis cuts in from beside me.

"Cartwright had an illegal slide into home while I was covering the base. Took me out by the knees. It was dirty and it pulled me out for the rest of the game."

My head whips back to Kai. "You punched him for that?"

"Of course not." He takes a leisurely sip of his bottle. "I hit him with a pitch the next time he was up at bat. I waited for him to charge me at the pitcher's mound, then I punched him."

A laugh bursts out of me because, well, Kai doing anything like that seems entirely out of character.

A ghost of a smile tilts from behind his bottle. "This was before Max."

Ah. Of course it was. He told me he was a different man then, but I like seeing this bit of fire in him. And the way his jaw flexes when his attention falls to the minimal distance that remains between Travis and me tells me it's still in there.

The table is small, the bar is crowded. I'm not standing any closer to his catcher than he is to his brother, so even though I like this side to him, he's being really fucking dramatic.

Travis pops off the table. "I'm grabbing us another round."

Cody and Isaiah turn their backs to us, facing the dance floor once again to entertain themselves by checking out every woman who walks by, but Cody also does the same to a couple of the cowboys. Kai takes the opportunity to slide around the table to my now unoccupied side.

He leans on his forearms, sipping his beer, and he doesn't look at me when he tries to casually throw out, "Travis is a good guy."

*Here we go.* "Yeah. He is."

He nods, still refusing to look my way. "Close to your age too."

"Well, that's too bad. As I said earlier today, I'm into older guys."

His eyes flicker up to mine. "He likes you."

*He's a good actor.*

"Does that bother you?"

He exhales a humorless laugh. "Isaiah asked me the same thing."

"And what did you say?"

Kai straightens to his full height again, deliciously over-bearing as he stands over me. "I told him it would only bother me because you're here for Max."

"And is that the truth? Because of Max?"

The corner of his lip lifts in a smile he's trying to suppress. "If I were to tell the truth, I'd say it bothers me enough that I've been spending my entire evening watching you and plotting a way to get Monty to trade him."

I huff a laugh, a smile on my mouth mirroring his. "And you call me ridiculous."

"I've had my moments. I was a different man before Max came along."

"A man who punches other players mid-game."

"A man who *protects* his teammate."

I raise a questioning brow. "A man who now wants that same teammate traded."

"Well, we all have our limits now, don't we?"

"And I'm yours?"

His eyes trail my face, once again landing on my lips. "I think you might be."

*Fucking make a move, Kai.*

I know he wants to. I can see it from the frustration that's grown all night, but it's as if he's decided it'd make more sense if I were into Travis or any one of his teammates I've danced with, so he's held back. And I'm worried the boys' little game of forcing his hand has only revealed that Kai is no longer selfish enough to take what he wants.

That concern is only amplified when Travis returns to the table, the necks of bottles laced between his fingers. As he sets them down, Kai leaves my side, making his way back to the opposite end with his brother.

"So, are we leaving or staying if Cartwright and his team-mates are here?" Travis asks.

"Staying." Isaiah pins him with a look, a slight slur to his speech already. "Fuck that guy. He was a prick when we were kids playing travel ball and he's an even bigger prick now."

"Well, if we're staying, I'm dancing." Cody holds his hand out for mine.

The boys turn to look at their pitcher, waiting for him to step in, but all he does is trade his finished beer for a fresh one.

As one song ends and the next begins, one of the outfielders spins me into the next teammate's pair of awaiting arms.

Only this time the person who grabs me isn't one of the guys from the team. It's Dean Cartwright—the player from Atlanta.

"What's your name?" he asks, one hand on my lower back and his mouth far too close to my ear.

I swallow, looking around the dance floor for a familiar face, but I've had a fair amount to drink and he's spinning me a little too fast to catch a good look at anyone. "Miller."

A slow smile spreads across his lips. "Aren't you going to ask me mine?"

"I already know yours."

"Figures."

His lips spread in a slow smirk that I'd assume most women would classify as sexy. But the overly cocky thing doesn't do it for me anymore. Now I've got a smoking hot but unsure man on my mind, and I can't think of anything more attractive than the idea of him finding his well-deserved confidence. Especially with me.

I go to pull out of his hold, but his grip only tightens.

"What do you want?" I ask.

"I just want a dance. I've been watching you all night and wondering what the hell you're doing here with the Windy City Warriors."

I stare him straight in the eye. "My dad is the field manager."

His brows lift. "Monty's daughter? I had a deal fall through because your dad wouldn't sign me."

"Makes sense. He's always had good taste."

His laugh is genuine. "Snarky little thing, huh?"

"Can I go now?" I ask, trying once again to unsuccessfully pull myself from his grip without causing a scene.

"One dance, Miller Montgomery."

It takes me a moment, but I resign. "Fine. But only if you tell me why the entire team hates you so much."

His smile is devious as we begin to move once again. "I've known the Rhodeses since we were kids playing travel ball. May or may not have slept with one or two of Isaiah's girlfriends in high school."

"Isaiah doesn't have girlfriends."

"He used to. And it was a real easy way to knock him off his game before we played."

I can't hold in my disbelieving laugh. "So you're just a shitty person, huh?"

"I'm a competitor. If something as trivial as that could make my opponent have a bad game, that's on them."

"You're kind of the worst, you know that? I hope the pitch Kai hit you with was a fastball straight to the nuts."

A smile slides across his lips. "Thanks, doll."

My head is on a swivel, looking for the team, and I finally find them all gathered at a table, eyes locked on us.

"What are you doing here?" I ask. "Don't you have a game tomorrow?"

"You know my schedule already? Sweet of you. My stepsister is staying close by. Thought I might get her out of the hotel tonight. You might know her actually—" Dean's attention drifts behind my shoulder. "Oh wow." His hand falls further south, fingertips draped over the top of my ass. "I've never been able to fuck with Ace before."

"I'm playing nice, but don't you dare let that hand slip any further."

He simply smiles. "I should've said I've never been able to fuck with Ace until *tonight*."

*Huh?*

I can feel Kai's presence long before I see him. When he makes it to us, he pushes Dean's chest into the crowd, breaking the hold he has on me.

"Get your fucking hands off her."

# 15

# Kai

I'll admit, I've been wallowing like a little bitch all night. I know that Isaiah is only messing with me, trying to force me into acting like a deranged caveman by throwing Miller over my shoulder or some shit. But all it's done is reinforce what I already know—I don't have the luxury to be the kind of guy she would want.

There's been an infectious smile plastered on those red-painted lips all night. She's hardly left the dance floor. She's fun and magnetic and I want her to pull me into her orbit, but I'll wake up tomorrow and remember who I am. A single dad with no time on his hands to chase around a twenty-five-year-old.

I haven't taken my attention off her. I've tracked her every move like an obsessed stalker and maybe I am. God, I feel like a creep, but I can't help it.

I could handle Isaiah dancing with her because I knew he was fucking with me. In fact, I could handle most of the team dancing with her, even though I watched with unblinking attention, making sure not a single one of their hands dropped too low. It's even come to my attention that Travis was playing me, and there's a large part of me that's brimming with the desire to fuck them all up for it.

But instead, I'll go home and take care of my responsibilities.

I pat my brother on the back as our right fielder takes a turn with Miller on the dance floor. "I'm taking off. Keep an eye on her for me and make sure she makes it back to the hotel, okay?"

"What?" Isaiah turns around in his seat, giving me his full attention. "Don't leave, man."

"I've been pounding beers to keep me from saying or doing something I'll regret, so I think it's time I go."

"Fuck, Kai. We were kidding. We just wanted you to be selfish for a second and go get the girl."

Palm to cheek, I tap my hand against him. "Love you. Don't do anything stupid tonight. Let me know when you make it home safe."

I connect my fist with a few of my other teammates at the table, saying goodbye, but as I turn to leave I give the dance floor one more glance, only to see Dean Cartwright take Miller into his arms.

*You've got to be fucking kidding me.*

Jaw ticking, my blood heats. I can feel it flowing through every vein, rushing towards my fists. I've controlled myself since becoming a parent, but I'm pretty sure I'm about to publicly lose my shit over Max's nanny.

Dean is smiling like the pompous ass he is, and I can't read Miller's expression or body language. They're talking a lot though and I don't like it.

"Malakai," my brother warns, dragging out my full name.

"He better get his fucking hands off her."

Isaiah steps in front of me. "Don't."

I keep my eyes on the two of them as I move towards the dance floor. "I'm just gonna go have a word."

"Kai, if you fuck up your hand, Monty will literally murder me."

"I'm not going to hit him."

Dean's hand that was on her back drops dangerously lower.

*Okay, I lied. There's a chance I'm going to jail tonight.*

It continues south, resting just above Miller's ass that looks unbelievable in those tight jeans.

I don't see anything around me other than red, but somehow I keep my steps at a casual speed, even though there's nothing casual about the pure rage thrumming through my body.

"Get your fucking hands off her," I say, pushing his chest to break the contact he has on her.

He only wears an arrogant smile as he rights himself. "Kai Rhodes. Shocked to see you out tonight. Shouldn't you be at home with your son? Wouldn't want another absentee father now, would we?"

"What the fuck did you just say?" I step into him, but I feel the tug Miller has on my shirt.

Dean has been a nuisance since we were kids. He's known us long enough that I understand he's referring to my own father.

"Or let me guess. You're out here looking for a new mommy for your son."

This time it's Miller making a move, but I hold out a single arm to keep her behind me.

"Oh." Dean lights up, looking from me back to Miller. "Is this Max's new mommy? C'mon, Ace, she's far too young to force into that kind of life with you. You're better than that."

"Kai." I hear my brother's warning voice somewhere behind me, but mostly my ears are pounding with seething anger.

If he talked about me, that'd be one thing. But Max? Not a fucking chance.

I step into him, tauntingly knocking the side of his jaw with my knuckles. "You need another one? Maybe one on the left side to match the teeth I knocked out on the right?"

"Kai," my brother warns again, but it does nothing to pull my attention away.

"Wow, that was so much easier than I expected." Dean laughs like the arrogant little prick that he is. "Does your coach know you're foaming at the mouth over his daughter?"

I shake my head. "Fuck you. It's not like that. She's just the nanny."

I fucking hate the words as soon as they're out of my mouth.

He simply laughs. "Nice work. You can't even blame that fuck-up on me."

Turning, I expect yet dread the idea of finding Miller behind me, but she's gone. And I know with every fiber of my being she heard what I said.

I catch a flash of dark brunette hair over tattooed shoulders in the distance, exiting the main room and heading downstairs to the bathroom. "You're a piece of shit," is the last thing I say to an all too satisfied Dean before I chase after her.

She's quick but I'm faster.

"Miller!" I shout loud enough for her to hear me, but she doesn't slow down. "Where the hell are you going?"

"I can take care of myself," she yells over her shoulder. "I had that handled just fine before you came around and made a scene."

Is she fucking kidding right now?

"He grabbed you!" I do exactly that, circling her elbow to stop her.

"I can take care of myself!" She turns on me, anger evident. "How many times do I have to tell you that? God, you ignore me all night, then pull that? You're giving me whiplash."

"Ignore you all night?"

Fuck, it would seem that way to her, wouldn't it? Little does she know I couldn't make myself ignore her if I tried.

Yanking out of my hold, she charges down the stairs, headed to the women's bathroom, but my long legs eat up the distance to get myself in front of her and keep her from getting any further. I'm two steps lower than her, putting us at eye level.

She crosses her arms over her chest like a brat and fuck if that doesn't do something to me. "You gonna follow me into the women's bathroom now? I'm not sure why you're so concerned. I'm just the nanny, after all."

*Fucking hell.*

I soften my tone. "I didn't mean for it to come out that way. That's not what I meant."

"It's fine. I was the one who asked to see the old Kai." She moves to get past me, but I step in front of her, blocking her path.

"That's never been me. I just . . . fuck, I hated seeing his hands on you. If you want to know the old me, he was known to take care of his people no matter how recklessly he did it."

My people. *Her.*

I can see the moment she puts that little piece together.

"I don't need anyone to protect me. I've been on my own for a long time just like I'll be on my own again come September. I can take care of myself."

"Stop fucking saying that."

"Saying what?" she tests. "That I can take care of myself or that I'm leaving soon?"

I run an aggravated hand through my hair, my chest still heaving with anger. "God, you drive me out of my fucking mind, Miller. He was touching you."

"You know who else you saw touching me tonight? Travis. Cody. Your brother. I didn't see you do anything then."

My jaw works. "That's different. They're good guys. If you wanted to . . ." I shake my head, unable to even say it. "Dean Cartwright is scum. I've known him since we were kids. I wouldn't be okay with that."

"Do you think I need your permission?" She laughs without humor. "You are not my father. I can do whatever I want *with* whomever I want, and I don't need to explain any of it to you."

People pass us on the stairwell, suspicious glances thrown our way as we argue in the direct path to the bathroom.

My eyes narrow. "And he's what you want?"

She throws her hands up. "Oh my God! You're impossible. You need to go. I'm not your problem to worry about."

Turning, she heads back up the way we came, but I stop her, pinning her against the wall, the two of us meeting on the same stair. "Yes, the fuck you are."

She stares right at me, not backing down. "Kai, I am *not* your problem."

My attention dips to her lips. "Be my problem."

Swallowing, she tilts her head, testing me. "Then do something to make me your problem."

*Fuck me.* I'm so frustratingly into this woman, so I do just that.

I make her my problem.

There's nothing soft or sweet about the way my mouth crashes onto hers because there's nothing soft or sweet about Miller. She aggravates me, pushes me, challenges me.

And according to the way her mouth yields to mine—she *wants* me.

Cupping her face, she hums as my lips close over hers, like this kiss is the sweetest kind of relief. They're pillowy soft, just as I imagined, and her tongue. Her *fucking* tongue. Warm and wet and responsive as it meets mine, pulling a reassured groan from my throat.

It's almost too much. Too goddamn perfect.

Pushing into her, I take more, bending down and trying to steal as much as I can.

Miller's hands are over my shoulders. She scrapes her nails against my skin in the most electric way, before pulling at the ends of my hair as if she equally can't get enough.

"Fuck, Kai," she whispers against me, her hands roaming with appreciation. "More."

I couldn't tell you the last time I felt this way. Wanted. *Desired.*

Touched and taken care of.

Bodies are passing us on the dark stairwell, but I couldn't care less. I surge my hips into hers, pushing her into the wall, our mouths frantic as Miller slings a leg over my thigh to get me closer.

Goddamn, the cradle of her hips is perfect for mine.

I push into her, my dick painfully hard and searching for friction even if it's only from some denim.

She's so pretty. So shockingly *willing.*

I thought she'd fight me, battle me for control, but Miller is *compliant.*

So fucking compliant when I cup her ass and pull her other leg around my hip as well, her ankles crossing behind my back.

Her head falls back against the wall, exposing that slender throat, and I take the opportunity to lick down the column, biting on the delicate skin.

"God yes," she moans.

I suck and lick across her collarbone, tracing my tongue over the tattooed lines that meet her skin there.

"Fitting, Miller." I kiss my way over her jaw, finding her ear and biting it between my teeth. "You taste sweet. Like a goddamn dessert."

She swivels her hips, rubbing her pussy and making me grow impossibly harder.

I wonder if her pussy will taste as sweet as the rest of her.

Taking her mouth again, she moans sweet little sounds into my kiss, and that sound only deepens when I sweep my tongue inside again.

I know it's possessive and greedy, but that's exactly how I feel right now.

I want her. I want her for a lot longer than she plans on being here, and if there's any part of her that'd be willing to want me in return, I'll be selfish as fuck and take her.

Her body stills, and as if she can read my mind, she whispers against my lips. "Kai." She adds a soft kiss on my lips, pulling back to look at me. "I'm leaving soon."

Searching her face, I see it. The gentle reminder for me not to get attached because she isn't. She's giving me an out if I can't handle her, this. *More* than this.

Like a bucket of cold water, it works.

I'm worried about my son getting attached and I'm over here dreaming up ridiculous scenarios from a fucking kiss.

Exhaling, my forehead drops to hers, my eyes screwing shut with regret. I get her back on her feet as she searches my face, looking for my response to her words.

"I need to go back to the hotel and check on Max."

A defeated exhale escapes her lips, but she nods and follows me out of the bar.

# 16

# Miller

The elevator ride is silent up to our rooms. My lips are still tingling; my mind is still racing. I want him to pin me against this cold, metal wall and make me feel just how he did back at the bar, but the fact that my small reminder was enough to have him pulling away tells me it can't happen again.

I felt it in the way he kissed me because I've never been kissed like that—longed for. Needed. And I knew I had to give him the opportunity to take it all back if he couldn't handle more.

As my dad warned me, Kai gets attached, but I . . . I don't.

We stand at our respective room doors, each of us taking our time pulling out our key cards.

"So . . ." Kai finally blurts.

"So . . ."

There's a light tug at the corner of his lips, a bit of a stain from my lipstick there too, but he keeps his eyes down on the card in his hand, twirling it between his fingers. "Thanks for a fun night."

I huff a laugh. "Is that what we're calling it?"

That handsome smile is now directed at me. "It was nice to remember the old me for a second."

More like it was nice for him to remember he doesn't want to go back to the life he had before Max.

He holds the card to the door, blue eyes regretful. For the kiss? Maybe. Because he can't separate himself from his responsibilities and allow himself a selfish moment of fun? Possibly.

"Night, Mills."

"Goodnight, Kai."

He lingers in the hall until I go inside and once my door is shut, I hear his close seconds later.

I wash my face. I brush my teeth. I replay the evening in my mind over and over. That's not how I wanted his first night out to go. I wanted him to love every minute of it, to feel light without the pressure of responsibilities.

But instead, he felt responsible to hold back while his teammates gave him a hard time, felt responsible to defend me by almost getting himself in a fight. And was responsible enough to break our kiss, which only led to him regretting it all.

I thought it'd be easy. I thought I could remind him of his old self, no problem. But it's obvious now, Kai doesn't want to be his old self.

Pulling my sheets back, about to crawl into bed, a knock on our adjoining door sounds.

I halt my movements. *What the hell?*

Lingering by the door, my heart is thumping in my chest, knowing it's him on the other side, knocking in the middle of the night after that stupidly hot kiss.

*Did he change his mind?*

I look down. How much time do I need to change into something a bit sexier than the old, hole-clad tee I was planning to sleep in? God, and my face. I look like a glazed donut from my overnight skin care.

He knocks again.

*Fuck.*

Quietly, hoping not to wake Max, I crack the door that separates our two rooms.

Darkness surrounds him, but Kai stands in the doorway, shirtless with those tattoos on his ribs and thigh that surprised me the night I saw them at the pool. In only a pair of athletic shorts, his arms are braced on the doorframe.

I swallow, heat pooling low in my belly just from looking at him. "Hi."

His eyes slowly trail up my bare legs, until they meet mine. "Your dad is passed out in my bed."

"What?"

"Your dad is ass in the air, passed out asleep in the middle of my bed."

A laugh bubbles out of me, and Kai's lips curve at the sound. I peek into his room to see, and sure enough, Emmett Montgomery is sprawled out in the middle of Kai's bed while Max sleeps soundly in his crib next to him.

"It looks like you got yourself a cuddle buddy for the night."

Kai stares down at me with an unimpressed glare.

"Wake him up and send him back to his room," I suggest.

"I feel bad. He spent the whole night with my son and now he's . . . snoring."

"Well, where are you gonna sleep?"

He keeps his attention on me, hoping for me to put the pieces together. I know what he's suggesting but for once, Kai is going to have to ask for what he wants, even if it's for something as minor as a place to crash.

He clears his throat. "Would you mind if I slept in your bed tonight?"

"You wanna sleep with me, Baseball Daddy?" My tone holds as much suggestion as possible.

"I'm only wearing a thin pair of shorts right now, so please don't ask if I want to *sleep* with you while we're standing in the same room as your dad."

My eyes are twinkling, nodding into my room. "Come."

"Miller."

I chuckle. "Yes?"

"Please shut up."

He follows me into the room, closing the adjoining door, and the vibe instantly shifts.

Standing in the quiet hotel room, him without a shirt and me without pants, the overwhelming awareness settles over us both. We just shared a hot-as-hell kiss and are now about to crawl into bed together right after Kai stopped our moment.

He scratches the back of his neck. "Which side of the bed do you prefer?"

We both look at it.

"The furthest side from the door. That way if a murderer comes in, he'll kill you first."

His head jerks back. "And take out Max's only parent? You're cold, Montgomery." He follows me to the bed. "And why are you glistening? Did you work out in the five minutes I left you in the hall until now?"

I slip under the covers on my side—the safe side. "It's my skin care, thank you very much. You should probably look into getting some. I've heard they have specific lines for mature skin."

"I can't wait to give you shit when you're in your thirties."

*Except he won't know me then. He won't remember me then either.*

Kai takes off his glasses, setting them on the nightstand before flipping off the lights and slipping under the covers. His foot brushes mine and he allows it to linger there for only a moment before pulling away.

As if I wasn't already aware of our lack of clothing, with the darkness covering us, sheets hiding us, and our bare skin brushing as we make ourselves comfortable, the silence is practically screaming that I'm almost completely naked with the man whose son I'm watching for the summer. With the man I just made out with and tried to dry hump by a bathroom in a bar.

I half expected him to immediately turn his back to me and fall asleep, but he doesn't. He lays with one arm folded under his head, showcasing every defined muscle, with his eyes open but locked on the ceiling.

And because I'm nosy as hell, I ask, "Does your dad know you're in Texas?"

The silence somehow grows more tense. *Great fucking question, Miller.*

Too much time passes so I adjust, turning over and trying to sleep, hoping this guy is a freak who maybe sleeps with his eyes open and therefore won't remember that stupid question.

"No," he finally says in the quiet.

Slowly, I turn back to face him, but don't ask more follow-up questions that could have me putting my foot in my mouth.

He lightly laughs, but it sounds slightly pained. "He doesn't even know he has a grandchild."

*What the hell?*

"I haven't seen the man since I was fifteen or sixteen. Once my mom died . . ." He shakes his head.

It looks like he wants to tell me, but he stops himself, and it makes me wonder if he's ever had someone to talk to.

"Can I . . . can I ask what happened?"

Kai watches me, a teasing glint in his eye. "Is this all I had to do to finally get you all flustered? Talk about my shitty teenage years."

I smack him in the chest, but I'm thankful that he's able to joke around right now.

He chuckles. "My mom was already doing a lot of the heavy lifting in the family, so when she died, instead of stepping up, my dad drank himself stupid. Left me in charge of my thirteen-year-old brother when I was still a kid myself. I didn't even have a driver's license yet."

*Jesus.*

"Eventually, he checked himself into rehab and cleaned himself up, but he never came back. Last I heard, he was settled in a town only two hours from where we grew up and he had gotten remarried."

"Is it okay if I hate him for you too?"

"One of us probably should."

"Don't tell me you've forgiven him? I'm far too petty for your level of maturity."

"I think I'm at the point where I feel nothing towards him. Is that good enough for you?"

Kai's face is soft, no angry lines etched into his features. How annoyingly reasonable of him.

"Is Isaiah upset with him at least?"

"For me, I think. Now that he's older, he'll make comments about how he feels bad that I picked a college close to our hometown so I could help him get through the rest of high school. Stuff like that. But I probably would've done it regardless. The guy is my best friend."

"That's cute."

He pins me with a look. "Don't call me cute."

Between us, I find his free hand and hook my thumb around his, palm to palm before I rest my head against the back of his hand. "Thanks for telling me that."

He traces my face with his gaze, soft wistfulness washing over him. "Thanks for listening. I've never really had someone to tell that to."

"You should keep talking. You have a sexy voice, even when you're talking about your childhood trauma."

He simply shakes his head at me, smiles, and keeps talking. "I'm not angry, and I don't miss him, but I do miss how our family used to be. Everything was so different before my mom died, that the hardest part has been knowing what a good family unit looked like and no longer having it. I'm just trying to give Max a bit of what I lost."

And that's when it clicks. Kai is older now. He doesn't want to make up for the partying he's missing out on or even the freedom. He doesn't need to reminisce on his old life. He simply wants the family he once had. He wants to be enough for Max in hopes that he might not feel the gaps Kai has convinced himself exist.

"You're a good one, Kai. You know that?"

He sighs, exhaling an uncomfortable laugh. "Don't give me too much credit now."

"I'm serious." Which I very rarely am.

The room is dark, but my eyes have adjusted to the lack of light so that I can make out the blue in his perfectly clearly without his glasses as a barrier.

He's beautiful. Really, truly so handsome.

Turning on his side, he fully faces me, and once again his foot brushes mine, but this time he doesn't pull away. Instead, he covers my feet with his, tangling them between the sheets.

"The only time I've thought about reaching out to my dad was when I found out about Max. For a split second I thought I should tell him he was a grandfather."

"But you didn't?"

"Nah. Didn't need to. Monty kind of earned that title right away. Even though Max doesn't call him that, it would've been weird to give it to someone else."

*Oh, my heart.*

"Yeah," I exhale. "My dad has a knack for earning his titles when they aren't automatically his to begin with."

"He's a good man."

"The best of the best."

"Snores like a motherfucker though."

I bark a laugh.

The vibe in the air changes again when Kai lifts a finger to delicately tuck my hair behind my ear. "I want Max to think of me the way you think of him."

I melt into his touch. "He does. You're doing such a good job with him. I know you don't believe that all the time, but you are. And I would know. I've got the best dad out there."

"I'm worried I'm messing him up by having him travel with the team. I don't know what the fuck I'm doing. I try to pretend I do, but I wish I had the answers on how to do this parenting thing right."

"I'd assume every parent feels that way in some capacity. You've surrounded Max with so much love. The team adores him. My dad adores him. That's all you could ask for."

He looks like he wants to kiss me again and God, do I want him to. But then I watch Kai swallow, pull his hands away from mine and flip onto his back once again, tucking them underneath his head.

I mirror his position but with my hands folded in my lap.

"Have you been able to get any of your work done?" he asks.

Wow, quite the subject change. I've been blissfully detached from that part of my life for the past two weeks.

"Nothing in the kitchen, but I've been plotting some things for when we get home and I can experiment in the van."

"In the van? You have a kitchen in there?"

"A little one, yes. It gets the job done."

A beat passes between us. "I looked you up online last week."

My head whips in his direction, a teasing smile on my lips. "Just last week? I figured you would've done that the second I walked out of my dad's hotel room on that first day."

"Your food is beautiful, Miller. It's artwork."

He holds no humor in his tone, not allowing me to laugh my way out of an uncomfortable compliment.

Pulling my attention away once again, I find the ceiling. "It used to be."

"What's different now?"

"I have no idea. Suddenly, one day I couldn't do the most basic things in the kitchen. Things I've been doing since I was a kid. Nothing new has worked."

"Do you think it has anything to do with the James Beard Award you won?"

A smile lifts on one side of my lips as I look at him again. "Kai Rhodes, how much stalking did you do exactly?"

"Just enough to figure out you're a big fucking deal."

I shake my head, but he only continues.

"You are. The entire world agrees with me, so you can try to downplay it all you want, but I'm right. Have you always wanted to be this big-shot pastry chef?"

"No," I tell him honestly. "But I've always found myself striving for the next achievement. To be the best at whatever it is I take on. Whether that be in softball when I was younger, or now in my career. I've always chased the checkmarks."

"Why?"

I exhale a laugh. "God if I know. That's what we as a society have been conditioned to do, right? Keep striving for the next best thing instead of finding gratitude and peace where we are."

"Well, now that you've taken a break, do you feel any of that at all?"

"Gratitude and peace?" I turn to look at him. "I think I could find a lot of gratitude and peace while in bed with you, Kai Rhodes."

He bursts a laugh. "You have no fucking filter."

I smile at him, feeling an overwhelming comfortability to tell him everything. Much in the way he's never had someone to talk to, neither have I.

"The pressure," I continue. "It feels heavy. Suffocating, almost. When I first went to culinary school, I had plans to open my own little bakery one day. A place where people could get my cookies or cakes and I'd be able to watch the joy take over their faces when they took that first bite. But once I was in the industry, that goal didn't seem big or impressive enough. Instead, I went into the high-end world, and now the only people who eat my food anymore are critics or guests who've paid a ridiculous amount to do so. I watch people analyze every bite of what I've created instead of enjoying it, and if I'm being honest, it's gotten hard to put the same love into my food without second-guessing everything I do, knowing it's going to be judged instead of enjoyed."

The silence in the hotel room is suffocating. Kai lays only inches from me, but still, I won't look at him. Vulnerability is a sensation I like to steer clear from. My lifestyle isn't conducive to close and long-term friendships. I haven't had to be vulnerable with anyone in a very long time, and I've avoided self-reflection for years.

His oversized hand cups my face, turning my chin to face him. "Why do you still do the high-end stuff instead of simplifying things and opening your own bakery like you wanted to?"

I swallow. "Because what I do now is on another level. Yes, the hours are ridiculous and sure, the pressure of working in a high-end kitchen can be crippling, but I've made a name for myself. I think others look at my resume and find it impressive."

His eyes search mine. "Does what other people think really matter?"

There's only one person whose opinion of me matters and that's the man on the other side of this wall. After everything he's done for me, he deserves an impressive daughter. A daughter who excels in everything she does.

"Will you bake for me sometime?" Kai asks when I don't respond. "I promise not to judge or analyze it."

I chuckle. "First you want me to watch your son, travel with you, and now I need to cook for you? God, what else do you want me to do?"

His thumb trails down my jaw before sliding against my lower lip. "I want you to kiss me again."

*Oh.*

He stares at my mouth. "I really liked kissing you, Mills."

My body moves towards his without hesitation and, like a practiced dance, his arm slips between me and the mattress, pulling me closer to him. Our bare legs slide against one another, and he lifts his over mine to bring me nearer.

I lick my bottom lip, prepared for wherever he wants this to go. "I really liked kissing you too."

"But we can't do it again."

*Annnd never mind.*

"Because if I kiss you again," he continues, "I have a feeling I'm going to want to do it every time I see you."

I arch into him. "I don't see the problem with that."

"The problem with me kissing you is it's only going to lead me to wanting to fuck you more than I already do, and I don't do the unattached fucking thing like I used to."

"But the unattached fucking thing is so fun."

He huffs a laugh. "Yeah, but ever since Max—"

"You don't do casual."

"Nothing about my life is casual anymore. I've got someone else relying on me and my decisions now."

"Again."

Understanding floods him. "I have someone else relying on me *again,* and I don't have the space to be selfish. You said it yourself, you're leaving soon, and I've had too many people I counted on leave. I can't put myself or my son through that again."

Of course he can't. Not when he's trying to build a solid and stable environment for Max, while I'm simply having a good time passing through until I get back to my real life and career.

"I get it." I pull away a bit, giving him space in the bed.

"Where are you going?"

"Giving you space. You just said—"

"A man can cuddle."

My brows shoot up. "Cuddle?"

"Yes, *cuddle*. Or have you never heard of the term?"

I pause, hesitating.

"Have you never cuddled before?" he asks.

"No. I cuddle with your son. I've just never—"

"Have you never cuddled with a man before?"

"Can we stop saying the word *cuddle*? It doesn't sound right coming from you. You're huge and hot and you've said the word *cuddle* more times in the last thirty seconds than I have in my entire life."

A knowing smile lifts on his lips. "Miller Montgomery, you cold, unattached woman. Get over here and cuddle with me."

"Stop saying *cuddle*!"

He reaches out for me, but I teasingly pull away.

"Cuddle with me, Mills."

"Get away from me!" I wiggle away on the mattress.

Laughing, he chases after me until finally I give up my sad excuse of attempting to get away from him.

His giant body traps mine and on instinct my legs open around him. As soon as his hips fall into the cradle of mine, our matching smiles drop.

He uses his arms to keep himself lifted off me, just enough so that I can watch his attention once again drop to my lips.

"Kai." I swallow, my fingertips trailing over his abs, tracing the endless ridges.

His stomach contracts, sucking a sharp inhale, and it takes everything in me not to lift my hips and rub to feel exactly what I've been dying to feel.

He wants to kiss me. I want him to kiss me. I also really want to shed the few layers of clothing that separate where our bodies connect. But I can see in his torn expression that he's beating himself over wanting me and, though sometimes I'll put him through that torture because it's fun, I can't give him someone to miss. And after what he told me, it's clear he can't keep himself detached the way I can.

"Fine," I say, breaking the tension. "I'll cuddle with you, but only because I can't have you jealous of your son over that."

His forehead drops with a combination of regret and relief that things didn't escalate.

Kai flips onto his back, his arm out wide, nudging my head to rest on his chest. I do so, settling my arm over his waist.

This is new for me. I've never been in a relationship before and I'm not one to linger after a hook-up, but with him . . . I surprisingly don't hate it.

"Do you make every woman who shares your bed cuddle with you?"

"I couldn't tell you the last time I shared a bed with a woman."

I look up to find out what the hell he's talking about.

"I couldn't tell you the last time I was with someone. Well before Max, I know that."

*Well, fuck me.* My last bit of hope for a casual hook-up dies with those words.

"I could help with that, you know. It'd be a sacrifice for sure, having sex with you, but I'm a martyr that way."

He chuckles. "I don't need your charity."

"Why not? I could use the tax write-off."

Kai completely changes the subject. "Thank you for bringing Max to the field today. It meant the world to me."

"I can't believe none of his other nannies ever brought him."

"I never asked them to. I never talked to any of them long enough to ask."

"But you talk to me."

His blue eyes are soft. "Yeah, Mills. I talk to you."

I settle my head back into his chest, once again soothingly tracing the lines on his ribs.

"Besides being tempted to murder my catcher," Kai adds with a yawn, "today was a good day."

"They can all be good days."

His breathing slows and his words are barely a sleepy whisper when he says, "At least for the next six weeks."

# 17

## Kai

"Dadda."

The sweet scent of sugar fills my nose as I breathe a deep inhale.

"Dadda."

My body is melted into the mattress, my arms filled with . . . *Miller*.

Miller is in my bed, or rather I'm in hers.

Inhaling again, I pull her closer until her entire body is on top of mine with her head tucked into the crook of my neck.

She feels like heaven. Warm and cozy. She also feels like mine.

"Dadda."

My eyes shoot open to find my son at the foot of the bed, perched on Monty's arm, the two of them looking down at us.

Max is wearing a smile. Monty isn't.

"*Shit*," I breathe out.

I'm a thirty-two-year-old man getting caught in bed by someone's father.

"Well, I'm not sure how I'm going to scrub this visual out of my brain," he says dryly.

Miller stirs when she hears her dad's voice, but it's not enough to fully wake her. Instead, she nuzzles further into me, slinging her leg over my hips where I've got a raging case of morning wood going on. I could not be more thankful this hotel bed has a thick comforter.

"Dadda," Max says again, and Monty puts him on the mattress, allowing him to crawl over to us.

"Hi, Maxie." My voice is all morning rasp as he climbs over my torso. "I missed you last night."

He settles on my stomach, head on my chest, looking at a sleeping Miller. I wrap an arm around his little body so I've got them both as he cautiously reaches out to touch her septum ring. His tiny touch is enough to wake her and, as she opens her eyes, she looks right at my son, a sleepy smile blooming on her lips.

"Morning, Bug."

He smiles right back at her.

This moment would be a whole lot sweeter, the two of them cozy on my chest together, if Monty wasn't still staring down at me.

"Morning, Millie," her dad says.

Miller whips around, realizing he's here. "What the hell, Dad?" she asks, quickly covering herself with the blanket, not that there's anything to hide.

She's lucky she doesn't have to deal with a raging boner the way I currently am.

"Ace," Monty starts, heading back to my room. "I think it's time we have a conversation."

"I don't think we have to do that."

"Get your ass in here!"

Miller rolls her eyes, flopping over to the other side of the bed and taking Max with her, tickling his belly to keep him occupied while I go get reamed by her dad.

After I handle my business in the bathroom, I meet Monty in my room, closing the adjoining door behind me.

"It's not what it looks like," I tell him, finding a shirt to cover up my chest.

"I don't give a shit what it looks like. What you two do is none of my business but Ace, she's leaving in less than two months."

I pause in my tracks. "Why the hell does everyone feel the need to keep reminding me of that?"

"Because I'm looking out for you."

"Well, you don't have to do that. I only slept in there because your snoring ass was hogging my bed."

A smile ticks on his lips.

"I'm serious, Monty. Please don't waste your time giving me the overprotective dad speech. It isn't needed."

He holds his hands up. "This is not that. I just wanted to talk to you because Miller has a life she's going back to."

"Jesus, I know."

"Let me finish," he says. "Miller has a life she's going back to, a life she's worked her ass off for. You two are adults. Whatever you do in your free time is between you two, but I'm asking—no, I'm *telling* you, if there comes a time where you find yourself wanting to ask her not to go back to that life, that you talk to me first."

What the hell? I would never ask that of her. I know what this summer is to her. She made it clear last night when she gave me a moment to stop our kiss that she's simply passing through. She's got her entire life's dream waiting for her.

"It's not like that."

Monty shrugs. "Keep it in mind. Come to me if that changes for you."

# 18

# Miller

**Violet:** *Not to be the nagging agent, but please tell me you've been getting some baking done. You've got five weeks until your recipes are due to the magazine.*
  **Miller:** *Starting today.*
  **Violet:** *Starting?!*

Slicing the butter over my saucepan, I keep the heat low on my single burner stovetop. It's convenient, having a mini kitchen in my van, but the flames are a bit uneven, heating the pan at different speeds, so though I could brown butter in my sleep, I have to go low and slow when I'm experimenting in my little house on wheels.

We've been back in Chicago for a few days, just in time to experience the city's first heatwave of summer. Only last week it was humid and raining, but now it's scorching and miserable, and the van is hot as balls with the stovetop and oven roaring. But I don't have much of a choice than to get to work on figuring out these recipes, especially on the rare times Kai has a day off from baseball the way he does today.

Max is easy, and it's not that I can't work while he's awake and I'm watching him, it's just that I don't want to. I like hanging out with him, and I'd rather focus on our time together than stress over my endless string of failures in the kitchen.

Stirring the butter in the saucepan, I watch it melt when a knock at the door shakes my entire car.

*What the hell?*

Kai has never once come out here. He'll shoot me a text when he's about to head out the door and needs me to come inside to watch his son, and I can't think of any reason he'd be here other than—

"Is Max okay?" My words are rushed, my voice laced with panic as I slide open the door to my van.

"He's good," Kai says softly, holding up the baby monitor in his hand. "Taking his first nap of the day."

My exhale is brimming with relief—a new feeling for me. I've never been attached enough to worry about another's well-being, but knowing Max's story, knowing his mom didn't want to be in his life, has stirred a surge of protectiveness in me.

Kai stands outside, his bare feet on the concrete path that leads from his place to mine. Loose white tee, shorts that show off how cut his legs are. Backwards hat with those damn glasses. And that smile, smirking and sweet—a new look for the pitcher.

"What's with the aggressive knock?" I ask.

"It wasn't aggressive. It was normal. You just live in a fucking car. I barely touched the door and it rocked."

I lift my brow, a sly smile creeping across my lips. "The van has been known to rock. You should come in and give it a try sometime."

He shoots me an unimpressed glare. "Please stop talking."

Kai's attention falls over my chest and stomach, reminding me that I'm wearing only a bralette with a pair of pants that are thin and loose, not touching any of my skin in this godforsaken heat.

I don't cover up. Instead, I casually lean my arm on the headrest of the passenger seat, only putting me on display even more, allowing him to look because he wishes he wouldn't.

"What can I help you with?"

Kai holds up a couple of Coronas. "Brought you your favorite morning beverage."

"It's 10 a.m."

"Too late for you?"

Chuckling, I take one from him. "Not quite."

"Can I come in?"

My van is meant for one. That one being someone smaller than a 6'4" baseball player. I've got a bed, a mini kitchen, and a milk crate I use as a seat or for storage depending on the day.

"I'm not sure where your big-ass body is going to go, but okay."

"The bed looks good." Kai ducks his head, walking into my space. He has to fully fold in half to make it the two steps to my mattress where he lays out, his long limbs hanging off the edge.

"You're right," I say, pulling my beer to my lips. "My bed looks *real* good."

He chuckles, leaning on one elbow, ankles crossed as he props the monitor where we can both see Max sleeping just inside the house.

Kai looks light today. Maybe it's the day off from the field. Maybe it's the alcohol he's allowing himself to enjoy. Maybe it's the uninterrupted time he gets with his son, but I can't seem to pull my eyes off him.

"Your butter is burning."

Well, those words will do it.

"*Shit.*" I pull the saucepan from the flame as the van fills with that distinctly overdone smell. "Stop distracting me, looking all good on my bed while I'm trying to work. I haven't burned butter since I was a kid."

He folds one arm under his head, his smirk all smug before he pulls his beer to his lips.

Kai is a good-looking man. There's no way he's unaware of that fact, but sometimes it seems like he forgets. In the weeks we've known each other, my comments have gone from making him flustered and fuming to adding a bit of swag to his step. I have no issue hyping the guy up all summer if that's what he needs.

Turning off the inconsistent flame, I take a seat on the milk crate across from the bed.

"What are you making?" he asks.

"I was working on something new. A hazelnut and browned butter tart. Vanilla buttermilk ice cream. Caramelized pear. They'll be in season in the fall, in time for the article to come out, but"—I gesture to the burned butter—"I didn't get far."

"That seems like quite the undertaking for this tiny kitchen."

"I've made more extensive desserts than that in here."

"Maybe you're struggling because of the lack of space to create."

My attention darts back to him. It should be criminal to be that good-looking and so intuitive at the same time.

"Is this why you brought me a beer at 10 a.m. on your day off, Kai? To get me to figure out why I suck at my job so badly?"

"No." Another swig from his bottle. "You once told me the reason you're here this summer is because you owe your dad. You also told me you'd explain what that means over beers one morning so I'm here to collect on that promise."

"Actually, I told you if we got *drunk* together one morning, I'd tell you. One Corona isn't going to cut it."

"Yeah, well . . ." He nods towards the monitor. "I've got responsibilities. Single dad and all so one beer is going to have to do it."

The smile on my lips slowly slides across my face before I cover it with the bottle in my hand. Kai Rhodes relaxing in my van with a drink in his hand would've been out of the realm of possibilities only weeks ago, so I'll take the compromise. He looks good like this.

"You gonna spill, Miller, or what?"

"My dad gave up his entire career for me. His entire life. I owe him to make sure I do something with mine."

"That's what this is all about?" He nods towards the stovetop.

I don't respond, unsure if he's referring to my career choices or the fact I've stayed away for so long, working in kitchens all around the country, but he'd be correct on both counts.

Kai climbs off the bed, taking Max's monitor with him as he hunches over and hops out of the van. He holds his hand out to me. "Come with me."

I eye him with skepticism. "Why?"

"Because I'm about to have a heatstroke in that fucking van and I need to show you something."

"You're awfully dramatic, Baseball Daddy."

I place my hand in his, the calluses on his palm rough against mine. I held his hand in bed last week, but I don't remember the size difference being this comical. It's no wonder he can alter the path of a baseball as if it were nothing. It must be tiny in his grasp.

As quietly as possible, we enter the house. Max's toys and playmat take up the entire living room and I love that Kai doesn't give a fuck about crawling over them every day. This home is his son's home too and he's not trying to hide it.

There are endless dishes in the sink that I remind myself to tackle tomorrow. Piles of laundry he needs to fold. Knowing him, he's going to try to get it all done on his one day off this week, but I'll pick up the slack when he's back on the field tomorrow, and I'm sure he'll be annoyed that I helped. He's prideful like that, wanting to do it all on his own.

Kai ushers me in front of him, the two of us standing by the kitchen island, and that's when I see it. A brand-new professional-grade mixer sits in the corner of the counter, including dry ingredient storage filled with everything I could need.

"You can't keep baking in your van," he says. "It's too hot and you can barely move in there. Use my kitchen, even when I'm home and you're not watching Max."

I slowly step into the space, my hand roaming over the ivory mixer. "You bought this for me?"

"Well, you're not getting paid to watch my kid; I figured it was the least I could do."

My head jerks his way, a startled laugh escaping me. "I'm absolutely getting paid this summer. The Warriors are paying me."

"Oh." He studies my new work area. "I'll just return all this then."

"Don't you dare." I hold up an accusatory finger but all it does is bring his stunning smile to life. "It's beautiful, Kai. Thank you."

"Thank *you*. For taking care of Max." He pauses, his voice softer. "He really likes you."

"Well, the feeling is mutual." I look back at the mixer. "You didn't have to do this, though."

"You promised to help me find my balance in life. I thought I'd try to help you find your joy."

My heart cracks at that, opening in a way I don't want it to. He's too good, too kind. Too goddamn hot with that backwards hat and that tattooed leg exposed. Guy thighs . . . who would've known they were my new kryptonite?

"So, what's next?" He casually leans back on the counter, ankles crossed. "After your interview with *Food & Wine*."

What is next? I haven't thought that far.

My entire life, I've thrived on achievements. All-American softball pitcher in high school. Check. Top of my class in culinary school. Check. Named the best in my field by winning the highest honor in my industry. Check.

So, what comes after there are no more checkmarks left to chase?

"I . . . I don't know."

"Will your debt be repaid?"

"What debt?"

"The non-existent debt you owe Monty for adopting you. That's what you meant in Miami, right? You feel like you owe him for what he gave up for you."

For fuck's sake. Is it an older guy thing? A single parent thing? Or am I that obvious?

"I'm not that dense, Miller. You love him yet you're never around. Is that why you've stayed away? Because you feel guilty?"

"Can you not be so mature and intuitive for like two seconds?"

He shifts, stepping closer. "Miller—"

I hold my hands up to stop him. "I just . . . after everything he's done for me, he deserves to live the life he missed out on."

Kai's brows pinch. "The life he missed out on? He misses *you*."

"Don't say that."

"It's true. He never used to talk about you. Did you know that? He and I are close, and I thought you were a kid because Monty never talks about you. I think he missed you so much, it hurt him to bring you up. And now? In the weeks since you've been around, he hasn't shut up. He's beaming like a fucking dork. There's nothing to feel guilty about."

I don't respond because I don't have to have this conversation with him. I don't want to have this conversation with anyone, including myself.

He sighs, somewhat defeated. "Use my kitchen while you're here. Figure out your recipes. Learn how not to burn the butter like an absolute amateur."

"Shut up," I laugh, letting the tension drift away.

"But Miller, we're gonna have a real problem if this article and award you're so stressed about is due to some misplaced guilt. Like you owe your dad for what he's done, and you think you can repay him with accolades."

"I just want him to be proud of me. After everything, he deserves an impressive daughter."

"He has one."

I roll my eyes. "You hated me up until like five days ago."

"That's an exaggeration."

"Sorry, six days ago."

"You freaked me out."

"Yeah," I laugh. "Got that."

"No. I mean with how much Max liked you right away. That freaked me out. I'm worried about him getting attached."

*Wait. What?*

I figured it was the way I spoke my mind or my lack of childcare experience that scared Kai in the beginning. Not once did I think he was worried about me connecting with his son.

"The first thing that happened in Max's life was the woman who was supposed to love him left. I don't want him to get used to the people he loves leaving him."

"But I am leaving."

"So you've said." His exhale is resigned. "We'll deal with it when we get there. For now, I want him to enjoy traveling with the team as much as he can, and I think you're the key to that. He's happy. He's safe with you. We'll figure out the rest come September."

*We'll* deal with it. *We'll* figure it out. Not only Max.

His hand is on the counter right next to me as he leans back on his palms, and instinctively, I cover it with my own. Kai uses his thumb to trap my fingers, softly stroking the skin there.

"Why are you being extra nice to me?"

He doesn't look at me, only stares at our hands. "I have no fucking clue, Mills."

*Mills.*

Fuck me, every time he uses that name it seeps a little more into my veins, cracks a bit more of my heart.

Kai looms over me, his ice-blue eyes zeroing in on mine before they drop to my mouth. I want to knock that baseball hat off him, run my hands through his hair just to remember what it feels like.

"Why are you staring at my lips?"

"I'm not," he says, looking right at them.

"You gonna try to kiss me again, Baseball Daddy? I thought that was off the table."

He blinks, putting distance between us. "It is."

"Oh my God, Kai. You were going to break your own rule and kiss me!"

"No, Miller, I wasn't."

"I thought it was *Mills* now?"

He shakes his head. "You ruin everything. You know that?"

I can't hide my smile, needing to tease him for this. "How much do you hate yourself for wanting to lay one on me again?"

Hands on his hips, Kai's head falls back in frustration, looking towards the ceiling. "Trust me, if I ever kissed you again, it will be as my last and final resort to shut you up."

"Okay, I'll keep talking then."

He shoots me daggers.

"I love how much you hate that you're attracted to me."

Kai rolls his eyes. "Yeah, well, you and me both."

The baby monitor begins to light up, Max's cry wafting through the speaker.

Kai makes a move to his son's room but before he can leave, I put a hand on his chest to stop him. "I got him."

"But it's your day off."

I pop my shoulders. "I don't need a day off. I'll leave you to sit and stew in here over the fact that you were about to kiss your coach's daughter again." I go to grab Max, but before I'm out of the room, I add one more thing, so he knows this isn't one-sided. "And cover up your guy thighs. We're being professional here. I technically work for you, and I didn't even know I had a thing for men's legs until you came along with all that tatted skin and lean muscle."

"Me?" His head jerks back. "What about you? I get hard just *looking* at your legs."

We pause, the kitchen silent for a beat too long.

I burst a laugh, both of us unable to stop from smiling like lunatics at each other from across the room. "We're so professional."

# 19

## Miller

In the week following, I spend almost every hour of my day in Kai's house. Either in the kitchen or with Max, and when Kai gets home from work after the games I don't take his son to, I find ways to linger a little longer even though inspiration has yet to strike.

Clearly, it's a me thing if not even a stunning, state-of-the-art kitchen with brand-new tools can make me create.

But today is the day. I can feel it buzzing through my fingertips. Last night, while I was lying in bed, I saw it in my mind, visualized every step—my take on a deconstructed banana flambe.

In the high-end world, you've just got to list something as "deconstructed" and it's automatically double the price, which really makes no fucking sense if you ask me, but I don't make the rules.

One time I created a dessert simply called "flavors of a banana split." I served a deconstructed banana split spread across the entire table. Hazelnut chocolate on one end, strawberry mousse on the other. You had to put in work to get yourself a single bite, but the presentation was stunning, and I earned an award for what was essentially a giant, messy banana split.

Today though, I'm taking on the banana flambe.

At least that was my plan before Max decided *his* plan was to be clingy. He crawls as quickly as I walk over to the stove. I meant to work during his nap earlier, but there were so many things Kai needed help with around the house, I didn't want to ignore them. Even though he's for sure going to be annoyed I did the laundry and may or may not have given one of his used T-shirts a deep inhale.

The guy smells good. Sue me.

I look down at the floor, next to my bare feet. "Max, baby, what's up?"

He sits on the kitchen runner, both hands reaching up towards me. "Nana," he says.

I've come to learn that whatever that noise is that starts with an "N" sound and ends with a bit of mumbling is his version of asking for a banana. I've got a whole bunch sitting next to the stove that I bought a few days ago. They're on the brink of going brown, which is why today is the day I need to use them.

Peeling one, I get down on my haunches and break him off a piece. "Here you go, Bug."

His blue eyes are shining, his hair is still a little sweaty from his afternoon nap, but gosh dang it is he fucking cute.

The stovetop is heating up, but there's no way I'm working on this type of dessert with him so close. Seeing as a flambe requires me to set a fire, we're officially done with that idea for today.

Max chews on his banana while he contently sits on the ground, his brown hair all over the place.

"Maxie, do you want to go play with your blocks?"

He shakes his head.

"Should we maybe go outside and blow some bubbles?"

Another no.

"Okay, do you just want to hang out with me in the kitchen?"

Looking up, he smiles, mashed banana all over his baby teeth.

I chuckle, picking him up. "All right, my guy. Let's put you to work then."

I flip off the burner before standing him in the small contraption that keeps him upright and at counter height.

Leaning down on my forearms, I make myself eye level with him. "What should we make?"

"Nana!" he yells.

"You've still got your banana."

"Nana!"

"I can't make that banana dessert with you in the kitchen. The flames are big and hot and *oooh*—" I tickle his belly just to hear his laugh. "Kind of scary. So, we've got to think of something else with bananas."

"Nana!"

*Dear God. Big banana fan today.*

"How about—" I look around the kitchen for ideas. Bananas, flour, sugar. A Bundt pan too. I face him again. "Should we make banana bread?"

This sure as hell isn't going to count towards any of the work I need to get done, but I haven't made something as simple as banana bread in years.

Max claps his hands.

I guess we're making some motherfucking banana bread.

There's an old recipe floating around in my mind, one that I used to make my dad when I was a little girl. This bread is almost like a cake with the moist center and sweet add-ins.

Washing my hands then Max's, I load the counter up next to him, letting him see and touch as much as he wants. Unhinging the base to the mixer, I set it up right in front of him.

"All right. First up. We've got to mash these bananas."

I peel and toss them in the bottom of the bowl, but Max reaches in at one point to take a handful before smashing it into his mouth.

I nod. "I've never baked like this before, but I'm here for it."

Taking a fork in my hand, I set him up with a much smaller one that won't do shit, but at least he can feel like he's participating.

We mash the bananas. Well, *I* mash the bananas. Max just kind of rings his fork against the metal bowl.

"Excellent job," I reiterate. "Four eggs." I do that part. I don't think his little hands could quite grasp an egg yet. "And a bit of canola oil." Filling up one of the measuring cups, I hold it out for him to take, making sure to cover his hand with mine.

I want him to feel like he's doing this. Who knows, maybe he's learning. I would've loved to learn about the kitchen from my mom, but she wasn't around to teach me in the same way Max's mom isn't here to teach him.

We pour the oil into the mixture, losing a bit on the counter along the way, so I add a splash more for good measure.

We do the same with the sugar and salt. Adding in baking soda and a packet of instant vanilla pudding. No way in hell would I get away with adding instant pudding into a recipe for work, but we're baking for *fun*, something I haven't done in years. And it's especially fun when Max throws the flour into the bowl and a big flour cloud flies up because of it, coating him in a layer of white.

He laughs hysterically and I can't help but join him. His messy brown hair is dusted, his shirt is covered, but there's a giant smile on his face as he tries to suck in enough air to breathe through his laughter.

"Bug, I think we need to get you an apron like mine."

He giggles some more, and I adore the sound. Sure, his family unit looks a little different than what his friends might have when he gets to school. He'll probably notice that a lot of kids on TV have two parents, but Max has got it good. He's happy and I couldn't want anything more for him.

I peel his shirt off and let him live his best naked toddler life before adding a bit more flour to the mixture. Carrying both him and the bowl, I latch it to the base of the mixer, then let him help me turn it on.

His blue eyes go wide and his little mouth parts when he sees and hears the mixer start up. I don't watch the ingredients. I only watch him because I can't get over seeing him experience these things for the first time. There's so much joy on his sweet face and I find myself feeling the same way.

Happy and excited while baking.

About time I felt that again.

I'm typically a walnut girl when it comes to banana bread, but I opt for chocolate chips on this round. I let him drop them in from above, noting the two he puts into the batter is balanced by the two he shoves into his mouth each time.

I get the Bundt pan into the preheated oven, an odd sense of pride and . . . *relief* flowing through me because I actually completed a dessert that I have a good feeling I won't fuck up over the next hour while it bakes.

But then I turn around and see the absolute disaster we made in the kitchen. Max is back by the counter, continuing to eat the chocolate chips I pulled for him, and I can't help but smile at the view.

My culinary professors would have died if my station were ever this messy in school. I would have been screamed at, berated. I've grown a thick skin from my time in the restaurant industry. Cleanliness and organization are rules one and two in the kitchens I contract for. Other than my one single towel I keep over my shoulder, I don't touch anything. My hair is pulled back tight, my uniform is crisp, and my skin is covered.

But I've got a naked baby over here, my hair is messily on top of my head, and I couldn't feel more like myself.

A little over an hour later, I've got a piece sliced for us with butter melting on top when the front door opens. Kai comes strutting in, post-practice, sneaking up on his son from behind.

"Are you nakey?" he asks, tickling Max's belly and covering his cheeks with kisses.

Max wiggles in his grasp, laughing.

"Naked Maxie, what are you doing?" His dad picks him up, holding him to his chest. Max's little arms instantly go around his neck and I have to look away so I don't drool from watching Kai hold his son while wearing that damn backwards hat.

"Hi, Mills," he says.

I swing my attention back to him. "Hi."

He's got Max situated on one incredibly veiny forearm when he uses the bottom of his shirt to wipe the summer sweat from his brow.

He's got to be freaking kidding with that. How has he not been with anyone since Max came along? All he needs to do is stand at his front door, hold his son, and maybe take his shirt off. All the women in the neighborhood would come running. It's like watching single dad porn.

"What did you guys make?"

"What?"

An annoyingly smug, but well-deserved smirk slides across his lips. "What did you guys make, Miller?"

"Banana bread."

His brows lift along with an excited smile. "You finished a new dessert?"

It's cute how much he wants this for me. He might not understand the ins and out of it all, especially since he's asking if I'm going to feature banana bread made with instant pudding in my *Food & Wine* spread, but it's sweet, nonetheless.

"It's not new, but I did finish it without burning it so that's a plus. Max helped too."

"You did?" Kai asks his son.

Max decides to be shy, but I see the proud little smile he's wearing.

"Do you want to try it?" I ask.

"Absolutely. Have you had some?"

"Not yet."

"Well, you have some first then I'll go in."

"Why?" I laugh. "Afraid I'm trying to poison you or something?"

"No, but you worked hard on something and didn't fuuu . . . dge it up in the process. You should try it."

"I like to bake for other people."

And I haven't baked for someone other than critics in far too long. It's almost as if I forgot that my favorite part of baking is feeding the people I love. I'm not always great at expressing my feelings, so I tend to tell them through their stomachs.

It's no wonder nothing has worked out lately.

"Max first though," I say, blowing on a tiny bite to get it ready for him.

He opens his mouth wide for my fork and hums when it hits his tongue.

"Okay with those rave reviews, I think I need some," Kai cuts in.

I get him another forkful.

"You're not going to blow on it for me?" He wears a devil-ish smile, but mine is a whole lot naughtier.

"Oh, I'll blow something for you. All you have to do is ask."

"Jesus," he laughs. "Give me the freaking banana bread."

I'm not sure why, but I don't hand him the fork. Instead, I guide it to his mouth, feeding him.

His eyes stay locked on mine, his lips wrapping around the utensil and there's something so oddly erotic about it all.

"Miller." He chews, his eyes going wide. "Oh my God, that's amazing."

"Really?"

This is what I missed. Seeing the pure joy when the sugar hits someone's tongue.

"Yes. That's the best banana bread I've ever had. I don't even know if you should call it bread. It's more like cake and I want to eat the entire thing."

"Wow."

"No, I'm serious. Give me another bite."

Chuckling, I do just that, feeding him again.

He moans and holy hell if I don't have to squeeze my legs together at the sound.

"You've got to try it," he insists.

Using the same fork that was in his mouth, I take a bite. I can feel him tracking me as if he's having the same thought I am about my lips being exactly where his just were.

And wow, he's right. It is good. It's *really* good. I think it might be better than the version I used to make when I was younger.

"You're right." I take another bite before reaching up to pinch Max's exposed belly. "Nice work, Bug."

Kai's big hand curves around the back of my neck, pulling my attention to him where I find his gaze all soft. His thumb softly strokes the pulse point on the side of my throat before he gives me a tender squeeze. "Good job, Mills."

*Whoa.* An odd rush of emotion sneaks up on me, over-whelming my senses.

What the hell is that about?

I can't remember the last time I was told I was doing a good job in the kitchen, and Kai said it so matter-of-factly. So confidently. It makes me want to bake more so I can hear it again.

And without a fight, I agree with him. I did do a good job.

# 20

# Kai

The warm, sweet smell of sugar hits me as soon as I'm out of the shower. It's the same smell I've been greeted with every day since Miller made that banana bread. She hasn't stopped baking, keeping my house constantly filled with fresh pies, pastries, and other desserts, and I've been bringing them to the field, needing to get them out of my house before I'll no longer be able to fit into my baseball pants.

But I love it. I love seeing her work her magic in the kitchen. It's as if she got bitten by the baking bug and can't stop. Apparently, nothing she's made so far is helping her with the recipes she needs to create for the *Food & Wine* article, but she's genuinely happy in the kitchen again and I can't help but note the difference on her face from the first night I found her in there, distraught from too many failed desserts.

Wrapping a towel around my waist, I turn the corner to find Max decked out in a tiny apron, sitting on the kitchen counter facing Miller as she talks to him while plopping dollops of cookie dough onto a sheet. She's all denim today, back in her usual cutoff overalls. I've realized she only has maybe four or five pairs that she rotates through, but these ones might be my favorite, showing off her thick thighs.

Max catches me eavesdropping, making his blue eyes shine and his smile grow. I should go back to my room and put some clothes on, but I just want to be around them.

"What are we making today?"

"Chocolate chip cookies." Miller keeps her back to me, continuing to portion out each one.

Cupping my son's cheeks, I give him a kiss on his head before reaching over, about to do the same to his nanny until it hits me midair on the way to cradle the back of her head that I'm out of my fucking mind right now.

*What the hell am I doing? Way too comfortable. Way too fucking comfortable.*

Thankfully, she doesn't pick up on any of that as I fist my hands back at my sides.

"Well, technically they're M&M cookies." She motions towards the cooling rack where a dozen cookies are ready. "You can take them to the boys at practice today."

I'll take them to my teammates, but no way in hell are they going to be the first ones to try them. It's one of the perks of Miller living with me.

*Next* to me, I mean. Living next to me. Though I hate that she sleeps outside, and I've made that perfectly clear on multiple occasions.

Snagging a cookie from the cooling rack I take a bite and, not surprising in the least, they're fucking amazing. "So good, Miller."

That smile bursts on her face as she continues to work. I know this isn't the high-end stuff she's typically praised for, so the compliment might seem mute, but I see how proud she gets from knowing how much those around her love what she's making.

There are perfectly placed M&Ms on top, and from a quick glance, you'd assume Max is helping with that part. But I'm certain, judging by his hands already inked in yellow, orange and green, that the M&Ms he's helping with are going straight to his mouth.

I pick him up off the counter, hoping to pacify the sugar rush first thing in the morning, and finally Miller's attention follows, looking at me for the first time today.

Her gaze starts at the arm my son is perched on, then it travels lower to where the towel meets the bare skin around my hips. I watch her trace my tattoos with her attention before her eyes bounce over my abdomen as if she's counting each muscle on her way up to my chest.

"My eyes are up here, Montgomery."

"Yeah, I know."

I chuckle. "You almost done sexualizing me?"

With her eyes, she retraces the same path. "You keep walking around here in nothing but a towel and the answer to that will continue to be a resounding no."

Finally, her attention finds mine but all she does is bite her lip and waggle her brows, never one to shy away from letting me know how attractive she finds me.

It feels really fucking good to be looked at the way she looks at me, especially by a woman like Miller. Beautiful, successful, could have any man she wants but is looking at *me*.

"So, what should I call these when I give them to the boys?" I change the subject. "M&M cookies?"

Miller brushes my son's hair out of his face as he sits perched on my arm. "We're calling them the Max and Miller cookie. The M&M cookie. Sorry, Baseball Daddy, but you're out on this one."

"Actually, I'm also an 'M'. My full name is Malakai, so I guess I count too."

"Your name is Malakai?"

I nod.

"Malakai Rhodes," she says, as if she were testing the way it feels on her tongue. "That's a good name."

It's an especially good name when she says it in that deep, raspy tone I look forward to hearing every day.

"I guess these could be named after you two then," she continues. "M&M. Max and Malakai. That has a nice ring to it."

*And Miller.*

*Max and Malakai and Miller.*

But I don't say that out loud because my mind is already creating too many ridiculous scenarios seeing this woman with my son in my home, especially when she has no desire to stay.

Sundays without a game are always nice, but there's rarely a day that goes by during the regular season that I'm not at the field. Today is an easy practice day, everyone coming to the field to work on what they need. Most of the guys get a bit of batting practice in, but I have a designated hitter who takes care of those duties for me, and I'm sure as shit not the guy who is going to be throwing out 50–60 mile per hour lobs over home plate.

These days are typically spent with me rushing through a bit of physical therapy in the training room after flying through a handful of pitch sequences, trying to get back home as quickly as possible. At least, that's how it used to be. But over the past month, I've taken my time, watched my teammates bat while we all shoot the shit before I sink into my PT, letting it do what it needs to do.

There's been a shift. I'm enjoying the game again, every part of it. I'm *content*, which is an odd thing to feel after stressing for the last ten months, convinced I wasn't doing enough as a parent.

But Max is happy. I'm happy, and there's a common denominator as to why.

"Goddamn, Trav," my brother says in disgust. "You look like you've never swung a bat in your life."

"It's Sunday," Travis calls over his shoulder as he squares up at the plate once again. "I'm over this. I'm tired and ready to go home."

"New rule! You hit a homer, you get a cookie." Cody holds up the Tupperware container full of Miller's cookies from our side, behind the batting cage.

Travis's brows shoot up from under his helmet before pointing his bat to left field and the next pitch that comes his way is sent sailing into that exact section. Travis tosses his batting gear and jogs over to snag a cookie, his eyes rolling back with an over-the-top moan when it melts onto his tongue.

"If I knew my daughter's baking would've had you guys hitting like this, I would've had her overnight me desserts years ago." Monty joins us, taking a cookie for himself.

"Hey!" Isaiah calls out. "You've got to hit a homer for a cookie."

Monty levels my brother with a look. "I don't have to do shit. I raised the girl, and I could bench your ass if I felt like it, Rhodes."

Isaiah gestures towards the Tupperware. "Have all the cookies you'd like, sir."

Cody guards Miller's cookies, treating them like a sacred prize to be earned as the team turns back to face home plate, watching the next batter.

I find my way next to Monty. "You gonna ever stop scaring the shit out of my little brother?"

"Nah. That's just how our relationship works. I love the little shit, but I don't need him to know that." He takes a bite of the cookie in his hand. "Goddamn. I almost forgot how good she was at this."

"Yeah," I exhale. "For a moment, I think she forgot too."

I can feel Monty's stare lasering into the side of my face as I watch the field, pretending to not be acutely aware of Miller's father watching me.

"What made her start baking her old recipes again?" His tone is laced with suspicion.

"Not sure."

"Why aren't you looking at me?"

I shake my head, eyes on home plate. "Still not sure."

Monty is my friend, but I'd be lying if I said he wasn't intimidating. I'm already paranoid he's going to accuse me of getting too attached to his daughter or think I'm trying to convince her to stick around town when the last thing she wants is to settle.

"Ace, why is my daughter baking this kind of stuff every day instead of working on her recipes for the article?"

He's clearly not going to let this go, so finally, I turn to face him. "I think maybe it's Max."

Monty squints in confusion.

"I think she likes showing Max the basics, letting him help in some capacity. He's been in the kitchen with her every day." A smile cracks on my lips. "She even got him his own little apron with dinosaurs all over it. I'm sure she'll get back to working on the other stuff soon, but for now, they've been having fun doing this together."

A soft grin slides across Monty's face. "Good. This is the stuff that makes her happy, not all that frou-frou bullshit people pay her to make."

*Huh?*

My brow lifts in realization. "Were you planning this?"

"I don't know what you're talking about." He takes another bite to keep himself from speaking as he faces the field, pretending to study the batters.

"You want Miller to quit her job, don't you?"

"I didn't say that."

"But you're thinking it."

"I want my kid to be happy, just as you want yours to be. Do I think she'd be happier making this kind of stuff every day instead of living in the stress of high-end restaurant life? Yeah, I do. Did I know she wouldn't be able to help herself from feeding the people she loves? Also yes. Did I think spending a whole summer with your sixteen-month-old would make her go back to the basics, knowing he wouldn't eat any of that fancy stuff? Maybe I did."

I burst a laugh. "You're a shit disturber, you know that?"

"I'm a dad," he corrects.

Crossing my arms, we mirror each other, both of us staring out at the field. "She named those the Max and Miller cookies. M&M."

"Hmm."

"What?"

"Didn't say anything."

"You hummed."

"A man's allowed to hum."

"That was a suspicious hum."

"It was a normal hum. You're just being paranoid and want to find ways to keep talking about my daughter."

I scoff. "You were the one who brought her up first."

His mouth curves slightly on one side.

"Hot Nanny alert!" Cody calls out. "Did you bring us more cookies?"

I follow his line of sight to find Miller frantically racing up the stairs of the dugout and onto the field with my son slung on her hip.

My heart instantly sinks at the sight.

"What's wrong?" I shout. "What happened?" I run to her, meeting her in no time though it feels like forever before I can get my hands on them both. Panic laces my veins as I check my son up and down. "Is he okay?" My attention flips to her, my palm brushing over her hair. "Are you okay?"

"Max is fine."

My stomach drops in relief, like I just plunged from the top of a roller coaster, and I have to let it level out before I can speak again. "Are you okay? What's going on?"

"I think he's about to walk." She sucks in a deep breath which tells me she ran here from the parking lot. "We were playing outside, and he was using the water table to balance when all of a sudden he let go and looked like he was going to take a step in my direction, but I scooped him up before he could. I don't think I was supposed to do that. All those online mommy groups would probably berate me for it, and I'm pretty sure every one of your parenting books would call me unfit, but I couldn't let you miss it."

Miller is frenzied, her words stumbling out without a single breath as she searches my face for my reaction, as if I truly thinks I might be upset over her stopping him.

"Jesus." Flipping the brim of my hat to the back, I drop my forehead to hers, half-heartedly laughing in relief. "You scared the shit out of me."

"You're not going to call me unqualified and refuse to let me watch him for the rest of the summer because I stopped him from walking?"

Pulling away, I brush her hair away from her face, tucking it behind her ear. "If you're unqualified then so am I." My brows furrow. "And do you really think I own a single parenting book?"

A laugh bubbles out of her.

"You drove all the way into the city?"

She nods against my palm as it rests on her cheek. "You can't miss his first steps."

*Fucking hell.*

Now that the adrenaline is settling, my chest physically aches because of this woman. She's too good to us, too good to *me*.

"Maxie!" my brother calls out, breaking the spell of being around her and reminding me my entire team is watching, including Miller's dad. "What are you doing here?"

I exhale, finally looking away from her and back to the guys behind me. "Apparently, he's about to walk."

There's a frenzy of noise stirring by home plate. This team has been there since the day I found out my son existed. They've been stoked for every milestone, and this one seems no different.

"Bring him over here and let's see it!" Travis shouts in our direction.

"Yeah, let him feel like his uncle, walking onto home plate after running the bases!"

"Well, if we're shooting for accuracy," Monty cuts in. "Maybe let him step onto second since Isaiah hasn't rounded that base once in the past five games."

The team bursts again, giving my brother shit.

"Geez, Monty." Isaiah holds a hand to his chest. "Go ahead and admit that you're obsessed with me, keeping track of my stats like that."

A slight crack of a smile tugs at the corner of Monty's lip.

Miller hands my son off to my brother before she finds Kennedy with an adorably excited wave. She takes her place with her dad, and Monty slings an arm over her shoulders, standing together to watch. The rest of the boys can't resist, leaving their spots behind the batting cage to create a half circle around home plate.

I get down on my haunches right behind it, facing the third base line when Isaiah puts Max down only a few feet from me. My son has still got a death grip on my brother's fingers, using them to balance himself, but he's staring right at me all giddy with baby teeth.

"C'mon, Bug, let's see it." I hold my arms out wide for him. "Come get me."

Isaiah pries his fingers away, but holds on for a moment, letting Max balance himself before he fully lets go. This is typically the time Max crumbles to his butt to crawl, but he keeps his eyes right on me, wobbly knees trying to keep him upright.

No one speaks. It's utter silence on a field that only moments ago was rowdy as hell with a baseball team giving each other shit. Now, they simply stand behind me, waiting on pins and needles for a sixteen-month-old to make his move.

"Max." I gesture with my hands. "Come on. You've got it."

Hands in the air to balance himself, he shakily steps his right foot forward. It touches the ground before he does the same with the left.

I can feel the smile widening on my face. "There you go. You're doing it! Keep going!"

The boys behind me are stirring with excitement. The anticipation feels similar to that of an important ninth inning when we're down with our best batter at the plate, looking for a walk-off win. I figured for them, it's simply a toddler's first steps. But for me, it's the not so gentle reminder that he's good. He's growing and I'm not messing everything up. So, even though I've been waiting for this day for months, I didn't realize the boys would be just as excited as I am.

I once assumed I didn't have anyone there to celebrate the good moments with, and I couldn't have been more wrong. I've had these guys the whole time.

Max is flailing about like one of those blow-up guys you see at a car dealership, but he's able to maintain his stability. He steps forward with his right foot, wobbles, and steadies himself before bringing his left foot forward too.

"Yes, Max!" The first cheer resounds behind me.

"Good job, Max." The smile on my face is splitting. "Two more big steps and you're here."

God, my chest could burst from the amount of pride that's flowing through me. He's doing it. He's really fucking doing it.

Then his little feet, decked out in checkered Vans, take two more steps onto home plate, right into the cradle of my outstretched arms.

The team goes nuts behind me.

"So good, Bug!" The laugh I exhale is full of relief as I hug him close to my chest, covering him in kisses.

When I stand with him in my arms, the boys cheer louder than I've ever heard. The noise is almost deafening as they jump onto each other, pushing one another in the chest like we just won some massive game or something.

"Let's fucking go!" Isaiah tosses his head back, arms out wide.

I'll remind him about cussing in front of my kid later; for now, I want to celebrate.

The noise is too much for him and Max's face melts, his lower lip wobbling before he lets out a giant wail.

"Oh buddy," I soothe, trying to cover up my chuckle. I pull him into my chest, running a hand over his hair. "It's okay. They're just excited for you."

The cheers settle immediately. It takes a second but soon enough, Max's face pops off my shoulder to look at them all once again and his chubby-cheeked smile is back, though his blue eyes are rimmed in red.

The boys cheer again, keeping their volume at a less frightening level, and as they smother my son with attention, I glance over my shoulder, looking for Miller.

She was standing with Monty, but now he's alone.

"Take him for a minute," I tell my brother, handing off my son.

I slip behind the batting cage, headed straight for my coach. "Where'd she go?"

An annoyingly knowing smile lifts on his lips. "She just left. Asked me if practice was over and said she figured you wanted to take Max home with you."

Before he can add any more, I take off to the dugout, jumping over the stairs and jogging down the hallway where she originally came from. I can see the frayed hem of her cut-off overalls as soon as I'm in the tunnel that leads to the offices, clubhouse, and eventually the parking lot.

"Miller! Hold up."

She turns on her heel as I continue to chase after her, the spikes from my cleats clattering against the floor.

"Where are you going?"

She throws a thumb over her shoulder, gesturing towards the parking lot. "Home."

*Home.*

"I mean, to your house," she corrects from down the tunnel.

I keep jogging and as soon as I can reach her, I pull her into my body, both arms wrapping around her shoulders. "Did you see him?" I ask, my words slightly muffled against her hair. "Did you see him walk?"

She nods against me, her arms snaking around my waist. "He did so well."

"Thank you. For bringing him to me. I'm so glad I didn't miss that."

"I promised you."

I linger a little longer than I probably should, but there's no one around to remind me to stop getting so fucking attached to this woman, so I stay, holding her in a hug for another moment. Eventually I pull away, my hand still cupping the back of her neck just to give myself permission to touch her in some way. I don't know what else there is to say, but I also don't want her to leave.

"Cody wants you to give him baking lessons," is what I come up with.

"Really?"

"Yeah. You know how he is, always trying new things."

"I'd love to teach him!" There's so much excitement in her tone, so much eagerness on her face.

"I'll let him know. You guys could do it at the house sometime."

"That'd be great." Her green eyes sparkle under the fluorescent lights of the hallway. "The only time I've gotten to teach people is in the kitchens I contract for but that's all high-skill stuff. I think it'd be fun to teach someone the basics. Well, someone other than Max." She finishes that with a soft laugh.

Miller is glowing. I mean, she's beaming like a fucking glowstick at the prospect.

I stroke my fingers against the nape of her neck, reminding us both that I'm still touching her. My other hand comes up to cradle her jaw, my thumb brushing over the soft pillow of her lower lip as my body subtly slants over hers.

"Kai," she whispers.

"Hmm?"

"Are you going to kiss me?"

"Thinking about it."

"What happened to your no-more-kissing rule?"

"Wanting to break it."

She nods, the movement causing my thumb to tug at her lower lip, pulling it down, and fuck if I don't want to slip that into my mouth and suck on it.

"I've always hated that rule," she says.

But before I decide what I'm going to do, the tunnel fills with echoing voices from my teammates headed this way from the field. Miller takes my hand that was on her lips and places a chaste kiss on the inside of my palm before dropping it to fall back at my side.

We keep our attention on each other as bodies swarm past us, headed to the clubhouse.

I get a few taps on my ass as they walk by, Miller is given a few "Hot Nanny" calls which I hate, and my brother gives me a wink over her shoulder as he takes Max into the clubhouse with him.

I scratch the back of my neck, knowing I need to go.

"So . . . um, Max and I won't be home tonight. We have family dinner."

"Oh, with Isaiah?"

"No, with my friends, but for some reason we call it family dinner. It happens every Sunday night and I go when I'm in town."

"Okay. Well, have fun, and I'll see you later." She gives my hand a quick squeeze, turning back towards the parking lot.

"Hey, Miller." She once again stops for me, and I'm stuck here rubbing at my neck like a nervous dork. "Would you want to come with me?"

That naughty smile is back. "In what sense are you asking me to come with you?"

"Get your teenaged-boy mind out of the gutter. Would you want to come to family dinner with me?"

"Do you need help with Max?"

"No."

I can see her tensing from here, maybe thinking my invitation means more than it should. Truly, I have no idea what it means other than I want her there.

"If it makes you feel any better," I continue. "The only reason I want you there is so I can prove to my people that I can go a whole month without firing a nanny. It has nothing to do with me enjoying your company whatsoever."

She bites back a smile. "And just how many of *your* people will be there?"

*If she goes, all of them.*

"Five or six. Give or take depending on if Isaiah shows. And they all assume we're fucking so heads-up on that."

"If it were up to me, they'd be right."

I purposefully ignore her because I'm already battling with myself here and her constant approval isn't helping me fight the urge.

"I'd have more fun if you were there," I add. "Remember that fun you promised me? You know, because I'm an over-worked and overtired single dad that doesn't know how to let loose."

"Cheap shot, Rhodes, but fine, I'll go with you."

A way too satisfied grin lives on my lips.

"Stop smiling. It's creeping me out." She once again heads for the exit. "You're driving. I'm much better as a passenger princess, so pick me up at home."

I watch as Miller leaves, getting back into her van, and fuck do I love that the term *home* keeps slipping from her mouth.

# 21

# Miller

This house is nice. Similar to Kai's place, which is only ten minutes away, but a bit bigger. On the short drive over, I learned that the owners are a local NBA player and his fiancée, and that I'd also be meeting another guy who plays for Chicago's NHL team as well as *his* fiancée.

I'm nervous.

I was hesitant to agree when Kai asked me back at the stadium, but those nerves have only amplified on the ride over here. Meeting the closest friends of the dad I'm nanny-ing for doesn't exactly seem like the no-strings-attached summer I planned for. In fact, this dinner feels very stringy.

At the same time, there's an odd pressure sitting on my chest, hoping they'll like me. I can't recall the last time I was concerned about acceptance. I never stay in one place long enough to worry if I'll make friends or not, but this feels different and I'm not sure why. It shouldn't matter if Kai's friends like me or not because, in less than a month's time, they won't remember me anyway.

Kai opens the front door without knocking, reaffirming how comfortable he is with these people, and I enter first with Max slung on my hip. But two steps into the foyer, when I hear voices, I stop.

"Go ahead." He motions towards the back of the house. "I think everyone is in the kitchen."

I don't move.

"You okay?"

I nod.

"Miller Montgomery." He turns toward me. "Are you . . . *nervous*?"

"No."

He chuckles. "Oh my God, you are. Miss 'grab my tits if it'll help you calm down' is nervous for a little family dinner."

I can't even get in on the joke right now. That's how off I feel.

His face softens. "They're all nice people, Mills."

I straighten my shoulders, determination set between them. "I'm sure they are. Let's go."

Kai's confused stare burns into the back of my head, but I'm not going to reveal that I'm nervous because I don't really have friends. No need to explain that friendship leads to connection which leads to heartbreak when I inevitably leave for the next city. Because then he'd ask why I'd be nervous if that were the case and I'd have to try to figure it out for myself why I want *his* friends to like me of all people.

I'm the first to see everyone as I stand in the entryway to the kitchen with Max on my hip.

"Hi!" He waves to the four other people in the room, but I stay frozen in place when all eyes land on me. Then Kai's hand finds the small of my back and an odd amount of peace washes over me from that simple gesture.

That's Kai though. Stable. Dependable. Always there when you need him.

But this summer, he's needed *me*. To help with his son. To make him let loose. And now, the tables have turned for the first time in our . . . whatever our situation is.

The group of four glance around each other in the kitchen, unspoken conversations taking place, before a tall man with a chain around his neck and tattoos decorating his arm splits into a cheeky smile. "Well, aren't you three the cutest little family we've ever seen." He finishes that with a few brow pumps aimed at the man at my side.

We do look domestic as hell, me holding Max, and Kai carrying the lemon meringue pie I whipped up.

"Miller, right?" asks a woman with blue-green eyes and curly hair.

I hold my hand up in a small wave. "That's me. The nanny he wasn't allowed to fire and is now sleeping with."

A man with equally vibrant eyes chokes on his drink.

"Yep. I like her," says the first man with the tattoos.

"She's giving you guys shit," Kai corrects.

A blonde woman with a spring in her step bounds right towards me. "It is so great to meet you! I'm Indy," she says, gesturing behind her. "This is my fiancé, Ryan. Welcome to our home! And that's my best friend, Stevie, and her fiancé, Zanders."

I mentally engrain those names the best I can.

Man with ocean eyes and freckled cheeks: Ryan.

Woman with those same attributes: Stevie.

Tattoos and chain: Zanders

And the blonde ball of sunshine: Indy.

"Can I say hi to this little guy?" She holds her hands out for Max and he finds his way into her arms. "And let me take that from you." She grabs the pie from Kai. "Did you make this, Miller? It looks amazing. Do you want a drink? I made margaritas! Come in, make yourselves comfortable."

After hellos are said, the room seems to settle, giving us a moment to join.

I keep my voice quiet so only Kai can hear. "She seems . . . friendly."

"She will make you her . . . *bestie*. Is that what you girls call it?"

I chuckle. "I don't fucking know."

"Well, she will make you her friend even if you try to resist, so my advice would be to just go with it."

A small curve settles on my lips at the idea of that.

Kai's thumb rubs a circle against my lower back in his naturally soothing way. "Do you feel a bit better now?"

"They called us cute."

"How dare they." His head jerks back. "The last word I'd ever use to describe you is 'cute'."

"Exactly. God, you know me so well."

"Stevie, how's the senior dog center been?" Kai asks.

"It's been great. With the team's partnership"—she points at Zanders—"donations have been amazing and adoptions have been consistent." Her brow raises. "Why are you asking? Are you looking to adopt?"

Kai chuckles. "One day, I promise I will. Once I officially retire from baseball, you'll be my first stop."

"Deal."

Indy uses her fork to point to the almost finished lemon meringue slice on her plate. "Miller, I'm going to need this recipe. Actually, I think I'm going to need you to just come over and teach me sometime. I've never gotten meringue right."

"I'd love to. Teaching is one of the favorite parts of my job."

"Perfect." She brings her margarita to her lips with a smile. "We'll make a girls' day out of it. Stevie, you in?"

"Absolutely."

I sit back in my seat with a smile on my lips, and Kai's palm slides over my thigh under the table, giving it a squeeze. When my attention drifts to his face, he's got a soft grin on his lips and shoots me a discreet wink.

Tonight has been great. The nerves disappeared almost immediately.

It also helped when Rio, Zanders' teammate, showed up and brought the humor. It's my favorite way to break the ice.

But it's been especially great because Indy and Stevie are nice girls, and it's comforting to see how much the guys care about Kai and his son. Ryan was even the one to take Max upstairs and put him down for bed in one his guest rooms where, apparently, they keep a crib for nights like this one.

"And the wedding?" Kai asks Ryan and Indy. "How's the planning?"

Ryan slips his hand into Indy's, looking right at her when he says, "Great. We're getting close. September twelfth."

"Miller, will you still be in town?" Indy asks, pumping her brow in Kai's direction. "Kai has a plus-one."

"Okay, matchmaker," he mutters under his breath.

I freeze for the first time at the table because dinner with his friends already felt too intimate and attached but attending his close friend's wedding is a whole other category.

"I won't be, unfortunately. I leave at the end of August."

My eyes flick to Kai and he's not smiling.

"Speaking of marriage and husbands," Rio begins, starting on his second slice of pie. "Miller, are you looking for one?"

"No, she's not," Kai quickly declares at my side.

"Dang, Daddy, I just meant because the pie is so good, I'd marry her for it."

Kai leans close to me but speaks loud enough for Rio to hear. "He didn't mean that because of the pie."

Rio sighs. "You're right. I didn't. I just want to find somebody to love me. Is that really so much to ask for?"

"Aw, Rio," Indy coos at my side. "I love you."

"Thanks, Ind. At least somebody does."

"So do I," Stevie pipes up.

"I love you too, man," Zanders adds from the head of the table.

Rio looks right to Ryan. "And Ryan, what about you?"

Ryan glances around the table, pretending to have missed the entire conversation. "What are we talking about?"

Indy playfully smacks him in the chest and while more laughter and conversation flows around us, Kai reaches between us and pulls my already close chair even closer to his.

"Having fun?" he asks in a hushed tone.

We lean into each other, each of us resting our cheeks on our palms and looking at one another.

I nod with a smile. "I am. Thank you for bringing me."

He watches my lips as I speak, tucking his lower one between his teeth.

"Thank you for coming. I think this is my favorite family dinner yet."

"Oh, yeah?"

"Yeah. Mostly because of the pie."

I give him a gentle swat on the upper arm.

"And because of the girl who made it."

He looks at my lips and I look at his before the front door opens, breaking our moment.

"Isaiah?" Kai asks, when his brother comes waltzing in.

"Sorry I'm late!"

Indy stands from her chair. "I'm so glad you made it! Let me get you a plate. We had tacos. You good with everything?"

"You're an angel, Ind. Thank you."

Isaiah goes around the table, swinging his arm around Ryan, Zanders, and Rio as he greets them all, then pops a kiss on Stevie's cheek as he walks by.

"Stevie, you're looking beautiful."

"Get your own girl, Rhodes," Zanders reminds him.

Isaiah takes a seat on the other side of Kai. "Working on it."

"What are you doing here?" Kai asks.

"It's family dinner."

"You haven't been to one in weeks. And why are you so late?"

Isaiah leans in closer, for only me and his brother to hear.

"Did you know that Kennedy isn't wearing her ring anymore?"

"What ring?" I ask.

"Ken used to have a giant diamond on her ring finger," Kai explains. "It hasn't been there all season."

"You knew? Why didn't you tell me? And how the hell did I not notice until today? I stare at that girl all the time."

"I figured you saw."

"Well, I did today, and now you're looking at a changed man."

Kai and I both burst out laughing.

"Excuse me, I'm serious about this."

"That's why you're here," Kai realizes.

"I'm a family man now. All these years, I didn't really have a chance in hell because she was engaged, but now, I have a shot."

"You *technically* have a shot."

"This is happening. As of today, you're looking at a one-woman man. I was just filling my time all these years, waiting for her to be single."

"And by 'filling your time', you're referring to filling your bed?" I ask.

He gives a quick nod of his head. "Yes, exactly."

Kai and I are wearing fully amused grins, watching his playboy brother turn into a love-struck yet hopeful idiot.

"You can't blame me for doing my thing when she wasn't available, but now that she's single . . . ." Isaiah shakes his head, pointing at himself. "Changed man."

Indy puts a plate of tacos down in front of Isaiah before giving his shoulders a squeeze. "Happy you're here, Isaiah."

"I'll be here every week!"

I lean into Kai. "Where's the restroom?"

He points behind us. "Down that hall. Second door on your right."

"I'll be right back."

Ryan and Indy's home is stunning, modern, and clean, but with plenty of bright pops as well. I take my time looking at the artwork on the walls as I walk down the hall. I use the restroom, and as I'm washing my hands at the sink, I can't help but stare at my child-like grin in the mirror because tonight was fun. These people are fun. I couldn't tell you the last time I had dinner around a table where the conversation was about something other than menu changes, seasonal fruit, or current food trends.

It was nice to have a meal where I was simply Miller instead of Chef.

Turning, I dry my hands on the small towel when my attention drifts to the framed piece of cross-stitch hung on the wall. The embroidery on the crisp piece of linen is bright and feminine. The lettering is done in cursive, using a dark pink thread and surrounded by tiny flowers and hearts.

*Please don't do drugs in our bathroom*, is hung proudly on display.

It's so out of place in this dark and moody restroom.

I love it.

On my way back, the conversation continues in the dining room so I slip into the kitchen to grab another margarita. For being in a stranger's home, I feel oddly comfortable enough to help myself. Kai's friends are laid-back and easy to be around, and it's comforting to see how much they've welcomed both him and Max into the fold.

I give the blender a quick pulse to re-mix the frozen margarita before opening the cabinet to grab a new glass. Except, the shelf at eye level is empty and the only available cups are up high, almost out of my reach.

Lifting on my toes, I stretch as tall as I can, tension pulling the straps over my shoulders and causing my cutoff overalls to ride up my ass. My fingers graze the bottom of the shelf I need to reach and I use my other hand to push myself off the counter. I'm so close to getting my hand around a glass when a vein-corded arm reaches over me.

"I've got it," Kai says before his hand stills on the cup, both of us suddenly hyperaware of our proximity.

His body crowds mine from behind, enveloping every inch of my skin, and when he finally takes the glass from the shelf, he sets it down, but doesn't back away. He keeps his stance, bracketing his palms against the counter on either side of me.

Dropping back on my heels, every inch of his front touches my back. "Thanks," I somehow say.

"Mm-hmm." His chest rumbles with a hum and I feel the gravel through each nerve in my body.

My shorts are so far up my ass right now, but I don't even care with Kai's body covering mine. Giving him permission to stay, I slightly lean back, my head resting on the broad plane of his chest.

He inhales and speaks in a whisper, his friends in the next room over. "You smell nice. Sweet, ironically."

"How is that ironic?" I chuckle. "I bake for a living."

"Because you like to pretend as if you're all spice."

I know what he's doing, trying to break down my defenses, bringing me to a cozy family dinner after his son took his first steps. Telling me he knows I'm sweeter than I let on. But I allow it, letting myself indulge in the idea of simple days when I know soon enough, I'll be back to the chaos of chasing life's checkmarks in a stressful kitchen.

Wandering, his hand skims over my bare thigh, fingertips grazing the hem of my frayed cutoffs. He follows the line of fabric, the pads of his fingers dusting my bare ass before he pulls the material down to cover me again.

"These fucking legs, Mills."

Involuntarily, I arch into him. He feels good. He smells good and I'm really tired of his no-kissing rule.

Kai's hand splays over my lower stomach to keep our contact. "Today was a good day."

It really was. Simple and good.

Turning, I look at him, our lips almost brushing. "They can all be good days."

His eyes bounce to my mouth.

"Really? In my kitchen? Next to the food?" Ryan stands in the entryway with his hands full of dirty dishes. "At least use a spare bedroom. We've got three more besides the one Max is sleeping in."

Kai takes a step back and I create more distance. The last thing I need is his friends comparing their situation to Kai's while they're getting married and having babies, and I'm over here only allowing myself to indulge in his lifestyle for my brief stay.

"You guys could sleep here, you know?" Ryan sets the dishes in the sink and starts to clean them. "That way you don't have to move Max."

And dear God, that sounds couple-y as fuck, spending the night at his friends' house after we've all had dinner and drinks together.

Kai quickly glances my way, most likely noting the look of absolute terror on my face. "Thanks, man, but we leave on a road trip tomorrow, so we should get back."

It's one of the few times I'm thankful he can read my mind.

Max is still passed out on his dad's shoulder by the time we get to the front door of their house. Kai unlocks it, standing back to usher me inside.

But I can't go in. It's almost as if there's a force field keeping me out. After tonight, things feel too sticky, too connected for me to go inside with him.

Running my hand over Max's hair, I place a quick kiss on his little forehead.

"I'm gonna . . ." I toss my thumb over my shoulder towards the side gate that leads to his backyard. "I'm just going to go to bed."

"Mills." Kai's tone is somewhat begging. "Please don't sleep out there."

God, that plea hits me right in the heart, cracking a bit more of the armored shell that surrounds it.

And for that reason, I take two steps backward toward the side gate and slip into the backyard without another word.

"Miller," he whisper-shouts. "Are you serious?"

I get myself inside the van, immediately locking the door behind me, needing to create some sort of barrier from the domestic, homey, and settled feelings that have invaded my chest tonight.

I just need to sleep it off. Maybe I'll take a drive tomorrow before the flight and remind myself that there are places other than Chicago, the city I'm leaving in a month. I just need a bit of fresh air to remind me who I am, that I don't care about his friends' opinions of me or the fact that I'd really like to see those girls again. I can be by myself for a moment, just the way I'm used to living.

Shaking it off, I reach for my toothbrush next to my sink, but come up empty.

That's weird. I put it right back where I always do after I used it this morning.

Searching around my tiny van, I don't find it anywhere. Nor do I find my skin care, my toothpaste, my goddamn slippers.

**Me:** *Did you steal my toothbrush?*

**Baseball Daddy:** *You didn't even say goodnight.*

**Me:** *Malakai Rhodes. Where's my toothbrush?*

**Baseball Daddy:** *Oh, she full-named me.*

**Me:** *Kai!*

**Baseball Daddy:** *Next time, don't leave before saying goodnight.*

**Me:** *Goodnight. Happy? Where's my fucking toothbrush? And all my other shit.*

**Baseball Daddy:** *I think I saw it in my guest room. Can't be sure, though. You should probably come inside and check.*

**Me:** *You're going to move me into your house without asking? Seriously?*

**Baseball Daddy:** *I've told you I don't like you sleeping outside.*

**Me:** *You're annoying.*

**Baseball Daddy:** *Back door is unlocked.*

As soon as I step through the back slider, I find Kai already stripped down to his boxer briefs as he stands in his kitchen, ankles crossed with the electric tea kettle heating up next to him. "Chamomile tea? It's good for the nerves."

"I think I hate you again."

He simply wears a proud smile.

I charge right past him towards the guest room. "I know what you're doing, Kai. Dinner with your friends, moving me into your house."

"I'm not doing anything. It was dinner, a meal you eat every day. And big surprise, I don't like you sleeping outside. That's all entirely casual and rational stuff. If you're over-thinking it, then that sounds like a you problem."

I don't have the energy to argue with his completely sane logic. Maybe I am overthinking it all, but this weird ball won't unfurrow from my chest. It feels like homesickness which makes no goddamn sense. I don't have a home to miss.

Kai's guest room is the first door to the right past the kitchen, across from his spare bathroom. One of his team shirts is folded neatly on the duvet for me to sleep in and my slippers are lined up next to the door. Quickly undressing, I leave my underwear on and slip his shirt over my head. Kai's huge and I'm not, so this shirt is practically a dress falling around mid-thigh.

Stomping across the hall to the bathroom like a child, I find my toothbrush and toothpaste sitting in a cup by the sink and my skin care thoughtfully laid out on the counter.

Through the mirror, I find an almost naked Kai behind me, long arms hanging onto the top of the doorframe, satisfied grin on his lips as he watches me brush my teeth.

"You're annoying," I mumble past the suds in my mouth.

"It's a wall. The only difference between you staying in my house and outside of it is a wall. The other part, where you're convincing yourself that because you sleep in a place with wheels it'll keep you detached from everyone around you, that's on you."

I pin him with a scowl through the reflection. "It's my home, and I'm going back out there tonight."

"It's your *car*, and if you stay inside the house, I can finally lock the back door again."

"What are you talking about?" I spit out the toothpaste. "Why haven't you been locking the back door?"

He shrugs. "I didn't want you locked out of the house in case you needed . . . something. I haven't locked it since the first night you stayed out there."

My eyes shoot up through the reflection, instantly finding his. Standing there, toothbrush in my hand, his gaze wanders down my length in the mirror, watching the way his shirt drapes over my body.

Kai clears his throat. "I'll be in the kitchen." And with that, he and his shirtless body leave me to finish my night-time routine.

When I'm done, I find him leaning against the kitchen counter with a mug in his hands. He's stunning and sleepy and I'm trying my hardest not to think about the single wall that'll separate his bed from mine tonight if I stay in his spare room.

"Tea?" he asks, holding up his mug.

He would like tea, this family man who wears glasses and raised his younger brother. My original notions of him being overbearing and uptight could not be further from the truth. He simply cared too much, loved too hard. He almost cried tears of joy from watching his son take his first steps today for goodness' sake.

"I'm okay, but thanks."

I can sense his anticipation, expecting me to bolt. It's my thing, after all.

I told myself I would get my stuff and go right back outside, but I find my feet glued to the kitchen floor. As much as I don't want to admit it, experiencing the simple joys of Kai's life today was the most fun I've had in a while. Here I am, supposedly showing this man how to have a good time when a Sunday night dinner and a toddler's first steps beat anything I could come up with.

His attention drops to the mug in his hand as I lean on the counter opposite him. "Why were you so hesitant about meeting my friends?" he asks.

"I don't know."

His eyes flick up to me. "Don't lie to me. Tell me why."

*Okay, him understanding me enough to know when I'm lying is quite annoying.*

"I don't really have many friends."

He pins me with a look, silently asking me to elaborate.

"I'm on the move so much that my relationships are always temporary. It's easier to go into each new city with that expectation already in place. It hurts less to leave that way."

"But tonight, those were *my* friends. Why was that difficult for you?"

I shake my head. "Stop."

Frustration thrums through me. We both know what he's doing. He's picking away, trying to get me to admit that I care. That I'll *still* care when I leave.

"Why, Miller? Why can't you admit that you wanted them to like you? That there are ties here in Chicago that are going to make it harder for you to leave this time around."

I pin him with a scowl. "Don't."

Setting his mug down, he steps towards me almost predatorily. Fingers raking through my hair, he pushes it behind my ear. "It'll be hard for you to leave this time around, won't it?"

"It doesn't matter. I'm leaving regardless."

His nostrils slightly flare at my words, his icy eyes holding mine. "I hope those words burned while coming out." The pad of his thumb traces my lower lip. "Because your armor is awfully annoying."

"So are you."

His attention is glued to my mouth. "Please don't sleep outside," he softly pleads. "I don't sleep well knowing you're out there."

His hand drops to my throat and I swallow against his palm.

"Tell me you'll stay," he continues.

There's really no argument left. I nod, breathless. "I'll stay."

"Good."

Tilting my chin with only his knuckle and thumb, he lifts my face up and presses his mouth to mine. It's soft and intimate. A bit tentative, but only until I arch up and eagerly meet him. With a bit more confidence, his hand slides around the back of my skull, fingers threaded through my hair as he kisses me.

"What was that for?" I ask, searching for air.

"I like you vulnerable, Mills."

"Well, don't get used to that. That was a one-time thing."

He chuckles. "Then I better make it worth it."

His mouth is on mine, this time with urgency. He grips my hip, instantly pressing himself into me, and I meet him there, rolling against him while he wears nothing but a pair of briefs. Kai releases a desperate moan into my mouth, the sound sending heat pooling between my legs, and I'm over here wanting to do everything in my power to hear it again.

He nips my bottom lip. "What did I tell you about these fucking legs?"

"That you get hard just looking at them?" The confirmation is pressing into my lower belly.

His fingers skim my thighs, lifting his shirt to see them better.

"You're the one who didn't leave me any pants to wear," I remind him.

A wicked grin tilts on his mouth. "I'm a smart man."

Kai lifts me onto the counter. The cold surface sends a shock to my system, goosebumps scattering my legs that instantly open around him. Inviting him closer, I drape my arms over his broad shoulders while he inches my shirt up over my hips to expose my soaked underwear.

"*Fuck,*" he curses when he looks down to see it. Head falling back and eyes towards the ceiling, he lets out a deep sigh. "This is why I wasn't supposed to kiss you."

"Why?" I keep playing with the hair at the nape of his neck, grinding my seeking hips into the air, needing something. "Because every little thing you do makes me wet?"

"*Jesus,*" he groans. "Because now, all I can think about is fucking you."

"Then stop thinking about it and do it."

He chuckles without humor. "You're so much fucking trouble, Miller." His eyes meet mine again, our noses brushing. "What happens if I become addicted?"

"Then lucky us, we still have a month to indulge in that kind of addiction."

"You really think I could quit you after it's all done?"

I nod with enthusiasm, hoping to convince him. "I'm easily forgettable."

"You're a little liar tonight, huh?"

Hooking my ankles around the back of his thighs, I pull him into the cradle of my hips. "Just don't let it mean anything and we'll both be fine."

A flash of annoyance passes over him before he gives in and seals his mouth to mine.

Inhaling, I pull him closer, deepening the kiss. My entire body is on fire as his palms coast over the raised skin of my legs, grabbing my ass, his tongue slipping easily into my mouth.

He rolls his hips into mine, his erection giving me just enough friction that a needy cry slips from my throat.

Kai swallows the sounds with a gravelly groan of satisfaction. "Goddamn," he exhales, pulling away for only a second. "Who knew you'd sound so pretty when you whine?"

I arch into him. "You could've heard it weeks ago if you weren't so stubborn."

His hands slip under my shirt, palms engulfing my bare back as they run the length of it. He crosses his arms, holding me to him as tightly as possible with a kiss that feels far too intimate for a casual hook-up, but I forget all about that notion when his hands start exploring, running over my hips and curving over my stomach. He flicks my nipples with his thumbs, hard and sensitive for him.

"Do that again," I beg breathlessly.

He does, rolling them before he pinches them between his fingers.

"You like that?" he asks, though he doesn't need the confirmation. I think he just likes to hear me ask for it.

I quickly nod, my eyes pleading as our foreheads rest against each other, swirling breaths shared between us.

He smiles wickedly. "You like when I play with your tits, Mills?"

"*Yes*," I hiss through another pinch that sends a throb straight to my clit.

"You think I could make you come just from this?"

Before tonight, that would've been a resounding *no*. I'm the kind of woman who needs a shit ton of warm-up before and if I ever come. We're talking toys and a whole lot of direc- tion when, most of the time, I finish myself later.

But if there's anyone who could get me off from a little nipple play it'd be this man, who has a whole confident side I'm starting to see.

"I think you should try," I suggest with a kiss.

He chuckles lightly before molding his mouth to mine again, our tongues tangling. I pull him closer, but every inch of our somewhat clothed bodies is already touching, and still, it's not enough. I want us naked. I want him inside of me. I'd let him fuck me right here on this counter where I could replay it in my mind each and every time I baked in his kitchen.

He squeezes me in his palms, rolling my nipples between his fingers as our lower halves continue to writhe into each other. My ass is barely on the counter with how hard we're dry-humping, my hips seeking his with every thrust.

Quickly, he removes one of his hands from my shirt, pull- ing off his fogged-over glasses and tossing them onto the counter, but instead of replacing his fingers on my sensitive nipple, he cups my hip, pads bruising my flesh with an almost painful but desperate grip as he moves our bodies together.

We both look down and watch ourselves grind against each other.

"Fuck, Mills." His breaths are labored. "You feel incredible."

I toss my head back when he pulls my nipple between two fingers. "Please don't stop. Please. Please."

I'm so wet, so close. I can feel my body pulsing, ready to come just from grinding on his dick.

His hand curves around, cupping my ass to keep me in place as he ruts into me, his cock brushing my clit with every roll.

"*Yes*," I cry. "Yes, Ace. Right there." The nickname slips off my tongue without thought, but I'm a panting mess right now, and can't be held accountable for my actions.

"Jesus." His hand slams against the cabinet next to my head, looking for leverage. "Call me that again."

"Ace? You like when I call you by your nickname?"

His face falls into the crook of my neck with a nod. "It sounds pretty coming from you. Especially when your pussy is soaked and rubbing on me."

He continues to slide us together against the edge of the counter, kissing my neck and collarbone, mapping out my jaw before biting my ear.

Every muscle in my body tightens with that, my hips moving instinctively as he hits my clit over and over.

Then I fall, right over the edge. Still clothed on the kitchen counter, I come from a bit of dry-humping and nipple play.

Hot-as-hell dry-humping and nipple play, might I add.

When he feels my body tense with an orgasm, Kai's hold on me tightens, keeping himself right where I need him. Lifting his head from my neck, he watches me fall apart.

"Fuck yes," he whispers, mesmerized.

Utterly fascinated, his attention never leaves me as I moan and shutter my way through it. He watches so intently, as if he'll never see me come again and needs to commit it to memory, but fuck, if this is how my body responds to his with our clothes on, I need to know what it feels like to touch him without.

Chest heaving, my entire body slumps as I come down, tired muscles falling limp and thankful that he's holding me upright. Catching my breath, I fall onto his shoulder, mindlessly playing with the dark hair on the nape of his neck. My body absent-mindedly rubs against his, still on edge from my high when I feel his erection slide against my inner thigh.

I cup him, stroking my hand over his length and ready for everything else.

"Miller." His voice is ragged, desperate. "Stop."

*What?*

Lifting from his shoulder, my breaths are still labored when my eyes find the bulge in his briefs that I know has got to be borderline painful at this point. "But—"

"Please." His ice-blue eyes are pleading with me. "All I can think about is fucking you right now, but you're out of your goddamn mind if you think any of this could be easily forgettable for me." He shakes his head, running a palm over his disbelieving face. "I think I'm ruined by simply watching you come, so please, do me a favor and go to bed." Fixing my shirt, he gives me one last quick kiss. "And for the love of God . . . lock the fucking door."

# 22

# Kai

My start this week is tomorrow night in Boston. We got into the city this afternoon and Isaiah immediately took Max and all his stuff, declaring he was having a sleepover with his nephew tonight.

Even though I strive to spend as much of my time off with my son, it's good for us both that he creates his own relationships, especially with the people who will be in his life forever.

So, with my evening free, I knock on the door between my hotel room and Miller's. Bouncing on my toes, nerves rattle through me because it's been a couple of days since we've really spoken.

Well, other than the night following our moment in the kitchen. I hadn't talked to her all day, so she snuck back into her van that night to sleep. Ten minutes later, I barged in, threw her over my shoulder, and put her ass right back in my guest room, reminding her she wasn't allowed to sleep outside anymore.

For once, I had someone there to celebrate the good moments with me. When Max took his first steps, she was there. And then that evening, with my friends, she fit in seamlessly. And sure, there were some ulterior motives to that dinner.

When the time comes, I want it to be hard for Miller to leave and not just because I've enjoyed having her here, but because it's one of the most important parts of life. Finding people that make your heart ache when they're not around. Having a place to call home.

Instead of Miller being the one to get lost in the fantasy of her sticking around Chicago, *I* was the one who did. In what world am I supposed to simply be okay with her leaving?

How the hell am I supposed to forget what her laugh sounds like? What her lips taste like?

I want her. *Fuck*, do I want her. Any sane, straight man would jump at the opportunity of having her as an unattached fuck buddy the way she wants, but my brain forgot how to do casual all the while my dick is praying I'll remember.

So yeah, I'm mad at myself because I don't understand how to have her while knowing that one day soon, I'll have to let her leave. And instead of growing up and telling her that, I've resorted to avoidance.

I knock on our adjoining door once again, but she still doesn't answer.

I try her phone with no luck.

Finding both Monty and Kennedy's contacts, I individually shoot them the same text.

Kennedy and Miller seem on the brink of becoming friends regardless that she likes to assume she doesn't have any. I can see how excited Miller gets anytime Kennedy is around. She's the only other woman on the road with us, so maybe they're hanging out now?

**Me:** *Happen to know where Miller is?*

**Kennedy:** *No, but your brother won't stop sending me selfies of him and Max, asking if I want to come over and play house with him.*

She forwards me a couple of the images of my brother and son on the floor, playing with toys. The pictures are clearly Isaiah's newest form of a thirst trap. His playboy thing has never done it for Kennedy, so I guess he's going with the family man route and seeing if that lands.

**Me:** *Want me to tell him to leave you alone?*

**Kennedy:** *I've got it handled. I've been dealing with your brother for years. When it comes to Isaiah Rhodes, my favorite thing to do is to humble him.*

**Me:** *Have fun with that.*

**Kennedy:** *I always do.*

In a separate text thread, Monty responds.

**Monty:** *Why?*

**Me:** *Weird answer. Is she with you?*

**Monty:** *What are your intentions with my daughter?*

Okay, he's definitely with Miller. Grabbing my hotel key, I leave my room and head towards his.

**Me:** *This new overprotective dad thing doesn't track. She lives in a van, and you're cool with it. She travels all over the country alone for work. No way are my intentions your greatest concern when it comes to her.*

**Monty:** *I'm asking a simple question here. So defensive, Ace. I've already caught you in bed with her once. Anything else I should know?*

*Fucking hell.*

Taking a few turns down the hallway on our floor, I find Monty's room and knock.

"Yes?" he asks, cracking the door only slightly.

"Miller here?"

"Anything you're wanting to tell me?"

"Dad, stop," I hear Miller scold from the background. With her hand around the door, she opens it fully, exposing her pretty brunette hair and olive-green overalls. "He's been like this all day."

"That's because you two have been acting like strangers. Something clearly happened."

*Well ... shit.*

Miller ignores him, her eyes tracing my clothes, fully dressed and ready to leave the hotel. "What's up? Need help with Max?"

"No, he's with Isaiah tonight, but I was wondering . . ." My eyes flit to Monty standing behind his daughter, big arms crossed over his chest. He uses two fingers to point to his eyes before directing them my way, telling me he's watching me. "Can you fucking stop? This is weird, Monty."

Miller whips around, but he plays it completely cool. "I have no idea what he's talking about."

I roll my eyes, redirecting them towards the tattooed beauty. "I was wondering if you wanted to go somewhere with me."

"Where?"

"It's a surprise."

Her greens sparkle. "Baseball Daddy, are you proposition-ing me to have some fun?"

"Something like that."

Miller turns back to her dad. "Do you mind?"

"Have her back by curfew."

Her eyes narrow. "In what fucking world would I have a curfew? I wasn't asking for permission. Stop being weird. I was just asking if you mind if I don't finish our movie."

"Nine p.m. sharp," is Monty's only response.

We're both exhausted of him. "It's already nine-thirty."

Grabbing her denim jacket from the couch, Miller pats her dad's arm. "You should probably rehearse that for next time. I'm sure you could do better."

The typical smile he wears around his daughter finally cracks through. "I've always wanted to play the overbearing dad watching his daughter leave for a date. What would make it more believable next time?"

"I'm not sure, I've never had one." Leaving the hotel room, she offers her dad a quick wave. "See you tomorrow."

"Love you, Millie."

"Love you."

Together we walk to the elevator. "Never had what?" I ask. "An overbearing dad or a date?"

"Neither." She stops in her tracks, turning in to face me. "This isn't a date, right?"

"Oh, I know you better than that. I wouldn't dare take you on a date. That's way too much commitment for you, Montgomery."

When our rideshare drops us in the North End of Boston, my hand immediately finds the small of Miller's back, ushering her towards the bustling building. I'd rather hold her hand, lace our fingers together, but I have to take it slow with her, keep her from overthinking it all.

A line of patrons spills outside and wraps around the corner, and once we get to our spot in the back, Miller takes her time checking out the red brick buildings, trying to piece together where we are.

It's clear this is Boston's version of Little Italy, with their Italian flags and string lights draped over the cobblestone roads from building to building. There's another bakery across the street that's as busy as this one, but Rio told me they only had cannoli and that I should bring Miller here instead.

"Are we getting dessert?" she asks as we inch closer to the entrance. Her eyes widen comically when she looks through the windows, spotting countless glass cases filled with sweets. "Holy shit, this is exactly what my heaven looks like."

"*Your* heaven, huh?"

"Yeah, we all have our own versions. Mine looks a lot like this but without all those bullshit glass cases in the way, but somehow, the desserts are still always fresh." She finally breaks her staring contest with the bakery, turning her attention back to me. "What would yours look like?

"I can ask for anything I want?"

"Anything."

"Well, I'm not sure what it would look like, but you'd be there and every time we were alone, your clothes would magically disappear right off your body. It'll be my first request when I get into my heaven. In fact, it'll be my favorite part."

She startles with a laugh, and for a woman I find to be funny, my ego grows at a stupid rate every time I get to hear it.

The line starts to move again, and she goes ahead of me, closer and closer to getting inside. From behind I wrap a single arm around the front of her shoulders, the size of my hands and the veins that accompany it contradicting the soft floral lines on her tanned skin.

"I'm sorry I've been avoiding you," I say softly, my mouth close to her ear.

She grasps my forearm, giving it a squeeze. "It's okay. You're apologizing with sugar so clearly, you're forgiven."

We step forward with the line, this time making it inside the building, the smell of cinnamon and chocolate hitting us the second we walk through the door. Miller's lips curve in a childish smile and it's so beautifully genuine, I can't help but watch her instead of the endless glass cases of pastries, cookies, and cakes.

"Okay, what is this place?" she asks.

"Do you remember my friend Rio who you met the other night? He's from Boston and told me about this spot. It's mostly Italian desserts, but they have some French options and traditional American pastries as well. With my travel schedule, I know it's hard for you to find time to get some work done, and these desserts aren't as fancy as what you'd normally make, but I was thinking maybe you might get a little inspiration for those recipes. Who knows, maybe something will spark an idea."

Miller stands still, not saying anything, which is strange. The girl is full of quick one-liners.

And my moment of confidence, thinking this was a good idea, has flown right out the window. "Or we don't have to think about work at all and we could just get something that looks good to take back to the hotel."

"No," she quickly says, shaking her head. "No, this is . . . this is really thoughtful of you." Her eyes flick to mine. "It sounds like the perfect idea. It also sounds a lot like a date."

I scoff. "Clearly, you've never been on a date before if you think this is what they're like. This is a work meeting, Mills. Stop getting ideas. Be professional."

Her eyes crinkle, her smile returning as she faces the desserts again and we move up in the line, closer and closer to getting our order in. Standing in front of me, she leans back, absent-mindedly resting against my chest as she continues to window-shop.

And I'm smiling like a thirty-two-year-old child on Christmas morning because there's been a good amount of easy touching for a business meeting.

"What do you want to get?" Her voice is almost a whisper, like it's a secret only between us.

I fucking love seeing her like this. The smile and excitement she's wearing now is how I envisioned her probably looking when she was a little girl and discovering her love for baking.

"Well," I say, pulling out the folded paper from my back pocket. "I did a little research."

"You did a little research?" she asks with a laugh. "Did you also print out your MapQuest directions to get here, old man?"

"Shut it."

Her eyes are shining and her lips are pinched to keep herself from laughing.

"As I said, I did some research and made a list."

"You made a list. On a piece of lined paper. With a pen."

"You gonna just keep explaining everything I'm doing or . . ."

"There's a notes app in your phone for a reason, Malakai."

"Anyway." I hold the paper in front of us, my arms caging her in. "Let's get all of these and anything else you want to try."

As Miller looks over my notes, comparing it to what's in the glass cases, we continue to move up in the line. All the women working behind the counter are small, older, and Italian. They also don't have time for any of these tourists' shit, expecting orders to be given the second a guest makes it to them. If there's a delay and patrons continue to peruse, a string of Italian words, presumably curses, echoes throughout the bakery.

I check over the glass cases, making sure I didn't miss any must-have desserts. They all look amazing, and I'd take one of each if we'd have room at our table. But I've also been so completely spoiled by the baker living in my home that this outing is more for her than it is for me.

"Tiramisu was my mom's favorite," I say, pointing to the Italian cake when we pass it.

"The woman had good taste, I see."

"Good genetics too, huh?"

She laughs. "*Great* genetics."

"Next!" the woman with olive skin and gray roots hollers from the cash register.

Miller simply hands her my list of desserts. "These please."

The woman's lips tick up in an uncharacteristic way as her eyes scan the sheet. "I like you guys," she states before taking off to box up our desserts.

"See," I whisper, my hand snaking over Miller's hip, fingers splaying over her lower belly. "My paper came in handy. There's no way we would've gotten that kind of response if we handed her a fucking phone."

She chuckles, her hand covering mine before calling out, "Can we add a tiramisu too please?"

"You got it!"

Miller simply shoots me a knowing smile over her shoulder all while doing a terrible job of making sure I don't fall for her.

Miller sighs a happy little sigh. "That was the best hour of my life."

Four giant pastry boxes sit on the table between us, still completely filled with only a few bites taken from each dessert. We had torrone, biscotti, éclair, and something called a lobster tail that was out of this world. I wish I could keep eating, but I'm stuffed.

"What was your favorite?" I ask.

"I don't know if I could choose. What was yours?"

"I don't know if I have a favorite dessert, but I did like watching you dissect them all like a mad scientist before each bite."

"I was working, remember? This is a business meeting."

"So . . . did you feel any spark?"

Her eyes flicker to me from across the table, a small smirk playing on her lips, and though I was referring to inspiration for work, we both know there's always been a spark between us.

Her attention falls back to our table of desserts. "I think so."

"Good." Grabbing the leg of her chair, I pull it, dragging her to sit next to me and letting her know our business meeting is officially over. "Tell me everything."

She picks up a cannoli. "I was thinking I could make a dark chocolate cylinder, like this shape, filled with a smoked hazelnut praline cream." She points to the slice of chocolate praline pie. "Similar to those flavors, but without the heavy texture. I could do a chocolate paint on the plate, garnished with a pulled sugar piece and finished with a scoop of salted sheep's milk ice cream." She pauses to catch her breath. "What do you think?"

My mouth only gapes as I look at her.

"I know. I know. Who the hell would want sheep's milk ice cream, right?"

"Your mind just created that? Out of thin air?"

For once in her life, Miller seems shy.

"That sounds incredible, Mills."

"Yeah?"

"Yeah. Damn."

"Well, as long as I don't fuck it up when we get home, I'll have one recipe down. Two more to go." A relieved smile tilts on her lips as she looks around the still busy bakery. "Thank you for bringing me. I love it here. How fun is it to watch people take that first bite?"

She's watching someone try a pastry right now, but I'm only watching her. I don't get that same enjoyment she does because I'm not a creative. I don't have a product to give to the world in hopes they like it, but damn, I could watch Miller watch others eat all fucking day.

"Would you ever want to open a place like this?"

I'm aware I'm playing with fire. Asking, in a way, if she'd ever stay in one place long enough to do so.

She pins me with a look, letting me know how obvious I'm being, but she plays along. "If you asked me that seven years ago, the answer would be a very easy yes. But now? I couldn't see it. I work in Michelin-level restaurants all over the country. I recently won an award that most chefs strive for their entire life and never get. I have a three-year waitlist of kitchens wanting to hire me. I make good money and, even though you don't like when I say this, I feel like I owe it to my dad to do something important with my life. And, no, desserts aren't important, but I've tried to make myself important in the industry. I don't exactly have the luxury to change directions at this point in my career. Don't you agree?"

Wow. I don't know if Miller has ever been this vulnerable with me. Not only to divulge what's going on in that pretty little head of hers, but to ask my opinion on it.

So, I choose my words carefully. Anything too deep and personal might send her running.

"No, I don't agree with you at all. I think you could change directions a hundred more times in your life, and you'd never be too stuck to do so. Life is about finding your joy, living in a way that brings you and others happiness. So, I guess the real question is, does your career make you happy? Is this job your dream job?"

She pauses, thinking on it for a moment. "I'm good at it, so yeah, it's my dream now."

Not exactly the answer to my question, but enough for me to understand. This is what she wants out of life. This high-level career she succeeds in, never staying in one place for long.

There are things I want to say: Just because you're talented doesn't mean you owe it to anyone. The only thing you owe your dad is to find your happiness. Move to Chicago. Don't leave Max.

Don't leave me.

But I promised Monty I'd talk to him before I ever asked that of Miller, and I care too much about her dreams to ask her to give them up for me.

Miller grabs her fork and dips into the tiramisu, taking a massive bite. She sighs around it as if the ladyfingers and chocolate are the answers to all her questions. "What was your mom's name?"

"Mae."

"Mae," she says wistfully. "Another 'M'."

I can't help but smile. I only got her for fifteen years, but she is the best woman I know. "I wish she could've met Max.

He would've had her wrapped around his chubby little finger."

"Aren't we all?" Miller agrees, tilting her head and leaning her chin on her palm as if she could sit and talk to me all night.

It's been nice finally having someone to talk to, but I'm afraid the loneliness is going to be that much more obvious when she goes.

"What was she like?" she asks.

"She was . . . funny. Strong. A no-bullshit kind of woman which she had to be, raising my brother and me. But she was also soft when it came to us." My hand finds her thigh under the table, running over the olive-green fabric. "She was a lot like you."

I fully expect Miller to crumble. To insist I'm being too sentimental around her, but I don't care. It's the truth.

"I'm glad Max gets to be around a woman like her. Like you."

Eyes searching mine, I hold strong, refusing to be intimidated by the hard shell she pretends to wear.

Miller exhales and drops her head to my shoulder, hand slipping over mine.

I count it as a win. Another moment of vulnerability Miller leaned into instead of covering with humor.

"What was your mom's name?" I ask.

"Claire."

"Claire," I repeat. "Do you miss her?"

"I don't really remember her. I was so young when she died, but I miss the idea of her. I've never really known what it's like to have a mom."

A rush of emotion hits me like a freight train, welling in my throat, both for her and for my son. Will Max feel that way? Will he miss out on the idea of a mother? I try to be enough for him, I really do, but it's hard to be both. The good and the bad parent. The mom and the dad. It wasn't until a month ago I finally felt as if Max was getting it all and that's because the woman at my side waltzed into our lives.

"But my dad did a good job filling in," she continues. "Much in the way you are."

Fuck. I have to look up towards the ceiling to keep myself in check, to keep any welling tears at bay. It takes a moment, but eventually I'm able to swallow down the lump in my throat and place a kiss on Miller's head as she continues to lean on my shoulder.

She takes another forkful of tiramisu, filling her mouth, and I use the pause to change the subject.

"We should probably get back from our business meeting," I say as she tilts to look up at me.

A bit of mascarpone lingers on her lower lip, and I can't help myself from cleaning it off with the pad of my thumb, sticking it in my mouth and sucking off the remnants that were just on her.

She tracks the movement, her green eyes hooded.

Miller only nods in agreement, both of us knowing it's past time to get out of here.


I'm so accustomed to Miller being the forward one, the confident one. Confident enough she'd make a move.

While we're in the elevator on the ride up to our hotel floor, I'm all but praying she does. I'm hoping for some dirty innuendo, or for her to straight up jump me because it'd give me an excuse to give in to what I want.

I want *her*.

There's no denying it any longer; I want this girl more than I've wanted anything in my life. Sure, I want her for more than the next few weeks, but she's made it clear I can't have her for any longer than that. So the question is, can I keep myself detached enough to not entirely crumble when she goes?

We stand side by side in the elevator, so much quiet tension in this tiny metal box. Miller doesn't make a move, doesn't say something sexual to cut the tension. She lets it linger, lets me choke on it.

But we both know it isn't her responsibility to once again declare how much she wants me. The ball is in my court, and after I've stopped us not only once, but *twice*, I'm the one who has to make a move. She's not going to put herself in the position to get shot down again, and I truly don't believe she'd try anything when she knows my fears of growing attached to another person who is leaving.

Her hand is right beside mine, dangling only an inch from my own. I want to pin her to the wall, press the emergency stop button and fall to my knees. It'd be fitting if I'd finally make a move and it's in an elevator, seeing as this is where it all started.

But before I can it dings, the doors open, and Miller exhales a defeated sigh before exiting and heading straight for her room with a bit of speed to her steps. She doesn't waste any time, pulling out her key card and holding it to the lock. "Goodnight, Kai," she says, opening the door. "Thanks for tonight. I had fun."

With that, she offers me a small smile, goes inside, and closes the door behind her, leaving me in the hallway.

*Fuck.*

Inside, I'm alone. My son's not here. The only person I'm responsible for right now is myself and I'm really fucking tired of being responsible.

I want to be reckless and impulsive.

I want the woman on the other side of this wall, and I'm done trying to convince myself I don't.

Why the fuck did I hesitate in the elevator?

For once, I'm not thinking about anyone else with this decision. I'm not thinking about my responsibilities. I'm not even thinking about my future self and how bad this is going to hurt when it's done.

So what if she wants casual? Whether or not we have sex, I'm going to be a mess when she leaves, so what's the point in abstaining from what we both want?

I'll pretend.

I'll fucking pretend. For her sake, I'll keep it casual on the surface, and when she leaves at the end of the summer, I'll wallow and bitch in private.

I can't deny it anymore.

So, with unsteady breaths racking my chest, I raise my hand to knock on the door between our rooms, but before I can make contact, it opens.

Hand on the knob, Miller is breathing just as heavy, green eyes dark and a bit unhinged. She already took her overalls off, standing in the doorway in nothing but a little shirt and panties.

I allow myself to eye-fuck the hell out of her because I've spent too many days pretending like she's not the only thing I see.

Her attention finds my balled hand still hanging in the air, a bit of surprise ghosting her face. "Why were you about to knock?"

"Why did you open the door?"

"I asked first."

"I was going to knock because I'm about to be selfish." Stepping forward, I cross the threshold between her room and mine, recognizing the metaphor of it all. "For once, I'm going to take what I want."

The corner of her lip lifts in a dangerous grin. "Finally."

# 23

# Miller

Stepping into my room, Kai's hands immediately sink into my hair, fingers tightening to tilt my attention up to him, lips hovering over mine. "Can I take what I want, Miller?"

Speechless, by both the untethered spark in his eye and his dominating yet uncontrolled vibe, I simply nod.

"Can I hear you say it?"

"*Yes*," I hiss when his fingers pull my hair in that delicious way. "You can take whatever you'd like."

"Good." He nips at my lower lip. "Now tell me why you opened the door."

"Because I was going to see if you've made up your mind about whether or not you want me."

His chuckle is a bit dark. "That's never been the issue and you know it."

With a single arm around my waist, Kai lifts me, my legs instinctively wrapping around him as his lips meet mine in a kiss that is so unexpectedly possessive, it startles me. I think I might be out of my body, looking down to see a man who is typically the last person to take what he wants, but has finally decided to be selfish tonight. But then my back slams against the wall, and I'm jolted right back into the moment to realize this is real and it's happening.

"Kai," I breathe against his lips. "Are you sure you're okay with this? Are you sure this is what you want?"

His eyes soften, his nose nudging mine.

"I don't want to hurt you," I continue in a whisper.

"I know." He places a tender kiss on my lips. "I know exactly what this is, and I want it."

Kai's tongue sweeps against mine as his erection rolls against my core.

It's dirty and needy and, quite frankly, not what I was expecting after visiting a quaint bake shop. But I think that's what he needs to make this fling work. The connection, the trust. Though he constantly said tonight wasn't a date, it clearly was, and maybe a sweet date beforehand is our solution.

But there's nothing sweet about this man right now.

"You wanna have some fun with me?" Kai rasps against my lips.

*Dear God.* Such simple words, but they unravel any previous concerns of protecting him. If he keeps talking like that, *I'm* going to be the one who needs protection.

"Please."

He smiles into my mouth.

Using the wall to hold me up, he grips the underside of my thigh, kneading the flesh like he's been dreaming of touching it. His other hand snakes down my back, over the curve of my ass, until his fingers slip under the hem of my panties.

But he doesn't go any further. He teases. He savors.

I'm on fire. Every part of me burns for him to touch me. And I mean really touch me, without any fabric between us this time.

His fingers fall lower, so frustratingly close to where I need them that I whimper into his mouth.

He chuckles. "Needy, Mills?"

"Yes," I whine. "I've touched myself so many times thinking about you."

His brows lift with interest. "In my house?"

"Right on the other side of the wall from you. That night, after the kitchen, I got myself off again just from replaying it in my mind."

"*Jesus.*"

Kai's hand is so big he palms my ass perfectly, squeezing before he slips his fingers under my panty line again, this time grazing over my entire pussy like it's a reward for being honest.

My head falls back against the wall.

"So soft," he hums against my throat as his mouth trails over it. "You're ready for it, huh?"

"I've been ready for it since the day I saw you in that elevator."

His middle finger circles my clit, coaxing the truth.

"I've wanted this since I met you."

He nips at my collarbone, smiling against my skin. "I know."

Usually, the arrogant thing doesn't do it for me, but Kai having a moment of cockiness? I'm fairly certain his fingers are soaked because of it.

"Thank you for that," he continues. "Not to get all sappy before I fuck you, but you make me feel like a man again and not just a dad."

*Good God.* I don't know where to focus first. On my hips grinding down on his hand, asking for a finger to slip inside, or the way the words *before I fuck you* sound rolling off Kai's tongue.

Or how this man is so easily vulnerable, it tempts me to be the same.

But because he knows me a bit too well already, he steers away from the sweet and sentimental stuff when I remain speechless.

"Have you been planning this the whole time, Miller? Ever since that elevator, where you wouldn't stop talking. You knew one day I'd have to pin you to the wall and make you shut up, didn't you?" He squeezes my thigh again, his other fingers rolling slow torturous circles over my clit. "And *goddamn,* these legs are going to feel so warm on my cheeks when I bury my tongue right here."

A finger slips inside, slowly working its way deep.

An unexpected gasp escapes from my lips, but I'm ready for him. I'm wet, judging by the sound of my skin as he works in and out of me. My entire body is hot, waiting for him to ease the ache.

He keeps his mouth close to my ear. "Are you clenching on my finger already, Miller? I've barely started and you're desperate, huh?"

Kai may have lost a little self-assurance along the way, may have had his sole focus on his son, but the man is clearly experienced even if he hasn't done this in a while. His hold on me, his words, they're brimming with confidence.

I love it.

He might not know it, but this is what I need in the bedroom. Someone else to take control. At work I'm in charge, telling others what to do, but here I want to turn that part of my brain off and simply comply.

I swivel my hips as Kai strokes inside of me.

"More," I beg. "Please, more."

He kisses me, speaking against my mouth. "Do you want more fingers, or do you want my mouth?"

"Both."

He laughs and it's a little evil. "So greedy."

Stroking through my wetness, he coats his thumb before he rims the entrance to my ass. Cautiously, he takes his time circling, warming me up before he slips it in, pushing just the tip inside.

My body crawls up the wall from the foreign feeling, but I take a breath to realize I might actually love it. No man has ever touched me there, but I'm not mad about the new sensation one bit. I especially love when he adds a second finger in my cunt and strokes in tandem as I drop back down and writhe against him.

"Still not enough?" he asks, absent-mindedly rocking his hips into the cradle of mine.

He's so hard and I just want to see it, feel it. Suck it.

"Miller." He nudges his nose against the column of my throat before licking his way down it. "Answer me."

I don't know how to answer. It feels like too much but not enough all at the same time. He has the best set of hands I've ever seen and knowing they're inside of me elicits some insanely hot visuals, picturing him pumping in and out.

"You need my mouth?"

"I need your dick."

He chuckles. "Patience, Mills. I want to get you off at least once first. Who knows how long I'll last once I'm inside of you."

Head falling to the crook of my neck, he finger fucks me while also thrusting his pelvis into mine, burying me against the wall. It's all I can do to hold on to his shoulders and hang on for the ride.

He smells good, feels good. I'm not sure if I've ever been so turned on in my life.

There's a part of me that doesn't want to come yet. This guy's got me hooked more than anyone else before and I'd rather my body not betray me by telling him in the first three minutes. But then he curls his fingers, and with the way we're positioned, the back of them strokes my front wall and I'm all but shuttering and falling on his hand.

"That's it," he coaxes. "Ride my hand, Miller."

My legs tighten around him, holding his hips to give my clit a bit of friction as he works inside of me. Heat and pressure coil in my lower belly. He strokes his fingers once more and I come.

I come so hard it's like I haven't been touched in years, when in reality, it was only a few nights ago I came on his kitchen counter then again in his guest room.

Hands gripping the fabric of his shirt, I ride my way through it, every muscle in my body tightening. My heart beats out of my chest which I'm sure he can feel against his own, and being the experienced man he is, he keeps his hips pinned to mine, allowing me the needed pressure. He doesn't change pace, he doesn't pull back, he maintains and lets my orgasm ride as long as possible.

"So fucking beautiful when you come," Kai rasps, his fingers still moving to make sure I've completely finished.

Our lips graze until I can finally speak again. "You're beautiful when you *make* me come."

He chuckles against my mouth.

When I begin to slump, he gently removes his thumb then his other fingers, fixing my underwear as if it's not about to be on the floor, and sets me back on my wobbly feet.

Not wanting to give him the chance to stop this again, I drop to my knees, palms grazing his body until they land on his thick thighs for support.

And dear God, my hands look tiny on him.

Kai looks down at me, all big and towering. "What are you doing?"

"I'm praying." Finding the button on his pants, I unzip. "What the fuck do you think I'm doing?"

His hand lands on top of mine to stop me. "If my cock goes anywhere near that mouth of yours, I'm going to be done, and I'd really like to be inside your pussy when that happens."

*Jesus.* How does he make coming too quickly sound hot?

"It's been a year, Mills." With a finger under my chin, he tilts my head up. "And I'd like to make sure you're thoroughly fucked before the night is over."

Backing away towards the bed, he uses a single hand to pull his shirt over his head, pants open and low on his hips, nodding towards the mattress.

"Come." His tone is all innuendo with a smirk that's all charm thanks to our little inside joke.

And I'm over here still on my knees. Literally and figuratively I'm on my knees for this man.

The guy is long and lean and defined. Not too bulky, but clearly strong, and on top of it all, he's so good. Kind. Thoughtful. Dependable.

And hot as hell with those glasses on.

"Stop eye-fucking me and get your ass on this bed, Montgomery."

*Damn.*

Standing, I make my way to the mattress, and Kai slaps my butt as I pass him.

"Good girl. You get a gold star for listening."

I fall onto the bed with a laugh. He's hot and commanding one second then funny and vulnerable the next. He hasn't even been inside me yet and I think I might be a bit obsessed.

*Whoa. No, I'm not.*

It's just sex.

I take a seat on the edge of the mattress. "Gold star, huh? Is that your version of a praise kink?"

He saunters towards me. It's the most swag I've ever seen this man possess as he makes his way to stand between my legs.

"Mm-hmm. Gold star lips." He tilts my chin up, meeting my mouth with his. "The way you felt on my fingers, I'd say you've got a gold star pussy." He finds the hem of my shirt, pulling it over my head before unclasping my bra with a single flick. His eyes go wide, shaking his head in disbelief. "*Jesus.* And gold star tits."

My hands run up the length of his thighs. "I also give some gold star head."

His neck cranes back with a tortured groan. Kai eyes the ceiling for three beats before bending down on his haunches, heels to ass, and eyes level with mine. Like some sort of gentleman, he tucks my hair behind my ear as he stares right at my mouth.

His palm trails over my jaw until his thumb presses against the seam of my lips, and the movement is anything but gentlemanly when he pushes into my mouth.

"Let me just see," he says, slowly working it in and out.

His ice-blue eyes are heated and hooded, contemplating.

In and out. In and out. And when he pushes in again, I suck, tongue rolling around his fingertip before flicking up the length of his thumb.

"*Fuck.*" He stands, pulling his hand away with a frustrated growl, towering over me as I sit on the edge of the bed. "Just a taste."

He barely lowers his pants and briefs, just enough to pull out his cock.

And . . .

"*Holy fuck,*" I hear myself say, staring right at him.

He's swollen and thick, throbbing in his fist as he strokes himself once. Twice. A bead of precum leaks from the tip and I'm entirely mesmerized by the way his thumb swipes it, rolling it around the head.

The man is 6'4" and his cock makes it seem as if a very average-sized hand is wrapped around it.

"Lick those pretty lips of yours and open your mouth."

Swallowing, I do as he says, tongue out and mouth open wide. Hand on the back of my skull, he guides himself inside.

I'm so full. It takes a moment for me to adjust to him somewhat suffocating me, but eventually, I gain my bearings, breathing through my nose.

"That's it, Miller. *Fuck.*" Getting my tongue involved, I flick the underside of his crown. "So good," he praises. "Just like that. So, *so* good. God, you're going to be the death of me, aren't you?"

I stroke and suck, using my hand on what doesn't fit in my mouth. He gives me complete control, though keeps one hand on my hair, petting and praising me as the other reaches down, testing the weight of my breast in his hand.

He rocks into my mouth, hips moving involuntarily with the sexiest noise of desperation I've ever heard. It echoes through my ears, coaxing me as I slip the hand that was on his shaft into his briefs, cupping his balls.

Kai jolts back, popping out of my mouth. He's more swollen now, angry veins decorating his shaft. "Jesus. Okay, I get it. Gold star head. Please don't embarrass me right now."

A satisfied smile lifts on my lips as I watch him regain his bearings, tucking himself back into his pants which is the exact opposite of what I want him to do.

But then he exhales and looks down at me, eyes tracking my almost naked body. He wanders, following my chest, my hips, my tattoos.

Kai shakes his head—his favorite thing to do when it comes to me, but this time it's not in annoyance, it's in disbelief. "You're so pretty, Mills."

His tone is so soft and sincere that it almost makes me blush. I'm not one to be shy regarding sex. But Kai is looking at me like I'm his favorite thing he's ever seen and the way his words are spoken it's as if he's thanking me for being here.

Which truly is so absurd.

The air shifts again as he approaches and takes me in a selfish kiss. He bends to my height as he works his lips down my exposed collarbone and chest. His tongue swirls around my nipple, his throat rumbling in a groan before he slips it into his mouth.

Kai sucks, my back bows, and when he repeats it on the other side, I'm all but falling off the edge of the bed and into his lap.

"Come here." His voice is hoarse, grabbing my ass, and pulling me to straddle him on the ground.

He sucks me harder.

"*Fuck*," I moan. "You're going to make me come from playing with my nipples again."

He smiles against my skin as he rocks my hips, rubbing me over his erection. And I swear to God if he makes me come again from dry-humping, I truly won't be able to look him in the eye. He's going to think *I'm* the one getting over a dry spell and comes on the spot from barely being touched.

Kai flicks my nipple with his tongue one more time before he meets my mouth. "I need to taste the rest of you."

Yep. Definitely going to come again because I sure as hell haven't been spoken to so freely in the bedroom before.

He's older, and has no issue saying everything that's on his mind.

It's incredibly hot.

"Please do."

He stands, carrying me to the bed. One knee lands on the mattress as he lays me down so gently, it's as if I'm precious cargo that could break. He then runs an explorative palm over my thigh. The top, back, side.

"That first day, in Miami when you were wearing those cutoff shorts." Kai kisses my neck. "All I could think about were your legs. I was supposed to be trying to figure out a way to fire you, but all I wanted to do was figure out a way to have them wrapped around my face."

I rub against him like a needy cat. "Looks like you found a way."

He nips and licks a path down my chest and stomach. "I've been dreaming of this. Every night as you slept just outside my house, I fell asleep after exhausting myself, trying to convince myself to leave you alone. But I fucking can't anymore. I want you. *Fuck,* do I want you. You've been torture, and I don't want to fight it anymore."

I'm arching, writhing off the bed just from some words and warm breath dusting my skin.

I want him too, but we can only have each other in this capacity.

Taking the waistband of my panties between his teeth, he snaps it against my skin. Every nerve in my body is sensitive beyond belief that even the snap of fabric has goosebumps scattering up my spine. With so much fluidity, he crawls down my body, using his strong legs to hold himself as he glides my panties down my thighs.

Fully exposed, I lie naked with my hair splayed over around my shoulders, watching Kai Rhodes stand at his full height with my underwear dangling on a single finger, his other hand scrubbing over his jaw in admiration.

"Goddamn," he exhales, shaking his head.

I open my legs a little wider for that.

Tonight feels like one big ego boost and I'm here for it.

Confidently, he slips my panties into his back pocket before taking off his glasses, safely setting them on a small table in the corner of the room.

Always so responsible.

"How much can you see without those?" I ask.

His attention trails my entire exposed body.

"Trust me, I'm seeing everything I've been dreaming about."

His steps are big and commanding, pulling my ankles to slide me to the edge of the mattress. He stands over me, running his palms down to the crease of my hips.

"I want you so badly, Miller."

That causes my eyes to dart to his, breaking my attention from where he's touching me. His words are so clear, so sincere. They sound like they're laced with meaning that goes beyond tonight. But I push that thought away. We aren't going there. We're just having some fun and he knows that.

"I want you too, Kai, so if you could take me now, that'd be great."

He chuckles, dropping to his knees. Expertly, he rests my ankles on his shoulders, right next to his ears before he pulls me by the hips, closer to him so my knees bend over his shoulders instead.

He kisses the inside of my thigh, his scruff providing the perfect texture on my skin. "You always have something to say, huh?"

He's got his arms wrapped around my hips, using his thumb to gently stroke over my clit. I almost buck off the bed. In fact, I probably would if he wasn't pinning me down with his arms. He rubs soft circles over the sensitive area before he uses said thumb to stretch my skin, exposing my clit and flicking his tongue over it just once.

"C'mon, Mills. Let's hear it."

Smug bastard knows I can't speak. I can't think.

"Where are those quick one-liners that are always spewing out of that dirty mouth of yours?"

He licks again, this time covering me with his mouth, sucking me and rhythmically flicking his tongue. Eating me out like it's a goddamn competition and he plans to win.

I don't respond because I can't. All I can focus on is the long, warm strokes of that talented tongue.

Where the fuck did he learn to do this?

Irrational jealousy zips through me, knowing there were other women before me. He's got a literal child, one that I care about, and I'm over here fuming because he had the audacity to have sex with someone before he ever met me.

He sucks again, twirling his tongue in the most insane way, and my jealousy is taken over by heat and desire and a bit of frustration that it's so effortless for him to make me putty in his hands.

"This is all I had to do to shut you up?" he continues. "Lick this pretty cunt to get you to stop talking?"

I simply fist the sheets and squeeze my thighs in response.

"Mmm," he hums, vibrating my entire core. "Yes, baby. Suffocate me."

I have no control over my body, so my hips take on their own life, rolling in tandem with his tongue, chasing my second orgasm of the night.

With a single hand flat on my belly, his tongue concentrates on my clit as two fingers from his other hand sink inside of me, curling forward, and I'm done.

I'm free-falling off the edge, my orgasm ripping through so hard that I'm convulsing, shivering, and shuttering on the bed. Every muscle tightens, down to my arched feet and curled toes that are currently resting on his back.

Kai keeps his tongue moving, but looks up as I glance down, ice-blue eyes dangerously watching me between my legs. He looks so goddamn good down there, I can't help but touch him, fisting his hair as I ride his face, taking every last second I can.

And finally, I suck in a breath of which the exhale sinks me into the mattress, limp and exhausted and I didn't even do any of the work.

He smiles against my skin. Smug and so well-deserved.

"So beautiful."

Kai places a soft kiss on my clit, gentle and tender, and once again he has my mind reeling. This guy is a walking juxtaposition. Dirty-talking confidence turned right back to the soft man who's gone through his life alone.

He stands, dotting a path of kisses on the inside of my leg before walking backwards away from the bed.

He's so handsome. So attentive.

"You've made me come three times since that night in the kitchen." My breaths are erratic as I try to calm down. "And I haven't taken care of you once. That seems awfully unfair."

Kai pulls a condom out of the back pocket of his pants. The one my panties *aren't* currently occupying.

"Is that how you think this works? Who the hell has been giving you orgasms only to expect them in return?" He shakes his head. "Don't answer that. I changed my mind. I don't want to know."

He slides his pants down, his cock tenting the fabric of his briefs.

"That's kind of how it works," I explain, unable to keep my eyes off him.

He laughs and it's entirely without humor. "Getting you off gets me off. You should stop entertaining boys with any other mindset."

He drops his briefs to the ground, and I can't breathe.

"In fact, you should stop entertaining other boys in general."

His thick, tatted thighs are rippling, the perfect V cutting down to his cock that's standing proud, tall, and thick. Entirely proportionate to his giant body.

More pre-cum leaks from the tip and he swipes it with his thumb, lubricating his fist as he strokes himself. He stands in front of me without a shy bone in his body.

He's stunning.

Pure masculinity, taut muscles, lean frame with a personality that's soft enough to lovingly raise a human on his own.

I think I'm seeing the old Kai tonight and that version scares me. The confidence, the self-assurance mixed with the new Kai—thoughtful, kind. He's a lethal combination, and not only does my body recognize it, but so does my heart.

He tears the foil packet with his teeth.

"Can I?" I ask, sitting up.

A small grin plays on his lips as he walks towards me, condom outstretched, cock jutting from his body, and I'm over here salivating, watching his muscles ripple as he moves.

Pinching the tip, I roll the rest of the condom over his shaft. I can feel how ready he is as he throbs in my hand. Kai's fist covers mine, using me to stroke himself again, his eyes fluttering shut as he repeats the motion.

"How long have you been keeping that in your back pocket?" I ask.

"Been carrying one with me since the night we went out in Texas."

"*After* that night, you mean?"

"No. I slipped one in my wallet before we left for the bar."

My brows lift. "For me?"

"It's always been only for you."

*Oh.*

My stomach explodes in a sensation I would assume people refer to as butterflies. I wouldn't know. I've never really had them until I started hanging around this man.

He nods towards the bed, telling me to back up. I do so, crawling back, but before he can climb onto the mattress with me, I flip, putting myself on all fours and facing the headboard instead of him.

His chuckle is dark and menacing. "You think that's going to help you?"

*Shit.*

"You think you'll be able to keep yourself detached because you're not looking at my face while I fuck you?"

The mattress sinks as Kai climbs on behind me. Thick thighs kiss mine and I hate how well he sees me, *knows* me and what my chaotic head is doing. One arm snakes around my waist, the other cupping my breasts as he pulls me up, my back flush to his chest.

He lowers his mouth to my ear. "Well, it doesn't matter if you see me or not. You're going to feel every inch of me. I'll be so deep, you'll be able to feel me in your fucking throat, and I can promise you, Miller, your body won't let you forget me."

*Jesus.*

The arm around my chest slips down between my legs, circling my clit. He bucks his hips, coating the condom in my arousal as he rubs his length over me.

He kisses just below my ear, nipping at the skin. "You think you can keep this casual, Mills?"

I nod frantically, hoping to convince both of us.

His laugh is silent but rumbles against me. "Best of luck to you with that."

And with those words, he adjusts himself, the head of his cock notching against my core. There's a moment where our breathing is synced, the anticipation heavy in the hotel room. He lingers there, allowing the moment to build before he lifts his hips and pushes inside.

"Oh *fuck*," I cry, crumbling forward towards the mattress, but Kai comes with me, blanketing my entire body with his. He holds himself up so as to not crush me, but I can feel how hard he's breathing, can sense the tension coiling through him as he gives me a moment and doesn't move.

Kai spreads his knees, using his thighs to open mine as I try to adjust to his size.

"Too big," I tell him, my words muffled into the sheets.

That fucking chuckle rumbles again. "I'm only halfway in, Mills."

With bewilderment, my eyes find him over my shoulder. "That can't be true."

"It is. I'm looking right at it. Goddamn, you should see us, Miller. You look beautiful, trying your hardest to stretch around me. It's really too bad you didn't want to see anything."

"I hate you."

He circles my clit and I moan.

"Keep telling yourself that." He continues to play with me, relaxing me into the bed. "Take a deep breath."

I do as I'm told, my body once again compliant. So compliant that Kai shifts his hips, slowly thrusting into me and when I feel his pelvis flush against my ass, I know I've taken him to the hilt.

He groans, nuzzling into the back of my neck. "So good, Miller. You feel perfect."

I try to ignore the sharp stretch. "Gold star pussy?"

He chuckles again, but this time it's light with amusement. "No question in my mind. Gold star pussy."

He decorates my spine with warm kisses, brushing my hair out of the way so he can extend those kisses up my neck.

"Does it still hurt?" he asks against my skin.

I shake my head to tell him no. The pain is more of a dull ache now, that delicious pinch of being too full, but this guy could split me in half, and I still wouldn't ask him to stop.

"Good." He pistons his hips and thrusts fully inside, his body still splayed over me, pinning me to the bed.

I whine into the sheets, hoping to muffle my sounds, thankful that the shared wall is with Kai's room.

His hands cover my bare back, rubbing against my skin as they travel down my arms until they reach my hands, intertwining our fingers. He holds me as he begins to move with pace, fully fucking me.

He feels insane. So incredible. So big. Warm. The way he rolls over me. God, he must look like a fucking porn star riding me right now.

His lips stay hovering next to my ear. "You've been like poison this summer, you know that? Seeping into my system and ruining me slowly."

I moan, lifting my ass to meet him in pace.

"Pretty. Fucking. Poison."

He continues to whisper dirty words into my ear, feeding me his cock over and over again. One of his hands leaves mine, slipping between me and the mattress until he finds my clit.

"*Ace.*"

"Mmm," he hums. "I love when you call me that. What do you need?"

"Flip me over. I want to see you."

He pauses. "Really?"

We're both terrible at holding strong on the pathetic rules we make for ourselves, apparently.

"Please."

He pulls out, the sudden emptiness hollowing my stomach, before he flips me onto my back.

Oh, this was a bad idea.

His steel-blues are dark with desire. His abs are contracted. Cock swollen. Skin glistening with sweat.

Kai opens my legs, putting one on his shoulder to give himself a better angle before he guides himself back inside of me.

We both groan as he fills me.

He slides in easier this time, my body ready and willing to take him especially now that I can see him. There's no question in my mind, I've never wanted anyone more.

He holds my hips while he fills me over and over again, placing kisses on the inside of my ankle as it rests on his shoulder. He plays with my clit. He squeezes my tits. Then he bends forward, folding my leg into my chest as he uses the leverage of the bed to fuck me into the mattress.

And, *Oh my God.*

I've never been fucked like this.

I'm at this man's mercy, and he's not holding back. Sweat beads on his brow, our skin sliding together as my hands

4

4

search for something to hold on to, my nails digging into his back.

"This is why you have Max," I somehow say. "I'm fairly certain you're fucking me right past my birth control."

"Miller." He halts his movements. "That's an inside thought."

"I don't have inside thoughts."

He simply shakes his head at me—his favorite move. Then he does *my* favorite move and snaps his hips to fill me again.

"I'd really appreciate it if we steer away from talking about me knocking you up while I'm rearranging your insides."

I raise an impressed brow. "Yes, Daddy."

"Jesus Christ."

Kai brackets my jaw with a single hand and kisses me roughly, his tongue sweeping into my mouth, no doubt to shut me up.

But then as his body falls onto mine, our movements change.

It's less frantic. We find a rhythm as Kai moves us together. Or kisses are slow and searching. His forehead rests on mine as he touches me, appreciating every inch of my skin. My fingertips press into his lower back as he moves over me.

We watch each other.

It's . . . *intimate*.

It's scary.

But I can't stop myself from climbing right back to the edge with him.

"I've wanted this for so long, Miller." He nudges his nose against mine, kissing me again.

And because I can't handle serious moments, I attempt to break the intimacy with humor.

"What? A whole five weeks? You have the patience of a saint."

He shakes his head. "A lot longer than that."

*Shit.* He's not referring to wanting my body. He's referring to wanting the connection we've created.

I should correct him. Remind him this is casual. Easy. Detached.

But this man deserves someone to fight for and stand by him. And though long term that someone won't be me, I let myself believe, just for tonight, that maybe I could.

He makes me want to be.

Kai slips his arm between my back and the bed, and we move together. I wrap myself around his body until we're both coming. He's buried into the crook of my neck as I have my third orgasm of the night and I'm kissing his chest and sweat-soaked skin as he finds his first.

My name sounds like worship as he chants it against my skin, kissing me softly as he comes. I've never liked the nickname *Mills* as much as I do when Kai says it while he's inside of me, lacing the word with gratitude.

And watching him come? I think I might do just about anything to see it again.

We're touching and stroking as we both ease back down, and when Kai pulls out of me, I've never felt so empty, losing that connection.

He plays with my hair as he lays at my side, watching me with appreciative eyes.

"Perfect," he murmurs.

I nuzzle into his chest like a stage-five clinger who needs to be held after sex. "You weren't so bad yourself."

His smile is soft against my skin.

I want to stay in this bed all night. Do that again and again. Maybe wake up to him between my legs.

But then my eyes shoot open to find his chest as he holds me, stroking my back.

*No offense to myself, but what the fuck am I doing?*

257

Clearing my throat, I pull away and gesture to the condom. "Do you need the bathroom so you can take care of . . ."

"You go ahead first."

My brow lifts, needing the humor back in the room. "Oh, so now you're being a gentleman after defiling me so perfectly?"

"Nah. I just want to watch your ass from behind as you walk away."

Giving him a playful swat, I lift myself, but Kai pulls me right back down, hands sinking into my hair with a kiss that feels so much more meaningful than it should after a casual hook-up.

"Thank you," he says against my lips, soft eyes searching mine.

I'm speechless.

I'm obsessed.

I think I'm in trouble.

So, I quickly pull away and scurry off to the bathroom, needing a moment to breathe.

*Don't give him someone to miss, Miller.*

And what about me? What am I doing to *myself*?

I stare at my naked reflection in the mirror. *He's just another guy in another city. I'll be gone in a month, and he'll forget all about me. I'll forget about him.*

I can't even look myself in the eye as I lie.

I have to fix this. Put the armor back on. It'll be better for us both in the long run.

Casual. Easy. Unattached.

Inhaling through my nose, I straighten my shoulders. I can do this.

Back in my room my bed is empty, so I slip under the covers, trying my best not to think about how amazing tonight was. How *right* it felt.

Kai comes back in from his room, sweatpants hanging low on his hips, headed straight for the bed. He lifts the corner of the covers to join me, but I stop him with a hand on his chest.

"What?" he asks.

"No sleepovers."

"You're kidding."

I simply shake my head.

He exhales a disbelieving laugh. "But we've slept in the same bed together before."

"That was different."

He contemplates for a moment, eyes wide with disbelief.

"Fine," he says, lifting the sheets over my naked body to tuck me in because of course he does. "I hope you're able to get some sleep with all the cartwheels your brain is doing right now."

Kai brushes my sweat-damp hair out of my face to place a gentle kiss on my forehead then a less gentle one on my mouth. "Goodnight, Mills."

I swallow. "Night."

He casts one final look at me over his shoulder before turning off my bedroom light and leaving. But he doesn't close the door that connects his room from mine, keeping that bit of an opening between us.

Flipping onto my back, I stare at the ceiling. Why does he have to handle everything so graciously? Why couldn't he throw a fit about not sleeping over or something else that might give me the ick? No, he just had to fully understand me once again.

How annoying.

Almost as annoying as the ache between my legs and the memories flooding my mind of him inside of me on this very bed.

There's a knock on the wall right behind my headboard coming from Kai's room. "Hey, Miller?"

"Yeah?"

"Thanks for the sex."

I burst a laugh. It's loud and unladylike and I don't give a shit.

This guy is frustratingly good, easing my tension with humor the way I usually do.

"You're welcome, Baseball Daddy. And I do mean *Daddy*."

I can hear his laugh from here. "Today was a good day."

*It really was.*

"They could all be good days."

He hums. "Yeah. Maybe."

There's only a thin wall between us, a handful of feet and an open door. Just enough distance that I've convinced myself is necessary. But in an odd way, it feels like he's still inside of me. Not physically, but as if he's etched his way into my soul. His scent is still on my sheets as I burrow into them. His touch still singes my skin.

He was right. There's no way I'll be able to forget him.

# 24

## Miller

The sun peeking through my curtains is what wakes me up, blinding and bright. Squinting, it takes me a moment to orient myself, remembering where I am.

Boston.

I'm in Boston.

I've woken up most of my adult life this way, needing to recall where I am, what city I'm currently passing through.

Rolling over, I'm struck with another reminder.

I'm sore.

I'm sore from Kai stretching my body.

*Because we had sex.*

Mind-blowing, made-me-come-three-times, better-than-I've-ever-had sex.

Flashes of his dark hair, wet with sweat, pass through my mind. His body, long and lean, knowing exactly how to take care of mine. And his words . . . *God*, he talks dirty in bed.

I squeeze my thighs at the memories.

My attention darts to the side table where he left his glasses last night, but they're gone, as are the clothes he left scattered across the floor. But yesterday's olive-green overalls are still right where I left them, so without fussing over a bra or shirt, I step into them, needing to cover some of my naked body, not knowing if Kai has picked up Max from his brother's room yet.

And right on cue, I hear the front door of Kai's room unlock. The one connecting ours is still wide open and it's only a few seconds later that he takes over the threshold, a coffee in either hand. He's wearing athletic shorts that cut well above his knees, showing off that thigh tat, with a gray tee and his glasses back in place.

He's so hot and put together at this early hour while I'm barely dressed with my hair still a mess from his hands running through it last night.

He smiles at me, all sweet and sexy, clearly not thrown off that I kicked him out of bed last night.

"Did you just wake up?"

"Yes." I turn away from him, using the full-length mirror on the wall to quickly throw my hair up in a knot. "It seems someone here exhausted me last night."

"Well, that seems fair." Kai occupies the space behind me, looking at me through the mirror. "Because you exhaust me on a daily basis."

I smile into our reflection. The last thing I needed was Kai coming in here talking about us making love or something like that. What I needed was for him to give me shit.

He bends to kiss my now exposed neck. "Morning."

"Hi." I find myself curving into him. "Did you bring me coffee?"

"A chai." He reaches the cup over my shoulder, putting it in my hand.

"How'd you know I like chai?"

"It's what you were drinking the first day we met, when your dad stuck me with your ass all summer."

A smile ticks on my lips. How observant of him. "Thank you."

Kai's eyes lose their previous cheery glint, replaced instead with concern. "Are you okay?"

"In regards to . . ."

"Are you okay with what happened last night?"

A slow grin spreads on my lips as I look at him through the mirror. "More than okay."

His worry washes away, his smirk taking on a boyish edge. "Yeah?"

"Yes."

"Would you be more than okay if it happened again?"

God, he's cute, all shy with his question.

"I'd love for it to happen again."

He's full-on smiling now, a smile I didn't know existed only a month ago.

A smile that seems hopeful, reminding me of what this man has gone through in his life, and that I can't be the next person to hurt him when I leave.

"But," I interrupt. "I think we should have some rules."

"Haven't we learned that we aren't very good at holding strong on those?"

I lift a single brow.

"Okay," he chuckles. "*I'm* not very good at holding strong on those."

"I think it might be a good idea, you know, to make sure we're both clear about what this is."

"Trust me, Miller. You've made it perfectly clear what this is for you and I told you I'm fine with it. I'll keep it casual."

"No sleepovers," I begin.

"Yeah." His tone is entirely unimpressed. "Got that one already."

"No kissing unless we're hooking up. No PDA."

He narrows his eyes through the reflection. "We've always been a little touchy though."

"Right, but now that we're sleeping together, I think that should stop. You know, to keep the lines clear."

"Just so *I* can keep things clear, are these rules to remind *me* what this little arrangement is, or are they a reminder for *you*?"

God, this man drives me nuts with how much he can wiggle his way into my brain and understand its patterns.

Sure, I don't want to hurt him, knowing how many people he's counted on only for them to leave, but more so, after last night, I think *I* need the boundaries these rules will enforce to keep me from growing attached when I don't have the space for that in my life or career.

I've never been worried about that before.

"And lastly," I shift, needing to include the most important rule of all. "This ends the moment I leave Chicago for my next job. There will be no grand declarations of love after all is said and done. We enjoy ourselves, but we remember exactly what this is. A summer fling."

"A summer fling," he repeats. "You drive away and it's over just like that?"

"Just like that."

Kai hesitates. "If that's what you want."

It is, and even if he won't admit it right now, it's what he wants too. Long-term, he and Max need someone grounded and safe. We both know that someone isn't me.

"You know." Kai's palm sinks into the side opening of my overalls, grazing my ribs and stomach. "I'm pitching tonight."

"I do know that."

"And baseball superstitions are very serious. I can't risk messing with them."

He drags his fingertips up my stomach before his thumb dusts over my already stiff nipple.

I fall back into his chest. "What are you saying?"

"I'm saying, I can't break routine." He kisses the sensitive skin just below my ear as he gracefully unhooks one of the straps on my shoulder. The fabric falls open, exposing my bare chest and Kai stares right at me through the reflection. "If I pitch well tonight, I'm going to assume it's because of last night and I'm going to have to spend the rest of the summer sinking into you every chance I get. You know, because of superstitions."

"And if you pitch poorly?"

He smiles against my skin. "We'll just have to keep fucking until we figure out what we did wrong."

I giggle at his logic. Yes, *giggle*. Like a schoolgirl with a crush.

Kai trails his hand over my breast and stomach, dipping lower. He takes his time exploring my skin, touching and kissing me before his middle finger grazes my clit. He rubs gentle, easy circles, working me up, but it's different from last night. There's nothing rushed or frenzied. It's slow and searching.

Reaching back, I hook my palm around the base of his neck.

Kai hums into my ear, and I'm about to drop this chai right to the floor so I can use both of my hands to explore him, but then there's a knock on his door and we both pause.

It's his brother and son, I'm sure.

Kai pulls his fingers from me before bringing them to his mouth and licking them clean, all while staring right at me through the mirror. "God, you taste good."

"Who the hell are you and where did this version come from?"

With a single hand, he reclasps my strap. "Been here the whole time. Just forgot what it was like to enjoy things for myself."

A knock sounds at his door again.

"And I've never enjoyed something as much as I enjoy fucking you." He finishes with a kiss to my temple before taking off towards his room, but he turns back to give me one more look through the mirror. "Now put some goddamn clothes on before you make me miss my game."

His smile is light and relaxed as he closes the door between our rooms.

All I can do is look at myself in the mirror and try to figure out who the hell is looking back at me. Because right now, I don't see any sign of the woman who showed up in Chicago five weeks ago.

"There's my guy!" I hear Kai say on the other side of the door.

"Dadda!"

"Did you have fun with your uncle?"

"Mmm, yeah," Max says, using a new word he learned last week.

"Oh, man." Kai exhales an audible breath, and I can't see them, but I can picture him holding his son tight to his chest. "I missed you so much, Max."

I look at my reflection again, but all I see is a woman who is completely soft over a little boy and his dad.

Isaiah laughs. "You were that bored without him, huh?"

Kai remains silent.

"Why do you look like that?" his brother asks.

"I don't look like anything."

"I almost forgot you had teeth, it's been so long since I've seen you smile like that."

"Stop."

"Oh my God, did you . . ." Isaiah drifts off. "Hot Nanny! Why is my brother smiling like an idiot?"

I hear his footsteps charging towards my door, so I get my ass in gear and race to it. I lock it just in time for him to jiggle the knob. "Miller Montgomery, are you responsible for this?"

I slap a palm over my mouth, not wanting Isaiah to know I'm in here.

He tries the door again.

"Isaiah, stop," Kai laughs.

"You're laughing. Why are you laughing? Why are you in such a good mood?"

"I'm not . . . I'm just glad Max is back."

"You got laid, didn't you?"

Kai doesn't confirm or deny.

"You did! Fucking knew it!" There's so much excitement in Isaiah's voice. He knocks on the door. "Hey, nice work, Miller!"

"Okay, you've got to get out of here." From the sounds of it, Kai is pushing his brother out of his room. "Thanks for watching him last night."

"If I knew I just had to babysit for Daddy to get laid, I would've done it fucking months ago."

"Language."

"Yeah, language," Isaiah deadpans. "Because my language is the most inappropriate thing to happen in this room in the last twelve hours." There's a smack of a kiss, most likely on Max's cheek. "Thanks for hanging out with me, Bug. Kai, I'm so damn proud of you."

"Please shut up."

The door closes, but I can still hear Isaiah in the hall. "Miller, I know you're in there, and I'm proud of you too, girl!"

The team bus parks in the private lot of Fenway. It's mid-afternoon and the game doesn't start until seven, but there's plenty that needs to happen beforehand.

Typically, Max and I would stay back at the hotel when the Warriors are playing an evening game, but Kai wanted to show his son one of the most iconic parks in the league before he takes the mound.

Lingering back, I watch as the two of them take their time getting off the bus. Now that Max is walking, he's adamant about being on his feet at all times.

Max's backwards hat matches his dad's, and his little jersey shares the same name and number as the one Kai will be wearing tonight.

Kai's tall frame is bent to hold his son's hand, Isaiah on the opposite side holding Max's other. Travis and Cody are chatting and giving each other shit, but also walking so incredibly slow, as if it were second nature for them to move at Max's speed now. In fact, no one is left behind. The entire team is moving at the pace of a sixteen-month-old.

An unfamiliar burn pricks the back of my eyes. I don't know why I would get emotional over it, but this group is so good to each other. They're so good to Kai and his son.

After spending so much time in kitchens with majority male staff, I was hesitant to spend my summer with another group of guys, but these ones proved me wrong.

I'm going to miss them all when I go.

"You all right?" My dad swings an arm over my shoulders as we keep pace behind his team, taking our time getting inside.

"Allergies, I think." Clearing my throat, I swallow whatever the hell is going on with me.

My dad's eyes bounce from me to Kai to Max. "Yeah," he says. "Sure."

"How do you feel about the game tonight?"

"Good. I always feel good when Ace is starting. Not to mention he seems to be in an exceptionally good mood today."

"Is he? I hadn't noticed."

My dad chuckles and it's knowing and annoying. "You, on the other hand, seem entirely in your head. What's on your mind, Millie?"

"Trust me, Dad, you don't want to know what's on my mind."

"All right. Well, did you have fun last night at least? Where did Kai take you?"

"To a bakery in the North End. He took me in hopes I'd get some inspiration for work since I can't bake while we're on the road."

My dad slightly shakes his head. "He's a good one."

I find Kai again. He's wearing a proud smile, looking down and watching his son walk into Fenway with him. All eyes are on him tonight as he takes the mound, but he's only got eyes for Max.

"Yeah," I exhale. "He is."

I can feel my dad's stare burning into the side of my head. "Do you know what you're doing there?"

"Yes. I've got it handled. Don't worry, I won't hurt him. We have rules in place to make sure of it."

He squeezes me tighter. "And what about you? Are you going to get hurt?"

I huff a laugh. "Of course not."

"Of course not," he repeats dryly. "Because you, Miller, don't let yourself get attached enough to get hurt, right?"

"Right."

"Well, for both your sakes, just be careful, yeah?"

A week ago, he would've left me out of that statement. He would've told me to be cautious for Kai. Now, he sees it as clear as I do.

There's potential for me to be in as much trouble as his pitcher.

With the team in the clubhouse, Max with his dad, and *my* dad in a coach's meeting, I wander the maze of the visitor's side of Fenway until I find the training room.

And when I open the door, my shoulders sag in relief to find it empty minus the one person I'm looking for.

"Kennedy, I need to talk to you."

She's organizing the tape, each one labeled with which player it's for, because of course they all have a unique tape preference.

She peeks over her shoulder, her copper ponytail swinging. "You okay?"

"Yes." I frantically pace the room. "No."

A single brow raises as she turns around, arms crossed over her chest, leaning back on a massage table. She's in her typical uniform of a Warriors polo, black yoga pants, team-issued sneakers, and topped with a make-up-less face, showing off her freckles.

"Look, I know we don't really know each other, but I don't have anyone I can talk to about this. And you're the only other woman on the road and—"

"Miller, do you want to be friends?"

I pause in my tracks.

"Is that how it works? You just say it like that?"

Kennedy pops her shoulder. "Hell if I know. I've spent almost every day of the past three years with a bunch of dudes. I don't have many girlfriends."

A smile ticks up on my lip. "Same here."

"So . . . friends?"

I hop my ass on a training table. "Friends. Now, I need to tell you something."

"You fucked Ace."

My mouth drops as Kennedy takes a seat on the table across from me.

"How did—"

"Oh please. That guy is walking around here today like his shit is made of gold. It's obvious something happened between you two. Besides, he's been pining after you since you got here."

"Uh, not exactly. He wasn't all that excited when I first showed up."

She laughs and it holds no humor. "Yeah, well, I'm sure he wasn't all that excited that he wanted to sleep with Monty's daughter knowing how close the two of them are, but we all see how he looks at you." She checks her nails as if this is the most mundane conversation of all time. I like that. I feel less frantic with how undramatic she is about it. "So, what's the issue?"

*What is the issue?*

"I . . . I don't know."

"Was it bad? Is it small?" Kennedy's eyes widen, leaning forward, finally invested. "Oh my God, does Ace have a micro penis?"

"No! Trust me. Size was not the issue. Have you seen that man's hands? He's very . . . *proportionate*."

"Damn. I work on those hands. How are you walking today?"

"No clue."

"So, it was good then?"

I shake my head. "It was perfect."

Kennedy's face softens. "Is his magical giant penis confusing you?"

"Maybe? But I don't know what I'm confused about. It's casual and we both know that."

She pauses, choosing her words carefully. "Do you want it to be more than casual?"

"No. Absolutely not. Casual was my idea. I have a full-blown career waiting for me to get back to in a few weeks."

She pops her shoulders as if this is the simplest of solutions. "Then keep it casual. Stop overthinking it. Ace is a big boy, and you've made it clear what this is for you. Have fun and enjoy the frustratingly good sex while you're still here, and when the time comes for you to leave, you get back to your life."

Wow. How utterly simple. It's the exact advice I would give myself if I were thinking straight.

"Besides, we don't let men get in the way of careers we love," she continues.

"You're right." I give a single, confident nod. "Damn, I should've gotten a girlfriend years ago."

"That advice was easy. I would give my left kidney for frustratingly good sex right about now."

"Well, Kai does have a brother."

She barks a laugh, falling back onto the massage table behind her. "Don't even go there."

"Isaiah is cute and very much into you."

"He's into everyone. And besides, that's an easy way to get fired. I sure as hell am not risking my career for a night with one of the players, least of all Isaiah."

"But you can be friends with them, right? You just can't date them?"

"Yeah. Casual relationships between staff and players are cause for termination, but a few years ago, a player's wife was hired on as a team photographer. That was allowed because of how serious their relationship was."

"Am I considered staff? If people find out—"

Kennedy waves me off. "Trust me, Miller, everyone already knows."

"What?" I laugh in disbelief. "How?"

"Because he looks like the old Ace again, the one that had a smile plastered on his face and was just happy and grateful to be playing baseball. That's the version I met last season before he found out about Max and convinced himself he was doing a shit job raising him. But I can promise you, there's not a person here that doesn't know why he's walking around on cloud nine today."

Checking her watch, she hops off the table and continues setting up the training room. "Besides, you're Monty's daughter. You can do whatever the hell you want, and no one is going to try to say otherwise."

My phone dings in my pocket.

**Baseball Daddy:** *Hey, you around? Would you mind coming to get Max? I gotta get ready.*

Sliding off the table, I swing my arms around Kennedy from behind. "Thanks, *friend*."

She chuckles. "You're welcome, *friend*."

I find Kai and Max outside of the visitors' clubhouse. Kai is already stripped down to his compression shorts, ready to go get stretched and taped, contacts in and messy brown hair pushed back from his fingers that keep running through the waves.

His smile is the first one to bloom when he catches me walking down the hall towards them, but when Max sees me, his facial expression lifts and mirrors his dad.

My lungs clutch at the sight. This is what I'm confused about. Why does the image of those two make my heart scream *mine*?

I jog down the hall, bending down when I get close, and giving Max space to run into my open arms.

"Ah, I got you!" I pretend to wrestle with him, tickling him to hear his laugh before I pick him up in my arms. I gesture towards Kai. "Give your dad some good luck."

"Dadda!"

Kai runs a hand over his son's head, brushing his unruly hair out of the way to place a kiss on his forehead. "I'll see you tomorrow, okay? Be good for Miller tonight. I love you."

Max falls onto my shoulder and I watch as Kai tracks the movement, a soft smile on his lips as his eyes bounce between us. Then he tucks my hair behind my ear, and I can see him contemplating bringing his lips to my forehead the way he did to his son.

The three of us could not look more like a family, standing so close with him touching me this way, longingly. Lovingly.

I clear my throat and take a step back to break the moment.

We've always touched. It's been easy, like another language between us, but now things are different. Everything seems to have meaning behind it when it can't.

I give him a thumbs-up. "Good luck out there."

Yes. Very casual. *Nice work, me.*

"Did you just give me a thumbs-up?"

273

I do it again as if it's not the lamest thing I've ever done. "Yep."

"I was literally inside of you less than twenty-four hours ago and you're giving me a thumbs-up?"

I choke on my saliva as an arrogant smirk lifts on Kai's mouth.

"Well, as I said, good luck tonight. I hope you have some . . . gold star pitching."

He bursts a laugh, so much bright joy coming through his smile. Kennedy was right. He looks different today. So light. And so, *so* good.

"Gold star pitching, huh?" There's a twinkle in his eye at the memories of last night, I'm sure. In the same way, I haven't been able to wipe the knowing smile off my face when those same memories have flooded my mind today. "Thank you for the luck, but I don't need it."

"No?"

"I've got superstition on my side."

"I wouldn't rely on that."

"Oh, I would. I know the kind of weight it holds. How important it is that I pitch well because of it."

I roll my eyes playfully. "Well, you're starting on a Friday night at Fenway, so I'll say good luck to you regardless. This is big and it only happens a few times in your career, so enjoy yourself."

He nods. "Thanks, Mills. I will."

We both linger, unsure how to end this. He seems like he wants to lean down and kiss me, but because of my rules, he can't.

So instead of doing anything, I turn, carrying Max towards the exit.

"Hey, Miller?" he calls out to stop me.

"Yeah?"

"I promise I won't text you to check on Max between

innings, but if you want to text *me* about how good my ass looks in my baseball pants, I wouldn't be mad about it."

My laugh comes easy. "I'll see what I can do."

Kai's smile is smug and excited and looks so damn good on him as he ducks into the clubhouse to get ready.

And that night, on the TV in the hotel room while Max sleeps soundly in his crib, I watch his dad's game. Kai starts each inning looking at the interior of his hat, running his thumb over something tucked into the corner, and by the end of the ninth, I watch as his teammates explode in excitement for him because he just completed his second career no-hitter.

Earning himself a new superstition.

# 25

# Kai

Our second game of the Boston series was earlier today. An afternoon start, which means Max came to hang at the field. The boy is so busy on his feet these days that he only made it three innings before Miller took him down to the training room and field offices, allowing him to run around for the remainder of the game. The two of them came back to the hotel before the buses so she could get him ready for bed, and I stayed at the field longer than usual, bombarded with questions over my no-hitter last night.

I can't explain what was going on with my body last game, but I was on. Every pitch felt fluid and strong as it left my grip. My shoulder wasn't humming with pain the way it typically does when I pitch late into a game. I felt electrified. Rejuvenated.

Yeah, I got laid, but can I really contribute one of my career-best games to sex?

It was great fucking sex, so yeah, maybe I can.

There was something about that night that reminded me of who I am, what I have to offer, and the idea that a woman like Miller could want me, even if it's just for the remainder of her time here, had me walking around as if I were invincible. Clearly, it translated to my game.

She, on the other hand, is entirely freaked out, and I'm not sure why. It was her idea, and I'm playing by her rules, but yesterday it was as if she thought every simple touch between us meant I was going to lock her down, wife her up, and put a baby in her just to keep her from leaving Chicago.

Her fucking rules. They're undeniably worse than any I had ever put in place. Now we can indulge in having one another, but only in the dark and never overnight. It doesn't feel like enough. But then again, I'm worried nothing will be enough when it comes to Miller Montgomery because no matter if I could kiss her in public or have her sleeping in my bed, the fact is she's leaving in three fucking weeks, and our fling ends then.

I know Max isn't asleep yet, but it's getting close to his bedtime, so when I enter my hotel room, I make sure to do it as quietly as possible.

But the two of them aren't in my room, so I make my way into Miller's and find them laying on the couch in the corner. Max is on Miller's lap with his head resting back on her chest. She's got a blanket surrounding them, but I can spot my son already in his pajamas as Miller reads him a story, speaking low and hushed.

They don't know I'm here, so I steal the memory, leaning on the doorframe to watch them together.

This version of her is so different from the one I met that first day. There's a calmness about her now. She seems centered here with him, or maybe that's just me projecting and she's only acting this way for my son's sake.

Miller reads, slightly adjusting her inflection to create different character voices, and Max loves it. He giggles when her voice takes on a masculine depth, and again when it goes high.

Miller turns the page before brushing my son's hair, running her fingers through it almost absent-mindedly. My son's little blue eyes are growing heavy as he melts into her touch and listens to her read.

And then my chest doubles in size when she presses her lips to the top of his head when she realizes he's drifting off.

It's so gentle and natural. Easy and done without thought. Exactly the way it is when I show my son affection.

God, they're fucking cute together.

I shift on my feet and the floor creaks, breaking the soft moment. Max's eyes shoot open once again when the two of them turn in my direction, finding me in the room.

They both smile.

"Dadda." Max reaches out with his only empty fist, grasping the air as if he's grasping for me.

"Hi, Bug." I step into the room, joining them when I get on my haunches next to the couch. "Are you reading?"

He points to the illustrated children's book in Miller's hand, making some kind of noise that starts with a "B" sound. His version of saying *book*.

"Yeah, you're right. That's a book." I make sure to enunciate the syllables so he can hear them all as my eyes drift up to Miller's, finding her just as sleepy and content as my son. "Don't you two look so cozy."

I brush Max's hair out of his eyes then I do the same to her because I don't give a fuck about her rules right now. She's only here for a little while longer so in this moment, I'm going to treat her how I want to treat her—as if she were mine.

"Was he okay today?" I take my hat off, dropping it to the floor because the brim is interrupting my view of them.

Miller nods with a sleepy grin before her eyes dart right to my hat where it sits upside down. "What's that?"

My attention follows hers to find the small photo tucked into the inner band. I pull it out to show her, the edges worn from me touching it during every game.

It's a tiny photo of Max when he was only seven months old. Just weeks after he came into my life and changed it forever.

Miller's face softens with a sigh. "You touch that before every inning when you're pitching. I saw it last night."

"Yeah. The umpires have to check it before each game to make sure there's nothing suspicious in my hat that could give me an edge, but most of them know it's in there by now. It's sappy and sentimental, but when I'm on the mound and stressed out, it's a good reminder that work isn't the most important thing in my life. He is."

She twists her lips, biting the bottom one. "You're a good dad, Kai."

I offer her a small smile, feeling a bit more deserving of those words.

"Let's go to bed." I say that to my son because sleepovers are against Miller's rules.

I want to tell her that her boundaries are bullshit, but I don't exactly have the freedom to say that when I decided to ignore my own boundaries just two nights ago. And here I am, in a world of trouble because of it. I can feel the painful goodbye lingering in my future, so yeah . . . maybe there's a part of me that wants her to feel a bit of that too.

With Max in my arms, Miller follows me back into my room. Our hotel stays have felt more fluid lately, as if our two rooms are intended to be one. If Miller is getting Max settled for bed, she takes him to her room to get him away from his toys and the chaos. And if we're all here together, she comes and spends time with us in mine.

As soon as we get past the door separating our rooms, Miller's phone rings. She pulls it out of her back pocket, skin cinching between her brows.

"Who is it?"

"Violet. My agent." She nods back towards her room before slipping inside and closing the door behind her to keep her conversation private.

Panic instantly floods me. Why would anyone from work be calling her? She's off for another three weeks. She's *mine* for another three weeks.

Taking Max to the chair in my room, I hold him against my chest so I can spend a little time with him before the day is over, attempting to not let my new anxiety interrupt our time together. He settles into me all sleepy before he points back to Miller's room.

"Mmm," he hums.

"What, Bug?"

He points to the door again. "Mmm."

"Are you trying to say Miller?"

"Mmm."

"Yeah, that's Miller." I rock in the chair, rubbing a hand over his back as I tilt my head to look at him. "Do you love Miller?"

He probably doesn't know what I'm asking, but he nods against me anyway, recognizing the question in my inflection.

Even if he doesn't understand what he just answered, I know my boy loves that girl.

"I know you do." I place a kiss on the top of his head. "She loves you too, buddy."

Minutes later, Max is passed out asleep in my arms, so I carefully place him in his crib, turning off most of the lights, but then the relaxed and calm vibe completely changes when Miller cracks the door between our rooms.

Stress is evident on her pretty face.

"I'm going to bed."

I catch the door before she closes it. "What's wrong?"

"Just tired."

Bullshit. She was tired before that phone call, but she's not anymore. Now she's upset.

"What did she want?"

"Kai—"

"Are you going back early?"

The question comes out so needy and desperate, and maybe it's against her rules to show that side of me, but I don't give a shit. I'm quickly learning I'm both of those things when it comes to her.

"No . . . no, I'm not going back early. It was about the upcoming article, but it's also not a big deal."

She forces a smile, but it doesn't look right. It's not light, devilish, or dirty. I don't recognize it at all.

I've seen Miller upset about work before, but mostly when she's having trouble in the kitchen. This stress on her face doesn't seem to be the same as that previous version. I can feel the distance she's putting up even though she's less than a foot from me, and that distance only grows when she says, "I'm going to get some sleep. I'll see you tomorrow."

And she closes the door on me.

What the hell was with that phone call?

Miller is the fun one. The wild one. The one who knows how to let loose when I'm too overwhelmed about life. So, an hour later, while I'm lying in the dark and see the crack of light under our door still shining from her room, I pull my phone out to text my brother.

**Me:** *You awake?*

**Isaiah:** *Yeah.*

**Me:** *You alone or do you have company over?*

It's my brother. I've got to ask.

**Isaiah:** *Alone. I'm changing my ways, remember?*

**Me:** *Sure. Would you mind coming over and hanging with Max for an hour or so? He's already asleep and I need to get Miller out of her room.*

**Isaiah:** *Sounds kinky. Does Monty know you're sneaking his daughter out of the hotel right under his nose?*

**Me:** *Please shut up. Are you coming over or not?*

**Isaiah:** *Geez. You go forty-eight hours without getting laid and you're a grouch again. Yes, I'm coming over.*

The door between our rooms is unlocked. It hasn't been locked in weeks, so I open it to find a wide-awake Miller sitting at the desk with her laptop open and notepad covered in messy scribbles. She's got one foot on the chair as she rests her chin on her knee, espresso brown hair pulled up in a knot as the light from the computer illuminates her face. She's sitting so close, as if hoping whatever information is on the screen will magically transfer to her brain, and even from the doorway, I can tell she's stressing over recipes.

"Mills, put your bathing suit on. You're coming with me."

She whips around. "Why?"

"Because I need to loosen my shoulder in the pool."

"But—" She gestures towards her computer.

"You don't have to put your suit on, but you're coming with me. In fact, I prefer you naked anyway."

She chuckles, rolling her eyes as she closes her computer. "Fine."

Once Isaiah is settled in my room, Miller and I find the pool. I thought this one would be an indoor one, seeing as Boston freezes over in the winter, but it's outside and on the rooftop.

She's in that forest green swimsuit again, and now that I know what's underneath, I refuse to hide my gawking as she leaves her towel on a chair and walks her ass to the pool. Her hips sway, her thick thighs rubbing together with every step, fucking mouthwatering with all that tanned and tatted skin.

"This is exactly why I needed you to come with me. This is the kind of motivation I was looking for."

"So you brought me out here just to objectify me?" she asks as she slips into the water.

"Yeah . . . obviously."

I follow behind, trying to adjust my growing erection in my swim trunks, but there's not a chance in hell it's going away being this close to her almost naked body now that I know what it feels like to be inside of her.

It's dark out and the pool is closed, but breaking and entering a hotel pool is nothing new for either of us.

Miller stays in the shallow end where she can stand, and I do a couple of leisurely laps while I allow her a moment to be in her head. I'm going to get in there in a minute anyway.

She's sitting on the top step of the pool stairs when I make it back to her.

"I need you to get more tattoos," she states as I crest the water.

"Where did that come from?"

"Just from looking at you. They look good on your skin."

"Well." I wade through the water to her. "I need you to wear less clothes."

"Where did that come from?"

I shrug. "Just from looking at you."

She smiles, a bit of that previous stress gone for a moment.

"Want to talk about it?" I ask, pushing my wet hair back.

"No."

"Okay. Why don't you talk about it anyway." Pulling her off the step, my fingers slide down her forearms, fiddling with her hands, and maybe it's because they're under the water or because no one else is here to see it, but she gives in to the physical contact.

Pressing my luck, I lean back on the ledge, ushering her to stand in front of me. I wrap my arms around her waist from behind, holding her close when she says, "I have to go to LA."

I freeze, panic zipping through me. "But you said—"

"Not for good. I'll be back, but the photographer for the magazine cover needs to get the photos shot and edited before September. I'll do the interview when I get back to work, but the magazine issue is releasing only two weeks later, I guess."

She drops her head back against my chest as if she's falling with defeat.

I don't like this. The idea of her leaving doesn't sit right. What if she gets there and doesn't want to come back? What if she gets back to her real life and realizes she's done passing through Chicago?

Wracking my brain, I search for a solution. "You have to be in that particular kitchen for the shoot?"

"No, but I don't have any kitchen connections in Chicago."

"Use mine."

Her head whips back as she looks up at me.

"Would mine work? It's just for photos, right? You said it yourself, it's nice to look at."

She furrows her brow. "Yes, but—"

"Then it's settled."

"Kai, are you sure? There's going to be a whole team of people involved. They'll take over your house for an entire day."

"If it keeps you from leaving then yes, I'm sure."

Miller's eyes soften, tracing my face before she exhales and falls against me again, but this time it's with relief. "Thank you."

Now that she's a bit more relaxed, I let my hands wander under the water, skimming against her ribs. "That's what had you so stressed out? That's no big deal."

"I think I forgot about what's waiting for me after this. What if I never get it back, Kai? What if I'm not good enough anymore? I've spent my whole life chasing this career and to end up where? Making chocolate chip cookies and banana bread for a baseball team? God." She buries her face in her hands. "This is too important for me to be fucking around all summer. I should've been focusing on work, and now it's coming up so fast and I have nothing prepared. I'm going to get eaten alive by critics and—"

"Hey," I soothe, running my hands up her arms to pull them away from her face. "Take a deep breath."

She does as I say while I trail my palms up to her shoulders, feeling the tension bunched there. I knead her flesh.

"You're supposed to be the fun one, remember? I'm the one who stresses."

She huffs a laugh, a bit of tension dissolving, but not enough.

I won't lie. Her words kind of make me feel like shit. I'm the reason she hasn't been able to work or practice in the kitchen. We've been distracting her all summer, keeping her away from this world she's worked so hard to succeed in, and now she's panicking because the weeks she was supposed to have been regaining her confidence in the kitchen, she's spent traveling with my team and taking care of my son.

I press my thumbs into the tension of her shoulders. "What is the worst-case scenario in all of this?"

She thinks on it for a second. "I never get my groove back. I'm never able to create a high-end dessert again. My waitlist of chefs dump me and I never get hired again. I'm forced out of the industry and end up working in the bakery department of a grocery store, decorating cakes for Karen's retirement party, but then of course, she fucking complains because the purple frosting isn't the right shade of violet. So, I cuss her out because there are worse problems in the world than her frosting leaning more eggplant than violet, causing me to get fired from there too and now I'm living in my dad's house and sleeping on his couch and he's devastatingly disappointed because he's given up his entire life for me and now I'm unemployed and couch surfing."

I can't help but laugh, which thankfully pulls one from her too. "Dramatic as fuck, Mills."

"It could happen."

"It's not going to happen. Even if you did leave the high-end world, you're still a badass baker. You'd open your own bakery or something equally as amazing. You don't get to where you are in your career out of luck. You're a hard worker and ridiculously talented. That doesn't just change."

I don't mention anything about Monty because it's completely absurd that she's worried about her dad's disappointment and I think she knows it too. That guy looks at his daughter like she hung the fucking moon.

"I need to get serious in the kitchen when we get home."

"Okay," I agree calmly. "You're right, but you can't do anything about it tonight. So, there's no point in stressing about it now." Bending down, I place a kiss on the top of her shoulder. "Am I the one who needs to remind *you* how to have some fun?"

She relaxes back into my touch, pressing her ass against the cradle of my hips under the water. "You're like a completely different man than you were at the beginning of summer."

"Yeah, well, in the last two days I got laid and pitched a no-hitter, so things are looking up for me." I trail my hands over her stomach and tits, barely grazing the pads of my thumbs against her nipples. "Besides, I told you, the old Kai was different. He had a wild streak."

"Hmm," she hums against me, her body coming to life under my touch. "And what did the old Kai do to have fun?"

Dipping lower, I toy with the strings of her bikini bottoms sitting against her hip. Finding the end of one, I tug. "He skinny-dipped."

The fabric falls open as she looks down into the water, and Miller is all but writhing against me when I pull at the string on her opposite hip, her bottoms floating away in the water.

It didn't take much and I'm hard as a fucking rock.

"Kai." Her tone is laced with warning, but the need in her voice is a whole lot louder. "We could get caught."

I nip her earlobe. "That's all part of the fun, baby."

I let my hand drift lower, skimming the skin of her belly before dipping my fingers between her folds. Palming her pussy, I give it a little tap under the water.

"This is the best pussy I've ever had, you know that?"

"Yeah?" Her voice is hoarse as she grips my forearms, partly to balance herself in the water, but mostly to keep my hand right where it is.

"I couldn't believe how tight and warm it was around me. You're all I've thought about since. How good you taste. How wet you get."

She moans, rolling the entire length of her body against me.

Nipping against the skin of her throat, I whisper, "I want to be inside of you again."

"Then do it." Her nimble fingers undo the tie at the top of my shorts, dipping inside to grip me.

Groaning, I drop my head to her shoulder.

She feels fucking amazing. Just as amazing as she did the other night. She strokes me in the water, grinding her ass against me in tandem.

I slip a finger inside her cunt and she almost falls apart from that alone. "You should fuck me, Kai. That'd be a good distraction from my stress."

"I don't have a condom."

"I don't care."

She doesn't know what she's saying. She's too turned on to be thinking straight.

"Yes, you do, Miller. You just don't think you care because your pussy is literally weeping on my fingers right now."

And I know I sure as hell care.

She grips my cock, her thumb rolling around the head as if her hand could change my mind. If my son, my constant reminder, wasn't sleeping just inside this hotel, maybe it could.

Her legs clench around my hand. "Then stop teasing me if you're not going to do anything about it."

I slip another finger inside her pussy, causing her to fall forward with a whimper.

"I'm not teasing you. I'm going to make you come. It just won't be with my cock."

"But I like your cock."

I chuckle. "I know you do." She twists and turns her hand around my shaft. "And *fuck*, it likes you too."

Miller leans up and kisses me, eager lips finding mine. I want to turn away, somewhat annoyed that she only kisses me when it's going to lead to more. Yesterday, before my game I wanted her to kiss me as I stood outside of the clubhouse, but she couldn't. And though I'm doing all sorts of mental gymnastics right now, when her tongue sweeps inside my mouth, I know there's no way in hell I'd actually stop her.

She makes quick work of my swim trunks, letting them float away in the water with her own suit. One swift tug of the strings on the back of her neck has her top falling down, and being the impatient man I am, I rip it off the rest of the way and throw it somewhere in the water to join our discarded clothes.

Her nipples are stiff when the night breeze hits them, pressing into my stomach, and my dick is equally as hard when it slides against her hip, searching for friction. I have to remind him we're not getting any tonight. We're simply making sure this wild girl remembers how to have some fun.

But then Miller grinds her body against me, and the head of my dick presses against her clit.

She whimpers into my chest, and repeats the motion.

"*Oh fuck*, Mills." My words are a breathy cry as I drop my head onto hers.

Fingers threaded through her hair, I tug to pull her attention up to me. "I need you to stop grinding your pussy on me."

"I can't help it."

I search her pretty face. She's a mess, falling limp against me, leaving her body at my complete control besides her seeking hips that are rolling against mine in the water.

"Fucking hell, Miller." I flip her around, pulling her back to my chest again, allowing my cock to follow the line of her ass until it slides against the folds of her cunt. I hiss from the sensation, rocking my hips against her as I slick my length against her core. "Use my cock to get off, but don't you dare put it inside of you."

She rolls her body, fully grinding against it.

My head drops back, eyes on the moon because holy fuck, that feels good.

She writhes down on me, needy and desperate, but I'm not going to fuck her without a condom. Instead, I find her thighs under the water and push them together, crossing her legs over each other to tighten her hold on my dick, creating a tight channel for my cock to jut into.

"Oh God." She rocks her ass against my pelvis bone, riding my cock without it being inside of her.

I can feel how warm she is even under the water. She's wet, but with her own arousal as she humps me close to insanity.

This is fucking torture. What the hell was I thinking? Every time she grinds, the head of my dick nudges her opening, and all I need is for one little slip and I'd be inside of her. Bare.

I'm never leaving my room without a goddamn condom again.

She's loud. She's naked. She's fucking perfect. We're in a public place with the city lights of Boston glowing below us. But there's no way in hell I'm stopping her. Watching and hearing Miller come has quickly become a new addiction, one I have no idea how I'm going to curb once she leaves me.

I rock my hips into her from behind and the head of my cock accidentally slips just past her opening.

We both freeze, and I'm thoroughly impressed by both of our restraint to not fully sink into each other right here and now.

"Miller—"

"Please."

Our chests are pounding with heavy breaths and waiting anticipation. I could take her right here. I could curve my hips forward and I'd be inside of her. Tempting as fuck, but I can't.

Instead, I yank her off me and lift her out of the water, sitting her on the ledge of the pool, bending her knees so her feet are planted on the cement.

Then I devour her.

I latch my mouth around her, flicking my tongue over her clit as I lick long, controlled strokes over her core.

"Oh," she cries, pulling at my hair. "Yes, Kai. Right there."

Looking up from between her legs, I find her with her head thrown back, her tits heaving under the moonlight. Her legs tighten around my cheeks, pussy pulsing against my tongue.

I think this might be what my heaven will look like, and if it's not, well, then I don't really want to go.

Miller is frantic, but loose, having no control over her body as she rocks her hips against my mouth, finding her orgasm. Her fingers tighten in my hair, her abdomen contracting as she moans so loudly, there's no way in hell we're not going to get caught.

"There it is," I whisper against her core and my words have her body shuddering.

"Kai . . . Kai, I'm coming."

Her legs tighten, clenching around me as her body shudders, and when her orgasm takes over, all I can do is watch.

She's all wet, contracting muscles. Flushed skin, dilated eyes. Fucking beautiful as she whimpers my nickname into the night sky. She rolls and writhes against me, looking for every last second as I taste her at the same tempo, letting her ride it out on my face while having the best fucking view to watch how stunning this girl is when she falls apart because of me.

My dick is throbbing, painfully angry that he's not getting any action tonight, but I'll take care of him in the shower when I get back to my room. Every languid stroke will be done with vivid memory of what it sounds like when Miller calls out my name as she comes.

She goes soft against the ground, sated and sleepy just as she was before that phone call. Exactly as I hoped when I pulled her out of her room.

I kiss her pussy, finishing with a gentle tap to the sensitive flesh.

"Feel better?"

She nods. "Much better."

"Good." Pulling at her arms, I lift her off the ledge and back into the water with me. "Let's get you to bed."

With her wrapped around me, I carry her to the stairs, putting her on a step to rest, but still deep enough that the water is covering her naked body in case anyone heard her moaning and has decided to come bust us.

Meanwhile, I swim across the length of the pool, gathering up our discarded swimsuits before meeting her back on the stairs. Retying her suit, I hand the pieces back to her, and while she gets redressed, I climb out of the water to grab her a towel, not bothering to get my naked body covered until I can cover hers.

My cock is making a proud display of how ready I am for a release as it juts out from my body. I try to ignore the ache as I bring a towel to her where she sits on the top stair, still as naked as the day she was born.

When I bend with the open towel, she doesn't just grab it. She grabs me too.

She pulls me down to her level until my ass hits the cement ledge of the pool.

"What are you—" but my words die on my tongue when I note the way she's prowling towards me.

And in one single motion, Miller flips her wet hair to one side of her shoulders and licks my shaft from root to tip.

"*Fuck,*" I exhale. "Mills, yes please."

With a smile on her lips, she opens them and slides my length into her warm, waiting mouth.

"Oh my God, baby, yes. Just like that."

Eagerly, Miller is on her knees on the top step of the pool, sucking my cock like it's a damn popsicle. I curl over her, gathering her hair in my fist so I can get a better view. Her tits bounce as she bobs on my dick, taking me so deep I hit the back of her throat.

"*Jesus.*" My eyes roll back.

With her hands, she wanders over my thighs, squeezing the muscle. She traces the inked skin on my legs and hips, before running her fingers over the small patch of pubic hair above my cock. The same cock which is being swallowed down in the most enthusiastic blow job of my life.

My hips thrust up as I cradle her skull, curling over to watch.

But then Miller presses her palms against my chest, ushering me to lay back against the cement ground. I do, leaning back on an elbow, one knee bent, foot perched on the ledge while my other leg dangles freely in the water.

My long body stretches out as Miller continues to work.

How the fuck did I get so lucky that I'm getting my dick sucked by a stunning woman under the summer moonlight? I feel like a fucking king.

And then she moans. She fucking *moans* with a mouth full of my cock.

I gather her hair again, holding it against her skull as I palm her head with a single hand, bouncing her at the tempo I crave. Miller whimpers against my length but keeps up. Lapping and licking, sucking the tip.

She's clenching her legs together on the top step as if this is turning her on so much she wants to come again.

Hand sliding down, she cups my balls and every muscle in my body fires, trying to hold my orgasm in. She strokes my shaft with both her hand and her lips, creating the most insane tempo and friction. Miller pops off me, using her saliva as lubricant as she jerks me with only her hand instead.

She peers up at me, those green eyes mischievous as her tongue darts out and flicks the underside of my crown.

"*Fuck.* You're killing me." My body jolts again, begging me to let go, but I want this to last as long as possible. I want to spend my whole night right here until someone walks in on us to reopen the pool in the morning.

She kisses a path down my shaft, using her hand in conjunction to stroke me. The sounds of our wet skin sliding together is the only thing you can hear out here other than my needy sounds. Miller licks the sensitive skin of my balls before she sucks one in her mouth, jacking me off simultaneously.

And she watches me the entire time like she's just waiting for the moment I come apart.

"I'm going to . . ." My words are stunted. "Gonna come."

She only continues, sucking and twirling her talented tongue until my thick and swollen shaft throbs in her hand.

In long jerks, cum decorates my abdomen, shooting out as Miller continues her movements. My entire body tenses and my lungs stop working as I come so hard my vision fades around the corners.

Somehow though, I can still see Miller between my legs. Smug and so satisfied like she's been looking forward to sucking the life out of me since the first day we saw each other.

I think she might be a little bit crazy. My favorite brand of crazy, but crazy nonetheless.

Once my dick is spent, I take a deep breath, falling back onto the cement ledge, entirely done for. Miller crawls over my naked body, her tits rubbing against my softening cock as she licks a path of cum off my abdomen.

All I can do is laugh in disbelief. How the fuck is this my life? "Where the hell did you come from?"

She straddles my hips, palms anchored on my pecks, and if my dick wasn't completely done, I might just say screw it to my condom rule and fuck her right here.

The power of a good blow job, I guess. Makes you do stupid things.

"That was incredible." I breathe.

"Told ya. Gold star head." She simply grins, all knowing, before she licks her lips as if she's tasting me on them again.

We both laugh, completely naked under the night sky, before Miller lays down on top of me, nuzzling her head into the crook of my neck while I hold her, running a palm down her bare spine.

I keep her there, even though we're teetering with getting caught, because I know as soon as we go back inside where we have two beds, she won't be in mine.

Too intimate. Too attached for her. Because lying naked under the stars after making each other come together isn't intimate as fuck.

"Thank you," she exhales against my neck. "For making me forget about real life for a second."

My eyes close at her words. This is real life. This is *my* real life.

As if I didn't already know, this moment is another reminder that I'm going to be fucking ruined when she goes back to hers.

# 26

# Kai

"Isaiah, you're coming over tonight." I grab my car keys, wallet, and phone from my locker stall after practice on our home field. "Cody and Trav, you too."

Isaiah struts out of the showers with nothing but a towel around his waist. "Why?"

"Because I said so."

Cody's brows shoot up. "Yes, Baseball Daddy."

"You're not allowed to call me that."

"No," Travis cuts in. "Only the coach's daughter is allowed to call him that."

"Yeah, well, for reasons I'm not going to discuss with you, she can call me whatever the hell she wants."

"Trust me, Ace. We all know why the coach's daughter gets to call you 'Daddy'," Cody says. "So why are we coming over?"

"Miller is working on some new recipes at the house tonight and I need people other than me to hype her up. So come over, eat, and sing her fucking praises with whatever dessert she puts in front of you."

"You should've just said that. You wouldn't have even had to ask me to come over. I would've just shown up." Isaiah throws his shirt back on. "Maybe you should invite Kennedy too."

"She doesn't want to hang out with the team outside of work."

"But she's friends with Miller now, so she'd probably be into it."

"Then go ahead and invite her."

Isaiah sighs in defeat. "She'll definitely say no if I'm the one to ask. Cody." My brother turns towards our first baseman. "Will you ask her?"

"Why?" he laughs. "So I can trick her into spending time with you?"

"Well . . . yeah. Exactly."

I grab my hat off the bench before leaving the locker room. "Come over around seven."

Before I hit the parking lot, I take a sharp left and round the corner to Monty's office. The door is slightly cracked already, so I rap my knuckles against the wood and let myself inside.

"Hey, Ace." He barely peeks up at me over his computer screen. "How's the arm?"

"Good."

"Did you get some time in the training room? Let the staff work on it?"

I take a seat on the chair opposite his desk. "I did."

Monty finally peels his eyes away from the computer. "I'm assuming you're in here because there's something you want to tell me."

I exhale a shocked and uncomfortable laugh. *Fuck my life.*

"*Want* to tell you?" I ask. "Not a chance in hell. Is there something I *should* tell you? Probably."

"Well, are you going to?"

Am I going to look him in the eye and tell him I'm sleeping with his daughter? Abso-fucking-lutely not.

"I'm gonna plead the fifth on this one, Monty."

He laughs to himself, clearly entertained by how uncomfortable I am.

I change the subject. "Are you free tonight?"

"I am. Well, I was going to see if Millie wanted to get dinner." He lifts a brow. "Or is she busy?"

God, this is weird. Six weeks ago, I thought I couldn't stand the girl, and now I know her schedule better than her dad. And he knows as well as I do that if she's not free, it's because she's with me.

"As far as I know, she is, but what do you say about having dinner at our—*my* house instead?"

A knowing smirk lifts on his lips at my slip-up. "I could do that."

"Great. And after, I need you to stick around for a bit. Miller is working on some recipes for work tonight. Well, she doesn't know she is yet, but I think it'd help her if you were there for that."

Monty leans back in his chair, folding his hands over his stomach, his tone full of suspicion. "What are you planning, Ace?"

I lean back too, sprawling my legs out in front of me. I guess if this man were anyone other than Monty, I'd feel uncomfortable being so honest, but more than being Miller's father, he's my friend.

"Look, the other night she got a call about work, and she was pretty upset because she hasn't had much time in the kitchen. That's my fault, so tonight, some of the guys from the team are going to come over and try whatever she comes up with. She needs to regain some of her confidence in the kitchen, and I know that more than anyone else, Miller wants to impress *you*."

He shakes his head. "That's ridiculous. I'm always impressed by her."

"I know. Trust me, I know, but . . ." *Fuck.* How the hell do I tell Monty about his own daughter who he clearly knows better than me? "She's putting a lot of pressure on herself to get back to the level she was at before she won that award and hearing it coming from you that she's doing a good job would help ease that burden, I think."

Monty pauses, a bit confused by my spiel, but eventually he relents. "Okay, I'll be there."

"Great." With a simple nod of my head, I stand from the chair, but he stops me at the door.

"I know you don't want her to leave, so why are you helping her do just that?"

*Well, shit.*

There's no way to answer that question without him figuring out just how fucking deep I am.

I sink into the chair again with a heavy sigh. "Because it's her dream, and I care about her too much to not help her chase it, even if that means I won't be there when she gets everything she's worked for."

Monty watches me, looking for any signs of bullshit, I'm sure. I wish I was lying. I wish I wasn't such a fucking sap that I could, in good conscience, do everything in my power to make her stay. But I won't be the reason she gives up on her dreams.

"You're good for her, Ace."

"No, it's . . . it's not like that."

"Oh, it's not like that, huh? So you're going to sit here and tell me you're sleeping with my daughter but it doesn't mean anything? Can't wait to hear that."

*Goddamn.* I should have never come into his office today.

"Hey, don't look at me." I hold my hands up in surrender. "If you want to have that conversation, you talk to your girl about the rules she made regarding sex."

Monty grimaces.

"Jesus. I can't believe I just said *sex* in front of you."

"Yeah, let's never do that again, especially in reference to my daughter." He sits back in his chair. "Even if you two are too blind to see it or are too stubborn to admit it, I know what this is."

"She's leaving." My two least favorite words that tend to fall from my lips whenever I'm looking for an explanation.

"She is," Monty agrees. "Are you going to be okay when that happens?"

I look right at him across the desk and lie. "I'll figure out a way to be."

His smile is full of pity. I'm now getting *pity* from the man whose daughter I'm sleeping with. Fucking great.

"You remember our conversation, right?"

He's referring to the time he requested I speak to him if I ever felt the urge to ask Miller to stay, to leave her dreams behind and settle into life with me and my son.

The urge is there every single day, but I won't ask that of her. It's not what she wants, and I don't have the strength to hear her rejection.

Miller doesn't allow me to show her how I really feel about her, so the best I can do is tell her through my actions. Support her dreams, help her chase everything she wants. I'll continue to do just that as much as it'll kill me in the end because unfortunately, I'm well aware that a simple life with me and my son would never be enough for her.

"I remember," I say. "But that's not what this is for her. She has so many opportunities waiting for her when she gets back to work."

Monty gives me an understanding nod. "What time should I be over tonight? Make sure it's early enough that Max is still awake. I want to see my little guy."

"Six?"

"I'll be there."

Once again, I stand to leave, but my eyes are drawn to the picture sitting on Monty's desk. Miller in her bright yellow softball uniform, kneeling with a pitcher's glove on her knee.

"How many of those do you have?" I gesture to the frame. I know he has one at home, this one at his Chicago office, and one he keeps in his travel bag for road games. I think he might even have one in his wallet.

"I don't know. Three or four."

"Why?"

"Why do you have a photo of Max in your hat?"

*Touché.*

"To remind me of what's important when the stress from work or life starts to become too much."

"Exactly."

Without hesitation or asking for permission, I take the frame off his desk and unclip the back. The photo is small, maybe only two or three inches in height and fits perfectly next to the one of Max in my hat.

Monty stays silent as I put the empty frame back on his desk.

"Shut up."

He laughs. "I didn't say anything."

I tuck the photo of Miller under the band, close to the one of Max, running my thumb over both of the edges. "How old was she here?"

"Thirteen maybe?"

"She looks happy."

"She was. She was a really happy kid, much in the way yours is."

Monty slides in the gentle reminder that I'm doing okay. It's his way of reassuring me that Max is all right. That I'm doing a good job, just like he did. But I'm only doing a good job right now because of the girl in the photo next to my son's.

I put my hat back on and leave his office.

My hands are full of groceries by the time I make it home. The house is empty and quiet, so after I set the shopping bags on the kitchen island, I make my way to the backyard in search of Max and Miller.

## Caught Up

My son's laughter echoes off the glass of the back slider, and I open it to find him in nothing but a diaper at his water table, splashing and clapping for himself when he dumps water from one small bucket into another slightly larger one. Miller sits on the ground and claps with him, cheering him on as he drenches himself in water, perfect for a hot August day.

When she catches my eye as I stand on the back porch, she offers me a small wave. Max follows her hand and, with a beaming smile on his face, takes off in my direction, arms up above his head as he races towards me.

"There's my boy."

"Dadda," he squeals.

I gather his wet little body in my arms, hoisting him up to sit on my forearm. Miller follows behind, and when I kiss my son, I'm beyond tempted to lean over and kiss her too. This is a normal, everyday moment, one I want to seal into my memories because these are the moments that matter.

But I don't seal it with a kiss because the soft, easy kisses are against the rules for her.

I nod towards the house. "Come."

"Malakai," she scolds. "Inappropriate."

Shaking my head, I let her pass by us, giving her a slap on the ass. "Get your dirty mind inside."

She finds the groceries on the counter. "Do you need help putting these away?"

I give her a second to rifle through them. She pulls out more flour, sugar, brown sugar, and milk. The best chocolate I could find from a local baking store. I purchased the most expensive vanilla extract on the shelf. I bought every kind of fruit the store had to offer.

"Nana!" Max hollers when she pulls out a bunch.

"What are you making?" she asks.

"I'm not. You are."

"I'm making what?"

"Whatever you feel like." I adjust Max in my arms. At almost seventeen months, he's starting to get heavy. "You haven't had time to create because we've been on the road so much, so I'm taking care of Max tonight and you're going to get to work. I know you do better in the kitchen when you get to see someone try your desserts and gauge their reaction. I figured maybe you should go back to what makes you happy, and bake for the people you care about, so a few of the guys from the team are coming over. Your dad too. Whatever you feel like making, we'll feel like eating."

She doesn't say anything, simply stares at the groceries.

"I hope that's okay."

Miller's nose takes on a rosy hue, but that girl doesn't cry. "More than okay." She turns to me with a crooked smile. "Thank you, Kai."

"It's the least I can do after stealing you away all summer."

She looks too soft, too vulnerable for me to resist, so I break her rules by cupping her head to pull her into my chest, placing a kiss on the top of her hair. Max, in my other arm, catches on and flops his body in half to place a sloppy one on her head as well.

She laughs, looking up to find my very proud son. "Thanks, Bug."

# 27

# Miller

**Violet:** *Please tell me you've got your new recipes locked in and you're back on track in the kitchen? Also, the* Food & Wine *photoshoot is happening next Tuesday. They'll be at the house at 6 a.m. to set up.*

**Me:** *Finalizing those recipes tonight. Kai planned a whole thing for me. It's really sweet. And Tuesday doesn't work.*

*Kai has a road game.*

**Violet:** *Can't you stay back from one? I'm sure he can handle one trip on his own. This is important.*

**Me:** *No, I can't miss it. How's that following Friday?*

**Violet:** *I'll check with the shoot coordinator. Chef Maven asked me what day you're planning to be in California. Can I confirm that it's the 1st? You'll be starting your drive from Chicago on Sunday the 29th, correct?*

**Me:** *Right. In two weeks.*

**Violet:** *Thank God. The food world is missing you, Miller. I have an inbox full of emails from food bloggers wanting to interview you about your little summer hiatus, not to mention I've already added another year of consulting gigs onto your schedule in the past couple of weeks!*

**Me:** *Great. Can't wait.*

**Violet:** *Your sarcasm is loud and clear, but you're blowing up right now, Chef. This is exciting. It's only the start of it all for you. See you in two weeks!*

"That's the one," Isaiah declares, pointing to the final plate I put in front of him.

He's deemed every single one of my desserts as "the one" tonight.

Cody moans around a mouthful, Travis's eyes go wide, and my dad is simply wearing a proud smile as he has all night. I've found myself looking for his approval first before checking in with everyone else.

"What's that one?" Isaiah takes another mouthful before going in for his third bite, but Kai knocks his spoon out of the way to fill his own because he hasn't had the chance to try it yet.

I wipe my hands on the towel that's draped over my shoulder. "That is a lemon curd glazed with strawberry. That slight shock you feel on your tongue is a homemade pop rock, paired with a rosé sorbet. There's also a bit of Voatsiperifery pepper in there which is a peppercorn that has a bit more herbal and floral notes to it. It's typically reserved for cooking, but I think it pairs well with the lemon."

The boys all stop their chewing, looking at me as if I've grown a second head. When I talk about a dessert with colleagues, I'm understood, but when I explain to others outside of the industry, it's as if I'm speaking another language to them.

"I have no idea what that means," Isaiah says. "But it's amazing and you should do this for the magazine."

"I think the flavor profile is a bit too summery for the fall release of the article, but I saw the strawberries and the lemon and thought, what the heck. I'll have some fun and experiment."

I've experimented all right. Making five new desserts for the boys to try. The dark chocolate cylinder filled with a smoked hazelnut praline cream that I thought of when we were at the bakery in Boston was an instant success, and I even impressed myself when I created a mozzarella cheesecake topped with a blackberry compote.

I didn't burn a single thing, didn't struggle with any part of it. I was happy and excited to feed the people I've come to care about more than I knew I was capable of. So much relief courses through me knowing I can still succeed in what I'm best at.

"Dad, what do you think?"

The one person I want to impress takes another bite of the lemon curd. "Phenomenal. As always."

I can feel my smile beaming under the lights in the kitchen, seeing him so proud of me. This is why I do what I do, to make sure he knows I'm doing something with my life that's made it worth him giving up his own.

I feel better today, like I'm on the right track to getting back to where I was before all the pressure hit, and I know a huge reason for that is Kai.

The fact that he would organize this for me—no one has ever done something so thoughtful. He played sous chef all night, getting me ingredients when needed and cleaning up after I was done using a bowl or spatula. He wore the proudest grin on his face the entire time and I've never loved being in the kitchen more than I did with him here next to me. The only thing that would've made it better was for Max to be sitting on the counter too, but it's long past his bedtime.

I was clean tonight, organized too. Nothing like I am when I bake with Max. I was more of the well-known pastry chef who helps kitchens earn Michelin stars, though I still had my tattoos showing, my septum ring in, and felt more like myself in the kitchen than I ever have before.

But the scary revelation is, I truly don't know how I'm supposed to go back to work without Kai's encouraging words quietly spoken in my ear or his hand resting on my lower back to check if I need anything.

Tonight was perfect. He was perfect because he always is.

And in two weeks, I won't have him next to me any longer.

I meet him at the sink where he's washing dishes, wanting to be wherever he is. I lean back on the counter, facing him.

"Great job, Mills," he says, a proud smile quirking his lips.

"Thank you. And thank you for tonight. This was . . . just what I needed."

"Feeling better?"

I nod, wanting to lean up on my toes and break my own rules, to press my mouth to his and thank him. He's so handsome, so kind. Cares so much for his people.

I want to hide myself in his home forever just so I can call myself one of those people.

*Whoa . . . no, I don't.*

"You're pretty like this," he says, continuing to wash the dishes I used. "Apron tied around your waist. Hair thrown on top of your head. Creative brain of yours at work. I love getting to see the polished pastry chef not so polished under her chef's coat."

"Well, lucky you, maybe tonight you'll get to see what's under the apron too."

"Maybe?" His eyes lighten with excitement. "We're past playing hard to get, don't you think?"

I lean into him. "You and me, Malakai, will never be done playing hard to get."

Bending down, he presses a chaste kiss to the top of my hair, chuckling as he does.

"Violet texted with a date for the photoshoot. Does the Friday before I leave work to have the shoot here?"

"You can do it whenever, Mills. Even if I have to go on a road trip, I'll figure out childcare for Max."

"You have a home game that night," I tell him. "I checked your schedule before I offered that date. There's something called 'Family Day' on the team calendar the following day. I'm not sure what that is."

Family Day also lands on my birthday, but Kai doesn't know that.

He swipes the sponge on the inside of a mixing bowl, not meeting my eye. "It's an event that team management puts on for all the families to come together on the field. Every team I've played for has hosted one. There will be food and drinks, that kind of thing. It's during the series against Atlanta." He finally looks my way. "Do you think you'll go to it?"

He doesn't have to say it, but I know he's never had anyone there for him at one of these events. I would guess Isaiah had always been too busy with his own season that they couldn't be there for each other, and yes, this year he'll have his son, but he's also going to have me.

"I'm sure your dad would want you there," Kai adds.

His tone is casual, easy, and detached, just the way I've asked him to be, but he shouldn't be detached when it comes to asking for someone to finally support him.

Hand on his forearm, I trace my fingertips up the thin skin on the inside. "I'll be there," I say with conviction. "For you."

I don't miss the way his eyes soften before drifting back to the island to check on his teammates and coach, reminding me that they're here, and maybe wondering why I'm suddenly okay with a bit of PDA.

I lean my head on his bicep, hand wrapped around his arm to hold him while he washes the dishes, forgoing my rules for the moment. "Thank you for tonight."

He leans his cheek on my hair. "I'd do anything for you, Miller."

# 28

# Miller

It's organized chaos outside of the stadium in Anaheim. The equipment managers are supervising the loading of the buses as the team finishes showering post-game. Fans are screaming, signs and jerseys in hand, hoping to catch sight of their favorite player before we head to the airport.

Typically, I'd be on the bus already and Max would be asleep, but he's been fighting a sickness over the past few days and his typical schedule has gone right out the window because of it. I'm equally as tired, dealing with a sick toddler on a road trip, and whatever it is Max has been fighting has finally caught up to me in the form of overwhelming exhaustion.

My head is pounding as I bounce him in my arms near the back entrance of the visitors' locker room. I'm trying to soothe him, but from what I've learned over the last few days, the only person he wants when he doesn't feel well is his dad. But Kai pitched tonight so I'm sure he's doing post-game press interviews and some amount of physical therapy.

"You're okay, Max. Shh." I run a hand over his back before lightly pressing his head into my shoulder, hoping it'll force him to rest.

It doesn't. He wails his little lungs, his cry deafening next to my ear.

"Dadda," he sobs, his ice-blue eyes rimmed in red as he frantically looks around the busy parking lot. "Dadda!"

"I know. I know. He'll be out soon."

He doesn't stop, somehow finding the lung capacity to scream even louder.

My dad shoots me a quick, worried glance from across the lot, but he's so busy going over scouting reports with the rest of the coaching staff that I simply shake him off, telling him I'm fine.

Everyone has a job to do, and this is mine.

But I have no idea what the fuck I'm doing. I know how to have fun with Max, how to figure out what he needs, whether that's food, sleep, or a diaper change. But I have no idea how to help him when he's this sick or upset.

I don't have that motherly intuition, and I'm not sure if it's because I lost my own at such a young age or what, but this might be the first time in my life that I'm bitter over the fact I didn't have her around longer to learn those instincts from.

When I excel at something, I have the satisfaction of knowing I belong, that I'm worth the investment. Whether that be the chefs that invested in me by selecting me for exclusive internships, or knowing that my dad invested his life by adopting me when he wasn't exactly in the position to take on that responsibility. At least I've made a name for myself.

But right now, I'm doing nothing for Kai or his son.

Fans line the roped-off area, keeping the walkway clear for the team to get to the bus, but most of the guys will take a moment to head over there, sign a few autographs, and thank the fans for staying so late.

They're staring at me like I have no idea what I'm doing with a seventeen-month-old still awake at 11 p.m., screaming bloody murder in my ear, and they'd be right. The insecurities are settling in fast because everyone here knows I'm not what he needs.

Just seven weeks ago, I was planning to spend my summer working on new recipes and ironing out my issues in the kitchen, but now all I can think about is trying to be enough for Max in hopes he might feel better. I know he's uncomfortable, you can see it clear as day. His throat is swollen and his nose has been running non-stop. But I'm not Kai, and Max isn't going to relax until his dad is out here.

My head is throbbing so fiercely that all I want is to fall into a bed and get a few hours of sleep when Kai finally walks outside, backwards hat and contacts replacing his glasses. Looking annoyingly handsome and put together while I feel like shit.

His son's cry is a beacon, pulling his direction to us immediately.

"Come here." Kai takes Max from me, bouncing on the balls of his feet as he tries to settle him. "You're okay," he whispers. "You're all right, Bug. I've got you."

Max's wail softens to a sniffling cry as he melts into his dad's shoulder.

"Did he not sleep at all?" Kai asks me, his tone a bit curt.

I simply shake my head, too tired to say much of anything, and too embarrassed that I couldn't help.

Kai sighs with frustration. He's gone three nights without getting a full night's rest, so not only is he as exhausted as me, but I think he feels guilty that he's putting his son through a grueling travel schedule during a sickness. Add that to the fact he kind of pitched like shit tonight and the Warriors lost due to a run he gave up while he was still on the mound.

Kai looks at me, and I can sense his fingers itching to pull me into him. I want him to. I want to say "screw it" to my dumb rules and fall into him because I need his comfort right now. I've become more and more reliant on it.

But as soon as the words are on the tip of my tongue, one of the team's media coordinators taps him on the shoulder.

"You're kidding me," Kai states because he knows what he has to do without being asked. "My kid is sick. Let me just get on the fucking bus."

He's clearly frustrated. Kai rarely cusses in front of his son.

"Sorry, Ace." The coordinator cowers a bit. "You've dodged fans after your last two starts. Unfortunately, I have to insist that you do your rounds tonight before we leave."

Kai's cool gaze is almost murderous, and my heart goes out to the poor media relations guy who is simply trying to do his job.

I hold out my hands. "Do you want me to take him?"

"No." I'm not surprised by his quick answer. He's been on edge for days, and maybe I deserve for him to be upset with me. I haven't been any help.

Kai slips the jacket off his shoulders and uses it as a blanket to cover his son. "This is bullshit," is the last thing he says before plastering on a smile and beelining it for the horde of fans whose noise level is growing with excitement as he gets closer to them.

The poor coordinator gives me a sheepish grin before he corrals more of the players and directs them to do their rounds. Luckily for him, none are as resistant as Kai.

Other players join the mass of fans, but through the crowd I see Kai putting on his handsome smile and using his only free hand to sign some autographs. There are male fans over there too, drooling over him, but all I notice are the women. Women who are fawning over little Max in his arms. Women with blatant signs declaring how much they'd like to wife up the single dad on the team.

I hate them all and I don't care how childish that sounds.

I hate that eventually he's going to meet someone who will give him the kind of commitment he needs. I hate that one day he'll complete their family.

And I hate that the woman he chooses won't be me because I'm simply a summer fling passing through.

"Millie," my dad calls out, pulling my attention, and waving me over to the team bus. "You okay? You look like you might be sick."

*Spot on, Dad. That's exactly how I feel.*

He touches my forehead with the back of his hand. "Your head isn't too warm."

"I'm just running on fumes at the moment."

"Why don't you sit up front with me for this flight so you can get some rest?"

"No, I'm fine. Kai just worked all night. I can't leave him with a sick baby."

"Well, *my* baby is sick, and I'm worried about you."

I breathe a half-hearted laugh. "I'm almost twenty-six, Dad."

"And you'll always be my baby."

This guy is a walking juxtaposition, I swear. Tall, built like a tank, covered in tattoos, and the softest guy I know.

"Come on." He continues up the steps of the bus. "We've gotta get to the airport."

Instinctively, my attention finds Kai one more time before I get on the bus. He's speaking to a woman with long auburn hair, and she's of course gorgeous. Decked out in a jersey with his name on it. He says something to her and whatever it is causes her head to fall back in laughter before she tucks her hair behind her ear and looks up at him through her lashes.

I know that look. I've *used* that look.

But it's directed at Kai so now not only am I tired, but I'm also fuming.

Handing off her Sharpie, she turns around and collects her hair to one side, allowing him to sign her jersey, and when he's done, you'd think he'd move on. But no, he stays to speak to her some more. She points to Max, who is finally relaxed, and whatever she says puts a smile on Kai's face, one that I'm used to being the main recipient of.

And then my blood begins to boil when she slips a piece of paper into his free hand—her number, no doubt.

# Caught Up

I'm not the kind of girl who simply sits back and watches her man get hit on. I've also never had a man to claim before, and although I'd like to walk right over there and claim Kai for myself, he's not my man either. And I'm the one who made sure of that.

I shouldn't feel possessive, I don't have the right to, but I can't help it. I'm oddly rattled. This woman doesn't know anything about him.

She doesn't know that he raised his brother or that he tried to retire the same day he became Max's only parent. She doesn't know what he tastes like or that his glasses fog up when he kisses for too long.

I get it. He's absurdly attractive and a professional athlete. I know that selfless single dad thing has to do it for other women the way it does for me, but he's not available.

*Right?*

Since when am *I* jealous? I've never been attached enough to be jealous.

And why am I spiraling, imagining this random redhead as Max's new mom?

I bet she'd know how to make him feel better when he's sick. I'm sure she would've been able to get him to stop crying in the parking lot. She's most likely a lawyer or a doctor. Even worse, she's probably a *pediatrician* who owns a lot of cardigans and comes from a giant family who would love to welcome those two into their fold.

Family is the most important thing to Kai, and I'm sure he'd love a big one to raise his son around.

God, she's perfect. I hate her so much.

This is why I need girlfriends. I can't exactly bitch to my dad about how much I hate Kai's red-headed future wife or that, regardless of me leaving town soon, those are *my* boys, and I'm not prepared to share.

So I text the only girlfriend I have.

**Me:** *Kai's future wife is stunning. I hate her. She also has red hair and I'm real close to hating all gingers because of it.*

**Kennedy:** *I have red hair.*

**Me:** *I know. That's why I'm giving you a warning. But at least you're not trying to seduce the man I'm sleeping with by asking him to sign your jersey or give him what is most likely fantastic parenting advice which is conveniently accompanied by the phone number you slipped into his hand.*

**Kennedy:** *Uh-oh. Are the fans making you jealous?*

**Me:** *I'm not jealous. But yes.*

**Kennedy:** *Why? You and Ace are just sleeping together, right?*

**Me:** *Right.*

**Kennedy:** *I gotta finish cleaning up the training room, but sit with me on the plane? We can talk about all your confusing feelings on the flight to San Francisco.*

**Me:** *Can't tonight. Max isn't feeling well, but let's get lunch or something tomorrow.*

**Kennedy:** *Deal, but wait. Did you save my number in your phone? I'm honored, Miss Unattached.*

**Me:** *Yeah. Yeah. You know what this means, right? We're in a committed relationship now.*

**Kennedy:** *Omg. Am I your first?*

**Me:** *You popped my committed relationship cherry, Kennedy Kay.*

**Kennedy:** *Double honored.*

I give Kai and his son one more long, lingering look. He's still talking to that same woman, and before I can look away, he turns to catch me staring. Kai stands locked still, watching me while she continues to speak to him, and our eye contact is only broken when I eventually offer him an understanding smile and turn back to the bus.

I don't want to understand it, but I do. Kai will eventually meet someone who will settle down with him, and we both know that someone won't be me.

# 29

## Kai

"This one was a little too inside, but your speed was good." Harrison, one of the pitching coaches, uses his cursor to move the stilled image around, showing me all angles of one of my pitches tonight.

I'm trying to focus on the computer, showcasing my post-game pitch breakdown, on the flight from Anaheim to San Francisco, but there's a woman in the aisle opposite me, holding both my sleeping son and all my attention.

The baby Tylenol finally kicked in, thank God, relieving some of Max's discomfort and allowing him a bit of rest. Miller is overly exhausted, but Max wouldn't go down in his crib, always being a bit needy when he doesn't feel well, so she's trying her hardest to get an hour of sleep in an uncomfortable airplane seat while my son naps on her.

Having a sick toddler is no fun. Having a sick toddler while on a work trip? Absolute nightmare.

The past three days have been rough. Guilt gnaws at me over putting my sick son through my travel schedule. I should've left him home, but I felt just as guilty over the idea of leaving Miller to watch him full-time, especially when he's not feeling well. That's not her responsibility.

It's moments like these that I feel selfish as hell for keeping my job, and if it weren't for her helping me, I couldn't do any of it.

Harrison moves onto the next pitch in the sequence so we can analyze it together, but when I catch Miller attempting to readjust out of the corner of my eye, using the fuselage to rest her head against, I can't sit still any longer.

"Sorry, but can we do this in the morning?" I gesture to the seat across the aisle from me. "Max has been sick."

Harrison peeks over. "He seems fine to me. Miller's got him."

"And she needs a break." I try to keep my tone even when, in reality, I'm annoyed and short. I get that the organization has bent over backward to make my situation work, but these are the moments that matter to me. "Look, I'll wake up an hour earlier tomorrow and meet you for coffee or something, but tonight I just need to take care of my family."

He agrees but is clearly frustrated over it, and I know he's just trying to do his job. I did lose us the game tonight, so I don't have much room to be making demands, but he gives in, taking his iPad and heading back to the front of the airplane to sit with the rest of the coaching staff.

I'm fucking drained. Wrecked by the lack of sleep due to my son being sick while fighting the overwhelming desire to treat the nanny temporarily living in my house like she's here to stay. But right now, I just really want to hold them both.

With the plane dark and quiet, most of the guys trying to get a bit of shut-eye before we land, I stand from my seat and sneak my way across the aisle.

Trying my best not to wake Max, I slide one arm under the bend in Miller's knees, the other under her back before I gently lift her in my arms, turning to steal her seat. I get her settled onto my lap so I've got them both.

"What's wrong?" she asks, not even opening her eyes as she buries her head into my shoulder, Max still melted onto her chest.

"Nothing," I whisper. "Get some sleep."

She breathes deeply through her nose, nuzzling herself further. "Why aren't you working?"

"Because there are more important things than work, Mills."

She doesn't respond, and yeah, maybe I said that in a way that referred to her work as well.

She buries herself deeper, running a hand over Max's back. "You holding me like this in front of other people feels pretty intimate."

I quietly chuckle. "Yeah, well, sometimes I don't give a shit about your rules, Miller, and right now is one of those times."

"Why haven't you tried to break the one where you sleep in my bed?"

*Wait . . . what?*

I play with the hair framing her face, pushing it out of the way so I can see her better. "Do you want me to break that rule?"

"I'm just wondering why you haven't tried."

"You're confusing the hell out of me, Montgomery."

"I'm confusing myself too."

I readjust my hold on them. "I haven't tried to sneak into your bed mostly for your sake, because I'm fairly certain if we start having sleepovers, you're going to low-key fall in love with me and I know how adamant you are about this remaining a fling."

A sleepy smile lifts on her lips. "I missed you."

Her jade green eyes shoot open at that, and I can't help but quietly laugh at her exhausted candor.

We've seen each other every day since she got to Chicago, so that's not what she's referring to. But taking care of a sick Max has been done in shifts, both of us too tired to do anything together once he's finally asleep.

"Told you, Mills. You're already falling."

"I don't fall in love."

Those words instantly change the playful vibe. She wants a no-strings-attached kind of life, and the deeper we get into this, it's clear the only life I'm complicating is my own.

She continues our hushed conversation. "I'm sorry I couldn't get Max settled down tonight."

My eyes flicker to my sleeping son who is very much settled down in her arms.

"I think he hates me," she continues.

"What are you talking about?"

"I tried to get him to sleep, I really did, but he didn't want me." Her voice cracks, the words whispered but watery, and her greens are glossed over in a way I've never seen. "I didn't know what to do."

A single but shocking tear rolls down her cheek, and I swiftly wipe it away with the pad of my thumb.

She's clearly more exhausted than I assumed because Miller is not a crier.

"He kept screaming and crying and I really think he hates me, and you hated me when I first got here, and I just know you'll both love that redhead."

*What the fuck is she on about?*

More tears fall from her closed eyes, and I clean them up, reminding myself not to give her shit tomorrow once we've both gotten some sleep. Knowing Miller, she's going to cringe at the reminder that she was so vulnerable.

But I love it. Whether she wants to acknowledge it or not, Miller is, at the bare minimum, attached to my son. I couldn't tell you how many times I've broken down from worrying that I'm not doing enough, and I know firsthand that you only react like this if you care.

"That wasn't on you. He's needy when he's sick and for some reason, I'm the only one who can calm him down. It's always been that way."

My brother, sitting in front of us, peeks his head through the opening between the seats. "He's right. One time, I was babysitting while Kai was at a charity concert and I had to walk into a completely silent auditorium during a violinist's solo because Max was going to make me go deaf from his wailing, but of course, he was perfectly fine once Kai had him."

"Stop eavesdropping, you little creep."

He ignores me, wearing a mischievous smile. "Miller, you're a beautiful crier."

"Shut up, Isaiah. Turn around and forget this ever happened."

I try to hold it in, but I can't keep my body from shaking with a silent laugh.

Isaiah catches my eye, giving me a knowing smile before he turns forward again. What he knows or why he's looking at me like that? No fucking clue.

"Miller," I whisper. "If you're this sad, I have a shoulder you could lean your legs on."

She cackles. Yes, *cackles*. It's adorable, which is a word I would never let her catch me calling her out loud.

"Hey, I'm the one with the dirty teenage boy jokes." Her smile falls again as more tears continue to cascade down her cheeks. "I'm just tired, and you were upset with me after the game."

Exhaling, my head drops back. "I wasn't upset, not with you. I pitched like shit. The press wouldn't stop asking questions and then having to go talk to fans . . . I'm tired and I knew you were tired. I wanted to give you a break. I didn't mean to take it out on you or make it feel like it was your fault." Running a hand over her hair, I usher her head back to my shoulder. "And he loves you, you know?"

When she looks up at me, Miller's eyes are an even more vibrant green from the red that surrounds them.

"I've never seen him so smitten."

*Which makes two of us.*

"You think so?"

I chuckle. "Yes, Mills. He's passed out and drooling on your overalls. I think it's safe to say he's in love."

She looks down for a moment, running a hand over his dark hair. "Okay." Sniffling, she composes herself. "Are you going to make fun of me tomorrow for having an overly-exhausted cry?"

"Oh, absolutely."

She lightly laughs, regaining some of that spirit that makes her who she is, before nuzzling back into my shoulder.

"Thank you," I whisper. "I know I don't say it enough but you're so good with him."

"Do you think I'm better than the pediatrician lady with all the cardigans?"

Confused, I tilt to get a better look at her. "Max's pediatrician is a man, and I don't think he's all that into cardigans."

"The redhead." Miller yawns. "The one who gave you her number after the game. Do you think Max will like her?"

Wracking my brain, I look for something to piece together. *Cardigans. Doctor. Phone number.*

Phone number . . . the red-headed woman who slipped me a piece of paper after the game? I assumed it was her phone number, but I didn't check before I tossed it in the trash outside of the bus.

"Miller Montgomery." A smirk lifts. "Are you jealous?"

She shakes her head to tell me no.

"Little liar."

"Shh," she hushes, burrowing against my chest. "I'm sleeping."

I can't stop the grin from spreading on my lips. Miller Montgomery is jealous, which feels like the opposite of a no-strings-attached kind of emotion.

It's just after 2 a.m. when I get into my hotel room in San Francisco. Max slept through the entire flight, thank God, never once waking up on the bus ride to the hotel or while I set up his travel crib in our room. For him, I hate red-eye flights and the team has rearranged our travel schedule to avoid them this season; however, sometimes we don't have a choice and have to get to the next city.

After brushing my teeth, I flop onto the bed, completely drained from the past few days.

But there's a woman on the other side of this wall from me who's equally as worn out, and I can't stop thinking about how upset she was over thinking she wasn't enough for Max. That's not something you worry about if you're "just passing through".

Grabbing my phone off the charger, I shoot her a text.

**Me:** *Are you okay?*

A minute passes before she responds.

**Mills:** *Yeah, I'm good now.*

**Me:** *Good. So, what are you wearing?*

I hear her laughter through the wall.

**Mills:** *Wouldn't you like to know.*

**Me:** *I would. That's why I asked.*

She sends me a picture of her in bed, fully covered from head to toe. Oversized sweatshirt, baggy sweatpants that I think might be mine, glistening from her night-time skin care. Clearly ready for sleep and God, do I want to be in there next to her.

**Me:** *If I ask you something, will you tell me the truth?*

**Mills:** *Well, I don't make a habit of lying to you, so go for it.*

**Me:** *Why were you upset over Max?*

There's a hefty pause before I get a response.

**Mills:** *I'm not sure. I just wanted to help him. To be enough for him, I guess.*

**Me:** *Is that because you love him?*

**Mills:** *Yeah. I do love your son.*

And she thinks she doesn't fall in love when she's already done it once this summer.

**Me:** *Can I ask you another question?*

**Mills:** *Shoot.*

**Me:** *Were you jealous tonight?*

Three gray dots appear then disappear, repeating that pattern a couple more times on the screen.

Finally, she responds.

**Mills:** *Yes.*

**Me:** *Why?*

**Mills:** *Would you believe me if I said I'm not sure? I've never been jealous before. I've never cared about anyone enough to be.*

**Me:** *But you care about us?*

I'm too much of a coward to suggest only me. At least if I throw Max in there, I know she won't be able to fully say no.

**Mills:** *More than I knew I was capable of.*

Fuck, my heart feels like it's about to explode out of my chest. I want to bust through the door between our rooms and pull her into my bed, to let myself believe she's mine for more than the summer. But Miller made these rules, so she's going to have to be the one to break them.

Before I can respond, Max starts to stir and it's not long after that his cry begins to fill the room.

Quickly, I stand from the bed. There are times I let him cry himself back to sleep. Him being sick is not one of those times.

"Come here." I pick him out of his crib as his wail gains volume. "Shh. It's okay, buddy. I got you." Bouncing on the balls of my feet, I pace with him.

He cries as I hold him. My arm is throbbing after a night of pitching, but if I put him down, neither of us is getting any sleep, and that includes our neighbors who share these thin walls. So, I walk the length of the room. I rock him, rubbing his back until his screaming cry settles into a sniffle as he tries to find a comfortable position on my shoulder.

I take him back to my bed instead of his crib. Maybe this way I'll get lucky, and he'll be able to get a couple hours of rest.

Keeping him towards the middle of the mattress in case he rolls, I occupy one side, facing him. He uses my bicep as a pillow while he continues to cry, but this cry is the one he uses when he's trying to settle himself back to sleep.

Rubbing his back, I make soothing noises, attempting to help calm him down, when the door separating my room and Miller's opens.

She peeks inside and catches my eye.

"Sorry," I whisper from the bed. "We're keeping you up."

She simply shakes her head and comes into my room, closing the door behind her. Lifting the comforter on the other side of Max, she slips into bed with us.

"Mmm," Max hums, trying to say her name when he rolls over to look at her.

"Hi, baby." Miller brushes his hair from his face before running her hand over the length of his back, soothing him.

She settles her head onto my open palm against the pillow, her eyes lifting to mine. "Is this okay?"

Typically, I hate someone else getting these moments, even the tough ones, but with Miller there's no envy. It feels right that she's here.

My words are desperate, but hopeful. "Please stay."

She nods against me, gently stroking Max's back and softly kissing his head until his little cry dissolves and he falls back to sleep.

I have no idea what she was worried about earlier, but it's obvious to me that this wild woman is my son's calm. And in a lot of ways, I think I might be hers.

Scooping my hand, I pull her in with my son sandwiched between our bodies, tangling my leg with hers, and draping my other arm over her waist in hopes to keep her close.

I liked seeing Miller jealous tonight, but she doesn't need to be. I know this picture, the three of us, will dissolve as soon as she leaves, but for now, I plan to steal every second while pretending there's no end date to us in sight. Because unfortunately for me, I know no one else will ever compare to how complete she makes both me and my son feel.

# 30

# Miller

We've been back in Chicago for a couple of days, and I've been working hard in the kitchen. The photographer for the shoot comes at the end of this week, which means my return to work is just around the corner.

Tonight, I have the house to myself. Kai, Max, and my dad are all at team dinner. I'm used to being by myself—having empty hotel rooms or house rentals whenever I'm on the road—but I hadn't realized how *lonely* I was until I got to Chicago. Until Max and Kai.

Mixing bowls, dry ingredients and baking sheets all line the countertop in Kai's kitchen as I try to work in this rarely quiet space.

I remember exactly what it feels like to have a chef breathing down my neck while I'm trying to create, or what it sounds like to be yelled at in front of my peers because one of my sauces didn't meld to the right consistency. As I've grown in my career, I've become my own motivation. Providing my own internal voice to push me when I'm messing up.

But looking around Kai's kitchen, I don't care about those voices. I don't want to hear any of them. I don't want to hear the clatter of pans or the communication among the line staff. I don't want to feel the heat from the stove's flame or the pressure of a head chef looking for his next order.

I only want to hear Max's incoherent words and Kai's soothing timbre telling me I'm doing a good job, two things I won't have when I leave this place.

Turning the flame off on the stove, I remove the half-melted chocolate. I untie my apron, throw my dish towel onto the counter. What a waste of my night. This is all I'll be doing once I get back to my busy life, and I have no desire to do it now.

Kai invited me to team dinner and I turned him down because I decided to work, but if I can be completely honest with myself, I don't give a fuck about work. I only have them for a few more days, so what the hell am I doing here alone?

As I pull my phone out to call him, wanting to know where he's at so I can join, a text comes through.

**Unknown:** *Hi! This is Indy. Kai's friend. This might sound strange, but I want to get drunk tonight, and my best friend can't support me in this because she's pregnant. So, would you want to come over and have a drink with me?*

Indy—the blonde ray of sunshine who hosted Kai's family dinner. Meeting up with Kai and his teammates sounds nice but I like the idea of having a girls' night even more. I've never been a part of one of those.

I've only made one girlfriend this summer, but she's so busy that I rarely see her when we're on the road.

But like me, Kennedy isn't used to being around a lot of girls so maybe she'd want to join too, and more than anything, I need to talk through the bullshit going on in my head.

**Me:** *Count me in. Any chance I could invite one more drinking buddy?*

**Unknown:** *The more the merrier! See you soon!*

"We're going to do it right out there." Indy points towards the backdoor slider, leading to her backyard. "It'll be small. Around fifty people. Perfect for us."

I'm surprised fifty people is enough for them. Her fiancé, Ryan, is a well-known basketball player and she's a social butterfly. It's fairly obvious judging by how welcoming she's been to me, someone she's only met once, and to Kennedy, someone she hadn't met until tonight.

"I can't believe I'm going to be in Ryan Shay's wedding," Rio sighs. "A dream come true for me, really."

"You do know you're standing on *my* side, right?"

Rio waves Indy off. "Semantics."

Indy chuckles and brings her cocktail to her lips, clearly unaffected by her best guy friend wishing he was a grooms-man instead of standing next to her as a bridesmaid.

Stevie, the only sober one of us, sits on the couch with Kennedy while Rio, Indy, and I take up the floor in Indy's living room. Kennedy picked me up on her way, and an hour in, Rio busted through the door to join our girls' night.

"Miller, when do you head out to LA for your next job?" Stevie asks.

If I wasn't three sheets to the wind right now, that question would've sobered me up.

"Sunday."

"Wow," she exhales. "I didn't realize it was so soon."

I sense all pairs of eyes on me.

"How do you feel about that?" Kennedy asks as she takes another sip from her drink, clearly knowing better than anyone else here that I'm struggling with the idea.

I roll onto my back, eyes on the ceiling, holding my cock-tail above my head because well . . . I'm drunk and I don't know what I'm doing. "Do you want the sober answer or the drunk one?"

I tilt my head back to see Stevie's brows furrow as she rubs her belly. "The drunk one, obviously."

"There's a part of me that doesn't want to leave."

"Then don't." Rio's words seem so simple.

"It doesn't exactly work that way," Kennedy says. "The girl is a world-renowned pastry chef, who has a three-year-long waitlist of kitchens she's going to be working for."

"Four years now." I point to Kennedy over my head. "But, yes, exactly."

"What's keeping you from wanting to go back?"

Whipping my head to the side, I immediately find Indy, who's wearing the biggest shit-eating grin from her question that she seems to already know the answer to.

I narrow my eyes at her. "Okay, Miss Romantic. Why don't you tell me, since you seem to already know."

"Because you're in love with Kai."

"Wrong. I'm not."

"Well, I know you're in love with Max and you can't even try to deny that one."

Exhaling, I drop my head back to the floor, holding my drink on my stomach. "I am. God, I love that kid so much. Is that weird?"

Indy, sitting cross-legged, looks down at me. "No, Miller. That's not weird. Sometimes we can't explain how or why we love who we love. We just do. You don't really get to tell your heart what to do."

"Is that the alcohol speaking, or are you really that much of a romantic?"

Stevie laughs. "She's love's number-one advocate. Drunk or not."

I sit up on the floor to face the group. "When I look at Max, I think about him going to his first day of school and how much I know Kai is going to cry over it. I think about the friends he's going to make and I just hope that they're good people. Those aren't normal thoughts just a nanny should have, right?"

Looking up, I find everyone watching me, expressions ranging from knowing smiles to glossy eyes.

"Miller, I don't think you've been *just a nanny* to anyone in that family," Kennedy says.

"Fuck my life." Rio pounds back his drink before going into the kitchen for another. "I'm going to be the only single one left, and that was so fucking adorable that I don't even mind it."

Indy squeezes my leg. "It's okay for the important things in your life to change, you know?"

Stevie nods. "And it's okay to change directions even when you've spent your entire life headed on a one-way street."

"It's not that simple. This is everything I've ever worked for. Everyone in my industry knows my name. I've won awards that people strive their entire lives to achieve, and I'm only twenty-five. People don't just walk away from that kind of a career."

"They do if they don't love it anymore. If they love something or someone else more." That's Kennedy who speaks up, and to say I'm shocked that she's suggesting I leave my job is an understatement. Kennedy is all about her career. She doesn't even hang out with the team because she's worried it'll tarnish her reputation or that the boys won't take her seriously.

Rio comes back into the room with whatever is left of the tequila, which isn't much, handing Stevie another water.

"I don't know what I'm doing," I drunkenly admit. "Everything is so messy. I was just taking a break from work, and now I'm head over heels for Max and I'm having the best sex of my life with his dad."

"There we go!" Stevie sits up straighter. "That's what we want to hear. After we saw you two together at dinner, we knew this was going to happen. Give us the details. It's good?"

"It's *so* good."

"I knew it. I told you!" Indy points at Stevie. "You've seen Kai's hands."

"The hands are a tell," I agree.

"Goddammit." Rio shakes his head. "It's official. I'm the last one."

"I don't know what I'm doing. Who fucks the single dad of the kid they're nannying for?"

Stevie pops her shoulders nonchalantly. "I fucked a hockey player on the team I was working for."

Indy points to Stevie. "I fucked her brother."

"I'm not fucking anyone," Rio sighs.

Kennedy takes a long drag of her cocktail. "My ex-fiancé is fucking my stepsister."

As if a record scratched, the whole room freezes in silence, all eyes on her.

"Okay, you win," Stevie says. "But you should probably expand on that."

Kennedy holds up the bottle of tequila before taking another swig. "My ex-fiancé ended our engagement because I wouldn't quit my job after last season. His ego was too fragile for his partner to be traveling with a bunch of male athletes, so he called it off. Then in a turn of events, right before *this* season started, I found out his new girlfriend is my stepsister. And just last month, I learned via a picture of a ring on Instagram that they're now engaged."

*What the actual fuck?* I'm attempting to school my expression, but I'm too drunk to keep my jaw from hanging slack.

"Oh!" She laughs with a dark edge, not showing any sign of weakness. "I'm not done. Said engagement ring was the one I had picked out, but not the one I was proposed to with. However, he did trade in mine for my stepsister's, and now I get to spend every family holiday with the two of them for the rest of my life." She raises her cocktail glass in a cheers.

Kennedy isn't hurt, but she is pissed. I can see it in the way she tells the story. She's tiny in stature, but quite frightening when she's mad.

"Damn." Indy stands from the ground. "I think we need more alcohol after that."

Rio clears his throat. "You know, if you need help moving on—"

"Rio," Stevie scolds with a laugh. "No."

"I'm just saying, Kennedy, take it from me, in this group you don't want to be the only single one the way I am. We could help each other out here."

"Isn't Isaiah part of this group?" she asks. "He's single."

I lift my brow mischievously. "Right. He is."

"Oh, no. Absolutely not. Don't look at her like that." Rio points between Kennedy and me. "If Isaiah, of all people, settles down before me . . . It's not going to happen. You two. Stop giving each other ideas."

"Don't worry, Rio," Kennedy cuts in. "I wouldn't even give up my career for my fiancé. The last thing I'm going to do is throw it away over Isaiah fucking Rhodes."

Stevie yawns again, rolling herself off the couch. The poor girl has been a champ tonight, hanging out with us while sober and exhausted. "This pregnant lady needs to get to bed. That was fun, and Kennedy it was great to meet you. Ind, I'm taking a guest room!"

"Okay!" she shouts from the kitchen. "See you in the morning." Indy makes her way back into the living room. "Rio, you're staying, yeah?"

"Yes! And I'm sleeping in Ryan Shay's bed."

"No, you're not." She turns to Kennedy and me. "I have two more guest rooms. You can each have one."

My drunk brain does not want to shut up tonight. "I think I want to go back to Kai's. I don't have too many nights left, and I want to spend them at his house."

"Wow, okay." Indy's eyes widen. "That was way too fucking cute."

I've never been one to like the word *cute*, especially when it's directed at me, but there's just something about that Clark Kent lookalike that has me feeling like a marshmallow these days.

"Kennedy?" I ask. "He has a guest room."

One that I've been staying in, but drunk me doesn't want to sleep anywhere other than Kai's bed.

"I'm fine with that. Ace is probably the only player I'm cool with seeing outside of work."

Unfortunately, it's late, I know Max is sleeping, and I don't know if Kai would be able to pick us up without waking him.

With a buzz in my head and a drunken smile on my lips, I pull out my phone.

**Me:** *Hi.*

He responds immediately.

**Baseball Daddy:** *Hi, Mills.*

**Me:** *I miss you.*

**Baseball Daddy:** *Are you drunk?*

**Me:** *If I say yes will you still take advantage of me later?*

**Baseball Daddy:** *Nope.*

**Me:** *Then I'm stone-cold sober, and I want to come home, but neither Kennedy nor I can drive.*

**Baseball Daddy:** *. . . because you're drunk.*

**Me:** *Nope.*

**Baseball Daddy:** *I'll come pick you up.*

**Me:** *What about Max?*

**Baseball Daddy:** *Isaiah is sleeping over. He can stay with him.*

**Me:** *Okay!*

**Baseball Daddy.** *Okay. See you in ten.*

**Me:** *Are you mad at me? You seem mad at me.*

**Baseball Daddy:** *Why would I be mad at you?*

**Me:** *I don't know, but you're putting a period mark after every sentence.*

**Baseball Daddy:** *I always use period marks. Would you rather me use an exclamation point instead?*

**Me:** *Maybe! Let's see. Give it a try.*

**Baseball Daddy:** *Isaiah is staying with Max! I'll be there in ten minutes! Kennedy can crash at my house if she wants!*

**Me:** *Jesus. I get it. Stop yelling.*
**Baseball Daddy:** *I hate you.*
**Me:** *You don't hate me.*
**Baseball Daddy:** *You're right. It's just about the opposite of that. Stop texting me. I need to start driving.*

If I was a little more sober, that text might freak me out, but drunk and loose Miller doesn't mind it one bit.

# 31

# Kai

After knocking on Ryan and Indy's door, Rio is the one to answer.

"I thought this was a girls' night?"

He pops his shoulders. "It is."

"Are Ryan and Zee out of town?"

"Yeah, they're in Indiana for the night, picking up a crib that Zee's dad saved for him."

Following Rio inside, I find a very drunk and very goofy Miller lying on the ground of the living room, laughing with Indy and Kennedy.

I lean my shoulder on the doorway. "Stone-cold sober, huh?"

She finds me and that smile on her lips only grows. "You're so hot."

"Okay," I laugh. "Let's get your drunk ass home." Bending down, I scoop her up and hoist her over my shoulder. "Ind, I'm blaming this on you!"

"That's fine! Miller, let's do it again."

Miller lifts her head from my back and points at her. "Yes!"

"Ken, you okay to walk?"

Rio steps up. "Because if not, I can help with that."

"Rio, I love you, man, but Kennedy would eat you alive."

He shrugs. "That sounds nice."

Kennedy wraps her long red hair into a bun on top of her head as she follows me out of the house. "I'm a big fan of you guys!" she calls over her shoulder.

"Same here, sis!" Indy shouts.

Damn, drunk girls really do become best friends by existing in the same room.

Kennedy gets herself in the back seat of my truck while I get Miller in the passenger side. Reaching over her body, I click the seat belt into place.

She runs a palm over my face, drunk and so touchy because of it.

"Yes?" I ask.

"I like you."

A laugh rumbles in my chest. "I like you too, Mills."

"Will you kiss me?"

"You don't want me to kiss you casually, remember?"

"I changed my mind."

Maybe she did. Maybe she didn't. But there's not a world in which Miller Montgomery could ask me to kiss her and I would deny her.

With my hand still on the buckle, I lean in, nudging my nose against hers. She smiles and as soon as her lips curve, I press mine to hers, stealing the grin right off her face. A sweet little mewl rumbles in her throat so I kiss her for a moment longer before pulling away.

She licks her lips, grinning again before she rests her head back on the headrest. "Thank you."

"You're welcome, baby." I simply shake my head at her with a laugh, close the door, and round the side to the driver's seat.

After going through the McDonald's drive thru and spending more money there than I thought was possible, the girls sober up a bit, and when we get back to the house, Kennedy is the first to walk inside.

"You're kidding me," she says while Miller and I are still on the front porch.

"You didn't tell her Isaiah was staying here, huh?"

Miller groans. "I completely forgot."

Entering the house I close the door behind us, only to find my brother looking like the biggest fucking dork sitting in the living room with a giant grin on his face. "I didn't know *you* were staying here too."

Kennedy rolls her eyes. "I never would have agreed to it if I knew you were here."

Isaiah holds a hand over his heart. "You always know just what to say to make me fall, Kenny."

I know how hard Kennedy has worked to be taken seriously. There's not a guy on the team who doesn't think she's the best athletic trainer we have, but my brother can't *not* flirt with her even if his life depended on it.

"Kennedy, do you want me to drive you back to the city?" I offer. "I can take you home if you don't want to stay here."

She turns back to analyze my brother. "No, it's fine. Just don't be weird about it, okay?"

Isaiah perks up. "So, it looks like we're sharing the guest room. I'm a cuddler, Ken, and I prefer to be the little spoon."

"I just asked you not to be weird about it."

I gesture to the back door. "Isaiah, you're in Miller's van outside."

Kennedy's face splits in a victorious smile.

"Fine." My brother punctuates the word. "But I'm making you breakfast in the morning, and you're going to like it. How do you like your eggs?"

"Poached. Soft."

"Wonderful," he deadpans. "I guess I'll go watch some YouTube videos on how to do that because I have no fucking clue how to poach an egg, but I can promise you, they're going to be perfect. So, good luck not falling in love with me tomorrow, Kennedy Kay!"

Isaiah takes off to the backyard, rattling the house as he slides the door closed.

Kennedy turns back to us with a smile. "The guest room is this way?"

"First door on your right. Bathroom is across the hall."

"Does your brother actually like her?" Miller quietly asks once her friend is out of earshot. "I can't tell if he's joking half the time or not."

"Oh, he likes her. He only acts this fucking weird when he's got a crush." I slide my fingers between Miller's, pulling her down the hall to my room. "Come with me."

Opening the door, I let her wander in first. She takes her time looking around, never having been in here before. Her rules of our fling haven't let us share a bed until that night in San Francisco when Max was sick. When we're home, we have fun in her room and I tuck her into bed before coming back in here to sleep alone.

There's not much to my bedroom. A dresser. An en-suite bathroom. A baby monitor and a picture of Max on the nightstand next to my bed.

There are a few more framed photos on my dresser. One of Isaiah and me the first time we played against each other in the majors, a few pictures of us as kids, and some with us and our mom. Then there's one of only her.

Miller goes right to it, picking it up off the dresser, and I can physically see her sobering up as she looks at it. "She's beautiful."

"She was."

"Mae, right?"

I nod, standing by the door and keeping my hands behind my back, beyond tempted to reach out and touch her. She looks good in here. In my room. In my home.

Miller puts the frame back, gently running her hands over the other pictures and taking her time looking at them all. "It's always been just you and Isaiah, huh?"

"Since she died, yes."

Her attention moves back to me. "You're a good brother to him. Raising him the way you did. Sacrificing your childhood and college choice to stay close to home."

"He's my brother. I'd do anything for him."

She smiles softly. "Just how you'd do anything for Max."

"And you."

Her eyes flick to mine and a shy blush warms her cheeks. She's not one to be shy, but the girl is drunk and I'm seeing a whole new open side to her tonight because of it.

"I'd do anything for you," I repeat. "You know that?"

"I think I'd do anything for you too."

I'm not showing it on my face, but if I were to wear the expression my heart is feeling right now, I'd be grinning like an idiot.

She continues to look at the framed photos of my family. "Did you ever have anyone to talk to about everything you were going through? Losing your mom so young then having to raise both yourself and your brother?"

She might not know what she's doing, but tipsy Miller saying whatever she likes is cracking my heart wide fucking open, when I've been telling myself for weeks to keep it guarded with her as best I can.

When I don't respond, she looks back at me standing by the door.

I shake my head to tell her no.

"You can talk to me, you know."

"I know I can, but for how long? You leave in less than a week."

Miller's soft smile slightly falls before she turns back to my room, ignoring my question and continuing her tour. "You don't have a TV in here."

Worried I ruined the vibe, I pop off the door, coming up behind her and snaking my arms around her waist, lips dotting the skin of her neck. "A TV is a distraction. When you're in here, your attention should be on sleeping or on me."

She chuckles, her head falling back to my chest. So drunk and so in need of sleep.

"Go brush your teeth and get ready so I can put your ass to bed."

She stumbles her way to the bathroom and only a moment later, she pops her head out. "All my skin care is in here. And my toothbrush."

"It is."

"Why?"

"Because you've got only a few days left here and I'm done with your no-sleepover rule."

She looks back at her things then returns her attention to me. "That rule did kind of suck, huh?"

"All your rules suck, Mills."

She returns to the bathroom to get ready for bed. I can hear her brushing her teeth, the sound of the running water accompanied by her drunken humming. And when she comes back into my room, she's still wearing her clothes with today's make-up still on her face.

Miller sort of melts into the doorframe, watching me as I pull off my T-shirt, shoes, and pants, leaving me in only my boxer briefs.

"You're staring," I remind her.

"I am."

"You gonna change?"

"I need something to sleep in."

"Naked works for me."

"Works for me too, but I will jump your fucking bones if I'm left naked, Malakai, and you're the one who doesn't want to take advantage of me."

I shake my head at her—I always shake my head at her, but what's different now than the beginning of summer is I can't help but smile at her as I do.

I grab my previously worn shirt off the bed and toss it in

her direction. She strips, slipping my shirt over her head, swimming in it as it hangs mid-thigh.

Perfect, really.

She sways a bit on her feet as she stands in the doorway of the bathroom.

"Do you want help taking off your make-up?" I ask.

"Yes, please."

Turning her around, I usher her back into the bathroom. Her skin care is still lined up on the sink just as I left it earlier today, trying to replicate the way she had it in the guest bathroom. Lifting her to sit on the counter, I stand between her spread legs.

"You're going to have to tell me what to do."

She points to a bottle of clear liquid. "That goes on a cotton round."

I do as she says, squirting some onto one of her cotton pads.

Miller closes her eyes. "That'll take off the majority. Just wipe it off."

Hesitantly, I wipe at her cheek because that seems like a safe bet. A swipe of color comes off on the pad, so with a bit more confidence, I run it over her eyebrow and get a swipe of brown. I gently run it over her eyes as her mascara melts away, and I clean up as much as I can without leaving her looking too much like a raccoon. Then, I repeat the same to the other side.

"What next?"

She grabs another bottle, squeezing a pea size on my fingertip. "Just move that everywhere." She makes a motion with her hands, but that seems kind of rough, so instead I carefully swipe it across her jaw, using my fingertips to rub delicate circles until it starts to sud.

Miller is wearing a goofy smile as I work, and I can tell she wants to give me shit for this taking so long, but I ignore her and continue, making sure to get all the way to the edges of her face.

We go through the rest of her skin care routine, finishing with moisturizer, as she calls it, and when I put some on her skin, she takes some and rubs it on mine.

"For your mature skin," she says with a chuckle, swiping it over my face before dropping her hands to either side of my neck. "I missed you and Max tonight."

*Fucking hell.* She's got to stop, but I have a feeling she won't because she's buzzing with alcohol and her lips are real loose because of it.

"We missed you too." I rub the light purple cream onto her face. "Did you have fun?"

She nods with a childish smile. "I like those girls, and I like Kennedy. A lot."

"Good. I'm glad you two are becoming friends. I'm sure it's nice for her to finally have another woman traveling with us."

"Yeah, and it's nice to talk to someone when my head is a mess over you."

My chest rumbles in a laugh. "Your head is a mess over me, huh, Mills? I'm flattered."

"You should be."

When I'm done with her skin care, Miller wraps her hair in a knot, trying to secure a hair tie around it, but the girl is still drunk as a skunk.

"Let me have that." Taking the tie from her, I gather her hair in my fists, much in a way I've done a time or two before, as I make something resembling a bun, wrapping the hair tie around it twice.

Miller checks the mirror. "That looks terrible, Ace."

I smile at her. It does look terrible.

Her eyes find mine in the reflection. "Thank you."

"You're welcome."

"Cuddle with me?"

"I'm sorry, but did you just say *cuddle*?" I touch her forehead with the back of my hand. "What the hell did you drink tonight?"

"Shut up." She wraps her legs around my waist and her arms around my shoulders as I carry her back into my room. Once I've gotten the drunk girl in bed and the lights off, I remove my glasses and crawl in with her. Opening my arm out wide, Miller lifts her head, cradling herself against my chest like some kind of seasoned cuddler.

We don't talk. We simply lay together and I'm almost certain she's fallen asleep until she speaks into the silence.

"Tonight, I told the girls that sometimes I think about not going back to work."

I swear time stands still as those words leave her lips. My eyes shoot open, staring at the darkness, and replaying her words to make sure I heard them right.

I swallow. "Why do you say that?"

"I don't want to leave Max."

Goddamn, my heart is thundering against my chest, sharp pricks burning my eyes because this girl loves my boy so fiercely. It's something I wasn't sure would ever happen, to have someone else love my child in the way I hoped they would.

"But I have to go back," she continues.

Biting my tongue, I wait until I can find the right response. "Yeah," I exhale. "You do."

She tilts her head to look at me. "I do?"

"It's your dream, Mills. I won't let you walk away from that because of my son."

*Or because of me.*

She settles her head back into my chest. "The pressure to perform, to live up to the expectations, is scary. There's a part of me that battles with wondering if I'm worthy of those expectations, you know?"

"Pressure is a privilege, Miller. Expectations are high

because you're successful. If you were average, no one would be waiting on bated breaths for you. I think about that every night I take the mound. You just have to decide if your dreams and goals are worth the pressure. If you want to live up to the expectations set for you."

"I do. I want to be the best."

"Then do it."

That seems like the appropriate amount of encouragement for a result I'm absolutely dreading, so in a moment of selfishness I ask, "Does your career make you happy?"

She waits, flipping to look up to the ceiling, lacing her fingers with mine. "No."

Grinding my molars, I try my best to keep calm. There's a weird contradiction happening, me wanting her to find happiness, but in a way, glad that the thing that will take her away from me isn't it. But what the hell am I supposed to say? Encourage her drunken ramblings because her staying is exactly what I want her to do?

I promised her dad I wouldn't do that.

She's having fun this summer, which is the only reason she's questioning her job. Out of sight. Out of mind. That's all this is.

She'll remember it's what she wants as soon as she leaves here. Leaves me.

"But I don't know if it's about being happy," she continues. "I want to prove that I can do it. I want to prove that I'm worth the award I won. I want to prove that I'm doing something that justifies the fact my dad gave up his entire life for me."

And there it is.

"Miller—"

"Don't tell him I said that."

"Love isn't earned. Monty gave up his career because he loves you unconditionally. You don't have to pay him back by chasing accolades. That's not how it works."

"You don't get it, Kai. He gave up his entire life for me and he barely knew me. It's why I don't want you to retire yet. I don't want Max to feel like a burden the way I did."

"Miller." My tone is a bit sharp, mostly because I don't like her talking about herself in that way. "I can't think of a single person who would feel burdened by having you in their life."

"You did. When I first got here."

"Well, I changed my mind. Now I just feel lucky."

She doesn't have anything to say to that, so silence stretches between us for a long while.

"If I quit, I'd feel like a failure." Miller's voice shockingly cracks a bit, so I pull her into me, allowing her to speak her mind, drunkenly or not. "I thought I just needed a break this summer to get my groove back, but it doesn't simply feel like burnout anymore. It feels like I've spent my whole life chasing a career that I'm realizing, regardless of the awards and the prestige, isn't all that fulfilling. And over the last seven weeks I've been the happiest I've ever been, chasing Max around, spending time with my dad, being with you."

"Mills, you're twenty-five. You could change directions a hundred more times in your life, and you'd still never be a failure. You're too hard of a worker to ever be considered a failure. Life is meant to be spent chasing happiness."

She pauses and when she speaks again, it's simply a hiccup and the words, "I'm almost twenty-six."

I crane my neck to look down at her. "Define *almost*."

"I'll be twenty-six this week."

"Miller, when exactly is your birthday?"

"Saturday."

Four days. Her birthday is in four days.

"Why didn't you tell me? That's the day before you leave."

She shrugs against me. "I've never really had anyone to tell, I guess."

God, I know that sentiment all too well.

I pull her in closer. We're more alike than I ever thought possible. We've gone through our adult lives alone. Me because of the cards I was dealt and Miller because she has a hard time growing attachments when she bounces from city to city.

"Do you want more kids?" she asks, and the sudden change of subject startles me awake.

"Jesus. How drunk are you?"

"Just a little tipsy. That Big Mac really soaked it all up. Answer my question, Rhodes. Do you want more babies?"

If she would've asked me this back in June, the answer would have been a resounding no. Mostly because I didn't think I was doing a very good job with the one I already have, but spending the last seven weeks feeling like a family with the girl by my side has changed my view on it all.

If it were with her, the answer would be, "Yeah, I do."

She flips onto her belly, laying on me. "Yeah?"

"Yes. But next time, I'll be there for it all. I'll never miss six months again."

She crosses her arms over my chest, resting her chin there. "You deserve that. You also make really pretty babies, so you should keep doing that."

Chuckling, I tuck away the hairs that are falling out of her bun. "Do you want kids one day?"

"I never thought about it before, if I'm being honest. I've always been focused on the next goal, the next career move, and families aren't exactly conducive to high-end restaurant life. But if my life was different, I could see it. As long as they were exactly like Max."

My smile is soft. "He's a good one."

"The best one," she says with a sigh. "Kai?"

"Yeah?"

"Can we forget about some of my rules? For the rest of the week while I'm here? I just want to know what it'd feel like."

"You want to know how *what* feels like?"

"To be yours."

Watching her, I search for any sign she might take those words back when she's sober, but Miller's eyes are clear and bright. So, I lean down and press my lips to hers, kissing her in a way that isn't related to sex. Kissing her in a way that feels attached and full of strings because that's exactly what I am when it comes to her.

"Mills, you already are mine. Even if I haven't been allowed to show you, you've always been mine."

She settles back onto my chest. "Until Sunday. That rule has to stay."

That rule is the most frustrating one, but what am I going to do? Beg her to want me outside of this summer fling? Ask her to give up on her dreams to play house with me and my son forever?

She's too free, too wild to be tied down to me. She's too talented for me to ask that of her.

"Miller?"

She hums in sleepy acknowledgment.

"Today was a good day."

She smiles against my chest. "They could all be good days."

At least until Sunday.

Blinking awake, I find Miller's hair covering my face. Her ass is nestled into the cradle of my hips, her thick thighs melded to mine.

I lift to look at her.

She's still sleeping on my numb arm, fingers linked through mine. She's peaceful, warm, and looks like she belongs here, in my bed. I haven't had the privilege to wake up with only her since we became more, and somehow, I need to figure out how to make our next four mornings, our *only* four, last me a lifetime.

I kiss her inked arm, running my lips over the black floral lines, and for someone who lives so unattached, I'm surprised she was able to commit to something so permanent.

She stretches against me, her ass rubbing against the obvious morning erection I've got. "Good morning."

Her voice is even raspier than usual and it has my already hard dick standing at attention.

I pull her body closer. "Morning, Mills."

She's putty against me, still sleepy and so fucking pretty.

Languidly, she writhes against me, still waking up, but I can tell by the way she's moving she woke up turned on.

"I had a dream last night," she says. "Well, it was kind of a nightmare."

"Oh yeah?" I kiss the skin under her ear, my hand dipping under the hem of my shirt she's wearing. "Tell me all about it."

"I was in bed with a giant baseball player. Wears glasses. Tattoo on his thigh."

My palm drifts to her bare tits, running over the pebbled skin. "He sounds attractive."

"He was, but when I asked him to take advantage of me, he turned me down."

She rolls her ass against my cock, and I pull her tighter against me to do it again.

"What a dick. Clearly, he doesn't know what he's missing."

"Clearly." Her voice is breathy, and a moan laces her words when I tweak her nipple. "So I think it's only fair if you take advantage of me this morning to make up for that guy. Really stick it to him by sticking it *in* me, you know?"

I chuckle against her, my fingers tracing delicate circles over her stomach, running my palm over her smooth skin. "Is that what you want, baby?" I dip lower, my fingertips trailing over the top of her panties. "You want me to fuck you in my bed? You want to know what I'd be like if I got to wake up to you every morning?"

A little moan escapes her as she nods frantically, her thighs rubbing together as I toy with the hem of her underwear.

"You want to regret spending the last seven weeks sleeping in a bed that wasn't mine?"

"Yes." It's barely a puff of air, already so turned on simply from waking up.

The tip of my pinky slips under her waistband, running along the smooth, warm skin there before pulling out.

"Please," she begs, writhing on the mattress next to me and pushing her ass back into me. "Please, Kai. Don't tease me."

"Don't tease you, huh?" I nip at her earlobe, dipping my hand into her panties, my fingers grazing over her pussy. "Why not, when it makes you this fucking wet?"

She's soaked, dripping on my fingers already.

"Please." This time she bends to pull her panties down, kicking them off with her feet, and leaving her in only my shirt.

"You're so polite in the morning." Reaching behind me, I pull a condom out of my nightstand drawer, and as quickly as possible, I drop my briefs to sheath my cock in the latex.

"You want me to fuck you like this?" I ask, pulling her back to my chest.

She lifts her leg without hesitation.

"*Fuck*, Miller." Grabbing my cock, I run it over her core, coating the condom in her arousal before tapping it against her clit. "Honestly, this makes me hate your rules even more that we haven't been doing this every morning since you got here."

She rumbles the prettiest little whine. "Well, to be fair, you thought I was a lunatic when I first got here."

"Sorry to break it to you, but I still think that."

She chuckles, but her laughter dies, turning into a gasp as I wrap my arm around her leg, lifting her knee to her chest to give myself better access. I notch the head of my cock against her opening before pushing inside.

Groaning, I fill her. "How are you so fucking tight? And so goddamn wet."

We lay together, me inside of her but not moving other than our erratic breathing.

"I do a lot of pussy exercises, so that's probably it. Gotta keep her in shape."

I laugh into her hair. "Please, for the love of God, shut up."

She presses her ass into me, willing me to move and I do, thrusting into her from behind. I keep my arm under her, holding her to me, my other hand circling her clit as we find a rhythm.

"You're so perfect, Miller," I whisper into her ear. "So mine."

Her throat rumbles in the sexiest, most agreeable moan.

"You like hearing that?"

"Yes," she exhales.

"You're mine, baby."

She moves against me quicker so I pick up the pace, fingering her clit with a faster tempo.

I know the words are moot to her, simply thrown out in the heat of the moment, but to me, they're the most truthful words I can say.

If she'd let me have her, she'd be mine. I love the girl, and I try to show her through my actions, but if she ever gave me the green light, I'd tell her too.

"Kai," she cries, her body contracting. "I'm—"

She can't say anything else before her orgasm racks through her, always so fucking pretty when she comes. I want to commit the image to memory, every shudder, every moan. Knowing it's all I'll have of her in just a few days.

I continue to move inside of her, her pussy squeezing me as she comes apart.

"Are you close?" she asks as her chest expands with desperate inhales and exhales.

My breathing is labored too as I continue to thrust into her, loving how fucking warm she is and wishing this condom wasn't in the way so I could feel all of her. I haven't wanted to be that intimate with a woman before, and I especially haven't wanted that risk since Max came along. But with Miller, I find myself wanting everything.

"Can I taste you?" she asks.

I pause my movements, my cock throbbing and needy inside of her. "What?"

"I want you to fuck my mouth while you're kneeling over me."

*Jesus Christ, this girl.*

Pulling out of her, Miller sits up to take her shirt off, leaving her naked in my bed with her pussy still fluttering on my fingers from her orgasm. She situates herself back on the pillow, close to the headboard with an all too excited smile on her lips.

*How the hell is this my life?* I've come to ask myself that every single day.

That smirk of hers turns dark as she watches me remove the condom, tossing it aside before I climb over her, my knees on either side of her face, trapping her below me.

I raise a brow. "Are you sure about this?"

Her tongue darts out, licking the tip of my cock, nodding with excitement like the little minx she is.

"Goddamn," I exhale, shaking my head in disbelief. "I'm fucking obsessed with you."

Her smile lifts. "As you should be, Malakai."

I nod downward. "Put your mouth on it."

She guides my cock into her mouth, and I use the headboard for leverage, fucking her face just as she asked me to. Miller moans around me as if this is the hottest thing to ever happen and when I look back over my shoulder, she's got her thighs rubbing together, already needy to come again.

It was only a few months ago I was exhausted, wrung out, and on the brink of quitting my job just to get me through the day. And now, I've got the sexiest woman I've ever met below me who's not only a champ in the bed but has also brought so much light and fun back into my life.

I truly don't know how I got so fucking lucky to have her attention on me, but I'd do just about anything at this point to keep it.

# 32

## Miller

**Violet:** *Today is the big day! This is everything you've worked for. Are you excited?*

**Violet:** *Also, prepare to hit the ground running when you get back to work next week. Not only is Chef Maven stoked about having you consult at Luna's, but your* Food & Wine *interview is scheduled after you've settled in for a week there. Oh, and I have a mini virtual food-blog tour set up for that initial week as well.*

**Violet:** *Somehow, this break you took has made you even more sought after. Not even I could've planned this kind of positive press. We're all ready for you to be back and see what kind of inspiration you've been hit with.*

**Violet:** *Miller?*

**Violet:** *Why aren't you answering?*

Max is playing outside, trying to catch the bubbles Kai and Isaiah are blowing in his direction. I watch them all together through the glass of the backdoor slider.

"Chef."

Max smiles up at his dad, his blue eyes squinting with a full-tooth smile.

"Chef."

He crawls over to where Kai sits, climbing onto his lap as his dad tries to teach him how to blow an exhale against the bubble wand.

"Chef Montgomery."

Snapping out of it, I turn to find Sylvia, today's photo-shoot coordinator, looking at me as if I've lost my mind. Maybe I have.

I clear my throat. "Yes?"

"I was asking where you want the crew to put those?"

She points towards the rack next to the sink where Max's sippy cups and silicone plate lay to dry.

The kitchen is pristine. Kai was up before Max or I were awake to make sure it was spotless because, of course he did. He's done everything in his power to help me succeed in going back to work.

The only things left in the kitchen are the dishes Max used for breakfast this morning.

"I um . . ." I look around for a place to put them, but that's where they belong. Because this is someone's house, and yes, a toddler lives here.

"Just put them on the floor or something," Sylvia says, frantically waving her clipboard around. "The photos will all be from the waist up, so they won't be in the shot.

Her assistant bends at his knees to put the dishes down.

"No! Don't," I call out. "I'll take them."

I gather them in my hands, awkwardly holding Max's cups and plate so I can find a safe spot for them that's not the floor. But looking around, there's no free space because the kitchen has been overtaken and turned into a photo-shoot set.

Lingering in the opening of the hallway that leads to Kai's room, I watch as Sylvia and the photographer go over the different shots the magazine is looking for. Three different people work on the lighting. Another assistant preps glass mixing bowls with ingredients for me to appear as if I were working in front of the lens.

The house is chaotic; ten or so people, whom I've never met, mill around Kai's kitchen, working their hardest to make it appear as if we were in a high-end restaurant instead of the house occupied by a single dad and his son.

Nothing feels right. From the moment the first person shoved inside the front door with their equipment, I regretted my decision to do this here. How the hell am I supposed to look at that magazine cover when it releases in the fall, knowing this kitchen holds some of my favorite memories, none of which relate to the life or career that will be featured in the article.

This is the place where Max and I baked cookies together for the first time. Where I fell in love with the basics of baking again. Where Kai and I were so desperate to touch that we literally rode each other's bodies on the counter.

And now it appears as if it's never been used before, with blinding bright lights and strangers frantically running around.

As I hold Max's dishes, my attention slides to the backyard again. The three Rhodes boys have been outside all morning, keeping Max busy and away from the chaos of the house. Compared to the frantic kitchen, outside looks like a whole other world.

*My* whole other world.

The life I've built during my summer hiatus sits on the other side of that glass while I'm immersed back into my regular life. But now that family outside feels like my new normal while this, the chaos of a kitchen that I was so accustomed to before, feels like a space I don't belong in anymore.

"Chef Montgomery," a shoot assistant says, and it takes a moment to register that he's speaking to me. I haven't been called Chef in so long. It sounds odd when I hear it now.

He quiets his voice. "Can I just say that I am a huge fan of yours?" His eyes are wide and excited. "I'm in culinary school right now, but I volunteered today because I was hoping to meet you. The way you combine contemporary presentation and techniques with an experimental approach to ingredients is . . ." He shakes his head in disbelief. "Inspirational."

"Thank you . . ."

"Eric."

"Thank you for that, Eric."

"No thank you, Chef. I don't think there's a person in the industry who isn't waiting on bated breath for your return to the kitchen."

God, I've been so out of touch with that world these past couple of months, I almost forgot what it was like to be spoken to this way. To be treated as if I were some sort of celebrity.

It doesn't feel right while I'm holding Max's things in my hands.

Eric might not be able to think of a single person who isn't excited for my return, but I can.

Me.

"My name is Miller," I tell him. "Just call me Miller."

His brows furrow in confusion, and the poor kid opens his mouth to speak, but no words come out. I doubt he's ever been told by a chef not to call them by their title.

"Eric!" Sylvia calls out, circling her hand as if she were telling him to wrap it up. "Chef Montgomery, we need you ready in ten."

"I have to get back to work, but it was an honor, Che—Miller."

I offer him a placating smile and when he moves out of the way, my view of the backyard returns, only this time Kai is looking right back at me from his seat on the grass.

*You okay?* he mouths.

I shrug because honestly, I have no idea how to answer that. And without saying anything, I turn on my heel and head down the hall to his room.

The same room I now consider mine until I leave.

As of earlier this week, every night is spent here in this bed with Kai. Every rule either of us put into place has since been thrown out the window, other than our expiration date, and each day that passes with my walls down, defenseless, I can sense him seeping in, taking over my every thought, my every action.

Where he is, I want to be, but each passing moment feels as if there were a giant countdown plastered on the wall, constantly reminding us that our time is up soon.

And today . . . today is the biggest reminder yet.

Closing Kai's door behind me, I place the plate and sippy cups on his mattress, not really knowing where else to put them, but not wanting anyone out there touching Max's things.

I couldn't tell you why I'm acting like this. Today is just about taking photos. I still have another few days until I have to be fully back in work mode again, to put on the armor that's necessary to survive in the restaurant industry.

It just doesn't seem right to let even a second of that part of my life touch this one.

As I stand in front of the mirror, parting my hair down the middle and brushing it back slick to my scalp, the door opens. And only a few seconds later, Kai overtakes the bathroom doorway behind me, looking at me through the mirror.

"Hi, Mills."

I secure my hair the way I always wear it in the kitchen, polished and controlled. "Hi."

Kai keeps his attention on me through the reflection. I watch as his eyes trail my hair that's in a style he's never seen. He watches me remove my septum ring and place it on the bathroom counter.

"I look different, I know."

"Just a little different from the girl who was double fisting beers on an early morning elevator ride."

My chest rumbles in a silent laugh, thankful he was able to pull one out of me.

"What's wrong?" Kai asks, because of course he would know something was wrong with me on the inside even when I'm laughing on the outside.

I shake my head to tell him nothing. This man just gave up his entire home to help me. He's spent so much time and effort supporting me this summer.

"This is wild," he says. "To see this part of your life. It's impressive, but also intimidating."

My eyes flick to him, a smirk on my lips. "You're intimidated by me, Malakai?"

"I've always been intimidated by you. By how free you are. How brave and confident you are in your own skin. So why do you look so unsure out there?"

My smile drops.

It's a great question. I've been confident in my career for years. I've worked hard to be the best, so why am I thrown off by a few pictures?

"It doesn't feel right doing this here," I tell him honestly.

His face morphs in confusion. "Why?"

Why? Because since leaving at eighteen, I never had a place to call home and while this stay is just as temporary as the others have been, this home feels important to protect.

I spin to face him, gesturing towards the bed. "They were going to put Max's things on the ground. You and I are constantly washing his dishes, his clothes, and they were going to put them on the ground to get them out of the way. Who does that?"

Kai chuckles. "People who don't want sippy cups in the background of their cover shot for a magazine that caters to a luxury lifestyle. I don't know, just a guess."

This time I don't laugh because I'm too in my head.

"Mills, come here," he breathes, taking a single step into the bathroom. He crowds me with his tall body, taking me in a comforting hug, and with a single hand he brackets my cheek, tilting my chin up for his mouth to meet mine.

It's unexpected but needed as both my body and my nerves melt into his touch.

Kai's tongue slides against the seam of my lips and I open for him, letting him take control. It's centering and calming in a way only he is for me.

My favorite thing about this man is how stable, how constant he is. He takes on responsibilities others don't have the strength to handle, including settling me in this moment. I somehow need to figure out how to steal some of his resilience for myself so I can take it when I go.

Kai finishes with a simple press of his lips against mine before pulling away.

"Thank you," I breathe.

"I'm so impressed by you, Miller. And proud of you." He chuckles, his forehead falling to mine. "I don't know if that's weird to say."

"Not weird." I shake my head. "Just what I needed to hear."

Kai has been adamant about me going back to work, encouraging me to do so, and helping me as best he can. There's a part of me that wishes he would ask me to stay, to continue whatever we've been doing for the last two months, but most of me is glad he hasn't. It would only hurt him in the long run, to open himself to asking for more because, at the end of the day, I don't have a choice. I have to go back.

I can sense him about to ask again, wondering what's wrong with me today, but thankfully, a knock sounds at the bedroom door before he can. "Chef, we're ready for you."

We separate as I turn back towards the mirror, sliding my hands over my hair to smooth it down, and Kai comes back into the bathroom holding my chef's coat, perfectly pressed by one of the shoot assistants.

I haven't worn that coat in months, and the only reason I feel okay putting it on again is because Kai is the one holding it open behind me, allowing me to slide my arms through.

Through the reflection, he leans on the doorway, watching with a proud smile as I slip each button through their respective holes.

This man has supported me all summer, eager to help me get back to work at the level I want to be. He's constantly reminded me what a great job I'm doing, which are words I almost forgot existed. There's no coddling in the restaurant industry, and it's not something I ever thought I'd need. But after two months with him, I can't imagine working without Kai's encouragement constantly filling the kitchen.

When I try to leave the bathroom, he wraps an arm around my shoulders, pulling me in to place a single kiss on my forehead.

Leaning back, I eye him. "Did you just give me a forehead kiss while I'm wearing my chef's coat?"

"Mm-hmm."

"I've made grown men cry while wearing this coat."

"Oh, I have no doubt about that, but girl bosses need forehead kisses too."

"Did you just say girl bosses?"

"Yeah, isn't that what you kids say?"

That finally pulls a genuine laugh out of me, instantly making me feel lighter, more myself. "I refuse to believe there's only seven years between us."

"Come on," he says, ushering me out of the bathroom. "Go do what you're best at so we can get these people out of our house."

*Our house.*

"And by 'what you're best at' I'm referring to you standing there and looking pretty for pictures. Nothing to do with you being a badass pastry chef."

With another laugh rumbling in my chest, Kai gives my ass an encouraging tap as he continues down the hall to the living room, leaving me in the kitchen.

"Behind the island, Chef." Sylvia points to my starting position.

Glass bowls of dry ingredients line the counter as I find my place, standing behind the kitchen island.

"We'll start with some action shots." She pushes an empty glass bowl in front of me. "One at a time. Crack an egg in there."

Sylvia turns to say something to the photographer, but all I can focus on is the living room behind them, where Kai, Isaiah, and Max watch.

Max catches my attention and points at me from behind the lens. "Mmm," he hums, the only part of my name he's gotten down. "Mmm!"

He squirms in Isaiah's hold and slips his way out of his uncle's arms, racing his way towards the kitchen. Dodging the lighting crew and photographer, he rounds the island.

"Mmm!" Max wobbles towards me, arms in the air for me to hold him.

My smile is the biggest it's been all morning as I bend down to get him. "Hi, Bug. Come here."

"No!" Sylvia snaps as I pick him up. "Put him down! You'll wrinkle your coat!"

I freeze right there in the kitchen, holding Max and staring at this woman in disbelief.

"Put him down." Sylvia turns away, speaking under her breath. "This is not a place for kids."

I don't move, as if hearing those words has stunned me into place. She's not wrong. The high-end restaurant scene is no place for kids. The hours aren't conducive, with late nights and busy weekends. And I'm realizing now, that's exactly why I've been off today.

I know the life that's waiting for me when I return, and even if I wanted to continue a relationship with Kai, to be there for Max in some capacity, I won't be able to. There won't be time to.

I've had critics and chefs fawning over me. I've had their attention, but now the only attention I crave is that of a little boy and his dad, but as soon as I leave Chicago, they'll go back to their normal lives—ones that I'm not involved in.

"You are wrinkling your coat, Chef." Sylvia gestures to me, the other hand on her hip.

Certain realizations sinking in have me beyond done with her attitude today.

"Well, that's what photoshop is for," I snap, holding Max closer to my body.

"I got him." Without realizing it, Kai is at my side, pulling his son off me. "We'll see Miller after she's done working, okay, Bug?"

Sylvia exhales in exasperation, shaking her head and repositioning the glass bowls.

Eric the intern offers me a pitying smile while the photographer looks at the screen on her camera, smiling at the images she's shot so far.

Then I find Kai and Max slipping out the back door to go outside again and my terrible mood is in full force.

Standing in the kitchen, an overwhelming yet terrifying realization sinks in. The possibility I was feeling this way has been there, lingering all summer, but right now it's as if a blurry fog has lifted and the sun is shining on the truth.

There's no part of me that wants to be in the kitchen.

I only want to be with them.

# 33

# Kai

Today is Miller's birthday and it started just the way I wanted it to—with my face between her legs.

I've turned into a goddamn sap over the woman. So much so that, when she left to meet up with Monty for breakfast, I spent my morning in the kitchen doing what she typically does by baking her a birthday cake.

Miller tends to tell people she loves them through the food she makes, so I figured since I wasn't allowed to tell her, I'd show her in the same way she does.

As I said, I've turned into a fucking sap.

But other than Miller's birthday, it's also Family Day. The Warriors organization opened a portion of the field off the third baseline for family and friends to mingle. The food spread is borderline ridiculous, offering any and everything someone could want, with an open bar for drinks and a photobooth for pictures.

Family Day tends to be my least favorite day on the calendar. Every team I've played for has hosted one. It's a bit awkward when no one shows up for me, especially when the rest of my teammates have their siblings, partners, and parents there. But before Max, Isaiah was my only family, and he was always in the middle of his own season. Last year, we had each other and this year, we have my son.

And though Miller is technically here for Monty, I know she's here for me too.

That notion was solidified when I parked my truck and

saw her for the first time since she left my bed this morning. She had a birthday breakfast with her dad then showed up here wearing a white pinstriped Warriors jersey with my name and number on the back. It's unbuttoned and open, paired with a tight tank and cutoff denim shorts that are doing all sorts of things for her thick thighs.

But as good as she looks, her mood has been shit since yesterday's photoshoot and I'm not exactly sure why.

Rounding the high-top table she's standing at, I slide my palm against her lower back. "Do you want to introduce Max to Trav's parents with me? They're wanting to meet him."

She shakes her head, pulling her cocktail to her lips.

"Why not?"

"Because that'd be weird for Max's nanny to be there while you introduce your son to your teammates' parents."

Head jerking back, I stare at her, but she keeps her attention straight ahead towards the outfield.

It's beautiful out here, golden hour in Chicago. The sky is all shades of orange and yellow, and the field is cast with a warm glow. But the woman next to me is all ice tonight, vastly contradictory to the bright light she's brought into my life this summer.

"You're not just the nanny and you fucking know that," I remind her in a stern whisper. "What the hell is up with you today?"

She shrugs nonchalantly and takes another sip of her drink, flipping her hair over her shoulders.

I lean down to her ear, speaking quietly. "Toss your hair over your shoulder like that again, will you. It's giving me flashbacks to a much happier Miller with a mouth full of my cock."

Finally, the smallest, most discreet smile pulls at her lips.

"Jesus," I chuckle. "That's what gets you to smile? Am I going to have to fuck the attitude right out of you, or what?"

"Probably."

I find Max walking the length of the field with Isaiah before my attention falls back to the girl next to me. She's got her drink mid-air on the way to her lips, but I snatch it out of her hand and finish it myself.

"Hey!"

"You're being a brat today." I swallow down her cocktail and set the glass back on the table.

She scoffs. "I'm a ray of fucking sunshine."

"You've had an attitude since the photoshoot yesterday, and you won't tell me why."

She continues to remain silent. We don't tend to keep things from one another, other than how I truly feel about her, so not knowing what's going on in that pretty yet frustrating head of hers is grinding on my nerves.

We've got *one* night left together, and if this is her form of distancing herself in preparation, I'm going to be pissed. *She's* the one who is leaving. *She's* the one who wanted to remain detached. If there's anyone who should be mentally preparing for her departure, it's me.

I'm the one who broke my rule of not having sex with her, all while knowing I was going to fall fast and hard if I let myself add another layer of connection to her, and that's exactly what happened.

One of the equipment managers catches my attention in the distance, placing two gloves and a ball next to home plate. He gives me a small nod in confirmation before rejoining the festivities.

"Come with me."

"Why?"

"Stop being so testy today and come with me." Linking my fingers through Miller's, I pull her behind. We pass by the staff and their families on the way to home plate, and I just smile and nod my head in greeting as if dragging my coach's daughter behind me is normal everyday behavior.

"I can be testy all I want. It's my birthday." Miller halts. "Wait. We can't go on the field."

"I already talked to our groundskeeper. They're going to drag the infield later tonight, so we're good."

"Good for what?"

Grabbing the two gloves, I hold the pitcher's one out for her.

Her skeptical gaze drifts from the outstretched glove back to my face.

"I want to see you pitch, Miss All-American."

She quickly shakes her head. "It's been a long time."

"That's okay. You can ease into it."

"I won't be very good."

I've noticed this about her. She has a hard time being anything but the best. It's an odd contradiction to the girl who lives unattached and carefree, floating from city to city. But when she has a goal in mind, she has this innate need to be the greatest to do it. All-American pitcher. James Beard recipient. As if the titles mean she's accomplished something instead of simply doing it out of joy.

"I don't care if you're good or not, Mills. I just want you to have some fun with me while I've still got you."

She hesitantly takes the glove.

"We'll play for it," I say. "If you get a strikeout, I'll stop asking you what's wrong. If you get a walk, you start talking."

The most discreet tilt happens at the corner of her lips. I toss her the softball and finish with a gloved tap of her ass, sending her on her way to the pitcher's mound.

She goes about forty feet from me, not quite the full distance of the mound to home plate, but more accurate to the distance she's used to when playing softball.

"Can I warm up?" she asks.

I chuckle, crouching behind home plate. So competitive. "Yeah, baby, you can warm up."

Miller tucks the too-long sleeves of my jersey into the bra straps at her shoulders as she positions her feet into the dirt, gaining traction.

I'm accustomed to being the one out there in her place, but she looks damn good on this field, especially while wearing my last name.

With the glove on her left hand and the ball tucked in it, she practices her mechanics once before going full-in on her first pitch. The glove delivers a loud smack against her thigh, but not quite as loud as the sound the ball makes, slapping into my gloved palm and coasting right over home plate.

Well, fuck, that was a pretty pitch.

"I think I'm ready," she says, opening her glove for me to toss the ball back.

"Yeah, no shit, Mills. I thought you were going to be rusty."

She simply pops her shoulders and catches the ball, retaking her position to pitch again, hell-bent on making sure she doesn't have to tell me what's wrong with her.

About ten minutes later, the count is three and two. The pitches her dad called as balls instead of strikes have barely been outside of the plate, and if there were an actual batter playing with us, there's no way in hell they wouldn't have swung.

I'm not ashamed to admit that watching my competitive girl is getting me hard. She looks so good out there with the empty stadium behind her, the sun setting in the distance, and a small sheen of sweat building on her forehead. I want to lick it off her, but the problem with crouching behind home plate with a raging erection is that a handful of my teammates have all gathered to watch us.

They're really killing the mood here, but at the same time, it's a summer evening on my home field. I've got my son, my girl, and my brother as well as Monty and all the other guys from my team. My whole family is here, and tomorrow, everything is going to change. So, I'll soak it all in while I still can.

"Full count, Millie," Monty says as I toss the ball back in her direction.

"That last call should've been a strike," she calls out. "You need glasses, old man."

Monty chuckles behind me, playing umpire. He's being much tougher on his calls than he probably would if this were anyone other than his own daughter.

Miller digs her toes into the dirt, repositioning herself. She pulls her elbow back, simultaneously rocking back on her heels before running through her mechanics, her arm swinging in a full circle. Her movements are so fluid, so practiced, even though she hasn't done this in years, but I understand what it feels like to have that muscle memory. To have a pitch so ingrained in your body.

The neon ball soars, pounding against my palm as I catch it. It's a close one, just on the edge of the plate, so I hold the glove closed exactly where I caught it, waiting for Monty's call.

I'd call it a strike and not just because I run the risk of not getting laid tonight if I didn't, but because that was a nice fucking pitch.

"Ball," he declares. "That's a walk."

"Bullshit!"

"Let's go!" I cheer, shooting my arms above my head in celebration as I stand, keeping my taunting smirk right at Miller, where she stands in disbelief.

Monty laughs in a teasing way, and you can see how much he ingrained this competitive nature and work ethic into his daughter.

"Those last two calls were terrible, Dad."

Isaiah's got Max's hand in his. "Killer Miller! You've got a hell of an arm, Hot Nanny."

Charging at her, I heave her body over my shoulder like a sack of sand. I take off towards first base, running the bases like I just hit a grand slam, one hand cupped to the back of her thigh, the other raised in a single fist.

"Put me down, Rhodes. You haven't run the bases once in your entire career. Stop acting like you know what you're doing."

I can't help but laugh. Competitive Miller is a feisty little thing.

"A walk?" I taunt. "Kind of embarrassing, Mills."

"I hate you. You had the ump in your pocket!"

Chuckling, I continue my jaunt to home plate. "God, I love winning so much."

"Put me down!" Miller smacks my butt. "Jesus. I forgot how hard your ass is."

"How the hell did you forget? I've still got your nail marks there from last night."

That finally pulls a genuine laugh from her.

"Gross." Isaiah covers both of Max's ears, turning him back towards the rest of the team's families and friends. "C'mon, Maxie. Miller and your dad are being annoyingly happy. We single men don't need to hear about that."

With too many people still by home plate, I carry her to the pitcher's mound for some privacy before setting Miller back on her feet. She's wearing that too-big grin again, much more of *my* Miller coming back after a day of sulking.

When she goes back to working six to seven days a week, twelve hours at a time, I want her to remember this. How it feels to be surrounded by the people that love her, that she loves in return. That life is so much more than the money you make or the status of your job. It's about chasing your joy.

But then Miller's smile drops when she falls into my chest.

"I hated everything about that photoshoot yesterday," she finally admits. "I hated wearing that coat again and hearing them call me chef. I'm supposed to be excited. My career is taking off, and I thought it'd feel like a dream. *My* dream."

I never know what I'm supposed to say when she talks like this. Do I agree? Disagree? I just want her to be happy, and up until the other night, I thought her career was doing that for her.

"If it didn't feel like a dream, then what did it feel like?"

She peeks up at me, her chin on my chest. "A nightmare."

I push her hair away from her face, coaxing her to continue.

"I've been in a bad mood since yesterday because I didn't expect it to feel that way, and that makes me angry. I'm mad that something I worked so hard for doesn't feel fulfilling in the slightest. I'm angry that time is against us, and I have to leave tomorrow." She covers her face with her hands, shaking her head. "I should be excited for what's waiting for me, but I'm not. And regardless of how I feel about it, I have to go. There are too many people counting on me to get back to work, and as you can see, I'm a fucking mess over it."

Pulling her hands from her face, I run my palms up her arms. "Miller—"

She keeps her eyes down on the ground.

There's a part of me that wants to lean into what she's saying, to get my hopes up, but I know these feelings will fade for her as soon as she's back to her routine. It's simply the last night of her vacation.

And the last night I can indulge in this fantasy.

"Sorry. I'm fine. I'm just having a moment." She takes a deep breath, composing herself, when her eyes land on Max off in the distance with my brother. "You know, sometimes I look at him and get irrationally mad at you because you were with another woman before me. The audacity you had not to think of me then, you know?"

A bark of a laugh escapes me as Miller breaks the emotional tension with humor per usual, a sly little smile plastered back on her lips. Just where it should be.

Wrapping an arm over her shoulders, I kiss her head. "You are the most jealous woman I've ever met. You know that?"

Her head jerks back. "You've met other women?"

"Charming as always, baby."

"I'm sorry I've had an attitude today."

"That's okay, Mills." I quickly take her mouth with mine. "You know I appreciate all your flaws."

"Well, shit. I wasn't aware I had any."

"Mmm!" Max hums, attempting to say Miller's name as he charges in our direction, his little legs working so hard to eat up the distance. "Mmm."

I was really hoping she'd get to hear him say her name before she leaves tomorrow, but he's not quite there.

"There's my favorite guy," she says, bending down to hoist him in her arms. "Are you hungry? I'm hungry. Let's go find us some snacks."

With my name on her back and my son in my arms, Miller stands in the center of the field, looking like mine.

She should be mine. *Ours.*

"You coming?" she asks me over her shoulder.

"You two go ahead. I've got to go talk to your dad."

"All right. See you soon." She takes one single step away from me before I slip a finger through her belt loop, pulling her back to me.

Craning my neck I kiss her, right there in the middle of the infield where anyone could see, because this is not just a fling. Nothing about our situation is detached. She's it for me and I don't know how the fuck to handle that.

Monty is leaning back on the dugout railing, chatting with the last person I'd expect to find at our family day, seeing as he's the third base coach for Atlanta.

"Hey, Ace," Monty says, nodding towards the man at his side. "You know Brian Gould, right? He's a part of Atlanta's coaching staff."

"Yeah." I hold my hand out hesitantly, still not quite sure why a member from the team we played against yesterday is here. "Nice to meet you."

"You as well." His shake is firm. "You've got a hell of an arm."

"Brian and I were teammates for the entirety of my career," Monty explains. "So, we were just reminiscing about the good ole' days."

Ah, this is making much more sense.

"Still such a shame." Brian shakes his head. "You retiring the way you did. You had so much potential, and you gave it all up."

"For good reason," Monty corrects. "Hey, Miller is here, so I'll finally introduce you tonight."

"Monty, can we talk?" I interrupt.

"Everything okay?"

"Yeah, but we need to chat."

Monty nods towards Brian and that simple motion has him walking off, creating privacy for only the two of us. I lean back on the railing next to him, both of us looking out towards the field.

"You asked me to come to you if I ever had the urge to ask Miller to stay," I begin. "And while yes, I want to beg her to stay, I'm not going to. We both know she can't, and I don't want her to feel obligated to me or to Max, but I am going to tell her she's always got a home with us, and I just wanted to let you know before I do."

Monty remains silent, his attention stuck straight ahead as he simply nods.

"I mean, if that's okay with you."

Until now, I haven't had a father figure in my life since I was fifteen. Monty has not only been a close friend, but a sounding board when I'm struggling. So even though the topic is about his daughter, I need him.

"Are you not going to ask her to stay because you don't want her to feel obligated or because you're afraid she'd say no if you did?" he finally asks.

*Well ... shit.* Of course, there are some internal fears surfacing here. Everyone wants to be wanted, and yeah, I'm scared to put myself in the position to ask someone to want me when I've grown accustomed to people leaving.

I don't ask anymore—for help, for someone to stay. I simply do it on my own.

But the hope of not having to do it alone, of Miller truly wanting to be with me, almost outweighs the fear.

"I don't want her giving up her entire life for me only to realize I'm not worth sticking around for."

Monty's head whips in my direction, but I keep my attention straight on the field.

"Then you don't know her at all if you can't see the way she looks at you, like you're the best damn thing to ever happen in her twenty-six years of life."

That earns my attention.

"You just might be," he continues. "After me, of course."

The emotional tension is broken with humor, much in the way his daughter tends to do.

"I'll speak from experience. She doesn't feel obligated to your son, so don't let that thought cross your mind. She loves him in the way I love her."

We find the two of them, slowly making their way down the food table. Miller gives Max a bite of cheese then finishes the other half of it herself before moving on to the next snack and doing the same.

She does love him. And he loves her.

"She's not my blood, but she's my girl," Monty says from beside me. "And she looks at your boy, who is not her blood, in the same way I look at her. I've seen it all summer. I watched her fall in love with two people at the same time, and it reminded me of myself when I met her and her mom. She won't be able to just walk away from that, regardless of if you ask or not." Monty finally looks my way, eyes welling with unshed tears. "I know I couldn't."

"Fuck, Monty." Pressing into my eyes, I will the emotion back. "What the hell?"

He chuckles, but it's watery and choked.

"All those times I asked you to come to me first, it's not because I thought you weren't worthy of asking that of my daughter. It's because I was looking out for *you*. Miller has this intense need to be the best at what she does even if it's not something she loves all that much, and I wanted to have this conversation before you put your heart on the line. Kai, she might not stay, but I can promise if she goes, it's not because of you. You need to understand that."

I exhale a long breath. "I've noticed that about her, her need to be the best. Like she finds her worth in checkmarks and achievements."

"Yeah," he says. "Has she ever told you what that's about?"

"Not explicitly, but I have a feeling it has to do with how you two became a family. I think there's some residual guilt there. As if she feels at fault for taking you away from the life you were living at the time her mom died."

Monty nods, keeping his eyes out on the field and not on me. He clears his throat. "Yeah, I've had a hunch that's what was going on. We've talked about it, but I don't think she's ever truly understood that nothing about our situation was a sacrifice."

Finding Max and Miller again, I watch as my son lays on her shoulder, delicately tracing the ink where her too-big jersey is hanging off.

"Do you love her?" Monty asks.

"I do. Very much so."

"She might break your heart."

"I'll love her anyway."

"I know you will."

"I mean." I pop my shoulders. "At times, I still think she's way too fucking much."

"Right? The things that come out of that girl's mouth? Who the hell raised her?"

A laugh spreads between us, the emotional moment put on pause as we watch my son and his daughter together.

Monty exhales a contented sigh. "Just know that I loved her first."

I nod. "And I'll love her always."

To the left of me, Kennedy comes bounding up the dugout stairs with none other than Dean Cartwright on her heels. I'd instantly be thrown off if any member of an opposing team walked through our dugout, but Dean of all people? Every one of my senses is on high alert.

I don't like the guy, but he's never done anything to me personally. However, he went at my brother for years while we were growing up, and after our mom died, I did everything I could to protect Isaiah.

Dean went to a rival high school and slept with any girl he learned my brother was dating, which gave Isaiah a real fucked-up complex when it came to relationships, never once having a committed partner who didn't cheat on him. He constantly talked shit to him on the field, and though my brother likes to pretend he's unaffected, the truth is, to his core, Isaiah is sensitive.

Therefore, I've spent years keeping Dean away from him

unless we're playing against Atlanta, as we are this weekend. Anyone who creates an issue with my brother is automatically an issue for me.

"What do you think you're doing here?" I ask, popping off the dugout railing.

Dean wears the most annoying smirk as he turns my way.

"Game is tomorrow, Cartwright." Travis steps up. "You're not welcome here."

"Yes, he is," Kennedy says. "What is wrong with you guys? It's Family Day."

"Exactly," Isaiah calls out. "He shouldn't be here."

Dean turns on my brother and that annoying smirk morphs into a Cheshire Cat-like grin. Knowing and pompous. He takes a step closer to Kennedy, which has my brother seeing red.

Isaiah takes quick, fluid steps towards the two of them, but I intercept, hands on his chest to keep him back.

"Get the fuck away from her," he seethes over my shoulder.

Kennedy's eyes are narrowed in confusion. "Why are you acting like this?"

"Yeah, Isaiah." Dean slings an arm over Kennedy's shoulder. "Why are you acting like this?"

"Get your filthy fucking hands off her or I swear to God—"

"Stop acting like a deranged caveman," Kennedy chastises. "He's allowed to be here. Dean is my stepbrother. Chill out."

I swear the entire stadium goes silent at those words. My brother's body is frozen under my arm as my eyes lock with Miller's across the way.

"Stepbrother?" Miller asks. "So, your sister is . . ."

"Yes," Dean agrees. "My sister is the heartless bitch. I'm Team Kennedy, so don't worry about that."

Miller's lips curve into a smile and I'm not positive what that's all about, but I'm sure she'll tell me later.

"Kenny," my brother whines. "Please tell me this is some sick joke."

"You're so dramatic. It's not a joke. Dean's dad and my mom got married when we were in high school. So be nice. It's Family Day."

"Yeah, Isaiah." Dean shoots my brother a wink. "Be nice. It's Family Day."

# 34

## Miller

"Are you okay?" I find Isaiah with a bowl of pretzels in his lap, sitting and sulking by himself in the dugout while Family Day continues on the field.

"No."

Taking the seat on the bench next to him, I pop a pretzel in my mouth. "You can't blame her for being somewhat related to the guy."

"I don't blame her for anything. She's a literal angel who can do no wrong in my eyes, but I can blame her mother for having terrible taste in men and marrying who I can only assume is the devil, seeing as Dean Cartwright is Satan's spawn himself."

I fall forward in laughter.

"It's not funny, Miller. This is the worst possible scenario."

"Nah. It could be worse."

He scoffs. "How the hell could anything be worse than Kenny being related to Dean motherfucking Cartwright?"

"They could've been sleeping together, so I count 'step-brother' as a win."

Isaiah's brown eyes widen as I watch the realization flash through his mind. "Oh my God, you're right."

Feet dangling off the bench, I snag a few more pretzels.

"Happy birthday, by the way," he says, nudging his shoulder into mine.

"Thank you."

"It's going to be weird not having you here, traveling with us. All the other nannies have sucked."

God, I don't want to think about another nanny. I haven't even asked Kai what his plan for childcare is once I go, mostly because there's no part of me that wants to picture someone else in my place.

"Do you . . ." I begin. "Does he know who is going to replace me?"

"No one yet. The trainers and some of the staff have figured out a schedule to help Kai for the rest of the season so he doesn't have to bring someone else on quite yet. And depending how deep we go into the playoffs, we only have a month or so of baseball left at best."

I quickly nod. "That sounds . . . good."

He swings an arm over my shoulder. "You're irreplaceable, Miller. No one else will ever be the Hot Nanny."

My chest rumbles in a silent laugh. "Always the charmer, Isaiah Rhodes."

"How are you holding up?"

"Not great."

"I assume you're a mess over leaving *me* and it has nothing to do with my brother or nephew."

"You're charming *and* brilliant now? You really are becoming a whole new man."

He chuckles. "Do you think you'll be back to visit soon?"

His question holds so much hope, and I know that hope is strictly for his older brother.

"I don't think so. Work keeps me busy, and at this point I have sixteen kitchens I'm scheduled to consult for. That's four years of bookings."

"Four years?" His tone is filled with shock. "Hell, I don't know what I'm even doing in four *days*, let alone in four years."

When I first opened my schedule to consultation services, I wanted every booking I could get. I didn't have much family or friends I was worried about penciling in. I had my attention laser focused on being the best, but now the lack of free time, the lack of a social life sounds dreadful.

And awfully lonely, if I'm being honest.

"Can I be serious for a moment?" he asks. "And you know this is important because I'm very rarely serious."

"You and me both."

"I know. We drive my brother nuts."

I pop another pretzel into my mouth as Isaiah adjusts himself on the bench, trying to get comfortable when getting serious makes him anything but.

"Malakai is the best person I know. He's my best friend and the best dad to his son. As I've gotten older, I've begun to realize everything he's done for me. No fifteen-year-old should've been left to raise their sibling. He got me through our mom's death. He got me through high school. He taught me how to drive. Hell, the guy even took me to buy my first pack of condoms." He chuckles to himself. "Which is ironic now, seeing as he's the one who ended up with an accidental pregnancy."

We find those two, Max tugging at the flips of dark brown hair curling out from Kai's hat.

"What I'm trying to say is that my brother deserves the world and for him, *you* are the world."

My pulse is thundering, my heart pounding in my chest. There's an odd contradiction happening inside of me. I want to be his world because he's quickly become mine, but the last thing I want is for this man to get hurt because of me. Isaiah doesn't have to tell me these things. I know how good his brother is, how much he deserves. It's what made me fall in love with him when I was trying so hard not to.

I realized it yesterday at the shoot. I didn't know what it felt like to be in love, and the realization that I am snuck up on me in the worst way possible. I leave tomorrow and I'm in love with Kai and his son. I'm in love with the life and friendships I built here.

And none of it matters because this was simply a pit stop to getting back to my real life.

"If there's any chance of you coming back to see them . . ." Isaiah shakes his head. "I don't know what I'm asking here. I'm just trying to repay Kai for everything he's done for me, and I've never seen him look at someone the way he looks at you. I've never seen him so immersed in someone else's orbit, and I don't know how you did that. If you found a crack and wormed your way in or what, but he's been so focused on Max for the last year that he forgot about himself. But you . . . you didn't forget about him. I'm asking that you don't forget about him when you go."

"Isaiah." My head falls to his shoulder with an exhale. "Trust me, I'll never be able to forget your brother."

I'll never ever be able to forget about Kai *or* his son. They've etched themselves onto my soul and unfortunately, I'll never be able to tell Kai that, to give him any sign of hope that I could stay. Tomorrow I leave town, and I'm hurting, aching at the homesickness that's already begun to settle into my bones.

It's one of our rules—no grand declarations of love.

I asked Kai to remember that we're simply a summer fling, and I'm praying for his sake that I'm the only one who forgot.

"Hey, are you Miller? Emmett's daughter?"

Looking up, a man that looks to be my dad's age comes hopping down the stairs into the dugout. He seems nice enough until I zero in on Atlanta's team logo on his quarter-zip.

Lifting my head off Isaiah's shoulder, I say, "Yeah, that's me."

"I'm Brian. Your dad and I used to play together in the majors back in the day."

"Oh, very cool. It's nice to meet you. Are you working for Atlanta now?" I gesture towards the logo on his chest.

"I am. I'd love to come and work with your dad someday, though. He and I used to make a hell of a pair. In fact, he was my catcher until he decided to retire mid-season while we were on a World Series-winning pace."

The smile on my lips falls. He retired that season because of *me*.

"He and I both would have our own rings if he stayed and played out that season, but he just had to call it quits. Absolutely wild to me." Brian shakes his head in disbelief.

"It was a . . . tough time for us then."

"Yeah." He exhales a humorless laugh. "It's a shame that his rash decision cost him his career."

Isaiah looks from the Atlanta coach to me. "What is he talking about?"

I shake him off, realizing Kai hadn't even told his brother about Monty not being my biological dad or how our family came to be.

"Emmett quit mid-season to adopt her." Brian gestures to me. "She didn't have anywhere to go so he left the league and started coaching at some tiny shithole of a college. He gave up a good chunk of change over it too."

I can feel Isaiah's attention burning into the side of my face, but all I can do is keep my head down, staring at my feet. As if I didn't still feel guilty all these years later over my dad giving up his life for me, this random dude had to remind me with an audience present.

"Your dad said you're some big-shot chef now." Brian continues. "Said you're going to be on the cover of some magazine soon. That's good to hear. At least you're doing something impressive with your life after he gave up his."

"Hey." Isaiah stands from the bench. "What the hell is wrong with you?"

Brian seems genuinely confused, as if he were simply stating facts and not trying to make me feel bad with his words.

"Isaiah, it's okay." I pull his arm back for him to return to the bench next to me. "He's right."

As much as the words burn to hear, it's exactly the reminder I need to get through tonight and back on the road tomorrow.

# 35

## Kai

Miller is looking out the passenger window of my truck, watching the city skyscrapers as we leave downtown to head home.

I don't ask what's wrong because we both know. She leaves in a handful of hours; the countdown on our time together hits zero in the morning.

Eyes flickering from the road ahead of me back to her, I reach over the center console, splaying my palm over her thigh. Miller exhales against the glass before she covers my hand with her own, holding on tight.

She smiles at me over her shoulder, but it doesn't reach her eyes.

Miller is the one to grab Max out of his car seat when we get home, holding him to her chest as we walk inside. She won't put him on his feet or let him go, and I understand that sentiment all too well. I do the same when I'm heading to the field for the day, but unlike me, when Miller leaves the house tomorrow, she won't be coming back.

When she starts for his room, I stop her, snaking my hand over her waist. "Hold up." I nod towards the kitchen. "I have something for you before we put him to bed."

The skin between Miller's brows creases, but with my son on her hip, and her looking like my fucking dream, she follows me into the kitchen.

Max claps enthusiastically, really boosting my ego as I put the cake I made on the counter right in front of a world-renowned pastry chef.

"Did you make me a cake?" she asks.

I look up to find her staring at it, bottom lip tucked between her teeth.

"It's your birthday, Mills. Everyone deserves a birthday cake."

She smiles the saddest smile I've ever seen. "I haven't had someone else make me a cake since I was a little girl and my dad tried. It wasn't very good, though."

"Well, keep your expectations low. I have a feeling Monty and I have similar levels of skill in the kitchen."

She laughs, but I can hear the emotion sitting in her throat. Today is hard for her and yes, in a way I wanted her leaving to be hard. I wanted her to feel so connected to a place or a person that it'd hurt in the best way when she had to leave them, but I fucking love the girl and the last thing I want is for her to be upset, especially on her birthday.

"The cake is from a box so we should be safe there, but I did have to make my own frosting. That's where the problem could be." Shyly, I scratch the back of my neck.

She takes a small swipe off the edge, offering a bit to Max on her finger, and as soon as it's on his tongue, his face scrunches as if this was the worst form of torture and not a sweet dessert.

"Oh, no," I grumble. "That's not a good sign."

Miller takes another swipe on the same finger, putting it in her mouth. She nods as if she were contemplating. "This tastes like shit."

I can't help but laugh.

Her green eyes soften. "Thank you, Kai. This is . . ." She simply nods, unable to add more words.

"The best cake you've ever had?"

A smile tilts. "Something like that."

Leaning over the kitchen island that separates us, I kiss her. "One more thing."

"One more thing?" She bounces Max on her hip, nuzzling into him. "One more thing, Bug?"

He giggles as I slide a small gift bag across the counter. Her attention bounces from it to me. "You didn't have to get me anything."

"It's small. Almost nothing, really."

Max reaches down, pulling out the dark yellow tissue from the top of the bag.

"Good helping," Miller encourages, dipping her hand in.

I watch her as she takes in the framed photo. Her face morphs, her tongue poking the inside of her cheek and her eyes taking on an instant sheen. She keeps her attention on it and when she blinks, the first tear falls.

"Mills—"

She shakes me off, continuing to look at the picture. It's a photo Isaiah snapped a couple of weeks back. Us on the couch in the living room with Max taking a nap on her and her using my thigh as a pillow. Her chocolate brown hair spills over my legs, and I've got my hand on her head, looking down at her like she's the best thing I've ever seen.

"Mmm, sad," Max says, pointing at a tear falling down her cheek.

She wipes it away. "No, baby. I'm not sad. I'm happy. I'm just crying because I love you so much."

*Fuck.* Now I'm going to start crying.

How the hell is this just *over* tomorrow?

I clear my throat. "I got the same picture framed for Max's room."

And for mine.

"And there's a card in the bag."

Miller shoots me a deadpanned glare, as if telling me that making her cry once today was enough. She sets Max to sit on the counter as she digs back into the bag and pulls out the birthday card.

It's simple, nothing flashy or extraordinary about it, but on the inside Max went to town with green and orange crayons. It's covered in his scribbles and at the very bottom, I signed it for him.

*Happy Birthday, Miller.*
*I love you.*
*Love, Max*

She exhales a breath of a laugh. "Did you make this for me?" she asks my son. "Thank you, Bug. This is beautiful. I'm going to keep it forever and look at it whenever I'm missing you, which is going to be all the time."

I watch her as she watches my son. She runs her hand over his hair, her attention flicking back to her card.

"Thank you." Those words are directed at me.

"Happy birthday, Mills. I hope it's your best one yet."

Her greens flick to me. "It is. Because of you two."

We don't usually do bedtime together. If I'm home in time, I put him down, and if I'm still at the field, Miller gets him to sleep. But tonight being her last night here, we both go into his room.

I change his diaper, get him in a pair of pajamas, and do a quick brush of his little teeth, but I hand him over to Miller so she could be the one to rock him to sleep. She's only going to have an hour or so with him tomorrow before she hits the road, so I'll give her as much time as she wants tonight.

They take a seat together in the rocker as I stand by the door, watching, trying to burn the image into my memory.

Max is so close to passing out for the night, so she doesn't even pull a book to read. She simply holds him to her chest, rocking back on the chair. Her face is etched in agony, knowing this is the last time she's going to do this with him. Her brows are pinched, her chin a bit wobbly.

"Miller," I whisper, but she shakes me off like she wants to feel the sadness, sit in it and let it consume her.

Max slowly lifts his head from her chest to look at her and she finds the strength to give him a smile. His little finger goes right to her septum ring, touching it cautiously.

"I love you, Max." Her voice is barely audible.

"Mmm," he hums her name, touching her face as gently as he can.

"You almost got it. One day I'll get to hear you say my name. You'll have to make sure your daddy records it for me when you do."

He looks right at her, his icy blues boring into her, and there's absolutely no misunderstanding when he says, "Mmm . . . Mama."

Miller's face falls. "What did you say?"

"Mama." Max grins, so proud of himself for saying a name I now realize he's been trying to say for weeks. "Mama! Mama!"

Miller's head whips in my direction. She's on the brink of an emotional meltdown while holding my son, who is looking at her as if every missing puzzle piece in his life has been put back together.

He settles himself back on her chest, quietly repeating the word over and over again while Miller rocks him and cries her fucking eyes out.

And I watch her heart break from the doorway while mine breaks for both me and my son.

# 36

## Miller

Once Max is asleep in my arms, I get him settled in his crib so I can get out of this room, bolting right past Kai standing in the doorway.

"Miller," he calls out, but I don't stop or slow, needing to get to the bathroom. Needing a second alone after what Max just said.

Before I can get away, Kai circles my elbow.

I turn to face him, and I know there's no hiding how upset I am from him. "I never asked him to call me that. I promise I didn't."

Kai shakes his head in confusion. "What? I . . . I know that."

This little boy, who I love more than I knew I was capable of, just looked at *me* and called me his mom. "I'm going to ruin him."

"What are you talking about?"

"His own mother left him, and now I'm going to leave him tomorrow, and he just called me that." I gesture towards Max's bedroom, tears streaming down my face.

"You're not leaving *him*, Mills. You're just leaving."

"This was supposed to be an easy summer. I was just going to help you so I could spend some time with my dad. I don't want to hurt him, Kai, and there's no way around that now. What the hell happened?"

I'm frantic, spinning out of control. I've never been one to get emotional, but these two boys have turned me into an emotional wreck.

Kai steps into me, cradling my cheek with his palm, attempting to calm me the way he always does. "What happened is he fell in love with you, and I think you fell right back."

I suck in a shuddering sob. "We had rules to prevent this kind of thing."

*Rules that didn't do shit to keep me from falling for them both.*

"No, Mills." He gestures between us. "*We* had rules. You couldn't have stopped him from feeling that way towards you, and I think a big part of me knew that from day one."

Of course, he knew. I remember him telling me how scared he was for his son to grow attached to someone else who'd be leaving. Regardless, I stayed, and look what happened.

"You were right, Kai. I should've left after the first night in Miami."

"Don't say that."

Hands on my head, I try to control my breathing. "I'm going to break his heart tomorrow, and I don't know how I'm supposed to live with that."

Kai swallows the distance between us, wrapping his arms around me to pull me into his chest. Sobs wrack my body then, knowing that he's got me. He'll settle me one last time.

"I haven't earned that title," I say into his shirt. "I haven't done anything to be called that."

"Yes, you have, Miller. Contrary to what you believe, you don't have to be the best to earn a name for yourself. I know you. I know you're having a hard time grasping what just happened because this wasn't a goal you set out to achieve, so yeah, you're feeling undeserving of the name. But what if I waited until I was the best possible dad to allow him to call me that? He'd be waiting for the rest of his fucking life."

I bury myself deeper into his chest. He's right about how I feel. I'm not good enough to be this boy's mom. I don't even know how to help him when he's sick. I don't have those natural motherly instincts.

"I see the way you are with him," he continues. "How much confidence you give him just by being there for him. How much you love him. Trust me, I know how fucking scary it is for someone to view you that way, and tomorrow when you go, I'll start straightening that out for him, but it's not because you're underserving of that name."

*It's because I won't be around to have it.*

Inhaling a calming breath, I step back from him. "I shouldn't have been so close with him this summer, Kai. I should've kept the line clearer that I was just passing through."

Kai's icy gaze hardens. "Why? So my son could spend time with someone who doesn't make him feel like he's the most important person in the world the way you have? Or so he wouldn't know what it feels like to be loved the way you love him? That's bullshit and you know it. Or are you saying that in regards to me? That you should've kept the line clearer with *me* that you're just passing through."

I should've kept the line clearer for *myself* because this hurts. Every word feels like an arrow straight to the heart, sharp and painful. This is exactly why I've remained detached because loving someone when your paths are running in different directions is the worst kind of torture.

Kai takes off his hat, placing it on the kitchen island, running an aggravated hand through his dark brown hair. "God, Miller, you try so hard to keep yourself detached. To live this lonely life, and I don't fucking get it."

I know he's speaking, but all I can see is his hat sitting upside down on the kitchen island. The same photo of Max is tucked into the inner brim, but now there's a new addition. I could pick out that picture anywhere. The bright yellow T-shirt is hard to miss after seeing it on my dad's desk every day this summer.

"What is that?"

Kai follows my line of sight, staring right at his hat. His exhale is defeated. "You know what that is."

"Why? Why would that be there? Why is it next to Max's picture?"

He doesn't answer me, so I pull my attention away from the picture to find him staring at me and it isn't until he has my full attention that he says, "Because when life or work gets too stressful, too overwhelming for me, I'm able to see who matters most. And that's you, Miller." He shakes his head. "And it's in there because I'm so fucking in love with you, it's too painful *not* to be able to see you every second of the day."

I shake my head frantically, as if the words will disappear if I do. "No, you're not."

We had rules that I needed him to follow. Rules that were set in place to keep me from hurting him. I can deal with breaking my own heart, but I can't live with breaking his. It's happened too many times in his life.

"I am." He throws his hands up in defeat. "I fucking love you, and I'm sorry that neither my son nor I could control how we feel about you. I'm sorry that this is the last thing you wanted to hear, but I'm not sorry that I do."

"Kai," I cry, fresh tears streaming down my face. "You can't. We just . . . we got caught up in this. We had rules."

"Fuck your rules, Miller!" he bursts, pacing the hallway that leads to his room. "I'm not asking you to love me back."

*But I do.*

"But I'm not going to keep pretending like I'm not absolutely fucking ruined from having you for the last two months. I know this is the last thing you wanted, but I'm not going to apologize. You're my favorite person, Miller, and for once I had someone for *me*. I had someone taking care of *me*. After being alone for so long, I finally had someone looking out for *me*."

"I haven't been taking care of you." I frantically shake my head. "You were the one taking care of *me*."

"You've been taking care of my heart, Mills, and I've been taking care of yours."

Using the back of my hands, I attempt to clean my face, but the stupid tears won't stop falling.

"Fuck," he breathes. "I didn't want to tell you because I knew it'd scare you, make you run. But I guess it doesn't matter anymore because you're leaving tomorrow anyway."

"You want a family to raise your son around. I don't have that, Kai." I swear I'm looking for anything to talk him out of his feelings. "I only have me."

"I only want you! We already have a family, Miller. My friends, the team, your dad. And you. I just want you."

"I didn't want to hurt you," I squeak out. "I knew I was leaving the entire time and I let you get attached. I let *myself* get attached, and now I'm just another person that's going to leave you."

Kai moves into the kitchen, hands braced on the counter in front of him. The kitchen where so much of my summer was spent. Where so many of my favorite memories were made.

"Miller, you're not just another person." He won't look at me, his attention locked on the ground, and I catch the first tear fall from under his glasses, hitting the floor. "You put me first when I forgot how to. You reminded me what it felt like to be important, to be chosen first. I know you wanted this to be easy and detached, but you're fucking in here." His fingers meet his chest, tapping it a couple of times, blue eyes meeting mine, and full of pain. "You're everywhere, and when you leave tomorrow, I'll still see you everywhere. In this kitchen. In Max's room. In my bed. There's nothing about us that's easy. This is fucking miserable, Miller, knowing there's a clock counting down the seconds until I don't have you anymore, but I'd do it all over again. I'd fall in love with you all over again. I'd break my heart all over again because loving you was one of the two greatest surprises of my life."

His other being his son and being compared to the most important person in his life has my head falling back, trying to catch my breath.

Kai's hands are fisted on the counter, shoulders low and defeated. He's bent over in agony, a physical representation of how I feel.

"If I could . . ." he continues, shaking his head. "I'd chase you. I'd spend every free day on an airplane to get to you, even if that meant I only got to kiss you once before I had to fly back to Chicago. I'd spend my off-season living out of a hotel or out of your fucking van just to be close to you, but it's not only me I'm making decisions for anymore. And because of that, I don't want you to say anything. Don't tell me if you love me, and fuck," he exhales a painful laugh. "Please don't tell me if you don't. But especially don't give me any hope because if you do, I have a feeling I'd chase you across the country until you were caught."

Unable to keep my distance from him, I slip under his arm to meet him chest to chest. "Kai," I whisper, short of breath and overwhelmed by his confession.

There's so much I want to admit, but when I search his eyes, looking for the right words, he simply shakes his head, begging for me not to say any of it. So instead, I lean up on my toes, pulling him down to meet my lips, kissing him in a way that I hope conveys just how much I love him.

Leaning back, I run both my thumbs across his cheeks before slipping his glasses off. He's so handsome, so mine. At least for tonight.

One last time.

"Please," I whisper, eyes searching his.

He chuckles, but it's stunted without humor. "We're past playing hard to get, Mills. You never have to ask."

Craning his neck, he takes my mouth in a searing kiss, simultaneously lifting me from the ground and carrying me to his room.

He lays me back on his bed so gently, so reverently, before settling between my open legs, never once peeling his lips from mine. His chest is already pounding against mine as I try to take it all in. Every needy kiss, every tender stroke.

It feels cruel in a way, to indulge in each other one last time. The awareness that this is it, this is the last time, is heavy in the air.

Kai guides my arms out of his jersey I'm wearing and all I can think about is that day at the field when he told me he liked seeing pretty girls in his jersey and liked to take it off them too. But he's not wearing that cheeky smirk he wore that day. Tonight, his face is tormented as he peels his last name off me.

When I take off his shirt, I follow with a path of kisses up his stomach and chest, his lean muscles contracting in the wake of it all. He cradles my cheek, pulling my mouth back to his, breathing labored against my lips.

Every movement is languid, focused.

We kiss for longer than we ever have. We touch and explore. We just do more, more of whatever will drag this night on as long as possible.

"Undo my belt," he murmurs against my lips.

I do as he asks while we continue to kiss, tongues stroking, searching for one another.

When his pants meet the floor, he undresses me in the same explorative way, kissing every inch of my skin and worshiping my body until we're both naked and writhing and wanting.

Kai's hips are settled against mine, his rigid length rubbing right where I want him as we kiss and ache.

He reaches to his nightstand next to me, but I put a hand on his to stop him.

His confused gaze meets mine.

"I'm on birth control."

"Miller—"

"Please, Kai." Stroking the side of his face, I hold his attention. "I need you, all of you. One time. For the last time."

His throat moves in a deep swallow. "Are you sure about this?"

"Yes, but only if this is what you want too."

He searches my face for a moment. "It is."

"I'm . . ." I shake my head. "I haven't been with anyone else this way."

"Me neither."

"But—"

He exhales a breath of a laugh. "When I said Max was a surprise, I meant it. You're the only person I've ever wanted to be this close to."

His fingers find me first, dipping between our bodies and running the entirety of my core. I can feel how ready I am by how easily he slides over me.

His steely blues close when he feels me. "So wet, Mills."

I open my legs a little wider for that, arching my back and running my pussy over his erection.

Kai uses his wet fingers to slick his cock, coating him in me. He settles on top of me again, holding himself up on one arm as I stroke his back, keeping him close.

He watches me with rapt admiration as he slicks himself against my seam, his lips dipping to taste mine again.

"Please let me say it," he whispers against me. "I've tried to show you all summer, so let me just say it on the last night I have you."

"Tell me."

He nudges his nose against mine. "I love you. God, I love you so much, Miller, it feels like it might kill me."

I quickly nod because he won't let me say it in return as I try to keep the lingering emotion held back, my hands running to his lower spine to urge him inside of me.

And with that confession, he tilts his hips and pushes inside.

Skin to skin.

Warm and tight and so breathtakingly full.

Our gaping mouths dust one another's, our beating chests rising and falling in sync.

"Oh my God," I exhale. "Kai, you feel—"

"Incredible. You feel incredible, Miller," he finishes for me. "I can feel every inch of you."

Everything about this feels attached. Not only the physical bond, but his heart and mine. It feels like we belong here, together, and the knowledge that I'm the reason this ends tomorrow has the burn of fresh tears welling at the base of my lashes.

I'm overwhelmed. With his body. With the way I feel about him. With the aching reminder that tomorrow it all ends.

Kai moves, slowly rolling his body on mine, his pelvis hitting my clit in the most delicious way with every slide. I hold him to me as the room fills with desperate gasps and panting breaths. He decorates my skin with soft bites and soothing kisses, murmuring how much he loves me, how thankful he is for me, how much I changed everything for him.

But can't he see I'm the one who's different?

I'm the one who has been completely unassembled and remade in the last eight weeks.

"Miller," he whispers, using his thumb to wipe the falling tears from my cheeks. "Don't cry."

I stroke the side of his face, holding eye contact. "I can't help it."

He continues to move inside of me, this overwhelming amount of love surrounding us both. Kai kisses my cheeks, cleaning up my face as the tears continue to drown me, suffocating my senses. He lifts one of my legs closer to my chest, hand cupping my ass to get himself deeper, closer, and I've never felt anything like it.

It's intimate.

It's connection.

It's love and it's terrifyingly painful because it's all going to end.

Kai pulls back to look at me and it's then I see the sheen over his eyes. He feels it all too.

"Miller," he says, making sure my attention is on him. "If you ever decide to stop running and make a home . . . Make it with me."

A choked sob escapes me, and all I can do is nod in agreement. If I ever changed my life, switched directions, it wouldn't be for anyone other than him.

We hold each other as our bodies move in sync, letting them say all the things I can't.

And that night, when Kai whispers that today was a good day against my skin, I don't tell him that they can all be good days.

Because for me, this was the very last one.

# 37

## Kai

"Ball!" the umpire calls.

*Fuck.*

I'm about to walk this fucking batter and subsequently walk a run in from the loaded bases . . . for a second time this inning.

Shaking it off, Travis stands from his crouching position, tossing me the ball from behind home plate. Even with his mask covering his face, I can see the concern in his furrowed brow.

"Come on, Ace," Cody calls from first base.

"Let's go, Kai," my brother adds.

Exhaling, I pace the mound but all I see is her.

Miller wearing my jersey and holding my son on this mound.

I'm a fucking mess over the visuals, the memories. And they only grow worse when I take my hat off and see her there too.

It's been one week.

One excruciating week since Miller drove away.

One week since I've started correcting Max every time he saw a picture of her and called her Mama.

One week since I started using the pillow she slept on in my bed instead of my own, praying that her sweet scent will somehow embed itself into the fibers and stay forever.

One week since this world I created, this little family I could finally claim as my own, dissolved, leaving me and my son with only each other once again.

It's also been a week since I've heard her raspy voice, heard her say my name. We haven't spoken since she left because I promised myself I wouldn't hold her back. I wouldn't guilt her into responding to me when she's got these amazing opportunities keeping her occupied.

Instead, I've resorted to using her dad to get information.

Did she arrive safely?

Is she sleeping okay?

Is she happy?

Those last two questions couldn't be further from my own reality, so for her sake, I hope she's doing better than I am. I hope she's finding everything she's looking for. I hope she's finding her joy.

Because I sure as fuck lost mine.

"Malakai, focus," Isaiah calls out from behind me.

The stadium is packed for this September afternoon game that holds our playoff hopes in its hands. We have the opportunity to clinch tonight, and I just walked in a run on the last at-bat.

God, they're going to ream me on the post-game recaps later, but I don't give a shit. All those times I told Miller that pressure was a privilege, that it was an honor to live up to expectations, make me feel like a fraud. Because I'm not living up to anything.

With my cleats dug into the dirt, Travis calls my pitch, giving me a four-seam fastball. I nod, straightening to align my fingers over the ball in my glove before looking over my shoulder to check for runners, but when I do, all I see are the bases I ran with her just last week.

When I was happy. When *she* was happy. When she was mine.

I shake off the image and run through my pitch, using my entire body to throw the ball before letting it leave my fingers. It soars right over the plate, right at the height the batter needs to send it flying into left field.

Which is exactly what he does, hitting a grand slam and changing the score to 5-0 before I've even gotten an out in this third inning.

Fuck.

The crowd boos. Loudly. Deafening, and I don't think it has anything to do with our opponents and everything to do with me.

Travis begins his jaunt to the mound, but Isaiah shakes him off, coming in from his position instead.

We both hold our gloves over our mouths to speak.

"Are you okay?" he asks.

"Does it seem like I'm fucking okay, Isaiah?"

"Yeah, you're right. Terrible question."

My entire fucking life fell apart seven days ago, and it wasn't due to a lack of love or wanting each other. It was simply because we were headed on two different paths that only crossed for a short two months.

Before my brother can ask anything else, Monty leaves the dugout, headed straight for me.

"God-fucking-dammit," I curse into my glove.

I couldn't tell you the last time I was pulled this early from a game. I played like shit in my previous start this week, but I made it a full five innings before the relief pitchers took over. Third inning is fucking embarrassing, and for the first time in weeks, I'm wondering what the hell I'm doing with my life.

Nothing makes sense without her. The team staff is taking turns watching Max until the season is over, but what am I going to do next year or the year after that? Hire some random person who will never care about my son the way she did? Why am I even doing this? Because I love it? Well, we don't always get to have the things we love now, do we?

Monty nods my brother away, and Isaiah gives me an encouraging swat with his glove before heading back to his spot between second and third base.

Monty exhales, holding his jersey over his mouth so he can speak without the cameras picking up on what he's saying. "I gotta pull you, Ace."

I don't argue. I don't complain. I simply agree.

"You've got to find a way through this," he continues.

"Yeah, sorry, I'll get working on that." My tone is entirely dry and Monty shoots me a warning glance, reminding me I'm not the only one having a hard time.

While I'm bitching and complaining about missing his daughter, he's also heartbroken over not seeing her every day.

"Sorry," I add more sincerely.

Monty's brown eyes search mine. "Go home. Go get Max and head home. You don't need to stay for the rest of the game or the press. Go take care of yourself and your son."

While standing in the center of the field with forty-one thousand fans watching me, my eyes begin to burn, my throat growing tight because I don't know how to take care of myself anymore.

I'm a shell of a human these days, barely showering or eating, only getting out of bed for Max. Having someone else to take care of while your heart is breaking is an odd relief. You want to wallow in self-pity but can't because someone else is relying on you.

But someone else is always relying on me, so that's nothing new.

"Pick up the damn phone and call her, Kai. It might help you."

I shake my head, swallowing back the knot in my throat. "I'll be fine. She's got more important things going on right now that she doesn't need to be distracted hearing how fucked up I am."

He watches me for a moment, then gives me one single nod of his head, my cue to take off.

I do just that. Jogging off the field, through the dugout to the clubhouse to grab my keys. I swing by the training room to pick up Max and find Kennedy playing with him on the floor. She volunteered to watch him for me tonight.

"Hey, Ace," she says as cautiously as possible. "How are you holding up?"

I groan. "Please don't pity me like everyone else. I can't handle another person looking at me like I'm about to break."

"Sorry, you're right. You got pulled in the third inning? Ouch. Hate to break it to you, Ace, but I only work on the body. I've got nothing for a bruised ego."

A huff of a laugh escapes me. "Thank you." Max walks himself over to me, hands up for me to hold him. "And thanks for watching him."

With that I turn to leave, only to stop in the doorway, looking at Kennedy over my shoulder. "Have you heard from her?"

Her face falls, so much pity that I asked her not to give me. "A couple of times, yes. I've texted to check in, but I don't get a response until it's the middle of the night. Then by the time I write back, she's asleep. She's busy."

*She's busy.* I know she's busy. I hate that she's busy.

"Thanks again for watching him."

Once in my truck, I drive away from the field, taking us home, all while trying to ignore the overwhelming, burning desire to pick up my phone and call her just to hear her voice one more time.

I get Max's dinner together for him, not worrying about myself because, as I've said, I've barely eaten this week. We do bath time and I get him cozy in pajamas.

"Max, can you pick out a book to read before bedtime?" I ask, taking a seat on his floor.

He makes his way over to his little bookshelf, picking a big colorful book about insects before dropping to the carpeted ground. He settles himself between my legs, his head resting back on my stomach.

Though most of the day, I feel like I'll never be okay again, I know I will be. I'll have to be for him and that gives me a spark of hope.

"Bug," he says, pointing to a cartoon caterpillar on the pages.

"Yeah, that is a bug. Do you know who else is a bug?" I ask him, tickling his side. "You're a bug!"

He giggles, folding himself over my hand that's tickling his ribs and it's the best sound I've heard all week. My smile is the most genuine one I've worn in that same amount of time.

Max stands to his feet, turning to face me, meeting me eye to eye. His little hands find my face, running over my cheeks, sliding along my scruff.

He outlines my eyes with a single finger, and I close them so he can. "Dadda, sad," he says, and my eyes shoot open at that.

His face is so concerned, far more concerned than any seventeen-month-old should be.

But I'm also not going to lie to him.

"Yeah," I exhale. "Daddy is sad, but it's okay to be sad." Wrapping my hand around his back, I help him keep his feet so he can look at me. "It just means we love someone so much that we miss them. That's a good thing."

"Yeah," he agrees, not really understanding everything I'm saying.

"We've got each other, Max. You and me." I pull him into my chest, holding him. "Do you know how much I love you?"

"Yeah," he says again and this time I can't help but chuckle.

"Do you know how much Miller loves you? I know she's missing you as much as we're missing her. You're so loved, Bug, by so many people. I don't want you to forget that."

He melts into my shoulder, curling himself close to my body, his cue that it's time for bed.

Standing, I get him in his crib, turning on the sound machine that sits on a small table next to his crib. Max follows me with his sleepy eyes.

He points to the framed photo that lives next to his crib. "Mama."

I swear the word takes the air right out of my lungs the way it has every day this week.

"That's uh . . ." I swallow hard. "That's Miller."

"Mama!"

"Yeah," I exhale in defeat, not saying anything else because truly, I don't want to correct him.

I lean over his crib to kiss his head. "I love you, Max."

After making sure the baby monitor is on, I turn the lights off and close the door behind me, heading straight for the fridge for a beer.

A Corona specifically, because that's all I have stocked, which feels like a big *fuck you* from the universe.

Taking a seat on the couch, I pop the top and take a swig, unable to block out the visual of the way Miller looked with her lips around that Corona the first day I saw her in the elevator.

God, I'm a fucking mess. How do people do this?

Fishing out my phone, I scroll, eager for an iota of information on the girl I'm desperately in love with.

The same girl who is off chasing bigger dreams.

Every night when Max goes to bed, I'm nose deep in my phone, typing in her name, and whenever those jade green eyes and dark brunette hair come into view, my stomach dips, wishing I could reach through the screen and touch her.

She's been interviewed at least once a day through different blogs. Violet truly kept her promise of filling her schedule when she returned to work. I'm annoyed *for* her. This is the pressure that set her off in the first place, but I know Miller, I know she can live up to the expectations if she chooses to, and judging by these interviews, she's doing exactly that.

Then there's the part of me that's thankful Violet has thrown her back into the thick of it because it's the reason I have a bit of her. I can read what she said that day, and yes, this hopeless, longing side to me is trying to read between the lines, searching for a hidden meaning. I'm trying to find the words "Miller Montgomery is moving to Chicago" somewhere in an article that's titled, "Miller Montgomery—Back to Business."

It hasn't been long since those insecurities of not being enough were drowned out by Miller. Those voices were quieted but never truly extinguished, lingering just below the surface.

They're there again, wondering, dreading the confirmation that she got back to her regularly scheduled life full of chaotic kitchens, traveling the country for work, and being interviewed for fancy magazines only to laugh at herself for ever believing she could get attached to this quiet and simple life with my son and me.

Mid-read of her latest interview, my phone dings with a new text.

**Ryan:** *Family dinner is happening. Thought you were coming by after your game?*

Shit. I didn't even realize. That calendar that I once stared at and memorized, the one that moved at the speed of light while Miller was here, is now moving in slow motion, days ticking down when it feels like I should be crossing off months.

So, yeah, I forgot that it was Sunday because how the hell have I lived through this pain for an entire seven days?

Or maybe subconsciously I made myself forget because the idea of hanging out with my friends, the same friends that are hopelessly in love with their partners, while I'm wallowing in heartbreak sounds like the last thing on earth I want to do.

**Me:** *Sorry, I spaced. I'll be there next week.*

Maybe.

**Ryan:** *Next week, me and my wife will be on our honeymoon.*

*Shit.* The guy is getting married on Saturday and I completely forgot.

**Me:** *I'm a terrible friend. Of course, I know that. I'm looking forward to Saturday.*

**Ryan:** *Don't sweat it. I know you're going through it right now. We're here for you if you'd let us be.*

**Me:** *I'll be all right.*

Before I can get back to Miller-stalking, a new text thread comes through.

**Indy:** *Ryan can bring you leftovers if you haven't eaten yet.*

**Me:** *Thanks, Ind, but I'm okay.*

**Indy:** *Love you and Max. Thinking of you both.*

I intend to swipe out of our conversation, but I can't help myself, hovering my thumb over the keyboard.

**Me:** *Have you heard from her?*

A pathetic amount of hope mixes with dread.

**Indy:** *I texted her the other day to tell her she was missed. She said work was kicking her butt, but she missed everyone here too.*

I begin to respond, wanting to tell Indy to relay a message for me, that Max misses her, that *I* miss her, but I talk myself out of it. If she's going to hear that, it should come from me.

**Me:** *Looking forward to Saturday.*

**Indy:** *Me too!!!!!!*

The idea of family dinner without Miller is bad enough, but to sit through my friends' wedding alone? God, that's going to be rough. I have six days to try to pull it together, to attempt not to ruin their day with my shitty attitude.

Any and all resolve leaves me when I mindlessly find her contact in my phone. It's staring back at me, taunting me.

Would it really be the worst thing in the world if I got to hear her voice? If I could just tell her how much we're missing her. Maybe I'd feel better if she knew. Maybe she'd feel better too. Or, and more likely, I just want to hear her say it back.

Without another moment of thought, I press her name and call.

My knees are bouncing with nerves as her phone rings. It continues to do so two more times, until finally on the fourth one, she answers.

My heart soars out of my chest at the knowledge that she's on the other line, that she can hear me. "Miller?"

I'm fairly certain my voice cracks on her name which would be real fucking embarrassing if I could feel anything other than excitement.

"Uh, no," someone finally says on the other end. "This is Violet, her agent. She's in the middle of an interview, at the moment."

Instant deflation.

"Oh, okay. Do you know when she'll be done?"

"I'm not sure. She's got a long night in the kitchen afterward. I'd guess she'll be free around 2 a.m. or so."

Two a.m. in Los Angeles which would be 4 a.m. in Chicago.

"Do you want me to have her call you then?" Violet asks.

"No. No, don't worry about it. I know she's busy."

"She is, but it's all very big and exciting things for her. And she's happy here. She's jiving well with this kitchen. She's got a bright future in the industry. Take it from me. I've represented a lot of chefs in my career, but none as promising as her."

This is what I wanted, for her to succeed. I just didn't realize it'd hurt so bad to watch from the sidelines. But taking myself out of the equation, I couldn't be prouder of that girl. It sounds like she's finally finding what makes her happy.

"Hey, Violet." I clear my throat. "Do me a favor and don't mention to her that I called."

She pauses on the line for a moment. "Are you sure?"

"Yes. Thank you. Have a good night."

"You too, Baseball Daddy."

I huff out a small laugh, knowing she saw my name on the caller ID.

I hang up the line feeling as if it were last Sunday all over again. Like I'm starting from scratch in missing her. Only this time, I have the confirmation that she's happy. That she's off succeeding, doing bigger and better things than I could ever offer her here.

# 38

## Miller

"How'd it go?" Violet asks, following me around the bustling kitchen as I hustle to prepare for dinner service.

"It was fine. The same as all the other blog interviews have been this week. Fine."

Stepping into the walk-in, I use the clipboard in my hand to take inventory of the fruit delivery Maven's restaurant received today, making sure the kitchen has enough to get through until its next delivery on Wednesday.

"Okay, great," Violet continues, stepping into the cold walk-in, head down, scrolling through her iPad. "Since the restaurant is closed tomorrow, I have another interview scheduled for tomorrow morning with this big-time blogger that goes by Pinch of Salt."

"Do you really think that's necessary?" I mentally inventory the shelves, counting crates of persimmons, pears, and figs. "I have my *Food & Wine* interview tomorrow afternoon, and I'm sure by now anyone who gives a shit is well aware that I'm back to work."

"Miller, we're *capitalizing*. Striking while the iron's hot."

"Well, I'd really like the iron to cool the fuck down so I can take a second to breathe. I haven't had a single moment alone since I got to LA unless I'm showering or sleeping."

"Yeah, about that." Violet continues, nose down, looking over my schedule. "What do you think about taking some phone interviews while you're showering? You know, really take advantage of every minute of the day."

I turn on her. "Please tell me you're joking."

"Of course I am. Did you leave your sense of humor in Chicago?"

*Sense of humor. Heart. Both are still there, I think.*

"I'll tell you what, I'll tell Pinch of Salt that it'll be a quick chat on Tuesday instead. That'll give you tomorrow morning off before your interview with *Food & Wine*."

I nod. "I can do that."

The walk-in door swings open to reveal Jenny, one of the two line cooks on desserts, holding a carton of raspberries in her hand. "Chef, we have a problem."

The kitchen is chaos behind her, busy bodies moving to get set up for the dinner rush.

"The raspberries that were delivered today are sour. Real sour."

I take one from the carton, holding it to my nose. She's right, they're far more sour than they are tart, but I pop it in my mouth to be sure.

*Shit.* They're bad, and I have a white chocolate mousse with a raspberry crémeux on the menu for tonight, one that I've been designing for the last two days and prepping all afternoon, minus the hour I took to interview with yet another food blogger.

"All of them are like this?" I ask.

"All of them. Maybe we can swap a blackberry crémeux instead? Those were also delivered today but they look good."

"No. It won't have the right flavor profile."

"Yes, Chef." Jenny's eyes refocus on her feet.

"That's not a bad idea, though," I quickly correct. "The blackberries are a bit too tart for that dish, but you're thinking on your feet. I like that."

Her lips slightly lift at the corners. "Thank you, Chef."

My eyes dart to the box of pears that were also delivered today. They're meant for the poached pear dish I have planned for Tuesday's dinner service, but I can figure out the future later.

"Get rid of the raspberries. Tell Chef Maven that we're pulling the mousse and swapping it for the poached pear dessert I planned for Tuesday. The pistachio soufflé stays. And would you mind going to the freezer and checking on the chocolate sorbet?"

"Yes, Chef."

"And please make sure Chef Maven knows why we're changing the menu. Your kitchen needs reliable suppliers and this one doesn't seem to be one."

"Of course, Chef."

Violet and I follow her out of the walk-in and my agent stays right on my heels as I continue to organize my station.

Tonight is my fifth dinner service at Luna's, Chef Maven's Los Angeles restaurant. While consulting, I'm not typically on the line unless I'm covering a call out, but I like to spend my first couple of weeks at a new job right here in the thick of it, figuring out how they communicate and what their timing looks like.

It helps me cater their menu to their kitchen.

"Violet, we're about to start service," I remind her while organizing my station.

My stack of clean dish towels are right where I like them and my knives are ready and laid out in the proper order.

"I know. I know. But I wanted to show you the *Food & Wine* layout. They sent it over to me this morning. It looks amazing and the photos are fantastic. Everything is ready to go. They just need to add your interview and it'll be off to the printers."

Violet is nose deep on her iPad once again, looking through her emails to pull up the article.

"Vi, would you mind showing me later? Tonight is kind of

frantic with a whole new dessert I wasn't prepared to introduce until later this week."

"Of course, Chef." She stops what she's doing. "Have you eaten today? You need to eat before the rush."

Luna's does a staff dinner every day before service starts. I, however, haven't been able to partake in one yet, seeing as I'm using that downtime to interview with any and everyone who wants a piece of me.

"I'll grab something."

Except, I'm not hungry, and I can't remember the last time I was.

I look over my station again, making sure that Jenny and Patrick, the two line cooks who are in charge of desserts, have everything ready for tonight.

Besides the poached pear that needs a bit of prep, we are good to go.

Through the pass-through window, I spot Chef Maven getting into position, my cue that doors are about to open and service is about to begin.

"Violet, I gotta get to work."

"Okay. I have your phone. Where do you want it?"

"Would you mind dropping it by the house rental? It's on your way home, right? I don't need it tonight."

"You got it! Have a great service."

"Violet." I point to my phone in her grasp. "Any important calls or texts?"

She hesitates. "An important email, actually. The photographer from the *Food & Wine* shoot emailed an image that didn't make the cut for the magazine. You should check it out. It's beautiful."

My heart sinks with disappointment. Another day without hearing from him.

"I'll look later. Thanks."

*　　*　　*

"I need two Lobster Bolognese all day," Chef Maven calls out to her line. "Jeremy, less truffle froth on the Bolognese. Your plating is getting crowded."

"Yes, Chef."

"Chef Montgomery, you've got two soufflés coming up. Table six and table ten."

"Yes, Chef." I eye the oven door, checking the count I currently have baking.

Maven runs a tight ship, but there's not a person on her staff who isn't top tier.

I chose this restaurant because I've been eager to work with Maven since she hosted a seminar while I was in culinary school. However, tonight is only the second night I've gotten the chance to work alongside her.

I've come to find out that Maven only spends two nights a week on her line, letting her second in command cover the rest. She works on ordering, menus, and prep during the day, then entrusts her line with dinner service while she heads home.

And they kill it. Every night.

"Chef Montgomery, I need one Bananas Foster all day."

For the first time today, my heart skips, my hands freezing on the plate I'm currently working on.

The Bananas Foster is rarely ordered. It's the off-menu vegan option, sauteed in a caramel-like sauce and served with a vegan butterscotch ice cream.

And I can't hear it ordered without thinking of Max because yes, something as simple as bananas has me missing him and our days in the kitchen together.

Just like that, I'm jolted right back to that tearful goodbye seven days ago. How much it hurt to drive away from Chicago after leaving everyone outside of the stadium. How Max's little blue eyes started tearing up, though he had no idea why, only that he saw me and his dad crying.

I'm convinced my heart has been ripped out of my chest and left with two boys two thousand miles away, and the only good thing about being so busy with interviews and line shifts is that, for the most part, I've been able to turn off my mind during those times and just work.

Reaching into my chef's coat pocket, I run my fingers over the cardstock, always keeping it with me. The card they gave me is the one and only birthday card I've kept in my life, never one to be sentimental, but those two boys have ruined me to the point where not only have I kept it, but I keep it as close as possible.

"Chef Montgomery?" Maven asks when I don't respond to her order.

I pull my hand from my pocket, quickly running by the sink to wash them. "Yes, Chef. Sorry, Chef."

With my hair slicked back and my chef's coat back in place, I attempt to focus on the task at hand—to get through this shift. Then to do it again tomorrow. Then again, every day after that, while I pray that this longing homesickness starts to ease.

Using the towel over my shoulder, I wipe the edge of the plate clean, delivering the Bananas Foster to Maven standing on the other side of the pass-through window.

"Beautiful, Chef," she says, eyes flicking to me before I return to my station.

She's not wrong. It's stunning. The problem is no longer that I can't do my job.

The problem is that now I don't want to.


The house rental Violet got for me is nestled in the Hollywood Hills, expansive and expensive with giant open windows so everyone in the valley below can witness just how lonely I am.

When I get back there after another late night at the restaurant, I only turn on enough lights to grab a shower and a glass of water, snagging my phone off the counter before walking right back outside to sleep in my van parked in the driveway.

This house may be beautiful, but it's empty without Max's toys littering the living room or the dishes piling in the sink. It's too pristine. Too perfect. It makes it far too obvious how much I miss them.

The van is just as lonely, but with it being such tight quarters, I can justify that the lack of space is the reason why Kai isn't in bed next to me.

God, I miss him.

I miss his smell, his smile—the tired one and the confident one. I miss his steady hold, and his overwhelming encouragement. I feel like I've been spinning off axis for the past seven days, but this was always the plan.

I was always going to be here, without him.

The short time before bed is the worst and best part of my days. It's when the loneliness starts to sink in because it's the only free moment in my day to think of them, to focus on them, though there's an ache in my heart and a hollowness in my gut every hour of the day due to missing them.

We haven't spoken since that morning I left Chicago. My dad checked in every few hours of my two-day drive and when I got to California and asked him why he suddenly decided to become a helicopter parent, he simply said, "*Kai asked me to.*"

Communicating would only make things harder. This is my life and that's his. Did I indulge in the thought that it could've been mine too? Sure. Am I still wanting it? Yes, absolutely, but I have responsibilities here. Responsibilities to these kitchens I'm scheduled for and a responsibility to my dad to do something impressive with the life he's given me. I'm also responsible for living up to the James Beard Award I won. Responsible to the editors who chose to feature me on the cover of their magazine.

This must be how Kai feels. Responsible to everyone else, constantly trying to do right by others, and rarely choosing things for himself.

He did make one selfish decision this summer though, and I've got to say, it was the best thing that's ever happened to me.

Climbing into bed, I pull the covers up to my chest before checking my phone for the first time today.

There are a few texts waiting for me, but before I read any of them, I head straight to the Internet to find the results from Kai's game this afternoon. Today was his second start since I left, and his last game wasn't his best.

And judging by the headlines, today's was worse.

The Warriors lost five to two, and Kai was pulled in the *third* inning.

A short video clip shows the moment he got pulled with my dad and him meeting on the mound. They don't zoom in enough for me to get a clear image of his face, but I can read Kai's body language perfectly. He's upset. Not mad, but emotional. My dad gives him a nod and Kai jogs off the field, straight through the dugout, to the clubhouse, and out of the camera's view.

That right there is my fault.

He's not okay because of me.

And as much as I can pretend during work hours, I'm nowhere near okay either.

Tears are already burning the backs of my eyes when my attention falls to the framed photo Kai gave me for my birthday. Me with my head on his lap and his son asleep there on the couch too.

I miss them. I ache for them, and I'm mad at Kai for breaking me this way, for making me feel when I spent so much of my life unattached and untethered.

I hate that I love him so much.

So what's the harm in one little text? One tiny text to remind him that I'm thinking of him.

I find my messages to do just that, but the time at the top of my phone blinds me with the realization that it's almost three in the morning. It reminds me that Kai asked me not to give him any hope.

It reminds me that summer is over.

Regardless of the late hour, a text comes through from Chef Maven.

**Maven:** *Sorry we haven't crossed paths much this week! Meet me at the restaurant tomorrow morning for coffee and we can sit down and go over your ideas for the menu?*

So much for that morning off I was hoping for. But it's probably for the best that I don't give myself time to think because thinking only leads to missing them.

**Me:** *Sounds great. I'll see you then.*

Finally making my way into my other messages, I find texts from Kennedy, Isaiah, Indy, and my dad.

Nothing from Kai. His way to move on quicker, I guess.

I could be sick just thinking about it. Them with another woman in their lives, someone else loving Kai and Max the way I do. That's what I should want for them, right? To have everything I can't give them. Everything they deserve.

Then why am I laying here crying in bed at the thought?

This is his fault too. I never used to cry. I never used to feel. Now it's like a dam has been broken and it's a non-stop flood pouring from my eyes when I'm not at work. I never needed anyone before them and now I'm laying here, a desperate, sobbing mess in the middle of the night in the Hollywood Hills because there's a baseball player in Chicago and his son who I miss. Who I love.

Who I can't have because nothing about our lives aligns.

Blinking through the blurry tears, I find my dad's text.

**Dad:** *I'm sure you saw the game recap. Give me a call some-time so we can talk. I miss you, Millie.*

I don't hesitate, calling him, needing to hear his voice, needing someone to tell me I made the right decision by going back to work because right now it feels all wrong. I know he of all people will find what I'm doing impressive. He'll find it worthwhile.

The phone rings until the call goes straight to voicemail because, of course it does. It's the middle of the night.

"Hi, Dad," I say into the receiver, clearing my throat in hopes he can't tell I'm crying. "Just calling to say hi and that I miss you. I *really* miss you. But things are going great here." *God, is my tone too telling that I'm full of shit?* "I have my inter-view with *Food & Wine* tomorrow afternoon, so . . . that's exciting. Sorry about your game."

I try so hard not to ask, but I can't help myself. "Is Kai okay? I hope he is." I exhale a sad laugh. "But I also hope he's missing the shit out of me because I'm missing him. And you. I miss you a lot, Dad. I wish you were here because I miss seeing your face. I got used to it this summer, I guess. I used to be so much better at this whole traveling year-round thing." *And I'm rambling.* "Anyway, call me when you can, and I'll be sure to answer. I love you. So much. Talk soon."

Loneliness sinks in again as I hang up and lay in my quiet van where only the sound of my sobs can be heard.

I hate it here, but this quiet moment is the only place where I can be honest about that.

I find my texts again, hoping something from one of my friends will make my self-pity shut up for a second.

**Kennedy:** *Checking in on you. How's the restaurant? Isaiah won't stop texting me about whether he should change his walk-out song and then proceeds to ask me what my favorite song is, you know, in case he wants to use it. And I miss you!*

Finally, a genuine laugh escapes me.

**Isaiah:** *Here with your daily dose of Max. He learned how to say "duck" yesterday but definitely pronounces his "Ds" as "Fs" so that was a fun treat to hear. I took a video for you. You're missed, Hot Nanny.*

He accompanies that with a video of Max sitting on his lap in the center of the Warriors' clubhouse.

"Maxie, what is that?" Isaiah asks, pointing to the book they're reading, which seems to be about a giant Mallard duck.

"A big fuck!" Max proclaims, so proud of himself.

The clubhouse erupts in laughter around him, and Max just sits there, clapping for himself, and the rest of the team joins in to cheer too.

Quickly, the camera pans to Kai, who is sitting in his locker stall shaking his head, a tiny smile fighting to break through before the video abruptly ends.

I watch it again with a smile on my face, catching Cody, Travis, and Kennedy all there, but then I pause the video on Kai.

Even when he's sad, he's devastatingly handsome.

I scroll down to Isaiah's second text.

**Isaiah:** *What do you think Kennedy's favorite song is?*

And lastly, a message from Indy.

**Indy:** *We missed you and your desserts at family dinner tonight. But mostly we missed you! I wish you were going to be here next weekend.*

Indy and Ryan are getting married next weekend. I wish my schedule allowed me to go, but I'll send them a gift in my absence.

For the first time in my life I have friends. I have people I ache for, people I miss. People who are all within a thirty-minute drive of each other while I'm out here on the other side of the country, trying to make a name for myself in this career that I once revolved my entire life around.

I don't know how so much could change in eight weeks. It doesn't seem possible. And it doesn't seem reasonable to make rash decisions based on those short two months. But the decision I made to come back to work, a decision based on years of hard work, feels like the wrong one. But it also feels like a decision that I can't change.

Climbing off the bed, I grab the framed picture Kai gave me for my birthday, bringing it to my bed. I leave it right there next to my pillow because I'm sad and pathetic and don't know how to handle all these newfound emotions.

This picture is all I have of Kai and Max while I'm off chasing a dream that feels more like a nightmare the longer I'm away from them.

# 39

## Miller

I wake, reorienting myself.

I'm in Chicago.

Kai's bed.

A smile immediately blooms on my lips until I blink away the sleep, looking around, looking for him.

Only I'm not in his bed. I'm in my van.

I'm in LA.

My stomach dips just as it did the first day without him because each morning, as I wake from my sleep, the realization sinks in that I'm two thousand miles away.

The realization that today I won't be baking in their kitchen, won't hear Kai's encouragement, won't get to kiss him. And I won't be playing outside with Max in the afternoon. I'll be at Luna's to meet with Maven over her menu changes.

Stretching, I roll my way out of bed but as my feet hit the floor, so does the framed photo I slept with, crashing with an undeniable crack.

*No, no, no.* I'm too fragile for this right now.

I cautiously pick it up. The glass from the frame is completely splintered with the center of said crack landing right over my face.

That seems fitting.

A pathetic whimper creeps up my throat because yes, now I'm the person to cry over a broken frame. I guess that's what happens when you start forming attachments.

I carefully place it upside down on the counter, promising to buy a new frame on the way back from my meeting with Maven. I unclasp the prongs, loosening the backboard so I can pull the picture out, hoping it didn't get scratched in the fall.

And as I disassemble the thing, Kai's handwriting comes into view, right there on the back of the photo.

Our names—*Max, Miller, and Malakai* are accompanied by the date and year with a small inscription below.

*I hope you're out there finding your joy because you're the reason we found ours.*

And just like that, on day eight, I'm ruined all over again.

"I've followed your career since I was in culinary school," I admit like the fangirl I am. "You did a four-day seminar on brioche. Mixing, shaping, proofing, baking, all of it, and I don't think I had ever been so excited about bread before."

"I remember that. I think I gained like thirty pounds going around the country and teaching that class." Maven brings her espresso to her lips. "You're impressive, Chef. I enjoyed watching you on the line last night."

"As are you. Your line is . . . well-trained." I blow on my chai tea latte, helping it cool.

"They're the best, and I'm looking forward to having you join us for the next three months. I can't wait to see what kind of changes you're thinking about for the dessert menu."

I pull out my notebook and pen, setting it on the table between us. The pages are filled with ideas on how to incorporate all the fresh California fall fruits. I don't know that it's inspiration that's struck me since I got here last week, but instead, a fear of allowing my mind to be quiet. To allow it the space to miss everything I left behind.

"There's a pomegranate dish stirring in my brain that I can't wait to play with," I explain as Maven flips through the pages of my notebook.

"Why haven't you opened your own patisserie? With your name on the project, there'd be a line down the block."

"I uh . . . never felt the desire to stay in one place long enough to do that. I liked getting to live in a new city every three months."

She nods, continuing to flip through my notes. "Do you still like it?"

"Huh?"

"You said '*liked*'. Do you still like it?"

Her brown eyes lift from the pages to find me sitting in silence.

I take a sip of my chai. "I won't lie, it's lost a bit of its luster."

She chuckles, closing the book and sliding it back to my side of the table. "My advice, after twenty years in the industry, stop giving your brilliance to other people. Put your name on it and own it." She pulls her espresso back to her lips, smiling behind the tiny cup. "After you finish donating a bit to me this fall, of course."

Chuckling, I tuck my notebook back in my bag.

"Sorry we haven't gotten a chance to sit down like this yet," she continues. "You know how hectic prep time is and I'm sure you've noticed I only work two dinner shifts a week."

Thursdays and Sundays, to be exact.

"Shannon, your second in command, is great too. The kitchen really respects her."

"She's a lifesaver, having someone I trust so much to run things while I'm not here. When I decided to open Luna's after my daughter was born, I promised myself and my family that work would come second. It's a hard balance to have. This industry isn't conducive to families, as I'm sure you know."

"Oh, I'm well aware."

"But I love this." She gestures around the dining room. "Running a kitchen, shaping a menu. Trusting my staff is the

423

way I get to have both." She finishes her espresso, pushing the saucer away from her. "So, what's your favorite part of all this, Chef? Is it the chaos? The gratification of getting through a busy night? The creativity? What's your why?"

There's no hesitation when I say, "Feeding the people I love."

Maven chokes on her own saliva with a laugh. "Then what the hell are you doing here? I couldn't tell you the last time I cooked for a loved one. Now it's all critics and fine dining . . . what do they call themselves? *Foodies*? But that's what I enjoy most, feeding the people who want *that* kind of food."

I don't respond, using my chai to keep my mouth occupied.

"This little summer hiatus of yours," Maven fills the silence. "You're named Outstanding Pastry Chef of the Year and disappear. You had the food world in a tizzy, Miller, and I'm honored to be your first kitchen back. But you've got to tell me, what the hell was that about?"

Do I tell her the truth about the burnout and the pressure? Will she look down on me for it? Judge me? Use it against me?

I tread cautiously, but honestly. "I was feeling a bit burnt out."

"Already?" she raises a single brow.

I pull my eyes from her.

"I hit that place about four years ago. Granted, I was fifteen years in at the time. I left and had my daughter. Found a new passion for life in her, but I still had this ache to be here too." She taps her finger against the tabletop, referencing her restaurant. "Do you mind if I give you a piece of advice? From one old chef to a fresh, young one?"

I laugh. "You're not old, but yes, please do."

"If you ever feel like you've truly lost your passion for this, quit. Your food will never meet its potential because *you'll* never meet your potential. This career is not for the faint of heart. You will be beaten down on the line, day in and day out. You know this. But if you're questioning if you made the right decision, you've already made the wrong one.

"Find your passion, Miller. Find what makes you excited to get up every morning and if it's not this, walk away."

*Well, fuck me, am I that obvious?*

"This is what I'm good at."

"Oh, you're fucking brilliant at it. But you know what's better than being the best at something you don't love? Being mediocre at something you do."

"It's really not that easy, Chef. I have a four-year waitlist of kitchens I'm scheduled for, just like this one."

"Do you have signed contracts? Has money been exchanged?"

"Just verbal agreements."

She waves me off as if saying I didn't owe anyone anything with only a verbal contract.

I don't have much more to add to that piece of the conversation because my mind has been doing cartwheels all summer knowing something has felt off for quite a while.

"All right Miss *Food & Wine* cover girl." Maven claps her hands, putting the big questions on pause. "I need to know about these top-secret recipes. And where did you end up taking the cover photo? They called to get my permission to shoot here, but then called back to say they had a set in Chicago."

*A set in Chicago.* I could laugh. They had a beautiful kitchen in someone's home with a toddler running around.

"I was helping my dad this summer in Chicago. He's a baseball coach and his starting pitcher has a son who needed a nanny for a couple of months. We took the pictures in his kitchen. Actually . . ." I pull my phone out of my pocket. "Violet sent over the layout for the article. They just need to add the write-up from the interview we're doing this afternoon."

Maven and I scoot our chairs closer as I scroll through my emails, finding the one Violet forwarded. As soon as I pull it up, the cover shot takes over the screen.

It's blurred in the background, but it's there. The kitchen I made so many memories in. I'm standing in front of it, chef coat in place, arms crossed over my chest.

But the most alarming part of this photo is how unhappy I look. Did no one else notice when they picked this shot?

"Wow," Maven exhales. "Stunning photo, Miller."

I don't respond, scrolling down to find the images of my desserts and the recipes that accompany them. There are more photos of me, whisking, cracking an egg. I look just as unhappy.

"Oh," Maven awes. "We need to feature that dark chocolate cylinder this fall."

The dessert I thought of when I was in Boston with Kai.

And once again, I want to cry, crumble, dissolve into nothing because he's everywhere.

He was so concerned about noticing my absence in his house, but I'm two thousand miles away and that man is embedded in every moment of my life.

As he should be.

I shake it off, trying to regain my excitement.

"Violet said the photographer sent over the shots that didn't make it. I'm sure there's more angles of the desserts there too. The mozzarella cheesecake turned out beautiful."

In my emails, I find the photographer's message with the subject line that says, "*Thought you should have this.*"

I click, letting them load, but once they do, I realize there are no photos of the desserts. No action shots or pictures of the kitchen.

Only one photo is attached. Me in my chef's coat holding Max with a smile so big, my eyes are almost non-existent. He's equally as happy in my arms, big gummy grin, and I'm looking at him like he's everything that's been missing from my life.

This must have been from when Max wobbled onto set, right before Sylvia lost it on me for daring to wrinkle my chef's coat.

It's undeniable, the joy on my face in this photo compared to the one that landed its way on the cover.

"Is that your son?" Maven asks, looking over my shoulder at the screen.

"Oh," I startle, forgetting for a moment that she was here. "No. This is Max. The little boy I was nannying for."

"Interesting."

"What is?"

"You look at him the way I look at Luna—my daughter, not the restaurant."

With my new frame in hand, I thank the rideshare driver as he drops me off in front of the house rental in the Hollywood Hills. Parking is a real bitch in LA, so I've been taking rideshares and leaving my van parked in the driveway here.

The driver takes off and I look up to see a giant man sitting on the front steps, tattooed elbows leaning on his knees.

"Dad?" I ask.

His smile grows. "Hi, Millie."

"What are you doing here?"

"I got your voicemail this morning. You sounded like you needed me."

I quickly nod, picking up my pace to meet him at the steps. "I do."

He wraps me up in a hug that's big and comforting. A hug that feels like home after telling myself for so long that I didn't have one.

"Missed you, my girl," he says into my hair.

"I missed you."

After convincing him and myself of my independence, like I could go through my life alone, it sure feels nice to admit how much I need him.

"What are you doing here?" I ask, quickly pulling away to get a view of him. "Is Max okay? Kai?"

"They're fine. That's not why I'm here."

"Don't you have baseball?"

"Day off. We have a game tomorrow, so I need to get right back to the airport after we have this conversation."

"What conversation?"

He gestures to the top step and we both take a seat.

"We've had this conversation a handful of times throughout your life, Miller, but I don't think it's ever really sunk in. I'm hoping it will now."

He intertwines his hands, leaning his elbows on his knees. "When your mom died—"

"Dad, we don't need to talk about this."

"We do." He takes a deep inhale, starting again. "When your mom died, I had my dream career."

"I know."

"What I thought was my dream career," he corrects. "Until my dream job walked right into my life, and suddenly, all I wanted was to be whatever you needed. I didn't care about baseball anymore. I didn't think twice about what could have been. All I saw was this little green-eyed girl who looked at me like I was her entire world."

He shakes his head. "Never once, to this day, have I ever viewed our relationship or how our family came to be as a sacrifice. It's been a privilege to be your dad."

His voice cracks a bit on the last word, so I slide my palm over his shoulder, resting my head there.

"Do you remember the first time you called me that?" he asks.

I shake my head. He's always been my dad. I can't remember a time when he wasn't.

"It was the first Mother's Day after your mother had passed and a mom from your kindergarten class was hosting a Mother's Day tea party for all the moms. I was so new, taking on this role and I didn't know how to handle it. I was pissed that she'd host something like that when your mother had only been gone for a few months. So, when all of the other moms filed into the classroom that day, I walked in too and sat right next to you."

I exhale a chuckle. "You were wearing this giant floppy hat with purple flowers on it. I remember that."

"Well, of course. It was a tea party. A hat was a requirement for a tea party and all the moms were doing it, so I did it too."

I melt further into his shoulder.

"They all looked at me like I was completely out of my mind, but I just sat there drinking tea and eating little biscuits and basking in the smile you had on your face." He shakes his head, his first tear falling onto the cement. "That became my new dream, seeing that smile every day.

"There was this one mom, she was a real piece of work. She was the one hosting the whole thing and she looked right at you and asked who I was in a tone that was so obvious she thought I shouldn't be there, but you didn't pick up on any of it. You just took a bite of one of those little cucumber sandwiches, looked her square in the eye, and said, 'This is my dad.' It was the first time you had ever called me that, and after the tea party I cried in your school's bathroom for a solid thirty minutes."

My eyes burn. "You never told me that."

He tilts his head, placing a quick kiss to my hair. "It was one of the best days of my life. One of the scariest too, because that name holds so much weight. So much responsibility. And all I wanted to do was live up to it."

My stomach hollows. I know exactly how he feels.

"Kai told me what Max called you."

I lift my head from his shoulder to look at him. Red nose and shiny eyes.

"It's hard to know if you're living up to the name. There are no tests you get to pass or checkmarks you can aim for. And for someone like you, someone who has chased titles as a way to prove to yourself . . ." He pauses. "Or to prove to *me* that you've accomplished something, I'm sure that's even scarier. You're an All-American pitcher, a James Beard recipient, but you'll never earn the title Best Parent because that award doesn't exist. You can only try your best and hope it's enough."

"I don't know how to . . ." I shake my head. "I have no idea how to be someone's mom. I was just supposed to be there for a quick two months."

"Do you think I had any idea how to be a dad?" he asks in rebuttal. "I was so far out of my comfort zone. I had gone from playing major league baseball to putting your hair in pigtails for school every morning. Do you think I knew how to do that? Hell no. I had to ask our neighbor to teach me. I had no idea how to deal with mean moms or mean girls in school, and don't even get me started on how terrified I was when you got your first period, and you asked me to take you to the store. My Google search was questionable at best because I was trying to find the answers to the questions I knew you were going to have."

We both laugh at that one. Talk about an awkward day.

"Or when you were sad about missing your mom, Millie. I was so afraid I was going to say the wrong thing."

"You were perfect, Dad. You always seemed so confident. Like you knew exactly what to do. I had no idea you were scared."

"I just figured it out as I went. One day at a time. I've only ever had one goal when it came to being your dad, and that was to make sure you found your happiness."

*I hope you're out there finding your joy because you're the reason we found ours.*

Kai's words written on the back of our family photo.

My dad nudges his shoulder into mine. "I'm not telling you what you should or shouldn't do with your life. I just don't want you to be so afraid to fail at something new that it keeps you from finding your happiness when you're the reason I found mine."

"Geez, Dad." Lifting the collar of my shirt, I use it to wipe at my face. "I thought you'd call me back today and tell me how proud you were of me for doing these great and impressive things with my life. I didn't think we'd be having this conversation."

"I'm always impressed by you, you know that. It really doesn't take a lot. When you were a kid, you got a Lego stuck up your nose and I found that impressive." He chuckles to himself. "But there are other avenues in life that are equally great and impressive. You don't need everyone to know your name for it to mean you're doing something great with your life. Trust me, when the right person knows your name, it's enough." He nudges his shoulder into me. "Or in your case when the right *people* know your name. Two to be exact."

Kai and Max.

"This is bullshit, by the way," I say, pointing to my tear-soaked face. "This is the worst part of learning you have feelings."

He smiles, wrapping his arm around my shoulders. "That's love, honey."

"I don't think love is supposed to feel like this. It's too overwhelming. Too consuming. I don't know how people get through life this way."

"That's because you, my girl, fell in love with two people at the same time. I've been there. It's a lot."

I suck in a shuddering breath, trying to get my shit together.

"Miller, when you think of Max, what do you want for his future?"

"I just want him to be happy."

"Would you ever expect him to repay you for loving him?"

"Of course not."

He looks up to the sky, the sun beating on his smiling face. "Exactly."

We've had this conversation before, but it hadn't sunk in until today. I didn't relate to him until today.

"I think you understand," he continues. "Leaving my career to become your dad doesn't seem like much of a sacrifice now, does it?"

I shake my head. "Not when I'm thinking of doing the same."

He turns to me, brown eyes soft, looking at me as if I were his entire world. I understand that sentiment more than I ever thought I would.

"Go find your happiness, Miller."

When I get back to Luna's for my *Food & Wine* interview, I've got an annoyingly giddy grin on my face and so much clarity on my mind.

I leave the kitchen to take a seat across from the interviewer, crossing one leg over the other. We shake hands, introducing ourselves.

"I feel honored to have landed this interview with you, Chef," she says. "I've been looking forward to it."

"I'm looking forward to this too."

"With the restaurant closed tonight, do you have any big plans after we're done?"

"I do," I admit with a smile. "I'm gonna go see about a boy. Two boys, actually."

# 40

## Kai

With Max already buckled in the back seat and my truck engine on, Isaiah finally pulls up to my house.

"He's alive," my brother observes as he hops into the passenger seat of my truck.

"Barely."

Isaiah chuckles. "Well, it looks like you showered, so that's a good start."

My brother turns around to say hi to my son while I pull out of the driveway and start the short drive to Ryan's house.

"How big is this wedding?" he asks.

"It's small. Fifty people, I think Ryan said."

"Too bad Miller couldn't make it."

If my truck reacted the same way my body does at hearing her name, we'd be parked, frozen in the middle of this street.

"I don't want to talk about her." My tone snaps.

I don't want to think about her. I don't want to miss her. That's all I've been able to do for the past thirteen days.

Out of my periphery, Isaiah's usual confidence falters. He's a sensitive soul and I know that better than anyone.

"Sorry," I exhale. "I didn't mean to snap at you. I'm just exhausted and I really fucking miss her."

"She misses you too, Kai."

My attention jerks to him before refocusing on the drive ahead of me. "Are you assuming, or do you know that as fact?"

My brother hesitates. "Fact."

"Have you talked to her?" Because what the fuck? I haven't even spoken to the woman I'm helplessly in love with.

He throws his hands up in admission. "Yes, okay? I've talked to her every day since she left, but I wasn't doing it to go behind your back. Before she left, she asked me to keep her updated on Max. So that's what I've been doing."

She wanted to be kept up to date on my son? Of course, she did. My girl loves my boy.

"Don't be mad at me," Isaiah continues.

I shake my head, trying to come to terms that my best friend has spoken to the woman I've spent every one of the last thirteen days torturing myself over not hearing from, not speaking to. "I'm not. I'm glad you're doing that. She deserves to know how he's doing."

"She tries not to, but a couple of times she's slipped up and asked about you."

"And what do you say?"

"That you're thriving. That you're killing it. That you're not wallowing in self-pity and don't have a real questionable eating and sleeping routine at the moment."

I shoot him with a deadpan glare.

"I tell her that you're missing her too," he admits. "Don't shoot the messenger."

"Nah, it's fine. She should know I miss her."

She should know I don't know how to do anything *but* miss her.

Isaiah hesitates, but I can tell from the lingering tension in the car, there's more he wants to say.

"What is it?" I prompt.

"Everyone is worried about you, Kai. The team, your friends."

"I'll be fine. Don't worry about me. That's not your responsibility."

He chuckles without humor. "So that's your responsibility too? You'll take care of it like you always do? How about you stop being such a fucking martyr and ask for help, huh?"

His voice raises with frustration, and my wide eyes swing to him once again, only this time in surprise.

"Whoa. What's up with you, man?"

"I'm frustrated. With you, and with myself for not seeing it sooner. You spent all of your teen years working odd jobs to feed me and never asked me to get my own job to help. You figured out how to get me through high school and into college without a penny to our names by sticking close to home so I could live with you. Then when life throws you new responsibilities"—he gestures to my smiling son in the back seat—"whom yes, we love and are so thankful for, you still can't ask me for my help."

"I just . . ." I shake my head. "I didn't want you to be burdened with any of that. I just wanted my little brother to be happy."

"And what about you? Why can't you be happy? Why haven't you asked me to help out with Max this off-season so you could go spend time with Miller?"

"Because . . ."

Well, I'm not exactly sure why I haven't.

"God, you're both so fucking annoying with this constant guilty need to do everything for others."

"What are you talking about?" Miller's guilt regarding her adoption isn't common knowledge, and I sure as hell haven't shared the information.

"You and Miller, you both do things out of guilt and it's annoying. You, because you didn't want me to feel the effects of Mom dying and Dad leaving. And Miller because she's trying to do all these big things to make up for Monty not being able to."

"She told you that? About their relationship?"

"No, this guy on Atlanta's staff was going in on her at Family Day a couple of weeks ago. It was weird, like he was mad all these years later because Monty quit and he kind of blamed it on her. I swear, Kai, there was a part of her that was hesitating about leaving the next day. I saw it, but I think that conversation solidified her decision to go back to work."

And just like that, a pathetic amount of hope blooms.

Hope that's irresponsible because it doesn't change anything about our situation. Miller is gone and I'm here.

"And also," he continues. "I'm kind of grouchy because I haven't gotten laid in almost two months. I totally get why you used to be such a grumpy dick. Becoming a changed man fucking sucks."

I huff a laugh, the tension drifting away until my eyes fall to the back seat where Max is.

"You'd really help me out with him during the off-season so I could figure out a time to go see Miller?"

He scoffs with a smile. "Of course, Kai. I'd do anything for you. You're my brother."

"Let's just . . ." I shake my head, more hope than I've felt in two weeks flowing through me. "Let's just get through this season and we can figure out the rest after."

"Deal."

I sneak a peek in his direction. "Love you, Isaiah."

"Yeah, yeah." He chuckles. "Love you too."

There's not much room to park at Ryan and Indy's house. Even though the guest list is small, it's still much bigger than their driveway allows, so I leave the truck a couple of blocks away and the three of us make the walk to their house.

There are caterers and coordinators buzzing around. Though this ceremony is going to be intimate, it's clear that no expense was spared.

We make our way to the backyard, where a flower arch

acts as the centerpiece for the ceremony. White chairs flank either side, leaving a center aisle that's also entirely covered in pink and purple flower petals.

The backyard screams Indy, all bright, feminine colors.

There doesn't seem to be set sides, so we pick a spot three rows back and wait for the ceremony to begin. Max sits on my lap in his little dress shirt and bow tie, smiling and waving at the handful of people who come up to say hi to him.

I recognize most of the people here. Some of Ryan's teammates I've met at gatherings at his house. One of Zanders' teammates and his wife who have been there too. Both Ryan and Indy's parents who I've come to know.

Lastly, there's a man standing to the right side of the flower arch, but not at the center where you'd expect the officiant to be.

The music begins and Ryan is the first one out, finding his way to the center of the arch. Contrasted by the lavender and pastel pinks behind him, Ryan wears all black. Black shoes, black suit. Black tie.

It couldn't be more fitting for him.

The crowd cheers when Ryan takes his place, and he offers a small fist pump in response, setting the tone for the casualness of their day.

Zanders and Ethan, one of Ryan's teammates, take their place up front standing behind him.

From my lap, my son waves at them and they each offer excited waves back.

Then the music shifts and all our attention slides to the back door of the house and, when it opens Rio, wearing a lavender suit, white shirt, and a lavender tie, struts out as if this day is for him, and him alone.

The crowd erupts as he slowly makes his way down the aisle.

My attention drifts back to Ryan at the front who is simply standing there, shaking his head with a not-so-suppressed smile on his lips.

Rio continues hyping up the crowd and when he gets to the front, he wraps his arms around Ryan. Knowing how much he loves the dude, I'm fairly certain he's losing his shit at the knowledge that he's in Ryan Shay's wedding.

Next is Stevie, hand under her baby bump as she smiles that sweet Stevie smile, making her way down the aisle. The groom peeks a look over his shoulder at Zanders, who is watching Ryan's sister as if she were his entire world.

When she gets to the front, she hugs her twin brother for a long while before taking her spot directly under the flower arch, but slightly back from where Ryan and Indy will be standing.

The music shifts and we all stand when Indy, wearing her white dress, appears with her dad at her side.

"Wow," I whisper to Max. "Indy looks like a princess, huh?"

From my arms, Max claps excitedly for her entrance.

She's beautiful. Stunningly happy smile on her face contrasted to her future husband standing up front and crying like a little bitch. Granted he's laughing at himself for being emotional and even Indy is giving him shit from down the aisle because Ryan used to be the least emotional man I knew.

Now, he's a blubbering fucking mess over how happy he is.

She stares only at him the whole walk down and when she and her dad meet Ryan at the front, they don't speak with their voices. Instead, Ryan signs something, Indy's dad signs back, the three of them laugh before her dad hugs his future son-in-law, leaves his daughter with him, and takes a seat.

The man that was standing off to the side steps up, using his hands to interpret everything Stevie has to say while she officiates. Ryan and Indy speak with both their voices and their hands the entire time as well.

I couldn't be happier for them. I can't think of two better people, but there's this selfish part of me that aches from watching them say their vows and walk back as husband and wife.

As beautiful as it is, this could be used as a form of torture. Going through a heartbreak? Watch your happy friends commit their lives to each other.

Isaiah pats me on the back after it's all done. "What do you say we go grab a drink?"

"Yes, please."

Max was a trooper during the reception, taking a quick nap on me during the toasts. Zanders' best man speech got everyone laughing, and Stevie's maid of honor speech was sweet and sentimental. The newly married couple had their first dance before the rest of the wedding guests joined.

The sun has set, the string lights over the dance floor giving enough light to see, but dim enough that it's moody and romantic. Drinks are flowing; the food was delicious.

My brother has taken it upon himself to dance with every single woman here, well aware from the bouquet toss that the only single women here are elderly widows. Regardless, Isaiah makes their nights, spinning them around the dance floor.

"Hey, Max!" Ryan ruffles his hair before clapping me on the back. "Hey, man."

"There he is." I clink my glass of champagne with his. "Congrats, Ry. This is amazing, and Indy looks . . ."

"Breathtaking." His wistful gaze is locked on the dance floor, watching his new wife dance with his sister.

"You two deserve each other."

I can feel Ryan watching me, eager to say something about Miller, I'm sure, but I deflect before he gets the chance to.

"Zee," I call out, waving him over.

Where Ryan will ask me personal questions, wondering how I'm doing, and thinking of ways he can help, Zanders brings humor to our friendship. And right now, I need him giving me shit far more than I need Ryan asking how heartbroken I am.

Zanders knocks his fist with mine. "I promise I won't bring up how terrible you've pitched for your last three starts. And I for sure won't remind you that you got pulled in the third inning last week."

I turn to Ryan. "Why is he here again?"

"Married into the family, I guess."

"You guys had your appointment this week, right?" I ask Zee.

Zanders' face lights up, a cheeky smile on his lips. Ryan's proud grin makes its timely appearance as well.

"It's a girl," Zanders declares. "And I'm stoked. Did you hear that, Max? I'm finally getting you a new friend."

Max giggles in my grasp.

"You're gonna be a girl dad, huh? Congratulations, man, that's awesome." I swing an arm over him in a hug.

"Did you know they make little hockey skates with tiny hearts on them? I'm going to get her those."

Ryan shoots him a knowing look.

"Okay." Zanders holds his hands up. "Maybe I've already gotten them. And maybe I've already stocked her closet with designer onesies. Sue me."

Ryan and I chuckle.

"Do you have a name? I know you had convinced yourself you were having a boy."

"The name has been picked since we found out we were going to be parents. Boy or girl, this was always their name." Zanders swings an arm over Ryan's shoulders. "Just had to run it by this guy first. Which we did at his rehearsal dinner last night where Mr. Unemotional started crying over it."

"Yeah, yeah. Fuck off."

"Her name is Taylor," Zanders explains to me. "After Ryan Taylor Shay."

Ryan's blue-green eyes take on a glossy sheen, but he bites it back. This day has been a lot for him, especially when less than a year ago the guy was a complete recluse, not letting anyone too close.

"Max and Kai!" Indy exclaims, joining our conversation. "I'm so glad you two are here!"

"You look beautiful, Indy. Tonight has been amazing."

Indy eyes me for a moment, and I can see the questions on the tip of her tongue.

*How are you?*

*How's your heart?*

*Are you going to curl up on the dance floor in the fetal position and sob in front of everyone because the girl you're in love with is off doing bigger and better things with her life than anything you could ever offer her?*

Okay, the last one was a bit specific.

Stevie slides in under Zanders' arm. "My feet are hurting, so if you want to get one more dance in with your baby mama, you better make it now."

Without a word, the two of them take off towards the dance floor.

"How about you, wife?" Ryan asks. "Can I take you for a spin?"

She smiles at her new title. "Please."

Indy looks back at me cautiously, as if she doesn't want to leave me and my son on the outskirts of the dance floor, sad and alone.

"I'll um . . ." I look around, trying to find something that can keep me occupied. My attention lands on the portable bathroom. "I'm going to go use the restroom."

I couldn't have picked the bar? Or the dessert table? I don't even have to piss.

"Let us take Max for a dance then." She takes my son before nodding towards their back door. "And don't use the portable one. Go use the one in the house."

"Are you sure?"

"Yes, Kai. You're family. Our home is your home." She gives my forearm a squeeze before she takes off with Ryan and Max to dance.

With my friends all occupied on the dance floor, I slip my hands into my pockets, head hanging low as I walk into the house to pretend to use the bathroom. As soon as I shut the back door, the music drowns and silence creeps in again.

Things feel like they did before summer began—me, alone, with my friends happy and in love. Only now, I know what it feels like to have what they have.

I feel equal parts jealous as I do grateful.

Jealous that I don't have it anymore, that I don't have her by my side to celebrate the good moments with. And grateful that I had the chance to love Miller, to be loved *by* her even though I never let her say it.

That's the part that's getting me through the dark days, the undeniable gratitude that I had her. Our time together was short, but it was everything.

I linger into the living room, wasting time, and trying to figure out just how long I should be inside. I pace, attempting to keep my mind occupied, when I spot a magazine on the side table by the couch.

And right there, the girl who has haunted my every waking moment is plastered on the cover.

It's her *Food & Wine* edition, but that makes no sense. It doesn't go to print until next week.

I'm eager to touch it, eager to know what the fuck this is doing in my friends' house. Eventually, I find the strength to pull my shaking hand from my pocket, taking a seat on the couch, and bringing the magazine into clearer view.

Miller looks stunning. Unhappy as fuck, but beautiful nonetheless. She's standing in her crisp chef's coat, arms crossed over her chest, hair slicked back, no septum ring in sight. My kitchen is blurred in the background and my stomach sinks at the memories.

Her and my son making a mess, having so much fun baking together.

The team coming over to try her creations.

Us, sliding our bodies together because we finally had to touch each other.

Leaning my elbows on my knees, I stare at the magazine in my hand.

God, she's impressive. I'm so fucking proud of the girl. As much as I've been hurting since she left, the pride I feel hasn't diminished.

After taking in every inch of the image, my attention finally slides over to the headlines.

*Zero-Waste Cuisine Takes Hold.*

*Six Tips on Poaching the Perfect Egg.* I should send those to my brother.

And finally . . .

*James Beard's Outstanding Pastry Chef of the Year Talks Family, Food, and Changing Things Up.*

Without wasting more time, I flip through the pages, looking for the article. I land on it halfway through the magazine.

### The Best Things in Life Are Sweet
*By Gabby Sanchez*

*I first met Chef Miller Montgomery in the dimly lit dining room of up-and-coming restaurant, Luna's (Los Angeles—Chef Maven Crown). We filled the potentially awkward opening minutes with small talk, both of us easing into the hard-hitting questions, but before I could get to them, Montgomery stopped me, fleeing to the kitchen to pull a baking sheet from the oven.*

*Returning, Montgomery proceeded to place a freshly baked chocolate chip cookie on the table between us before casually asking, "Should we get started?"*

*Here I was, sitting across from James Beard's newest Outstanding Pastry Chef of the Year, with an entry-level baked good offered to me on a small dessert plate.*

*There wasn't much that made sense to me that afternoon. Our interview took place in another chef's restaurant. Montgomery was casual and used words that an at-home baker could understand, distinctly unlike any James Beard recipient I had interviewed before. There was an approachability about the young chef, a relatability that so many long-time professionals lack, but every juxtaposition, every contradiction, disappeared when that chocolate chip cookie hit my tongue.*

*There are an immeasurable number of good cookies out there, but it's difficult to make the simple great. Montgomery not only made a simply great chocolate chip cookie, but simultaneously readjusted my scale on which all future desserts will be judged.*

*I'll admit, though this article was always going to be written in a positive light, when I walked into Luna's that early September afternoon, I was skeptical of the reputation Montgomery had earned. I was positive her name, pastries, and menu magic were that of another overhyped but ultimately underwhelming chef. But I'm proud to admit that when I left, I did so as a new fan, willing to travel anywhere the star chef is working.*

Taking a moment, I quickly look around the living room to see if anyone knows what the hell is going on. But no one is here with me. With my head back in the pages, I continue to read about Miller's work history, the internships she did overseas and in the States, the big-time names she's worked for, but it's the third page that has my heart beating far faster than what's most likely safe.

*But the most shocking revelation from our time together is when Montgomery admitted with a beaming smile that after earning the top honor in the industry, she's leaving it all behind.*

I reread that sentence three more times to make sure I got it correctly. What the hell is going on? My knees are bouncing so rapidly from the adrenaline coursing through me that I have to pull my elbows off them so I can continue reading.

*I was thankful I had my recorder on because my journalist hand had frozen mid-pen stroke.*

*"It's not my passion anymore," Montgomery admitted. "I took a summer hiatus from the restaurant industry and fell in love with a different kind of life. Baking is all about passion. If you don't feel it, your food reflects those sentiments. One of those art imitating life situations."*

*"And you've found a new passion then?" I asked.*

*"A new dream as I like to call it." She wore a meaningful grin at the statement. "One with balance, friendship, and a whole lot of love."*

I close the magazine for a moment. There's no way this is real. This has to be some kind of sick joke the guys are playing on me. Like they typed this up and left it in here for me to find, except . . . the pictures. The fucking pictures. From the first page to the last you can see the transformation in Miller, starting with the photos from that morning at my house and evolving into pictures I assume were shot at Luna's.

I reopen to see Miller's hair gradually falling to her shoulders as you move through the article. Eventually, she removes her chef's coat around the time she reveals she's leaving the industry. Her tattoos and beautifully bright smile are on full display by the time I flip to the final page.

*"Can we expect to find you consulting at kitchens in the Chicago area?"*

*"No," Montgomery said with a hearty laugh. "There's only one*

kitchen I plan on spending my time in and that's the one featured on the cover of this magazine."

Chef Montgomery has never owned her own restaurant or patisserie, so when asked if she had plans to change that, she simply said, "Yes."

"I feel it's time to put my own name on my work," Montgomery clarified. "I don't know yet what that will look like, but the biggest thing I've learned through my years of consulting is that it wasn't the type of food that had me excited to wake up. It was the teaching, the sharing of a craft I love so much. I'm excited to find ways to continue doing that in a capacity that's more suitable to my new life."

"And what about this new life has you so excited?"

"I'm looking forward to living in one spot. Having a place to call home. Having my dad close by and being a part of a community that supports me, who I support in return. Hearing the constant encouragement from the man I love, and I'm equally excited to cheer him on in his endeavors. But the part I'm most looking forward to is having the opportunity to bake every future birthday cake for the little boy who stole my heart this summer."

"How does it feel to know you're settling down?" I asked.

"I don't like the term 'settling down.' I didn't settle for anything. I simply stopped running when the two best boys I know caught me."

We continued the afternoon by swapping stories, her sharing that she was nervous for the new role she was stepping into but felt as if she had all the support from the people who mattered most. She revealed that she had three alternate desserts lined up to be featured in this article, but with her big announcement, she wanted to go back to the basics. She wanted to showcase recipes that the everyday baker could execute.

"My favorite part of baking is feeding the people I love," Montgomery said. "I hope these recipes will help others do just that."

We drank chai tea lattes as we spoke about life, family, and *food, and it was the first time I could recall an interview of mine that derailed so wonderfully.*

*I left our time together with a reminder so many of us in the industry need at times—there's life outside of the kitchen . . . and it's beautiful.*

I inhale a sharp breath, attempting to swallow down the lump in my throat as I move my attention to the recipes she worked so hard on this summer. Only now, they're simplified and meaningful.

*Banana (Nana) Bread—the one that got me back in my groove.*

*M&M Cookies—named after my favorite people.*

And finally, the one that makes my eyes burn.

*Mae's Tiramisu—for the woman I never got to meet but who raised two amazing men. I hope I follow in your steps by being a fantastic boy-mom.*

Closing the magazine, I shut my eyes because the tears are about to free-fall. Dropping my head back on the couch, I try to steady my erratic breathing.

I don't want to get ahead of myself, but the way I've taken it, Miller is coming back.

She's coming *home*.

I exhale a disbelieving laugh at the realization, a stupidly giddy smile living on my lips, because for the first time in thirteen days my world feels right.

"Not too concerned about those wrinkles, I see. Smiling like that." It's that raspy tone I love so much. The one that I haven't heard in far too long.

My lips only curve more as I keep my eyes closed, basking in the knowledge that she's back.

She's fucking back.

"You should probably hook me up with some of that skin care, Miller, because I have a feeling this smile isn't going anywhere."

She laughs that deep throaty sound and it's then that I finally open my eyes for the confirmation.

*There she is.*

Miller is leaning on the partition that separates the living room from the dining room, wearing a forest green dress that makes her eyes infinitely more vibrant. Hair down, tattoos on full display with this strapless number hugging every inch of her body. She looks so fucking good.

And she looks so fucking *mine*.

I adjust my glasses to confirm I'm seeing this correctly, that I'm not hallucinating after living in my own personal hell for the past two weeks.

But she's here all right, because it wouldn't be a Miller Montgomery entrance without her double fisting.

With champagne this time, but still.

"Double fisting again, Montgomery? A little late in the day for your drinking habits, don't you think?"

Her knowing smile grows. "I'm celebrating."

"Oh, yeah? And what are you celebrating?"

She holds both flutes up. "I quit my job."

Just like the first day I laid eyes on her.

Cautiously, I rise from the couch, not quite believing that she's really standing in front of me or that she might be back for good.

I don't make it far, needing to take a seat on the arm of the couch because if I get any closer to her, I won't be able to stop myself from kissing her, and I need the confirmation that she's here to stay.

"What are you doing here, Mills?" There's so much hope in my tone, but I need to hear it from her.

She sets the champagne glasses down on a nearby table, nervous hands fiddling. Miller is not a nervous woman, but sentimental moments are out of her comfort zone.

She steps between my open legs, and I hold her hands in

mine, taking away that nervous tick. But now my hands are shaking because I'm finally touching the woman I convinced myself I'd never get to hold again.

Miller exhales with a smile on her lips. "You said it was my choice if I wanted to live up to expectations, and I do. But now, the only expectations I'm going to worry about are the ones I set for myself. And the only expectations I have for myself are to be happy and to chase the things I want."

"And what do you want, baby?"

The term of endearment rolls off my tongue so easily, as if it hasn't been almost two weeks since I last called her that. But in my mind, it doesn't matter how long it's been since I've seen or spoken to her. We could've gone years and I still would've claimed her as mine the moment she decided she wanted to be.

She holds steady eye contact, so brave and bold while being vulnerable. "I want to open my own patisserie and teach classes there a couple of times a week. I want to watch as many of your games as I can. I want to wake up with you every morning. I want to live close to my dad. I want to read stories to Max every night before bed. I want to try my hardest to be who he needs me to be. I want to be the one to bake him cupcakes for his first birthday at school and for all his birthdays after that. I want to have more babies with you because you are such an amazing dad. But most of all, I want to be happy and you two make me happy, Kai. And I hope I make you happy too."

The words tumble out of her mouth, as if she spent her entire drive here rehearsing and needing to say them.

They're words I've ached to hear. A part of me always hoped she felt them, but I've been dreaming of the day she might voice them out loud.

She squeezes my hands. "But what do *you* want?"

Does she really have to ask? It's the same thing I wanted two weeks ago. The same thing I wanted all summer.

"You. Just you. I want it all with you, Miller."

Her beaming smile is back. "Just to give you a heads-up before you really make your final decision, I'm currently homeless, jobless, and my van is way past due for an oil change."

Chuckling, I pull her into me. "I can work with that."

She slants over me, but before I can kiss her, she stops with her hands on either side of my face. "And I love you."

My eyes dart to hers.

"I love you so much, Kai. Nothing about me leaving was because of you. I need you to know that. You're more than enough, more than I could've dreamt for. I loved you before I left, and I love Max and I've never felt so much at once that I'm fairly certain my heart is going to give out soon. I'm only twenty-six, Malakai. It's too soon."

Hand bracketing her jaw, I pull her down. "Don't worry, Mills. I'll go long before you, due to my old age and all."

"That would be best," she whispers against me, her fore-head leaning on mine. "Because if I go first and you meet someone else, I promise you I'll come back and haunt the shit out of her."

"I'm glad to know your jealousy goes beyond the grave, baby. Now please shut up and kiss me."

Palm cupping her cheek, I thread my fingers through her hair and pull her lips to mine.

It's as if every missing part of my life is entirely reassem-bled in that moment. Everything I've wanted for my life, for my son's life is wrapped up in this woman I love. This woman I thought I lost.

She makes the sweetest moan of relief and I part my mouth, taking her deeper before our tongues tangle, slow and measured as if we've both been dreaming about this moment for the past two weeks.

Miller's lower half melts into me, right into the cradle of

my hips, and I use my other hand to curve around her ass, keeping us pressed together.

She slides her hands over my shoulders as we kiss and touch and remind each other that we're here, in the same place, with no expiration date on our time together.

We have forever.

I pull away only slightly, needing to tell her something. "I love you."

She smiles into my lips. "I love you."

"Mmm," I hum. "You should probably say it again."

"I love you, Malakai, and I love your son."

Fuck, that's the one that does it.

Head dropping back, I look up towards the ceiling, taking a deep breath.

She runs a palm over my scruff, regaining my attention. "When I left, I hadn't fully come to terms that what I was chasing was no longer my dream, but as soon as I got there, I knew. I have a new dream now. You and Max are my dream."

I can feel my chest expand, as if it needs to make room for all the love in my life. Never once did that lonely fifteen-year-old boy ever think he'd be surrounded by so much support. So much love.

Love I didn't see before—from her, her dad, my brother, my team, and my friends. I have this huge support system backing me and my son. I have the family I had always hoped for.

"Miller." Wrapping my arms around her waist, I keep her close. "We were missing you before we even met."

She leans down to kiss me as I sit on the edge of the couch with her standing between my legs.

For a long time, I felt a bit broken from trying to be enough for everyone else. But once this woman walked into my life, she made me realize that not only am I enough for Max, but

I'm also enough for myself. And now I know, without a shred of doubt, that I'm enough for Miller too.

"Quite the party out there," she says, gesturing towards the back door. "Why aren't you dancing?"

My eyes track every inch of her face, basking in the knowledge that I'm going to have the privilege to see it every day for the rest of my life. "Because I only want to dance with you."

She leans back as if she were ready for us to join our friends, but I pull her into my lap, letting her know I need a few more moments with just her.

I grab the magazine off the couch.

"You featured a dessert for my mom."

"Do you think she would've liked it?"

"She would've loved it." My attention bounces back to her. "And you."

"Cute girl on the cover, don't you think?"

"Cute?" I scoff. "How dare you call her cute." I flip through the pages, finding her article. "This means so much to me, Mills."

She smiles in a way that is so sexy, so seductive, all I can think about is getting her out of here, peeling her out of that sinfully tight dress, and letting my body tell her just how much I fucking missed her.

"And you look stunning tonight."

"I'm sorry I'm late," she says. "I was hoping to meet you at the house before the ceremony, but the drive took me so much longer than I expected. I hit traffic in Nebraska. Who hits traffic in Nebraska?" She toys with the hair at the back of my neck. "I did the interview on Monday, but then I had to stay in LA for the photographer to take new photos and Violet was able to slip me an early copy before I left. I wanted to surprise you with it."

"This is the best surprise I could've asked for, but how much does Violet hate me?"

She bobs her head from side to side. "She's not stoked about losing her top-earning client, but she's happy for me. She apparently had her suspicions all summer long."

"And your contracts?"

"The only one that was set in stone was with Maven and she dissolved it on the spot when I told her I wanted to leave."

I can't hold back my smile. "This is really what you want?"

I know it is, but fuck if I don't love to hear her say it.

"This is what I want. This life together. The three of us. You keep me grounded, Kai, and I'll keep you wild."

I nod before sealing it with a kiss. "Deal."

A knock sounds at the back door of the house and we both turn to find Isaiah, Zanders, Stevie, Ryan, Indy, and Rio with their faces pressed up to the glass, watching us.

"Jesus, fuck," I exhale as Miller waves at them. "Did they all know?"

"Only Indy. I couldn't show up to someone's wedding without RSVPing."

"Mama!" Max calls out from the other side of the glass, and when we look back, Ryan's got him hoisted on his arm to get a good view.

His blue eyes are wide with excitement, looking right at the woman he and I love so much. He smacks the glass as if he it'll help him get to her.

"Max is here?" Miller asks on a gasp.

He claps in excitement. "Mama! Mama!"

Miller drops her forehead to mine, eyes closed in relief, speaking quietly. "Today was a good day."

There were so many times I said that this summer with the fear that they were going to all end, but now . . .

"They're all going to be good days, Miller."

I hold her, this girl I'm hopelessly in love with, and I only fall further when she places a soft kiss on the corner of my mouth and whispers, "Let's go get our boy."

With her hand in mine, I lead her to the back door, opening it to let her out first.

The small crowd is excited to see her, but she doesn't hesitate to go right to my son, and just like the first day they met, Max is eager to get in her arms, throwing himself off Ryan's body in her direction.

"Hi, baby," Miller whispers to him, a bit emotional as her forehead falls to his. "Oh, how I missed you."

She slightly bounces with him, taking her time. Our friends give them space, heading back to the dance floor with a squeeze of her arm or a wave of acknowledgment in her direction.

She smiles at them all, clearly looking forward to catching up, but right now her attention is solely on my son.

"Mama," Max whispers, his little fingers tracing her inked arm.

"I'm here, Bug, and I promise I'm not going anywhere."

Standing on the back porch, I lean against a pillar and watch them, trying not to cry. But this moment is everything to me. I watch as everything falls into place, when our family becomes whole. How do I *not* get emotional over seeing the two people I love more than anything, find that same love in each other?

Max doesn't have the vocabulary to express how much he missed her, how much he loves her, but you can see it in the way he looks at her, the way he melts onto her shoulder to hug her.

She's everything to him, in the same way she is to me.

Miller sways with him, dotting soft kisses against his hair.

"Kai! Miller!" my brother calls out from the dance floor, waving us over to join.

Miller's sparkling eyes bounce back to mine.

"You coming, Baseball Daddy?"

I chuckle but need a moment to gather myself, needing to

454

let the realizations sink in. "Yeah. Give me a second, and I'll be right there."

She leans up to kiss my lips before the two of them bound down the stairs to join our friends on the dance floor. With couples pairing off and the space filled, Miller helps my son stand his feet on the tops of hers. Holding his hands, she starts to move, the two of them dancing together.

Max is looking up at her as if she were his entire world.

Those two, this life . . . I don't know how I got so lucky that I now get to call those two mine.

The fear that once consumed me, that Max wouldn't have enough, that he wouldn't feel loved unless he was with me, it's gone. He has so much love in his life, and so do I.

Miller finds me over her shoulder, happy green eyes sparkling under the string lights. She gestures me to the dance floor, and though I love this view, I can't keep myself from them.

I scoop Max up, holding him on my hip before sliding a hand against Miller's lower back. Pulling her into us, she snakes one arm over my shoulder, the other over my son, pressing her cheek to my chest as we dance together.

"I love you," I remind her once again.

She smiles up at me, so content, so at peace. "I love you." Miller runs a soothing hand over my Max's hair, her attention drifting to him. "And I love you."

With our friends surrounding us, I finally got my family.

# Epilogue

## Kai


**Six months later**

"Max, which color pants do you want to wear today? Red, blue, or green?"

My son lays on his back in only his diaper and a T-shirt that says "Two Wild" in bold black letters, looking up at the three pant selections I've got on display.

"Gween!"

"Nice choice, my guy."

"Mama, gween."

As he lays on the floor, I slip his legs through his olive-green pants. "You're right. Green is your mama's favorite color, huh?"

"Yeah."

While I've got him sitting still in one place, and most likely the only time he'll be this way today, I take the opportunity to slip on his socks and checkered Vans.

"Who are you going to see today, Bug?"

"Mama."

I chuckle. "Yes, but you get to see her every day. Who else?"

"Zaya."

"Yep, your uncle Isaiah will be here. And . . ."

"Monny."

"Yeah. I think Grandpa Monty will be here any minute." I lift him off his back, placing him on his feet, all decked out for his second birthday party. "And why are all our favorite people coming over today?"

Max's smile widens as he uses both hands to point to himself.

"For you! Because it's your birthday, huh?" I give him a little tickle on his belly. "How old are you today?"

My son holds a hand up, showing off all five fingers.

"You're five?! When did that happen?"

He laughs at himself as I help him put three of his fingers down. "Or are you two?"

"Two!"

And how the hell is he already two?

My happy boy with so much energy, confidence, and bravery. He's thriving and I couldn't be more grateful.

"Should we go show Mom your cool outfit?"

"Yes!"

I stand from the ground, letting him put his hand in mine. "I think there might be a jungle outside waiting for you."

Max looks up at me, wide and excited blue eyes.

"Maybe even some giraffes and elephants and zebras."

His little smile is so sweetly hopeful as he hops around on his feet. Turning the corner to the living room, he stands slightly behind my leg, using it to shield his eyes. We stop walking and he peeks his little face around, as if he were nervous to see his birthday party.

There are endless balloons in all different animal prints, palm leaves draped all around. Banners hang on every flat surface, and the décor is finished with an array of giant toy animals you might find in the jungle.

I get down on my haunches next to my son, pulling him between my crouched legs. "What do you think, Bug? Is that jungle for you?"

He nods excitedly, but leans back on me, like he's not so sure if he should go outside yet.

But then he spots Miller at the dessert table, rearranging the endless display she's been busy baking.

"Mama!" Max pops off my chest, running his way outside to go find his mom.

I stand at the back door as I watch her scoop him up, resting him on her hip.

This is my favorite view—the two of them.

"What do you think of your birthday party, Bug?" Miller bounces him on her hip. "Is this all for you?"

"Yes," Max says, hiding against her shoulder.

"I think we should go explore."

I already knew they were close, but that bond has only strengthened since Miller officially moved in six months ago. A day hasn't gone by that she hasn't kissed him before bed or been with me to wake him in the morning.

Their love for each other is so evident.

Last month Max caught a little cold and, instead of me, the only person he wanted was his mom. My ego took a small hit but getting to see her confidence towards motherhood grow was well worth the blow.

I follow them into the backyard as Miller puts Max on his feet so he can play with the giant toy lion sitting on the ground by the dessert table.

"This looks amazing, baby." I slide my arms around her waist from behind, chin leaning on her shoulder.

"Yeah? Do you think there are enough balloons? I have more inside I could blow up."

I couldn't tell you where she'd fit more balloons. There's a balloon arch around the dessert and drink table. Over the photo backdrop. You walk through a balloon arch in the entryway of the house. I couldn't count how many giant gold number two balloons are floating around out here.

I chuckle. "Yeah, we should probably get more out here. I'm not sure if people will understand this is a birthday party."

She swats me in the thigh, but I catch her hand, pulling it to my lips. "It's perfect."

"Is it, though? I want it to be perfect for him."

I sway with her as we look down at our son, who has now found his way to sitting on the toy lion as if it were a horse.

"I'm fairly certain this is going to be the best day of his life."

My eyes drift back to the dessert table she's working on. A tiered cake sits in the middle, each layer a different animal print. Cupcakes, brownies, and mini pies surround the table as well, all done in some sort of safari-themed way.

"These look perfect, Mills." Reaching around her, I pop a mini brownie in my mouth. "Holy hell," I moan.

"Kai," she scolds with a laugh. "Those are for the guests."

"We should cancel. The three of us can polish these off."

"I worked way too hard on those not to share them." She turns back to the table to cover the small gap I made on her brownie plate before she finds me over her shoulder. "But yeah, they're good?"

Even after all this time and all this success, she still looks for approval from the people she loves, wanting them to love what she created.

I lean over her shoulder to kiss her. "They're amazing. Everyone is going to love them."

And when I say everyone, I don't just mean our friends and family. I'm referring to all of Chicago.

Back in October, Miller became the owner of a little brick building on the North Side of Chicago. She spent the winter months hard at work gutting the place and turning it into her very own bakery. M's Patisserie has only been open for six weeks and has yet to make it through scheduled business hours before selling out of her baked goods.

Violet, Miller's agent, went to work spreading the word about the James Beard winner's latest endeavor. She's been written about in travel and food magazines. Her business's social media already has an incredible following and each morning when they open, they're greeted by a line around the block of both locals and tourists eager to try her creations.

I wouldn't be surprised if she opened a second location by the end of the year, but for now, she's enjoying finding success in something she loves, something with her name on it.

Though, she has yet to admit who M's Patisserie is named for.

It could be for her own name or for Max, Me, or Monty. But when asked, she simply says it's named after all her favorite people.

The bakery has a back room that serves as a cooking class-room. On Tuesdays she teaches baking basics, but every Thursday, she features a specialty dish on her menu. They're the type of dishes she would've showcased when she was in the high-end restaurant world. She sells out every Thursday before noon then, that evening, she hosts a class and teaches people exactly how to make it for themselves.

That particular class is booked three months out already.

Miller works four days a week and entrusts the other three to her staff. And every day she comes home from work, she's wearing an exhausted but fulfilled smile on her face. It's the daily confirmation that she made the right choice all those months ago when she returned to Chicago. She came back not just for me or Max, but also for herself.

Sliding my hand down her lower back, I rest it on her ass. "Can I help with anything?"

"I think we're good to go."

Pulling her in, I kiss her temple. "He's lucky to have you and so am I."

She looks up at me, jade green eyes so full of happiness. "I think we're all lucky."

461

Just then Monty turns the corner, coming in through the side gate with a giant gift bag in one hand and a case of beer in the other. Because even though this is a two-year-old's birthday, all my son's closest people are well over twenty-one.

"Monny!" Max cheers when he sees him.

"There's my birthday boy!"

"Let me go help your dad."

Jogging over, I take the beer from his grip.

"Thanks, Ace. There's more in the car."

"I can go get it."

"I'll go with you," he says, giving me a look that tells me exactly why he needs to go back to the car with me.

We get the present on the gift table and the beer in the cooler before we make it back out to his car.

"Do you have it?"

"Eager," he laughs. "Yes, I have it."

Monty dips into his pocket, pulling out a small rust orange velvet box.

A few weeks after Miller moved to Chicago, I went to Monty's apartment and asked how he felt about me asking his daughter to marry me.

He cried a little, mostly out of joy, before pulling out a ring he had kept with him for over twenty years. It was the ring he was going to propose to Miller's mom with, but never got the chance to.

When he asked if I wanted to use it, there wasn't a moment of hesitation when I told him yes. This ring is not only beautiful and unique, but it'll mean more to her than any ring I could buy from a jeweler.

My hands are a little shaky with nerves as I take it from him but when I pop the lid, an overwhelming calm washes over me, knowing how right this is, knowing how much our family belongs together.

I was tempted to propose the second she came back, but with so many life changes happening for her at once, I decided to wait. Until today.

"It's beautiful, Monty."

"It's going to look beautiful on her. Her mom would be so proud of her."

Glancing up, I find Monty with shiny brown eyes, staring at the ring box in my hands.

"Are you sure you're okay with me using this?"

"I'm positive. It'll mean so much more to see it on her finger instead of it living in that box the way it has for so long."

Swinging an arm over him, I pull him into a hug. "Thank you. Not just for the ring, but for . . . everything."

He hugs me back. "I love you, Kai, you know that. And I love your son."

"Your grandson, you mean?" I ask in a teasing tone.

"I swear to God if you start calling me Grandpa at work, I will kick your ass. But yeah, I love my grandson too, and I'm happy you're finally making this all official."

"To Max turning two." Ryan holds his beer out to cheers with mine.

"To Kai and Miller," Zanders corrects. "For keeping him alive."

"Yeah, well we've got a pretty good support system behind us."

The backyard is full of our friends, including the team staff and Miller's employees from the bakery. The only people missing are the guys from the team, most notably, my brother.

Every year before the season starts, the team takes a trip together. They like to say it's for bonding purposes when in reality, it's an excuse to spend a few days drunk by a pool. This year they chose Vegas and, though Isaiah begged me to come, I made the very easy decision to stay home with my family.

With the season starting in a couple of weeks, I want to soak in as much time at home as possible. Max and Miller won't be traveling with us this year. With Miller's business taking off and Max getting older, it's time to transition him away from my hectic schedule.

The two of them will, however, come join us on the road for a night or two every month and that feels like a good enough compromise until I can be home full-time with them. And Miller's office at the bakery can double as a playroom so Max can spend time with her there. Between the two of us and the friends who have offered to help us fill in any gaps in our schedule, I don't think Max will ever need another full-time nanny.

Ryan looks around the party. "Miller's really stepping into this whole new mom role, huh?"

I find her sitting on a blanket with Stevie and Indy, baby Taylor laying on her back with Max watching his new friend adoringly from above.

The crew is growing and I'm excited for Max that he won't be the lone kid around here anymore.

"Dude, she loves it. It's wild to me that just six months ago, she thought she wouldn't be good at it. She's a natural, and every time I see her with Max, I get hit with the craziest baby fever." I shake my head. "I want to knock her up so badly."

"Yes," Zanders agrees. "Watching Stevie be a mom over the past four months is seriously one of the most attractive things I've ever witnessed."

We both turn towards Ryan, who is attempting to suppress his smile. He's going to understand how we feel real soon because they just found out Indy is pregnant.

He nudges me. "When are you and Miller going to have another?"

"I'm ready, but she's so busy with work and everything that we agreed we'd try once I officially retire."

"Stay-at-home dad." Zanders nods in approval. "Sounds amazing."

"I can't wait."

The truth is, in theory Miller and I are going to wait, but we aren't doing much to prevent it from happening now either. So, if we get hit with a surprise pregnancy, it won't be much of a surprise at all. And there isn't a person on the planet who could change my mind. I will be retiring once baby number two is here.

A bit of noise comes from inside the house, and I turn to find my entire team finally here to join the party.

"I'll be right back," I tell my friends. "I need to go check on my brother."

I welcome my teammates, pointing them in the direction of the food and drinks, before I make my way to the front entryway where Cody, Travis, and Isaiah seem to be having a private conversation.

"What's going on?" I ask, my tone suspicious. "And why are you guys so late?"

The three of them look to each other, silently communicating.

"Your brother is an idiot," Travis finally says.

"Trav, what the hell?" Isaiah shoots him a warning glance. "We agreed not to say anything today."

Travis simply shrugs.

"I don't know," Cody cuts in. "I think the whole thing is romantic."

"It's not romantic," Travis corrects. "It was a drunken mistake. A very dumb, drunken mistake."

Confused, my attention bounces between all three of them. "What the hell are you guys talking about?"

Travis looks right at my brother. "Just tell him."

Isaiah plasters on a smile that is so forced, it's clear he's trying to convince me I shouldn't be mad at him.

Then he holds up his left hand so I can see the wedding band living on his ring finger.

"What the fuck is that?"

"It's a wedding ring because . . . surprise! I got married!"

"You what?"

"Got hitched. Tied the knot. Took the plunge."

"I understand what it means to get married, Isaiah, but who the fuck did you get married to?"

"Oh, I love this part!" Cody pipes up.

Isaiah's smile is equal parts sheepish as it is thrilled. "Kennedy."

"Kennedy?" I ask in disbelief. "Kennedy Kay?"

"Kennedy Rhodes as of last night, but yes."

"But she . . ." I stutter. "She hates you."

"Well, you see about that. Turns out, after about eight shots of tequila, she doesn't hate me all that much."

I look back to the other guys, waiting for someone to tell me this is one big joke, one of their stupid pranks they like to pull.

It's evident by their expressions, it's not a prank.

"Wait, what? You're telling me Kennedy went to Vegas with you guys? She never goes out with the team."

"She was there for a different reason. We ran into each other on the strip."

"And you got married?"

"Yeah, we were both a little surprised over that part when we woke up this morning too."

"Kennedy will lose her job over this."

Isaiah quickly shakes his head. "She won't."

"You need to get this annulled and just pray that team management doesn't find out about this, because if they do, I can promise one of you is getting fired and we all know that someone isn't going to be you." I shake my head in disbelief. "I assume she's not coming to the party anymore."

"Probably not."

"I don't know what's more unbelievable," Cody laughs. "That Kennedy married you or that Dean fucking Cartwright is now your brother-in-law."

"Oh *fuck* me."

"Kai!" Miller calls from the backyard, Max's hand in hers. "Are you ready for cake?"

I turn back to my brother. "Take the fucking ring off before you go sing 'Happy Birthday' to your nephew. Miller can't find out about this today. I'm proposing tonight and the last thing I need is for my brother to steal her thunder over a drunken mistake."

"Mistake seems harsh," he counters. "I like the term, 'happy accident'."

"Is that what Kennedy is calling it?"

"Oh, no. She definitely called it a mistake."

Miller gets Max situated in a seat with his birthday cake on the table in front of him. He's got an adorably cute smile on his face, rosy cheeks from all the attention. I get the candle lit for him and make sure he's enough of a distance away while the entire backyard of our friends start to sing him "Happy Birthday".

I wrap my arms around Miller's shoulders from behind, holding her as we sing to our son. He's so giddy, his blue eyes scanning the crowd to see everyone who loves him.

When the time comes, we prompt him to blow out the candle, but he needs a little help so his uncle steps in to blow it with him and, when they finally get it out, Max sits up straight and claps for himself, urging the crowd to clap with him.

Miller laughs in my arms and I pull her closer.

Leaning down, I kiss the skin under her ear. "You and me, Mills, we're doing good."

She finds my forearm, holding me. "Yeah, we are, aren't we?"

Once the party is cleared out and only our closest friends remain, we let Max open a few gifts as we sit around in a circle and watch him do his thing in the center. Miller is curled up on my lap with a glass of wine in her hand at the end of another one of our good days.

"Wow!" Max exclaims as he pulls out a small wooden train from the gift bag Monty brought. "Twain!"

Every present he's opened has been revealed with a "Wow" and it has yet to get old.

"I got you a whole train *set*," Monty explains. "Your dad and I are going to set it up in your room tomorrow."

Max gets on his hands and knees, pushing the train around on the ground, making choo-choo noises the entire time.

"It looks like there's one more present," Isaiah says, holding up the tiny gift bag.

The nerves instantly take over and I feel my body tense.

Miller looks at me over her shoulder in confusion. "You okay?"

"Yeah," I exhale, shifting in my seat, trying to figure out how I'm going to casually get her off my lap so I can get down on one knee.

Isaiah looks around the bag. "I'm not sure who it's from, though."

That seems like a good opening. "Let me see." I usher Miller off my lap and onto the chair. Taking the bag from my brother, I look inside, pretending I have no idea what this is.

"Max, come here for a second."

He leaves his train behind, shuffling his way to me.

I hold him close, showing him the inside of the bag before I whisper, "This one is for your mom. Can you go give it to her for me?"

On a mission with a smile, Max takes the bag right to Miller, holding it up for her. "Mama, you."

"For me?" she asks him. "But it's your birthday. Why am *I* getting a present?"

Her confused gaze finds mine, but I simply shrug her off.

"You'll help me open it, right?" she asks, and Max nods before climbing into her lap.

Miller sets her glass of wine down and holds the bag down in her lap so Max can feel like he's helping.

I make quick eye contact with both my brother and Monty, the two of them so obviously excited, as I find my way in front of my two favorite people.

"What do you think this is?" Miller asks Max in a high-pitched voice, not quite catching on to what's in the bag.

That is until her fingers graze the velvet box and her eyes shoot to me. "No."

I chuckle. "You're saying no already? I haven't even asked."

"Malakai." She tilts her head, her lip jutting out.

"What is it?" Indy asks from behind me.

Miller pulls out the small box just as I get down on one knee.

"Let's go!" Ryan cheers.

"Miller Montgomery," I begin, but she cuts me off before I can continue.

She points at the tear that's already falling down her face. "I hate you for this."

"It really wouldn't be a proper proposal for us without you telling me how much you hate me, huh?"

She laughs that watery laugh, and I carefully take the box from her hand.

"Miller Montgomery—"

"Yes! The answer is yes."

"Okay," I chuckle. "Thank you for the vote of confidence but I still got to get this out."

She hugs our son to her chest, her chin leaning on his head as I make this little speech to both of them.

"I wanted to ask you the second you came back, but I was trying to give you the space to grow into this new life without asking too much of you. But I can't wait any longer. There's no one else I want to raise him, and hopefully a few more babies, with. You're my closest friend and the person I have the most fun with. I love you, Miller, and I'm pretty envious that Max gets to call you Mom because I'd really like the opportunity to call you my wife."

She huffs a choked laugh.

I open the box and Miller's eyes dart to her dad when she sees the ring, clearly knowing its original intention.

With her tears falling quicker now, her attention comes right back to me where I'm kneeled in front of her. "What do you say, Mills? Will you marry me?" I glance down at Max. "*Us*?"

My entire world is looking right back at me, this family I've longed for, *dreamt* for, and the three of us have never felt more complete than when she takes a deep breath, smiles at me, and simply says, "Yes."

## THE END

# Acknowledgements

The most important acknowledgment is to you all—the reader. Thank you for reading, sharing, and reviewing my books! You all have given me a career I love, and I am so grateful.

Allyson—I'm pretty sure at this point, you'll be in every one of my acknowledgment pages, but this one especially. This book truly would not have come to life without you. The constant voice memos, texts, chats, and updated google docs. Thank you for reading all 30 versions of this manuscript and helping it become this story I love. So much of Miller's development is inspired by you. I'm so grateful to not only have you as one of my best friends, but also someone I get to share this whole writing journey with. Love you so much and I cannot wait to be neighbors with you and Marc. (Life goal unlocked!!)

Samantha—my wonderful PA. You're always there for me with whatever I need, whether that be work stuff or just a moment so I can vent. I appreciate you so much, and I'm so thankful to have you by my side.

Megan— my amazing alpha reader. Thank you so much for all your help and for hyping me up! So appreciative of you!

Erica— book three together! I love having you on my team and working with you is amazing. You're my first stamp of approval and I'm always eager for your opinions! Looking forward to many more books in the future!

Marc— thank you for the music. I'm so appreciative of your help in making sure the playlists are spot on for each couple. It has been so fun to get to have you and Allyson alongside me during all of this!

Mom— the best baker I know! You've passed down your love of baking to me, and I felt it was only fitting to finally have a baker in one of my books. Love you so much!

Thank you all for taking the time to read Kai and Miller's story! Now it's time for Windy City Series Book 4!